MW00830830

A
GRIMOIRE
DARK

D.S. QUINTON

ISBN: 978-1-7327723-3-5

Development Editor: Andrew Lowe

Copy Editor: James Osborne

Cover design: Jeff Brown Graphics

Interior formatting: Mark Thomas / Coverness.com

PROLOGUE

I n 1722, a great hurricane struck the city of New Orleans, the largest slave trading port in the South, destroying most of the city. Ships capsized or were thrown to splinters, sending the unfortunate to a watery grave. The dead were many and bodies were found for weeks: wedged in trees, buried in mud, under piles of debris dumped into swamps. For days after, bodies washed onto beaches and beckoned the living to them. The names of the people were lost to history, but the souls remained.

In 1788, the Great New Orleans Fire raged and destroyed over eight-hundred and fifty buildings on Good Friday. The poor areas built of wood and thatched roofs burned and the dead were many. Piles of ash containing wood and bone were scooped together and thrown to the swamps or plowed under the soft rotting soil. The wind moaned agony and the agony coated the fragile things; leaves of the mighty Eucalyptus, once silent and soft, rattled like fragile bones; false voices called out in the night, begging eternal rest. The names of the people were lost to history, but the souls remained.

In 1849, the Mississippi River breached a levee north of New Orleans. The city remained under water from May to late June. Coffins and bones emerged from the low, water-logged soil and floated the streets, disturbing the living, but reminding the dead of what they once had. The remains were reburied without ceremony, sometimes stacked three bodies deep with a layer of rock on top to weigh them down. The bodies were mixed and lost to history, but the souls remained.

The agony of the souls was cast upon the wind and the wind became their voice. The sensitive people heard the moans of the dead late at night and in their dreams, and soon, in an effort to quiet them, Spirit Hunters emerged. The Spirit Hunters, through some ability cursed upon them by the stars, were able to hear the spirits and, in some cases, coax them back to a state of eternal sleep. But not all souls yearned to sleep. Some souls, once awakened, would never rest and wandered the streets moaning their vengeance.

The Spirit Hunters learned through the years powerful magic, that if used with discretion, could tame or trick the spirits and put them to rest. The risk to the Spirit Hunter was the wielding of the great and terrible power, for it changed their own soul each time it was used. To protect themselves from unnatural outcomes, the Spirit Hunters hid the magic, and made it secret. Long years passed where the wandering souls were quiet, and the Spirit Hunters were all but forgotten.

Then, in 1963, a book was found wrapped in cloth, bound by twine, covered in burlap, tied with rope, in a hidden alcove, behind a false wall in a den, crowded with bric-a-brac, in an ancient home on a dead-end street, in the old section of New Orleans.

The book was thought destroyed or lost to the ages; some believed it never existed at all, or that it was *not* what was said of it, but that was their undoing. Obtaining a clear description of the book—to avoid it completely—was a fool's errand as it was designed for deceit; hiding its true nature.

Upon discovery of the book, a most unfortunate thing happened; someone read from it. And the spirits moaned that the dead would be many.

CHAPTER 1

A Dark Void

Hello? Is someone there?

Anyone?

Oh dear, what has become of me?

Whoever's there come close please. I cannot see and can utter but a whisper. My throat is so dry.

Hear how my voice quivers?

Where are you good soul? Alas, have pity and don't leave me here all alone.

I fear I am lost in the darkness; a terrible void of some type.

It is a cold place in which I have found myself; utterly without warmth or light. I dare not reach out for fear of what I might find—or, that I might find nothing at all.

Oh! Dreadful, dreadful state of mind! My heart is nearly bursting from my chest. I'm sure it will falter any second now!

What terrible thing could I have done to be cast into this abysmal place?

Hello?

What was that sound? A rustling of the wind?

Are you still there or do my ears deceive me?

Oh, how the mind plays tricks!

Come closer still please. I fear this dreadful place in which I have found myself and feel that I am fading; fading almost out of existence! Oh! the horror!

There's that sound again. Did you hear it?

It's as of leaves rustling across a thicket.

Oh, what a wretched state I am in! Dead! Dead I am sure! —if this is not Hades, then very nearly!

Are you the specter from my nightmares? The spirit who has haunted my mind? The one who cast me down?

Nay, I feel not the evil presence I... the presence I felt long ago.

I pray you will help me?

How I came to this state is beyond the capacity of my mind to recall, and what a wretched company you have found. I assure you—well, I believe—that I was not always like this. The actual state of my being— before the state in which you find me now—was quite sane I'm sure. Yes, I feel as if I was quite sane... but alas... something dreadful happened to me. I cannot recall it, but I am—

Why, there it is again. Did you hear it? A gentle rustling sound. A sound quite like that of leaves or of… parchment.

Yes, of course. That must be it. I believe I understand now.

I'm sorry, I cannot recall the events exactly, my mind is quite muddled. In fact, I fear you suspect the ramblings of a madman, quite incoherent, but… a peculiar feeling gnaws at my soul, there is something...

Despite my wretched state, I have a yearning to portray to you what I can, so the same terrible fate does befall you. Excuse me, does not befall you.

Yes, now that I state it, I am quite sure the telling of my tale is what is needed. I feel this to be true in the marrow of my bones, as if my life utterly depended on it.

However, I feel that my constitution is feeble and that I may not last the night. If the most terrible fate should befall me while we're on our… journey, I beg of you to soldier on.

But how would that be possible you ask? Soldier on with a voice lost to the winds of time and the void of death?

Yes, soldier on you must, for this voice is now upon the wind, and now that the words have been spoken, it must continue.

It's fate you see. Once the words are spoken, even just a whisper, the wind hears them and carries them on to their destination and will carry you along if you just listen and speak the words. But that is the key you understand, you must speak the words the wind gives you, for it is the only way.

Are you close? Are you comfortable?

Thank you.

As I recall, it all began with an unholy rain.

CHAPTER 2

A cold March rain began to fall on New Orleans, the Crescent City, wrapping it in a shroud of fog. It was a long, slow rain that drizzled and dropped its way down rooflines, into moss-filled gutters and eventually out to the streets.

At night, the rain formed a ghostly fog that hung like specters drifting through the streets, inspecting the living for any trace of humanity they chose to leave behind.

In the morning, the rain harnessed the smells of the previous night and hung them in low, wet clouds to be sampled by people who scuttered by. Sometimes the rain cleansed the city, most times not.

The following night, the rain drizzled on.

By the fifth night, the old gutters were filled and overflowing, dangling from roofs where the downspouts had clogged. Moss grew everywhere in the Crescent City and straining gutters were common, but when the Live Oaks began creaking their waterlogged limbs, people began to talk.

By the tenth night a heavy stench hung about the city. Not the common *humanity on high* stench that was so common in the tourist areas; that could be washed away with hose and broom. By the tenth night the city gave up hints to its long and violent past; the stench was of death and the first of many bones floated to the surface of the low, soft soil.

*

Del absently fluffed at her tight curly hair as she watched the droplets follow a lazy, miniature stream down the window of the cab. She fingered the scar that ran up the right side of her neck and under her ear. Her jaw muscles tightened reflexively.

The view of the city was blurry through the raindrops and gave it an otherworldly feel, as if it were a watercolor painting, or old photo of the city that used to exist, hidden just beyond the real one. That city existed in her mind as a city in black and white—as an old photo would portray—dead and rotting, but somehow lingering on.

She chewed at a broken nail and tapped a worn sneaker against the floor. "Can't you go around?" she said. "What about Brouchard street up on the right? Is that open? I'm going to be late."

"Sorry miss," the cabbie said, "dis infernal rain got all da lights a blinkin'. Ev'rbody got all switched up. Ain't nothin' can be done but wait out da jam."

She heaved a sigh and sank into the lumpy seat. Fidgeting with her bandeau-style headband, she looked at the half-empty sidewalk. She could have made better time on her bike, but the cake wouldn't have survived her backpack.

Looking at her watch, she realized she only had a few minutes left and still had several blocks to go.

"Forget it," she said, looking at the meter. "I'll get out here."

She quietly dug through her pockets and felt a tinge of panic as she searched for coins. The cabbie watched her through the mirror.

She carefully counted out fifty-five cents for the ride, then added a dime at the last minute. She handed him sixty-five cents and smiled weakly at his face in the mirror.

She had no idea a cab ride was so expensive and vowed to plan better next time. She knew she couldn't afford such luxuries considering she had just started her first real job and was saving money for a house—although she had no idea what a house would cost—but the rain hadn't let up and she was late. It was important to get this package to the party on time and intact, so she had chosen the cab.

Del didn't go in much for birthday parties. Growing up most of her life in an orphanage, they were painful reminders of another year of not being wanted, of being passed over and generally being considered non-existent.

She had watched people for years through the windows of the St. Augustine orphanage where she had lived, hustling by with bags and boxes–some wrapped, but usually not. She guessed most items were household or work items, but occasionally she glimpsed the telltale signs of a pending party; a handful of balloons was obvious, or a brightly wrapped package, but they rarely had balloons or packages in the orphanage.

Over the years she had learned to tune those images out almost as soon as she saw them. It was an innate survival mechanism she had—defocus the image until it obscured into oblivion—that way it could have been a dream. The memory reel of her life so far had many obscured images like this.

Grabbing the carefully wrapped gift and small cake she stepped out into the blanket of fog before the driver could inch to the curb.

Hopscotching over the uneven cobblestones of the street, she easily avoided the larger puddles and any hidden items they may contain, cleared the curb and began winding her way down the sidewalk.

Her worn jean jacket did little against the cold mist and despite being a youthful eighteen, she shivered as she bent her head against the rogue gusts of wind.

The heavy fog-rain formed large droplets of water on her light-brown face and freckled nose. She ignored the drops as she ran up to the corner, turned right on Brouchard and cut through the next alley, coming out near the corner of the St. Augustine Church.

The orphanage, built in 1843, two years after the church's inception, served the poor and destitute of this part of the city. Maybe the location was the reason Del never had any real attempts at adoption— *Who was looking for another Creole girl anyway, especially from this part of town?* —or, maybe it was the fact that people seemed to be able to read her thoughts as if they were written on her face.

"Attitude girl! Straighten up and lose it." Sister Eulalie—the Mother Superior—would say as she grabbed a handful of her wild black hair and yanked her head up before the prospects walked through. "And lose the devil eyes."

Del would chew every nail those nights, dreaming of the day she would finally be rid of Sister Eulalie and the St. Augustine orphanage.

As she passed a streaked window that looked into the side waiting room, she saw a small flat face pressed against it, nose pushed flat, tongue lolling against the cold pane, eyes searching the sidewalk, and knew she was late.

Through the small windows of the double-doors, Del spied Josephine Soble sitting at the reception desk buffing her nails in secret. Del knew the desk well—and Josephine's habit—because she had spent much of her time there the last year.

When Del left, the task was assigned to Josephine, who seemed to despise this chore the least: pretending to care about the people who wandered into the orphanage, ensure they signed in correctly and see that they didn't steal any brats from the back.

Josephine did this happily because the alternative was to actually play with the brats in the back, and Del knew there was no greater punishment for her—well, only one.

The secrecy of the nail buffing was due to the nuns incessant preaching about the sin of vanity; one which Josephine relished in as often as possible as far as Del could tell.

Hurrying through the big double-doors of the orphanage, the antiseptic smell of old mop water and lye filled Del with a stomach-turning sense of the place she had just called home. She couldn't imagine how she had spent ten years of her life here. And she was determined to think about it as little as possible.

Josephine smiled as Del approached the desk. "You look cute, all dripping wet."

Del wrinkled her mouth at the comment but presented it as a smile. Josephine always said odd things like that.

Waving absently at the reception desk, Del signaled to be signed in, knowing that Josephine would do it for her. There was really no need for her to sign in considering she had left only a month ago, but she didn't want to irk the nuns. Josephine, also a member of the *does-not-exist* club, understood the need for compliance and wrote Del's name.

Del entered a small waiting room where the round, flat face turned from the window and screamed her name.

"Deh Beh!" Jimmy said with hands on his hips, "you 'ate!"

"What? Who says I'm late?" Del said with mock surprise.

Jimmy's eyes narrowed to sharp slants as he smiled with the knowledge of being able to provide Del an answer. "Me Deh, Yimmy says you 'ate."

"Jimmy? Jimmy who?"

"Yimmy Wawoo," he said thumbing his chest.

"Jimmy Lareaux? Oh, hmmm. I was looking for someone who has a birthday today. Who would that—"

"ME Deh! Yimmy Wawoo!" Jimmy said as his arms shot up in a victory pose.

"That's right, Jimmy Lareaux. It is your birthday today isn't it?

"Yeh, an you 'ate!"

"Only a few minutes!"

Tapping his watch for emphasis Jimmy said, "Sic minunds 'ate, Deh. Sic minunds."

"I'm sorry about that Jimmy. With all this rain, the streets are a mess. I took a cab to get here as quick as I could."

"Dah teets ah a mess? Why dah teets a mess?"

"I don't know, I think a tree fell down."

"A tee feh down? On you head?"

"No Jimmy," she chuckled, "nothing fell on my head. Except all this rain." She bent and shook her head sending water droplets showering over Jimmy.

"Bah! You a mess, Deh." Jimmy said slapping the water from his face.

"Not today Jimmy," Del said, giving him a wink. "Who's ready for some cake?"

"Dis guy!" Jimmy said thumbing his chest.

Outside, the rain drizzled on: gutters overflowed, top-heavy trees leaned precariously, and somewhere, a bone, carried by a torrent of water, bumped quietly along a street and dropped into a drain.

CHAPTER 3

F rank Morgan pulled his 1953 Chevrolet Bel Air in front of his office at 10:00 a.m. The convertible top would have been down had it not been raining. The chill March air was a relief for a man of his girth, and Frank Morgan, *Fat Frank* to his friends, was known around town for driving with the top down in all sorts of weather.

The car was a gift to Frank from his late wife as an early retirement gift from the New Orleans police department, and as *advertising* for his new detective agency. After solving the Glapion murders in '53, he enjoyed a bit of celebrity and had been encouraged to go out on his own.

In reality, it was his wife's way of getting him to slow down from the hectic schedule of police work—without saying so—in hopes that he wouldn't have a heart attack at his desk. Little did she know, she was the one with the bum ticker.

Although the car was now ten years old, it still gleamed candy-apple red like it had just rolled off the showroom floor. He scraped, washed and polished it on a weekly basis from the detached garage in the back of his modest house.

Turning off the car, Frank sat watching the rain as he brushed cigar ashes from the plateau of his stomach. Seeing no delay in the monotony of drizzle, he stepped out, covered his head with the morning paper and trudged up the stairs to his second-story office.

The small nondescript office sat directly over a satellite office of the *Times-Picayune* newspaper, where several reporters worked. Over the years they had learned to keep tabs on Frank and his investigations, picking up crumbs of stories wherever they could. Often, they would share a drink or two at the Lamp and Lantern Bar near the corner of Bourbon and St. Phillips Street, pumping him for information.

The second-story office was a converted flat made of two rooms, a small bathroom and one door leading outside to a covered walkway that ran the length of the building. The other top office space had been vacant for years, so no one ever walked outside his office window which looked out onto the street below.

At one point he had a secretary, but now only had a cleaning lady come every other week. She would complain about the overflowing ashtray of cigar stubs and the stacks of old newspapers—which he called his *research* material—and warned that she would find him burned up or dead under a pile of papers one day. To this he would simply nod and say, "As long as I'm in heaven five minutes before da devil knows I'm dead!" And pull a long draw from his cigar.

Today, the phone was ringing as he stepped through the door. Tossing his hat and coat onto an old wingback—the only waiting chair he had in the front office—he shuffled his girth through the inner door to his stuffed office and grabbed the phone.

"Yeah?" he said.

"Frang? It's Henri GeeOHM."

Frank recognized the deep, slow voice immediately. Henri Guillaume had been a sergeant on the force before Frank retired. After Frank left, Henri quickly rose to captain. He smiled at the sound of the heavy French-Creole accent that sounded slightly Jamaican, as he pictured the six-foot-two black man in his mind. A heavy accent could be expected in the poorer wards or deep in the bayou, but Henri was from an educated family. He dressed for a higher class but spoke like the down-trodden; just enough to make Frank feel there was another side to Henri GeeOHM.

"Cap'n, what I do ya fer?"

Slow, rhythmic words unfurled. "Frang, leesen, I was wond'ren could you run a call fer me?"

"Talk about. Like a regular call? You outta desk jockeys?"

"Frang, it's de'pouille—a mess! Da damn bones is floatin' up ever'where and me men are scattered. But dis—"

"Bones? You got more?

"Yah, yah, not since da 1800s we see dis many. We think they're old graves, but gotta run it, you know."

"Yeah, of course."

Frank remembered reading about a flood in the late 1800s that soaked the area for so long that bones from old grave sites started working their way up through the soft Louisiana soil. In a few cases, caskets—those unfortunate enough to be buried—popped straight up out of the ground due to the high-water table. Those were relocated to new burial vaults above ground, but there was a long-held belief that there were thousands of bodies buried in the soil that had nothing more than a layer of rock on them to weigh them down.

"So, it's a bone run?" Frank asked.

"No Frang, dis a body. A fresh one. Sounds like a gator 'tack."

Louisianans were no strangers to alligator attacks, Frank knew this. Besides the slave and cotton trades, the alligator trade in Louisiana had been significant in the late 1800s. The state still boasted the largest alligator ever killed, coming in at an astonishing nineteen feet and nearly 2000 pounds. Even more astonishing was that the gator was killed in the early 1890s.

"Surprised der's a body a'tall den."

"Yah, I know. Missin' da head I tink, but you run it, eh? It's out da Jean Lafitte way."

"Not exactly on my way home, Henri. That's a bit of a—"

"Drive da damn car faster Frang, you go, eh?"

"Yeah das fine. Let me write it down. I'll go da afternoon."

"OK Frang, tanks."

Frank leaned back in his desk chair, lit his cigar again and stared out the window. This wasn't exactly detective work, but it gave him something to do.

Prolly some poor drunk step off his porch last night and got et.

Frank shook his head slowly.

Dat poor sumbitch musta stank to high heaven to not get et up all da way.

He brushed cigar ashes from his plateau-belly again and watched the rain drizzle on.

He thought about a headless body lying in the mud of the vast Jean Lafitte Preserve and wondered if he really wanted this case.

Somewhere, from an unopened window, a faint breeze chilled the back of his thick neck.

He thought the answer was *No*.

CHAPTER 4

el looked at her watch and realized she was running late again. Jimmy had eaten more cake than he should have and had made a mess in the waiting room. He continued to thank Del for his drawing set while she quickly straightened the room.

"An den, I daw you a piduw of dah tee dat feh on you head." Jimmy cracked a wide smile.

"That tree didn't fall on my head, silly. But maybe it will fall on *your* head." She rubbed his messy hair.

"No, doan say dat Deh!" Jimmy covered his head with both arms. "I doan wan bad deams!"

Del had known Jimmy most of his life from the orphanage, and had sat with him more times than she could remember after he'd wake from a bad dream. When they were younger—when boys and girls stayed in the same large room—she could easily soothe him back to sleep by humming some made-up tune. She told him if he closed his eyes and listened quietly, he could hear the angels singing far off in the distance.

Some days, the older kids teased her for *singing retardo* at night, which meant singing nonsense words, but she usually ignored them. But the day she came into the room and found several of them playing *Ring Around Retardo*, with Jimmy crying in the middle of the circle, she pushed one of them down and stood fiercely over the girl until the others left. This earned her several swats from Sister Eulalie, but the kids left Del and Jimmy alone after that.

"Bad dreams? Why would you have a dream about a tree?" she asked, looking at her watch again and cleaning the last speck from Jimmy's face. "Oh, I'm really late. I gotta get going."

"I had a bad deam ast night, Deh."

Throwing on her damp jean jacket, she spied Sister Eulalie's old wrinkled face through the waiting room doors and her stomach turned sour. Sister Eulalie's eyes shone white against her black face, which looked like a deep shadow inside her white habit. She was watching Del with crossed arms.

"Jimmy, I really got to—I'm sorry, what did you say? A bad dream? About what?" She sent a tight-lipped smile toward Sister Eulalie through the window, who returned a cold and distant scowl.

"A bad deam Deh. About a… issad," he said after some thought.

"A what?" she asked, hugging him quickly and wiping away the last icing smear from his cheek.

Del could understand Jimmy better than most, but had to think about the word he was trying to form.

"Ah… iiissaad," he tried again. "He was bad, Deh."

"A… wizard?" she said, hurrying for the door. "Did someone tell you a spooky story about a wizard? Don't worry, if we see one, we'll just throw some water on him and melt him!"

"No Deh, dat—"

She closed the door, saying, "Bye Jimmy Lareaux. Happy birthday!" from the lobby. She ran out the double doors.

"—da ickad itch got mettad!"

Watching Del run down the sidewalk, Jimmy pressed his face to the same cold window and absently said, "Doan et da issaad eat you head."

*

Frank sat in the front window of the Treme Grill at the corner of St. Phillip and North Robertson streets, finishing his lunch of liver and onions.

This was his regular table when he came here, which was often since his wife passed, and the cook and two waitresses knew him by his first name.

The grill was just down from his office, and both sat on the edge of the Treme neighborhood, one of the poorer in the city. This meant the rent was right and the clients were plenty.

He brushed the breadcrumbs from his shirt, grabbed his cigar and dropped a five on the table. Stepping into the sodden air, he was surprised by a figure running out of the mist, nearly colliding with him.

"Whoa der!" he said, shielding his head with his newspaper.

"Frank! Oh my gosh, how nice to see you!" Del said.

"Del-bell! What you doin' runnin' dis rain honey? Not in trouble, are you?"

"No Frank, nothing of the sort," Del said. "Heading to my new job and running late is all."

"New job? You out da orphanage? Dat's great news!"

"Believe it? I'm finally rid of Sister Eulalie!" she said.

"Ha! Dat ole—"

"Careful Frank, she got good ears!"

"Heh, yeah, I guess. But not good enough to hear you sneakin' out all dos nights."

The side of Del's mouth curled slightly as she remembered the many nights she had slipped out of the orphanage and roamed the old city. It was a stupid thing to do, she knew—at least, that's what people told her—but she had never been afraid, nor had any trouble. In fact, the night seemed to shield her in an odd way, embracing her presence and sucking her in, as if they both fed from each other.

"Yeah, thank you again for helping me smooth that over with the sister! Hey listen, I really gotta run, I'm just—"

"Where you goin' honey?" He started walking. "My car's right down der, I'll give you a—"

"Down there? That's where I'm going. I started at the *Times-Picayune* last week and they sent me to help the reporters. I want to be a reporter one day."

"Talk about! Well let's jabber outta da rain, but I don't think Harry or Sal is in today. My office is right over them, and Friday is pretty quiet in that office. Thursday night bein' poker night and all."

As suspected, the newspaper office was locked tight. Frank invited Del up to his office to dry off and sat down heavily in the protesting office chair.

"When you get dried up, I'll run you home. Infernal rain ain't never gonna stop I 'spec. Anyway, I got a call I gotta run, so I'm headin' out any—"

"What kinda call? A crime scene call? Can I go with you?" she asked.

"Oh, I don't know honey, it's kinda out der. And I don't know if a young girl like you should be seein' such things as—"

"Come on Frank, please! What better way to learn the newspaper business but to ride along on a real call? I'll write up whatever you find and break my first scoop!"

"Well, I tink dis'll be a case ah accidental death, but death it will be. You sure 'bout dis?"

"Absolutely! No turning back."

Frank frowned slightly at the odd choice of words, but dismissed it as a cold draft raised goose bumps on his neck. He always ran on the warm side, and didn't remember his office being drafty before. He looked at the dark gray sky outside and wondered briefly how long the storm would last.

"Frank?"

Looking back at Del's expectant face, he was surprised by a strange color reflection in her eyes—mottled dark gray with black flecks. He blinked and it was gone.

Must have reflected through the window, he thought. "Well… OK den, let's go."

CHAPTER 5

T hirty minutes later Del saw an imposing sight rise in front of them as Frank pulled off Barataria Boulevard onto a dirt road and headed southwest into the Jean Lafitte Preserves.

She had made a few trips out of the city in the past, and knew that a short drive in any direction would lead a person to some form of water: Lake Pontchartrain to the North; Lake Borgne to the East which opened to a Sound then the Gulf; the Mississippi river snaking its way from the West and running south of the city. Any southerly drive led to more water: marsh, lake or swamp.

The sight in front of them cast a deep pall over an already gloomy day. Although the Jean Lafitte Preserve was officially established as an historic park and preserve in 1907, most people just thought of the area as uninhabitable swamp. Half the state of Louisiana fit the general category of wetland, which could consist of a river, lake, marsh or swamp. But once the low shrubs and grasses of a marshland gave way, the swamp took over and things changed: the land became wilder with narrow strips of land—barely qualifying as roads—winding deep into the murk; the trees were tall and twisted in all directions as if trying desperately to escape the stinking black water; Spanish moss hung from giant cypress trees in long, ghostly shreds, swaying slightly in the stagnant air; and then there were the sounds.

The dense swamp air compressed and reflected sounds in strange ways. Unseen wildlife inhabited every part of the swamp, producing a cacophony of barks, hums, growls, chirps and twitters. Combine all the sounds together, thread them through ancient groves, twist them around giant trees and warble them off murky pools and you hear the voice of a thing that should not have a voice; you hear the voice of the swamp.

"Damn, but there ain't nothin' out here 'cept gators and bones," Frank said, absently squinting through the windshield.

"Is this the right place? I don't even see phone lines out here. And is this a road?"

"Der was a phone outside dat ole broken down store turnin' off Barataria, but not much else dis far out. We gonna' turn around up here if we can find a place, less I gotta back us all da' way out. Maybe up around dis curve—"

"Hey look," Del said, pointing at a spot through the curtain of branches, "an old shack."

Frank crept the car forward, squinting. "Ol' shack is right," he said, clinching his cigar between his teeth. He braked the car nearly to a stop as he reached across and opened the glove box, pulling out a revolver.

Del eyed Frank as he slid the pistol into a shoulder holster.

Noticing her questioning look, he said, "Fer gators."

The sinking path that doubled as a road disappeared into the muck of the swamp just beyond the shack. They rounded the last curve of the swamp-road.

The shack was built on spindly legs of pine poles that had been driven into the soft ground, elevating the shack five feet above the ground. A gangplank of mismatched boards surrounded the shack in a sort of wraparound walkway. Near the front door the gangplank widened into something nearly like a porch that held a few odd chairs and was covered by a flimsy roof of rusted tin, supported by a scaffolding of boards and cables. The porch and gangplank held a myriad of miscellaneous items: gator skulls on high stakes facing in all directions; a string of Christmas lights that held a few old towels, a fish stringer and several small animal skulls hanging from twine, and a doghouse occupied by a family of raccoons.

A carpet of moss, leaves and branches covered the roof of the shack, which Del would have thought was abandoned except for a small curl of smoke that snaked its way out of a leaning piece of tin pipe protruding through the roof.

The area around the shack held the remnants of a life spent bartering, including an old truck piled with junk that was more in the swamp than out of it.

The time of day was lost to the murk and the fog-rain cast a dusky hue that hinted at a foreboding night to come. A strange sensation of movement emanated from the swamp as it pulsed from an unseen light source.

As they stepped out of the car, they realized the mysterious *pulsing* came from dozens of mirrors that hung from tree branches, slowly twisting in the dank air, reflecting the ghostly scene in all directions.

"Hallo!" Frank called out as he ascended the steps to the gangplank porch. "Anyone ho—"

He stopped short as the working end of a double-barreled shotgun poked out of the front door.

"Whoa now! It's da police," he said, holding up his wallet and expired badge. "Did someone call in a body?"

The shotgun disappeared and the door swung open. A grizzled hand waved for them to come in.

Frank poked his head inside the doorway as he knocked on the open door, waving at Del to stay behind him.

"Da door's open ain't it? Yeah…" said a voice from inside the shack.

Frank and Del stepped through the door of the shack and into the world of Blind Loo'siana Slim.

The grizzled old man sat in a rocker near a small pot-bellied stove. The shotgun rested across the arms of the rocker as he hummed a low tune that was barely audible.

Del drank in the strange scene in front of her. Here, in and old shack in the middle of the swamp, was a man dressed in his Sunday best. Slim sported worn, but pressed wool trousers, a white dress shirt made of heavy cotton, and a Bolo tie with an Onyx stone set in silver. The blue-mirrored lenses of his 1940s-style tortoise-shell sunglasses hid his eyes, but imbued his face with an air of deep knowledge and an odd sophistication. His alligator skin boots were polished to a high shine and drove a slow, hypnotic rocking against lightly creaking floorboards.

"Afternoon, sir. Name of Frank Morgan. Did you call in a dead body?"

"'Frank Morgan' you say? Alright… name of Slim. Loo'siana Slim. Yeah…" He rocked his head to a silent beat.

"Who's dat behind ya? Come up so I can hear ya," said Slim.

"Good afternoon sir, I'm Delphine Larouche."

"DELL-phine... yeah... das ol' name." At this, Slim set the shotgun aside and fumbled for a guitar leaning against the wall. Producing a glass slide seemingly from thin air he started picking out an old Delta Blues riff with haunting slide notes, and slowly sang.

"Del-phine / Del-phine / doan liiiiie to me / tell me wheerrre'd you sleep las' night?

"In da pines / in da pines / where da suuunn doa'never shine,

"I shiverrrr da ho' night through..."

Setting the guitar across the arms of the chair Slim said, "Yeah... das ol' name..."

Frank and Del exchanged glances as Slim's mirrored glasses stared off into a space somewhere to their left. He continued rocking slowly, mouthing the words, *Del-phine, Del-phine...*

Frank coughed. "About da body—"

"Come fer da body, didja?" Slim interrupted. "Bes' to let it lie, but I doan think the swamp want it back, you unerstan', yeah..." His head lolled into a lazy figure-eight pattern at a slow four-four time.

"Shoulda left it alone myself, but doan wan' dat soul hangin' roun you unerstan'... no... doan wan' dat hangin' roun atall..."

"Excuse me for asking, sir," Del said, "but how did you find it... I mean, if you're—"

"Blind, you mean? Yeah, my eyes went out a long time ago, but dat's NOT da only way to see, you unerstan'... not da only way..."

Del exchanged another questioning glance with Frank, only to turn back and see the mirrored blue lenses staring straight at her.

"I heard it, you see. Woke da other night wit a powerful fear. Laid still as da dead, listenin' you unerstan... yeah... den I heard it."

"Heard what?" asked Frank.

"I heard da most terrible, awful murder you can imagine!"

Del's pulse climbed at the thought of her first breaking story.

"Murder? Why you say dat?" Frank asked. "I thought we had a case of a gator 'tack?"

"Heh… if so, dat no gator you wanna find, no… My grann'on come to check on me yesterday and found me in bed, still as da dead. Thought I'd passed o'er in the night, but when he shook me, I bolt up like a demon, ya unerstan! I was in a trance or somethin'. Had to go deep in my head, in a song, you unerstan, when I heard da murder. Had to fill my head, so he couldn't find me."

"Not following you," Frank said. "So who couldn't find you?"

"Doan ask me to say da name. I woan say it! And you'd be best not to even think it. Leave dat body to da swamp. I'll deal wit da soul if it come 'round."

Del listened intently to the strange story, but thought there must be something wrong with the shack. She felt as if it were moving slightly under her feet, swaying so subtly that her conscious mind couldn't detect it, but her subconscious could. She felt the slightest wave of dizziness flush up her neck as her stomach started to turn sideways.

"Well, that's part of da job you see. I been sent out here to investigate a dead body, and that's what I aim to do. I understand if you don't want to see it. Just point me in the right direction and I'll take care of it," Frank said.

Slim rocked in silence, contemplating the two. His tortoise-shell sunglasses playing a trick of observing both Frank and Del at the same time.

"If I tell you, doan go gettin' lost. And DOAN be folleren no fifolets, you unerstan! I doan need no more lost souls out here then they already are!"

"Fifolet?" asked Del with a smirk. "What's that?"

Slim smacked his lips apart in disgust and adjusted in his rocker as his head rocked from side to side.

"Girl, you in Jean Lafitte swamp, you unerstan. Lotsa lost souls in da swamps, but this one is bad fer it, yeah...

"A fifolet is a lost spirit. Show up like a light... Blue light, Green light maybe, just floatin' off da path in da woods a way.

"DOAN FOLLER IT, you unerstan! No... People believe da fifolets lead 'em to treasure, cause ol' Cap'n Lafitte used to bury his treasure, then kill a slave o'er da treasure hole to protect it. But it's a trick, don't you know. Yeah, lotsa tricky things in da swamp.

"I saw one once when I was a piss-ant. Me and my little cousin was diggin' worms, not watchin' da sun and it got late. Purty soon my cuz' just started walkin' into da woods. I said 'Hey girl, where you goin'?' and she said, 'To catch dat fairy,' and I looked up and Lawd there it was, floatin' away all shimmerin' and lonesome. Didn't make no sound, but I could... feel it, you unerstan, yeah...

"Da fifolet... it'll just lead you on an on, just 'round another tree, then..." holding up his hands, "you just be gone."

Del shuffled from one foot to the other. Being raised in a church orphanage, she was not only taught the fear of God, but a bit about false idols and pagan beliefs. She knew how seriously Creoles took their legends, so she didn't want to say that she didn't believe in children's spook stories.

Frank cleared his throat through the cigar side of his mouth. "If you doan mind, I still need to look around."

Slim rocked, as if in a trance, for several seconds, then said, "Take da walkin' path, other side da road, pass an ol' chicken coop. Grann'on says it's just beyond."

Del spoke up. "You mean past all of the mirrors? Why are they out there?"

"Heh, you doan know nothin' bout da swamp, missy. Those mirrors all aroun' da house. They keep da Devil at bay, you unerstan... He's so vain, when he comes to take ol' Slim away, he'll stop and gaze at himself in those mirrors, purty soon, he get confused and forget how to find ol' Slim, yeah... then he go on his way."

The only response Del had was to wrinkle the side of her mouth and give a silent *hmpphh* through her nose.

"Doan sass me girl," Slim said, staring straight at her again. "I can hear you mighty young, yeah... mighty young... but there are things in this world dat gris alone cain't han'el. And you mind those things, you unerstan..."

"OK, Slim. It was nice meetin' you. We'll be on our way, but I do have one more question," Frank said.

Slim's mirrored glasses watched him closely.

"What makes you say murder? I 'spect there was a lot of screamin'. Horrible way to die, getting et up by a gator, but did you hear something to make you think it was murder?"

"Course I did. I heard da talkin'."

"What talkin'?"

"After I woke wit da fear, I heard two voices. First, I thought it was some drunks a fightin'. There was all sorts ah thrashin' and carryin' on.

"Drunks fightin'?" Frank asked. "Out here? You pretty far out for neighbors disputin'."

"They all types that live out here. Yeah... all types. But when da screamin' started, I knew some bad was bein' done. Da voices was all mixed up at first with other sounds. Lotsa splashin', jus' like you hear a gator do when he's eatin', tail a slappin' da water, rollin' over and over, but then da screamin' and hollerin' started from da one voice."

"And then?" Frank asked.

"An' then I heard da other voice. It was growlin'… and laughin'."

CHAPTER 6

'Six-finger' Eddie Bartlett awoke from his binge coma with a smashing headache. His mouth tasted like cigarette ashes and his pasty face looked like it had been used for the ashtray; pock-marked with splotchy red acne scars. The acne made little difference to Eddie's overall appearance; tall and gangly, his body was not coordinated enough for sports; thin and protruding, the bridge of his nose arched like a beak; his oversized Adam's apple made him look even skinnier than he was; and his bushy red eyebrows called to mind a lost tribe of Irish Neanderthal, or at least a problem of inbreeding.

He opened one eye to identify the room he was sleeping in. He was pretty sure it wasn't his apartment. *Freddie Blue's pad? Yeah, maybe.* Wherever he was, it stank like three-day-old wet laundry, mildewy and pungent. And the couch was itching him.

Feeling as if he had melted into the sofa pillow, he raised his head and realized that he had excreted so much sweat the night before, he had soaked the pillow. The mildewy smell was him.

Sitting up nearly caused him to black out as a wave of blood rushed through his head and caused his eyes to flash. Holding his head in his hands, he let the wave of dizziness pass and tried his eyes again.

Nice bender, dickweed. Get your shit straight, man.

"Yeah, yeah," Eddie said to the room. "Clean up my act, blah, blah." *Where's the coffee, Freddie Blue?*

Eddie slumbered to the small kitchenette, holding chairs for guidance and balance as his eyesight kept flashing with the change in blood pressure.

Sloshing coffee into a cup, he leaned against the counter and observed the dim apartment through despondent eyes. Sometimes shit just doesn't work out, but a real man just soldiers on. *Whatever.*

Gagging on the cold coffee, Eddie said, "What the fuck, Freddie, no hot Java my friend?" *What time is it?*

Looking around the small apartment, he spied a wall clock. "Oh shit! Ten-thirty?" *You're fucked dude. Kiss that job goodbye.*

He scratched at his neck and chest. *Fucking bedbugs, Freddie. Something's in your couch man.*

As resignation settled over him to another lost job, he sat down at the small kitchen table. *Just stop drinkin', dude!*

Yeah, I'm going to think about that.

After choking down the rest of the coffee, Eddie saw the note left for him on the table:

> *Ed, get your shit straight man. You broke the key in my*
> *lock last night and I think you stepped on your guitar. No*
> *more floppin here til you clean up.*
>
> > *F—*
>
> *And take a shower. You stink!*

"Whatever man!"

Eddie shuffled back to the couch looking for his guitar case. *Please tell me I didn't step on it. Please, please...*

Lying next to the couch, the flimsy black guitar case foretold a dire tale. A shoe-sized indention could be seen at the headstock. Quickly opening the lid, Eddie saw that two tuning pegs had been broken off, which meant unknown damage had been done to the neck. The guitar, his real passion and lifeblood, was unplayable.

"Oh fuck! Oh fuck! Man, not this..."

Slapping himself hard to emphasize each word, he sat on the floor and cried, "Get!" *slap...* "Your!" *slap...* "Shit!" *slap...* "Straight!" *SLAP.*

After several minutes lying on the floor, Eddie scratched his neck and chest again.

"Fucking BEDBUGS!!"

Stumbling his way into the bathroom, he turned the shower on hot and stripped off his stinking clothes. Looking in the mirror had always been painful. If he just wasn't so damned ugly, things would have been better for him. *Totally unfair,* he thought as he pushed at his springy red hair. Other dudes had it way easier in the world. Hell, some of the guys were only on stage because they had a great face and decent voice. Some even had shitty voices, but they still had better luck than he did. Fucking stars where shining on someone else the day he was born.

He looked down, flexing his pecs, but only saw his ribs. He was surprised at how skinny he had become. *Need a good woman to fatten me up,* he thought as he pulled his taut skin from his ribs.

He looked back in the mirror and slapped himself hard again. He watched as tears formed on his lower eyelids.

You're gonna let the music slip away. There's talent there, you know that. You could make it! It would be a shame to throw that away. A damn shame.

"No, it would be a sin," he said to himself in the mirror.

Stepping into the steaming water, he felt a modicum of stress leave his body. After drying, he stood in front of the mirror again, inspecting his itchy neck and chest.

Now what? he thought.

Reflected in the mirror, crimson against his pasty skin, was a bright red rash, starting on the left side of his chest and snaking its way up his neck. *These are not bug bites,* Eddie thought.

It looked like a pattern.

*

Sharon Frobije walked down Rue Blvd to the corner of Rue and St. Jean. She kept her head down, but was scanning the sidewalk from inside her hood. Her raincoat served two purposes: shield her head from the rain, and shield her face from anyone who may recognize her. Usually wearing sunglasses—she thought they would draw unwanted attention on a day like this—she worried about showing her distinctive, multi-colored eyes. She walked quickly on.

She hadn't worked this part of town for a while—how long she couldn't remember—but it always paid to be cautious. She entered the old family convenience store and scanned its inhabitants: a young clerk stocking cigarettes behind the counter, an old couple comparing the price of soup cans, someone in the back talking on the phone.

Sharon made her way towards the old couple and started browsing. *When opportunity presents itself*, she thought.

Leaning around the woman to grab a soup can with one hand, Sharon bumped into them both as her other hand slipped into the woman's purse.

"Oh, my goodness," Sharon said. "I'm ever so sorry. Clumsy me." She smiled politely and walked down the aisle with her can of soup and the lady's wallet.

Hearing the voice still engaged in its conversation, she browsed the next aisle while watching the clerk over the top shelf. The soup can and several other items fell into her large purse without a sound.

She casually walked toward the counter and asked for a pack of Camels. The bright-faced clerk set them on the counter, but before he could ring the sale, Sharon grabbed his hand with the pack in them. She looked at the cigarettes then back to him, making an obscene gesture with her mouth and raising her eyebrows in question. The blushing, stuttering clerk looked mortified. She rolled her eyes, dropped thirty-five cents on the counter, and walked out.

Back at her house, Sharon realized she was late. Her noon appointment would be there soon. She ran into her bedroom and checked her appointment list: *Séance – Dead husband,* the note read.

Stripping off her coat and blonde wig, she looked at her reflection in the mirror. She ran her hands through her red hair and bent forward, fluffing it slightly, and flung her head back. The natural bounce didn't disappoint, and she thought back to her high school graduation picture. A schoolteacher is what she had wanted to be; she was one of the smarter in her class after all. Where things went wrong she could no longer remember, but what a string of bad luck she'd had. The fling with the married professor had been blown way out of proportion, unfairly labeling her until she had to drop out of her sophomore year of college. She was shocked at the fallout; they were adults after all, and she couldn't help it if he didn't like his wife.

Mom and Dad didn't help much by claiming the incident to be the *'Embarrassment of a lifetime!'* and could only see fit to pay for her to go to a school out of the city, like she was a leper or something.

She didn't hold quite as much animosity for them as she once had. *Maybe* she could have done a few things differently. *Maybe*.

She touched the small crow's feet that were forming at the corner of her eyes and thought of how disappointed her mother had been.

What a waste, she thought. *Two more years of school was all you needed. What would your life be if you had just tried a little harder?*

She didn't have the answer, but also didn't like the feeling that was settling over her. She smacked her cheeks for color, adjusted her boobs and blew herself a kiss in the mirror. "You're a star," she said.

Throwing her séance smock over her shoulders, she felt a hot itchy rash on the back of her neck. As soon as she touched it, it seemed to inflame across her right shoulder and up onto her neck.

Great, now what?

She started for the lotion when she heard a knock at the door. Her appointment had arrived.

"Dammit!" she said as she grabbed her black Cleopatra wig from the stand and stuffed her hair underneath it.

I hope she's far-sighted, she thought as she went to the door.

CHAPTER 7

Frank and Del left the house and followed the walking path that started on the other side of the drive.

Although early afternoon, this part of the swamp was dark enough to use the flashlight Frank kept in his car. Walking slowly down the path, Del tried to count the number of mirrors she saw in the woods, but quickly lost track.

"Can you believe all these mirrors?" she said. "That's a crazy superstition. The Devil's so vain he'll stop to look at his reflection?"

"Lotsa folks believe dat stuff, Del," Frank said. "It's the belief in da thing that gives it power."

"But believing in something doesn't make the Devil real, Frank."

"Hush up now. Doan be talkin' about those things out here."

Del rolled her eyes again.

A short way up the path, Frank pointed out a sinking, rotted chicken coop to the left of the path, toward the water's edge.

A few steps further and Frank stopped. He shone the beam of the flashlight on a disturbed area at the water's edge, several paces off the path. Now in full detective mode, Frank scoured the area around them before taking a step. He progressed carefully, one step after another, ensuring that he did not disturb any evidence.

It was now clear that something terrible had happened here. A large, dark lump lay at the water's edge, and in the middle of a ten-foot square area that had been churned and flattened. Small piles of apparent flesh littered the area, and dark mottled spots glistened across the surrounding mud. It looked to Frank as if two animals had wrestled for their lives here, clawing and thrashing the ground to gain a hold over the other.

The body—if that's what it was—was an opaque lump of meat. Frank was certain it was meat, considering the way the ants and beetles were swarming over it. The subtle sounds of swarming insects added to the voice of the swamp. Frank thought he could hear faint tearing sounds as the body was torn apart by thousands of tiny mandibles.

Squatting close, Frank's nostrils were assaulted with the hot, putrid smell of rotting flesh as it floated on the air. He turned away and swallowed hard.

"Why doesn't it look like a body?" Del asked.

"Doan know. It kinda has the shape, but it's… too flat. It could be a body if it was… deboned."

"Come on Frank, really?"

"I'm not sayin' das what it is, jus what it looks like. Coulda been that it got so mashed up by the gator, it just doan look right."

Frank poked at the mass with a stick. The beetles scurried, but the ants were steadfast.

"Jesus, Mary and Joseph," Frank exclaimed. "Look at dis."

Frank knocked more beetles away and uncovered the remnants of a belt with a metal buckle. The belt was ragged on both ends.

He shone the light around the body and settled on a gouged area of mud. "Could be gator tracks. Pretty messy, but could be. I just don't understand why there's still a body here. Gator should've pulled it all down."

"Frank, what's that?" Del pointed several feet past the roiling mass.

Frank's flashlight swung toward the path as he stood up and took two steps closer.

"Some type of print or track, I think," he said. "I'll be damned if it don't have the stride of a footprint, but… the print don't look right. It's kinda… draggy, you know? Drug itself out da mud toward da path, but… where's the tail drag? Now how the hell…"

"Frank, what are *those*?"

He swung the flashlight beam back toward the body and noticed the small white objects Del was pointing at.

"What the hell…"

"Are those teeth?"

Carefully picking one up with his handkerchief, Frank held the three-inch long object up in the air and bathed it with light.

"It's a damn gator tooth," he said.

"Did it break off?"

"No. Well ain't dat da damndest thing. It looks like it just… fell out. See here, if you look close, you see dis ring line around da tooth? Dat's da gum line. This part of the tooth is the bitin' part. See how it's kinda smooth? From all da wear and tear. And then da line, then all the rest of da tooth—not as smooth, and look, it's hollow inside. This is da root. It should have a nerve here. Or at least what's left of da nerve. Can't imagine da bugs et it clean this quick."

Shining the light around the flattened area, they now saw a disturbing sight. The ground was littered with gator teeth that appeared to have simply fallen out.

CHAPTER 8

Frank watched the rearview mirror until they reached Barataria boulevard and were back on real pavement. After they found the gator teeth, he had quickly shuttled Del back down the swamp path and to the car. He hadn't said a word.

"OK Frank, what gives?" Del said finally. "What do you think happened back there? And what about old Mr. Slim? Crazy huh?"

Frank drove on for a while.

"Del-bell, I don't know what to make a dat scene. But don't go off assumin' he's crazy jus' because he's in da swamp. Lotsa legends and myths about da swamps around here, especially dat one!"

Wrinkling her forehead, she said, "But Frank, YOU don't believe them, do you? It's 1963 for heaven's sake. They're talking about us going to the moon!"

"I spect there's a good reason for what we saw. Gator most likely, maybe a killin', maybe even a ritual killin' of some kind. But I didn't like da look of it. And I have more faith that we'll learn da truth of that killin' then I do some bureaucrat is going to fly a can to the moon!"

They drove on for a while until finally crossing the swollen Mississippi. Foghorns and steam whistles called to each other up and down the river, lending a surreal, far-off feel to the Crescent City.

"Where you stayin' at Del-Bell? No sense you walkin' home. 'Specially with dis damn rain eatin' on people's nerves."

"That's OK Frank, I'm in 6th Ward, but way up Ursuline. I can just—"

"Where at in 6th Ward? I know it."

"Oh, I won't be staying there long," she said, voice trailing, "if I can help it."

"Watchoo mean honey? If you can help it?"

"Well, I just mean… I need to get out on my own, that's all."

Eyeing her sideways, Frank said, "You jus' got out da orphanage. What's da rush?"

She looked out her window at the gray, darkening day and wondered if the sun would ever come back out. "I just need to."

Frank's instincts told him to stop this line of inquiry. "OK, so where on Ursuline?"

"The old Prudhomme House. It's Mama Dedé's halfway house now. But like I said, I'm saving up for my own—"

"Mama Dedé you say?"

"Yeah, why? You know her?"

Frank considered this as he crept through the choked city streets. Another tree had fallen in a local city park and took down a bird's nest of power lines that had accumulated on the corner of two streets. The city was quickly fading to black as night encroached.

"Not sure… prolly lotsa Mama Dedé's in dis town, posen' n'such. Just like there's lots of Marie's claimin' dey a Laveau."

Del inspected Frank's face from the passenger's seat, but the dark streets hid his features. "You know I don't believe in that stuff. How is this city ever going to move forward if they don't let go of their voodoo rituals and spook stories?"

"Yeah, I remember you tellin' the Sister that you didn't believe you'd go to hell for sneakin' out also, but I bet it was hell after I left, wasn't it?"

"Sister Eulalie could be overzealous in her punishment, but that is of human making. There's nothing supernatural about it."

"Overzealous…" Frank whistled at the word choice. "Look at you. So, I guess the Church teachins didn't stick with you, huh?"

"I don't know… I guess some did," she said. "Be kind to others. You know, 'Do Unto,' and that sort of thing. I just don't know if it's all so… black and white, you know?"

"Yeah, I do know. Der's lotsa gray in da world."

They drove on in silence the rest of the trip. Frank didn't ask why she chewed her nails.

He eventually stopped in front of the Prudhomme House.

"Thanks a ton, Frank!" Del said, hopping out. "I'm going to write up everything I remember. Can I come by tomorrow? What's the next step? Oh, tomorrow's Saturday isn't it? I guess—"

Realizing that she wouldn't be letting this drop, Frank said, "Yeah, tomorrow's Saturday, but I'll be gettin' to da office around ten, so if you—"

"Ten o'clock. I'll be there."

"OK, den. Ten it is."

Frank drove off after watching Del go through the front door of the Prudhomme House, now a halfway house for girls, and let the events of the day play through his head.

Damn gator teeth jus' don't fall out, Frank. You know dat. What else could be da cause?

Frank could think of nothing from his days as a cop or detective to explain what he saw today, but a nightcap and a cigar might help him remember.

*

Later that evening, Loo'siana Slim stoked the fire in his stove as a cold chill settled over the shack. "Del-phine / Del-phine / doan liiiiie to me / tell me wheerrre'd you sleep las' night? /

"In da pines / in da pines / where da suuunn doa'never shine /

"I shiverrrr da ho' night through..."

He sang low and slow as his alligator boots rocked a rhythmic creak into the floorboards of the old shack.

Outside, the droning rain knocked at his roof, windows and door. Large drops, accumulating in the branches of the vast cypress trees that overhung the house, knocked harder or softer, depending on where the wind blew them.

He stopped his lonesome melody as a far-off sound caught his attention. The swamp had a voice all its own, and spoke in unison with the night creatures that lived within it, but this new sound was not natural to the swamp.

He quietly sat his guitar against the wall next to the pot-bellied stove and fingered the shotgun next to it. After several seconds he nearly withdrew his hand, until a gust of wind buffeted the tiny house and he felt the floor shift beneath him. He heard glass shatter far off in the swamp. Someone was breaking the mirrors that his grandson had hung for protection. A cold sweat broke over Slim's brow.

Donning a long leather slicker from the wall, Slim grabbed an old hat and stepped into the heavy drizzle.

Listening carefully, he first turned left out of the front door and walked slowly toward the rail. He felt the break in the railing where the steps would lead him down to the drive path—the same steps that Frank and Del had used just hours earlier—but turned left again and followed the narrow gangplank along the side of the house to the back. He faced the swamp in the direction of the old chicken coop, leveled his shotgun on the railing and waited.

Far off in the swamp, barely reflected in the blue mirrored lenses of his tortoise-shell glasses, a fifolet appeared and seemed to float above the water.

The shape, not more than a wispy cloud of mist, rolled and twisted in the air as if struggling into existence. The outer edge of its shape flickered in and out, like a bad T.V. reception. It took form as a man-sized mass, badly deformed, and moved as if stretching the rubbery skin of an egg sac.

It made no sound, but Slim somehow stayed fixed on its location, sensing a static-electric wave in the air. It hovered for a brief time, as if summoning the old man with the promise of treasure, but Slim did not move. He could not see the inviting light. He could only sense the impending danger as he stood listening.

The fifolet seemed to sense the obstinance in the old man and quivered rapidly in annoyance. When it did, a second fifolet appeared near it. The fifolet spirits, appearing as strangely lighted, dense clouds, emanated slow pulses of blue and green as they floated.

Slim heard the voice of the swamp fall silent. Not a toad nor cricket could be heard; even the raindrops seemed to hold silent as the ghostly lights approached.

Silence thundered in his ears and dread filled him. His skin prickled. There was something in the air.

He heard breaking glass again, only this time closer. He didn't know who or what broke the glass, but understood that by doing so, a path was being cleared for something else. He feared what it may be.

His mirrored-blue lenses tracked the floating shapes as they drifted soundlessly closer. A third fifolet, smaller than the others, fluttered down from high in the trees, perceptible only as the absence of color—a black void—and alighted on the low branch of a tree.

The unholy rain had swollen the swamp, which now lapped against the pine stilts of the shack. A slight gurgling of the water drew his attention down, and the lenses reflected the deformed, man-sized shape in the mist. When reflected, the shape stopped and shuddered as if going out of existence with the world, or trying to hide from direct observation. When the large, peculiar shape shuddered, so did the other two lights, as if all were bound by an unnatural union.

The black fifolet-spirit stayed perched on the low branch. The green spirit descended to the water's surface, sank below, then silently slithered up out of the mud. The larger blue spirit suddenly split in two, causing a smaller shape to cast off from it. The two blue fifolets were connected by long wisps of blue mist. The smaller thing quivered rapidly, excitedly, to its own existence. The larger shape reached out to pet the quivering thing in comfort.

The entire scene was reflected, silently, in the mirrored-blue lenses.

For several seconds, the ghostly spirit shapes held silent as if observing the blind man with curiosity. Finally, the two blue fifolets quivered again in unison, making the slightest warbling sound when they did.

Slim recognized the warble but detected something different in it. From the day his little cousin was nearly coaxed into the swamp by the magical sound of the fifolet, he was tuned to its vibration. To him it was a high-pitched, tinkling static; a vibration that set the fine hairs of his neck on end. He felt the voice of the fifolet before most people could see the shimmering apparition. Over the years, as he dealt with the many lost souls that wandered the swamps—some fifolets, some not—he learned how to ignore their siren call.

He sang softly under his breath.

"You come a callin'… / Knockin' round my door…

"You come a callin', wwooo… / Knockin' round my door…

"Good-bye you Devil, nooo… / Don't hear you call no more…"

Slim thought back to his traveling musician days, when he wrote this tune. Every honky-tonk and juke joint from Louisiana to Mississippi knew when Loo'siana Slim was in town—before he was blinded by a jealous lover and a handful of lye.

He remembered meeting another young guitarist, down on his luck and haunted by demons, who surely would have died on the road or in the back of a whore-house, had Slim not crossed his path that night in 1935. Slim, a veteran of the road, met a twenty-four-year-old Robert Johnson and gave him this tune to focus his mind away from the dark things that haunted him. The younger Johnson would go on to record a slightly modified version of the song as 'Me and The Devil Blues', only to die three years later.

Slim now sang a verse he had modified during his years dealing with fifolets.

"I'm wit' da livin'… / Six feet above da ground…

"I'm wit' da livin', ohhh… / Six feet above da ground…

"Don't hear you callin', nooo… / My soul doan want you aroun'…"

The blue fifolets warbled again as if accepting Slims invitation to pass him by, then a deep, throaty gurgle belched from the swamp. Slim heard a choked, mocking laugh bubble from the black water as the smell of rotten flesh filled the air.

The thing that rose from the swamp had masked itself and its offspring as fifolets to Slims demise.

Slim pulled the trigger on both barrels, blasting a hole in the silent swamp water and shattering several mirrors hanging in the distance. At this, the second blue spirit went into a wild, quivering convulsion and a deformed voice screamed ear-splitting gibberish. Slim threw his hands over his ears to scream, but not before he heard the large shape laugh a bellowing roar and smelled the stinking breath of death descend upon his face. A second later, a gaping maw tore out his throat as he called the name of his killer.

"L—!"

CHAPTER 9

Saturday

The next morning Del rode her bike through the drizzle. *Won't this ever stop?* she thought as she splashed through inch-deep water laying over the road with nowhere to go.

Several more trees had fallen through the night, and more neighborhoods were without power. The Treme area was typically the last to get services restored, but she was biking into better areas now and traffic was snarled here as well. People honked and shouted out of car windows and drove up on curves to get around. One person had tried to drive around a fallen branch and sunk their car up to the axles in the city park.

Del detoured to the orphanage to have breakfast with Jimmy before heading to work. Josephine looked up with surprise as she walked in.

"Del! What are you doing here?" Josephine looked over her shoulder through the interior double doors. "How's the outside world?" she asked with lighted face. "Do any—"

"I wanted to say hi to Jimmy before work. Why?"

Stepping between Del and the entry doors, she smoothed her jacket sleeves and said in a low voice, "You probably shouldn't go back there today, Del. Jimmy's in trouble again."

"For what? The sisters know he's just clumsy sometimes."

"It's not that. He's in bad trouble this time. He's been up all night singing some crazy song and he got all the young ones riled up and singing it with him. I tried to stop him but—"

"A song?"

"Sister Eulalie is whipping him in front of the class, but he won't stop!"

Del pushed through the doors that led to the waiting room and was opening the door to an interior hall as Josephine caught and pulled on her arm. Through a long hallway window, Del saw Jimmy standing in the middle of the cafeteria with his hands over his ears, crying as the sister yelled, "Stop that unholy singing right now, you vile boy!" She swatted him again.

Jimmy cried and squeezed his head with his hands. Tears and snot ran down his face.

"...da spit tay cat wit da mot'eatn ear. I can't stop singing! I can't stop! Aaaahhh…. Da mot'eatn ear, and da—"

SWAT!

"...baaaahhhhh,Ican'tstopit.ICAN'TSTOPIT!BAAAHHHHH…"

At this, Sister Eulalie grabbed Jimmy by the collar and dragged him from the room.

Del, watching through the cafeteria window, spun around and bumped into Josephine she was standing so close. "Oh my God! What was that about?"

Josephine caught her breath, looked up at Del and smoothed the arms of her jacket again. "Del, I'll be getting out soon you know, and—"

Del shook her off and began stalking the room. "I swear, I'm going to get Jimmy out of this place one day, and when I do, I'm gonna report that old biddy!"

Josephine watched in frustration as Del did not see her. A release of adrenaline suddenly fueled her words. "You know they're not going to release Jimmy to you. Not while you're in a halfway house, they ain't! He's never gonna be right anyway. Why do you care so much?" She bit her lip, regretting the last statement as soon as it left her mouth.

Del's eyes caught fire.

Josephine hadn't seen that look since the day Del caught them all dancing around Jimmy, taunting him. She remembered that it looked like two faces for a split second: one face, the angry young girl defending her only friend, the other face was of someone else, an older version of Del, weathered and wise, watching her life unfold from a distance. It was a terrifying sight that she never forgot. And she never teased Jimmy again.

"Don't ever…" Del clinched her jaw tight.

"I'm sorry, I'm sorry!" Josephine said. "I didn't mean that. I just don't know how—"

"Just tell me what he said. Who taught him that song?" Del stormed back to the waiting room.

"I don't know," Josephine said, following her. "But Del, it's…" looking around the room, "creepy as hell."

Del wrinkled her face in question.

Josephine leaned in. "I have the darn thing memorized 'cause the kids were singing it half the night. It goes like this:

Say your prayers my sweet little dear,
   Loud and clear so God can hear,
   If you don't, he'll soon be near,
   The man with the cat with the moth-eaten ear.
   I'll say my prayers and they'll be clear,
   Loud enough for God to hear,
   The split-tail cat will run in fear,
   And the Gris-gris man he won't come near."

Josephine watched as a look of shock fell over Del's face.

"Who taught him that?" Del asked.

"No one! At least, I've never heard it before. Creepy, isn't it?"

Del turned and looked out the window of the waiting room. The same window where Jimmy had patiently waited for his birthday to start. She watched the rain drizzle on, wondering what this meant and why these things always seemed to happen to Jimmy.

Interrupting her thoughts, the sizzling crack of a transformer announced its own death seconds before the lights went out in the orphanage.

Josephine jumped and ran to the dark cafeteria, where several little ones where already crying.

Del thought back to all the nights she had cried silently in this place. After being brought here by a social worker—an old woman who smelled of failing kidneys and three-day-old wash—she'd fallen into a deep depression and didn't speak to anyone for nearly a month. She only cried in the shower, so the sound of the running water would mask her sobs. After the first month, the nightmare of losing her parents was replaced by the harsh discipline of the nuns. She hadn't known punishment could be meted out so easily.

Her life would have gone on like that, sinking further into a darkness she felt deep inside herself, if Jimmy hadn't arrived at the orphanage. When he arrived, he reminded her of a little mouse that had been dropped into a cruel maze; a maze of ideas and expectations that was built from rules he would never understand. She felt drawn to Jimmy from the very beginning and decided that she would help him learn the maze the best he could.

Del sat in the feeble light of the window listening to the cries of the other children, wondering if this was a place of sanctuary or not. Either way, she felt certain she had to get Jimmy out of there.

*

Somewhere in the swamps of the Jean Lafitte Preserve, something resembling a body slowly bubbled to the surface of the soft, rotten mud. It was constructed of bones and flesh; it had arms and legs and something like a head, but it was an abomination at its core. The skin was that of a thing born from the swamp, leathery brown and lumpy, as if years of scar tissue had grown over foreign objects under the skin's surface. The thickness of the body was bloated in some areas and grotesquely caved in others, as if the organs had been poorly placed. The length of the body was indiscernible as the extremities appeared to melt away into the mud—or were still being formed from it.

It was surrounded by three fifolets: a small blue one—writhing itself into the rough shape of a disfigured animal—shivered in ecstasy and hovered close to the body; the green one—having pushed the body up out of the mud—stretched out and slithered a long circle around it, then disappeared beneath the brackish water; the black one—devoid of all color—fluttered up to a low branch and waited.

The beetles and ants did not molest the body, nor did any living thing come near it. The creatures of the swamp held their breath as the swamp itself sighed a low relief of having excised the hellish thing from its bowels.

The skin, as if reacting to the putrid air, suddenly began to move.

The blue fifolet shivered with excitement at the first sign of movement and floated down over the body, spreading itself out as if for protection. The skin, loose in some parts and stretched tight in others, undulated with life. The blistering skin never burst, but sometimes leaked a greasy substance where deep, dry-rot cracks existed. The black fifolet looked on from its low branch as one shiny black eye formed on its surface. The black eye watched the hellish scene, unblinking. The blue fifolet slunk off the body and writhed in ecstasy in the mud. It rolled over and over until a crude head formed from one end, and wisps of blue spirit formed a sort of antennae extrusion on the other end. The extrusion twitched in the dank air as if sensing its new surroundings.

The skin bubbled and hissed for several minutes. A sense of internal organ movement was reflected in the single black eye that watched from above. Some skin bubbles pressed outward and formed large tags, filling quickly with pus. The oversized skin tags, when filled to capacity, popped free of the body and hung from its sides by tenuous strings of sinew.

Suddenly, a violent gush of swamp water erupted from the body's mouth, expelling a stinking mash of rotten flesh and organs. The putrid mash lay steaming on the cold swamp floor.

Then the body pulled in its first ragged breath.

CHAPTER 10

F rank walked into his office shaking rain from his umbrella. Over the last two weeks, the cold drizzle had seeped into his core, and he felt a little stiffer each morning. He plopped down in his protesting chair and sat his cigar on the edge of an overflowing ashtray.

The old radiator heater hissed and groaned in response to the chair's complaints—two old mechanical friends complaining about the weather.

He opened the day's newspaper and read the headline:

COFFINS, COFFINS, EVERYWHERE!

The article described how a previously unknown Civil War-era cemetery had been found when four coffins had emerged from the murky depths and out of the saturated soil. The unfortunate residents, thrown from their final resting places—and in one case, scattered along a torrent of water—were found yesterday morning and were being attended by the local university historian and clergy.

His eyes jumped to another article that stated the police department had received several reports of missing persons, and that if anyone had any information, to call the NOPD immediately.

On the second page, below the fold, another article described an outbreak of strange rashes that were turning up across the city. Doctors theorized it was a bacterial rash due to an elevated mold count caused by the incessant rain. Citizens where encouraged to check for damp areas near windows and doors and use antiseptic cream until the rains cleared.

Frank lit his cigar again and fingered the alligator tooth he'd found yesterday. He needed to report his findings to the captain, but still wasn't sure what his report would contain. He doubted there would be much left of the body by now. There was hardly anything left of it yesterday.

As he rolled the tooth between his fingers, the radiator hissed a warm lullaby; the rain beat a low melody; Frank had just closed his eyes to think when the phone rang.

"Yeah?" he said.

"Frang? It's Henri GeeOHM."

"Cap'n, I was just getting ready to call you."

"Frang, what da hell happened out der?"

"Well, you got a dead body, dat's for sure. Did da recovery team get anything?"

"It's a damn massacre out der, da way I hear it. Why didn't you call me first thing? An where's da first body?"

"Whoa, da first body?"

"Yah Frang, dat's what I'm tellin' you. Da team couldn't get der 'til dis morning. When dey did, da grandson of da ol' swamp man was runnin' down da road screamin'. Dey took him back and da place was a horror show. Did you move anything?"

"No, course not. Twern't much left to move anyway after da ants and beetles had their fill. But what of dis first body business?"

"Some ol' swamp dweller. In a shack, Frang. He's dead and da first body is gone. In fact, not much a da second body is left da way I hear. Some small chunks, lotsa blood, but a real problem wit da head I hear."

"OK, cap, I'll head back out der, but I got a bad feeling about dis." Frank slowly rolled the gator tooth over and over in his fingers.

"Yeah Frang, I tink you're right. Keep dis between you and me for now. Only give your updates to me, no desk people."

"Sure thing."

"And Frang: no reporters, eh? Dey're sniffin' all over da bones now."

"Yeah, yeah, no reporters," Frank said just as Del walked through his office door.

Hanging up the phone, Frank saw Del's face and knew something had happened.

"Del-bell, what's wrong, honey?"

Del paced the office floor and recounted what she had seen earlier that morning.

"Yeah, I remember dat kid, Jimmy. Used to sneak out wit you sometimes, no?"

"Only a few times. Just when it was warm, and the moon was big. He always wanted to see the moon."

"Dat what put him on da bad side of da Sister you tink? Cause you was always standin' up fer him?"

Del stopped her pacing and stared out the window at the rain. "Yeah, I suppose. That and because the Sister thinks he's an abomination." Del stared pacing again.

"Come on honey, enough of dat. Let's take a drive. I gotta follow up on yesterday's thing. Cap'n just called and I'm afraid to say, but da ol' man we spoke with, he's dead too."

"What? How?" Del asked, confusion washing over her face.

"Doan know. Killed in a bad way it sounds."

"Isn't being dead bad enough?" she asked.

"No, honey. Der's far worse things than just bein' dead."

CHAPTER 11

S haron Frobije finished her last Tarot card reading for the night, closed the door on her customer and sank in front of her makeup table and lit a cigarette. The flickering candles cast competing flames to the matchhead in the three-way mirror.

Pulling off the Cleopatra wig and dropping her smock, she took the folded bills from within her bra and dropped the money on the table.

It had been a good night, she thought. Her fortune telling was always generic enough to pass, but she had hit a couple of specific points, and a fortunately timed wind gust just as she had finished *calling up the spirits* earned her a few extra dollars in tips.

Business had been good of late, probably due to the strange things that had been happening in the city, but certainly because of the deeply engrained superstitions of its people. Any time a bone was found, someone would come for a blessing; too much rain, a blessing; a bad turn of luck, a reading. And it went on and on.

But that fortunate wind, that had really helped.

Sharon walked to her front reading room; here her customers were greeted by the few old pieces of furniture she could afford. The walls were covered with drapes of silk and other material. Strange objects—some recently created by Sharon—adorned the shelves, and a séance table stood in the center of the room. She pulled an old book from a shelf, laid it on the table and opened it to a marked passage.

This was the one book in her possession that she felt had some actual magical properties to it, although she had never fully deciphered how to read it. Having stolen it years ago from an elderly couple while working as a cleaning lady, the book had a false cover and appeared to be the remnants of multiple books pasted back together. Some of the pages were written in French-Creole and were utterly unreadable to her; other pages seemed to be fragments of hand-written spells and incantations, and other pages—partially—seemed to advertise the strange history and abilities of one Jean Montanee.

Sharon smoothed back the old pages and read:

Of, or concerning Jean Montanee, circa 1850 —

Jean Montanee (Montanet), a free Negro of the Senegal tribe, originating from the deep Congo, recently purchased a respectable lot of land bordering Bayou Road, north of the city.

Easily recognizable by the ritual country marks and tattoos that adorn his face, he is considered by the native population as a priest of high standing in the Houdou religion, conjurer of the black arts and general healer.

If services are required, do not petition favors directly. Leave an offering of Absinthe or High John root and knock three times on the Bone Gourd—

There seemed to be more to the instructions, but those pages were lost from the book. She wondered where she may find more about this purported healer and wondered what, if anything, he had to do with her favorite passage in the book.

She then flipped to another heavily worn section, and although having these well memorized, reread the handwritten lines:

ϛεροε Ι – Verset I

Ηελλιοη σπιριτ ηεαρ με χλεαρλψ, γραντ ψου νοω φυλλ υσε ορ νεαρλψ,

Hellish spirit hear me clearly, grant you now full use or nearly,

Οφ μψ σουλ φορ υσε ανδ τοιλινγ, ατ τηε ωορκ οφ εϖιλ λορε.

Of my soul for use and toiling, at the work of evil lore.

Τηισ δαμνεδ σουλ ισ ριπε φορ τακινγ; ιν ιτσ χορε ωιτη τρεμβλεδ σηακινγ,

This damned soul is ripe for taking; in its core with trembled shaking,

Ηυνγερ–λυστ πανγ νεϖερ σλακινγ, βεγγινγ ατ ψουρ γηοστλψ δοορ.

Hunger-lust pang never slaking, begging at your ghostly door.

Υσε με σπιριτ, φυστ τονιγητ, τηατ Ι μαψ υνλοχκ Αβγελ σ δοορ;

Use me spirit, just tonight, that I may unlock Abgel's door;

ϑυστ τονιγητ, νο λεσσ, νο μορε.

Just tonight, no less, no more.

It was these lines that she used before important readings and tonight it had the desired effect. As soon as she had spoken the words, a heavy wind buffeted the house and creaked the timbers. Her customers were mesmerized the rest of the reading.

As she finished reading the lines, a strong wind creaked the house again, blowing a branch tip against a windowpane. Crushing out her cigarette, she realized that the branch had been blowing against the window the entire time she was reading, but the sound had faded into the background. Now it was more incessant.

Walking back to her bedroom to fix the offending branch, she stopped dead just inside the door. An ominous shadow lay upon the floor. Backlit from a ghostly lightning flash, silent in the distance, the shadow of a bird could be seen pecking at the floor.

Following the long shadow to its origin, she watched as a large black bird pecked three times at the window pane, a tap-tap-tapping in the unholy rain, then stared at her with one glossy eye. The bird, a raven, stopped its tapping when she entered the room. It sat quietly and watched her as she stared back at it. Finally, it turned and flew off into the night.

CHAPTER 12

Frank and Del left the house of Loo'siana Slim for the last time. They drove away in silence, following the same route they had driven the day before. The incessant rain cast a gray pall over the road, the swamp and the shack, which remained shrouded in a thick fog.

As they approached the Mississippi heading Northeast toward the city, Del could barely see the bridge girders that would support them over the swollen river. The fog-mist swirled in tattered shrouds from beneath the bridge in a slow curl that rolled over the creeping line of traffic.

"Damn, must be some kinda' jam up der," Frank said.

Del continued staring out the window, not hearing him.

"You OK, honey? Watcha dwellin' on?"

She worked to pull her mind out of a sluggish daydream—almost trancelike. Upon returning to Slim's house she had felt a heavy weight descend upon her. Even though she had only met Slim the day before, she felt a profound sadness at his death. She felt a heaviness of heart that she couldn't explain. An abnormal feeling of loneliness. An old vision, or memory plagued her mind. She felt sick to her stomach, as if an old secret were about to be exposed. When she was young, she'd get this feeling when she was sent to see Sister Eulalie. Not understanding the rules at an early age, missing her family, and not knowing what her future held made her sick to her stomach a lot. But the thought of getting in trouble beyond that tore at her dream of ever having a normal life again. If she couldn't stay out of trouble, no wonder no one wanted her. In the early days at the orphanage she thought the Sisters would all be like mothers to her, but that was not the case. She was happy when Sister Eulalie first took a special interest in her, considering she was the head nun, but she soon learned that the Sister had a sickness in her that could not easily be cast out. She'd said there was something unnatural in Del, vile, like Jimmy. Del said there was something unholy in Sister Eulalie.

"Del?"

She shook the feeling away as best as she could and looked at Frank.

"Do you believe in the Devil?"

Frank flinched in such surprise that a shower of cigar ash burst apart on his stomach as it was flipped from his cigar.

Slapping the sparks away, he said, "Course I do honey. What kinda question is dat?"

"Do you believe he talks to people?"

Eyeing her from the driver seat, he said, "Talks to people? Like you an' me doing now? I don't know—"

"In their heads, Frank. Do you think some people can hear him? Or... maybe are... tuned to listen for him?"

"Well now, I don't know about dat, honey," Frank said as he shifted uncomfortably in his seat. "I 'spect der are some people dat would like to think dey could call him up, ask a favor whenever. But if dey could, der'd have to be a terrible price paid, you know?"

Del continued looking out of the window, searching for something.

Finally, she said, "Ever since yesterday, I've had this sick feeling in my stomach. And I keep… seeing images of things… I think they're old memories, but I can't tell. Memories of a bunch of voices all talking or singing at once, but they're all jumbled up." She glanced over at Frank to read his reaction. "Either that or… or, someone's trying to talk to me." She laughed weakly.

Frank clinched the cigar in his teeth as he rubbed his chin. A deep puff sent a cloud of smoke around his head that mixed with the fog from the partially open window.

"Der's lotsa strange things people doan understand. You kinda scoffed at em yesterday, and that's fine if you doan believe. But," he looked at her with a furrowed brow, "not believen' doan make da bad things go away. And sometimes, it lets things creep in that aught'ena."

Del looked back out the window and wondered what things had been let to creep into her life.

CHAPTER 13

A Wretched Mind

Hello? Are you still there?

Anyone? I pray you've not abandoned me...

Oh, how my wretched mind churns these twisted thoughts! I fear that I cannot go on. Such a dreadful pall lays over my soul, you unerstan'.

Yes! A terrible, dreudful pall has been let to creep into my life. What abysmal things are let to creep into our lives? Powerful and terrible, yeah...

Yes, I recall now how it happened… it was a voice. Such a terrible, awful thing that was done to me, my mind had quite blocked it from my memory; never to be thought on again.

That voice called to me from the dark, you unerstan', yeah… called deep from the dark.

Then the voice spoke in my mind. From a black place… a black thing.

It was the Raven.

CHAPTER 14

In the dark of the night, Eddie Bartlett trudged through the drizzling mist and listened to the sounds float out of the French Quarter—the well-known jazz and blues music section of the old city.

The Crescent City's music heritage had been built on the strife and hard living of the people who had moved through this area over the last one hundred and fifty years. The destitute and downtrodden; the scorned and the hopeless; all left their song upon the breath of the city, and the city sighed deeply.

Having left his broken guitar at the repair shop, promising to pay for the repair when his next non-existent check came in, he took the last few dollars in his pocket and bought the cheapest bottle of whiskey he could find.

He knew he would have a cranking headache in the morning, but tonight, being only a third into the bottle, he felt as if his luck may change.

Walking up St. Louis Street, he saw the old St. Louis Cemetery

#1 loom in the murk. He knew from legend that the vault of Marie Laveau, the old Voodoo priestess, was somewhere inside. If he could find it, he might make an offering of part of his whiskey bottle and ask her for help with his life and music.

The cemetery was one of the oldest in New Orleans. Above-ground crypts, white as decaying bone, lay in repose in close, straight rows. The affluent lay in crypts of granite and marble, while flaking cement, peeling away from old brick walls, housed the less fortunate interred. Crosses and spires jutted up into the mist as lonely saints looked down upon the sinners.

Eddie wandered the rubble-choked alleys between crypts until he found one that was decorated with small trinkets and crude inscriptions on the sides. He sat down on a granite bench opposite the decaying crypt, took a large drink and closed his eyes. He felt particularly powerful right now, and was sure that his God-given gift of music was being felt by the spirits. He felt warm against the chilling mist and thought of how he could make the spirit of Marie Laveau hear him.

Along with the offering of a little whiskey—which he poured on the stoop of the crypt—he sang slowly into the night, watching the mist from his breath float away into the night.

"Black-girl / black-girl / don't liiie to me / tell me wherrre'd you sleep last niiight.

"In the pines / in the pines / where the suuuun never shines / I shiverrred the whole night through."

He took another long drink and closed his eyes, humming the tune under his breath.

Just as he was about to start another verse, he opened his eyes and watched his frozen breath float away from his body and merge with an eerie black mist that seemed to float against the prevailing wind. Tightening the grip on the bottle, he watched as the black mist became a bird, which now sat on top of the crypt he believed was the Voodoo priestess's.

He blinked his eyes, but the bird remained sitting, sitting above the dead chamber door.

The bird—a raven, he thought—looked down at him with one black eye.

Is this the Voodoo priestess? he wondered. *Is this how she travels back and forth from the land of the dead?*

"Marie?" he said quietly.

The raven adjusted its position above the chamber door and looked at him with the other black eye.

Thinking his introduction was too informal, Eddie said, "Voodoo priestess, Marie Laveau, help me please."

The raven cocked its glistening head, pecked three times above the chamber door and said, "Ask."

Eddie stared in amazement as he stood up. Had he really just heard the bird speak? A cold wind whipped through the cemetery, causing him to rock unsteadily. Oddly, the wind didn't appear to ruffle the bird's feathers at all.

The raven watched him patiently.

Eddie's mind reeled. *Ask? What should I ask for?*

Ask for help, dude! Get your shit straight!

This could be a once-in-a-lifetime, genie-in-the-bottle sort of thing. He had to think quick. *Don't fuck it up, Eddie. You won't get another chance like this.*

You have the talent! Just get clean, that's all you need!

Yeah, he could ask to get clean. Stop drinking. No more drugging.

That's what he should do. His fingers twisted around the neck of the bottle.

He should really do that.

But his drinking wasn't his fault. His parents had really fucked him up. It was because of them that he was like this, anyway.

Ask for them to pay, Eddie. Make something happen to them first.

But then what? What do I do then?

He shifted uncomfortably from one foot to the other, grinding gravel into dust, the way the question ground on his mind.

Ask to get clean. Forget the revenge crap.

Ask to get clean, but then what? Back to the same ol' slog? Beatin' the streets for a few bucks? Is that what he really wanted?

The raven watched him patiently.

Fuck dude, what are you doing? Ask for money, ask for fame, something! Don't just stand there! You're fucking up man! The bird's gonna fly away!

Eddie took another swig from the bottle and grabbed his head, rubbing it hard. His eyes were wide and watery, searching the dark gloom for an answer.

Fame... money... revenge... fuck!

The raven twitched.

"A song!" blurted Eddie. "A song that will make me famous!"

The raven tilted its glossy head; an amused, knowing tilt of its head.

The raven croaked, "Sing."

Eddie thought, *Sing? Sing what? That's what I—*

The raven began...

I call to you, by way of chanting—lest a demon voice be ranting,

Ranting in my wretched mind to call you up from days of yore.

I summon you to evil deed, your voice as one my mind will heed,

Seeking someone sure to bleed, to right a wrong done to my core.

Use me spirit, just tonight, that I may open abGel's door,

Just tonight, no less, no more.

Eddie didn't miss a word.

*

Somewhere in the Jean Lafitte swamp, a body that had breathed its first ragged breath just hours before sat up. The skin had stopped bubbling and had settled into a brown, leathery covering. The bones and tendons, mismatched and broken, had mended into a frail skeleton. The large skin tags had popped free of the body, excising foreign objects embedded within, encapsulating them in soft bags of skin that hung from the body by long strings of sinew.

A strange man now existed where the inanimate body had been.

The fifolets that protected the body went through their own transformation, each one different depending on their needs, but they could not exist without the strange man, for they were of the same essence.

Disoriented and weak, the strange man bent over and tasted the putrid swamp soil. He breathed deeply, inhaling the ancient spores that floated heavily on the air. He remembered this place.

Somewhere in a dream this place was known to him. Old images, some quite ancient, flooded his new mind.

The remaining blue fifolet, now with one formed eye, shimmered in anticipation and coaxed the strange man on. Its transformation was stalled; there was not enough energy for them all, not yet.

The strange man reached out to the blue shimmering object—hardly thicker than the surrounding fog—and felt its pain. His weak hand stroked a lump of spirit-cloud that may be its head, for the half-formed eye hung there looking on in anticipation. Another extruding lump of the thing shivered on its own when the man's hand passed through its essence. The shivering cloud-lump split from the main body of the blue fifolet and tried to exist on its own, only to fall lightly with a dead squish onto the swamp floor. The man coaxed the dead spirit back to the main form, where it was absorbed.

"Time…" the strange man said weakly. "I need to eat. Then you all will be restored anew."

CHAPTER 15

J immy lay in bed very still, fingers clinched tightly together, quietly
repeating his nighttime prayer over and over.

"Now I way, down to sweep, pway and pway fo Gawd to keep.

"Now I way, down to sweep, pway and pway fo Gawd to keep."

Occasionally he would stop and listen to his stomach growl, but
then he became afraid the bad song would jump back in his head,
so he said his prayers again like the Sister told him. He whimpered
lightly at the hunger pains of no dinner but covered his head so Sister
Eulalie wouldn't hear him.

The day had started with the terrible song he couldn't get out of
his head. He wasn't sure where it had come from. Maybe the sandman
had poured it in his ear when he was asleep the night before, but if he
had, that was a mean trick to play, and Jimmy didn't like mean tricks.

He'd thought that Del-bell was coming to have breakfast with
him this morning, but maybe she forgot. If she had, she would have
stopped the bad song from bouncing around in his head. Jimmy knew
he wasn't as smart as the other kids because of his *condition,* and

maybe the song got stuck there because he had less in his head than the other kids, but still wished Del had been there.

He loved Del very much and was sad when she left him and the orphanage. She said that she wasn't leaving *him*, but she left anyway. He wasn't sure what would happen once he turned eighteen, where he would go, but Del had always told him not to worry about too many things at once.

You can't think of too many things at once because it clogs up your head and the answers can't get in, she would say.

Since he didn't have many things in his head anyway, he didn't think he had to worry about it getting clogged up, but Del was usually right.

Jimmy still slept in the same bed he always had. Even though he was older and taller now—well, not that much taller—he had never been moved out of the room with the younger kids. That was OK with him, though. They didn't tease him as much as the older kids. At least most of them.

Jimmy lay there listening to his heartbeat, not realizing he was no longer repeating his prayer, when he heard the window in the coatroom creak.

He immediately thought it might be Del coming to see him.

The coatroom was off the back of the main sleeping area, a small closet where the kids hung their winter coats, rain slickers and kept their galoshes under a bench. It was also the one room that Del would sneak out of that the nuns hadn't found.

The other windows, one in the bathroom and one in a spooky broom closet had been found, but the window in the coatroom had an inside shutter over it. Everyone had forgotten it was a window. Del found it because she was so smart.

Jimmy lay very still and listened as hard as he could. *What if das Deh? Maybe she got stuck!*

Jimmy tried to figure out what he should do.

Don't get stuck, Deh!

That probably wouldn't help, because Del couldn't hear his thoughts.

I hep her! Hod on Deh, I hep you!

Jimmy lifted his head and looked around the room. Remembering what Del had told him before when they snuck out, he had to be quiet as a mouse.

Quiet da mouse, quiet da mouse, he thought as he snuck to the coat closet. Once inside, he giggled to himself at what a great mouse he made.

He moved the old coats from in front of the shutters. No one remembered who the coats belonged to any longer, so they always hung in the same place, hiding the shutters that hid the window.

He then opened the shutters and looked out the window.

Whe'd she go? he wondered. She wasn't stuck in the window after all.

He could barely see anything in the alley that ran the side of the orphanage. The old streetlamps at the ends of the alley barely cast their light to the middle.

Kneeling on the old bench, Jimmy pressed his face to the cold glass, just as he had done when waiting for Del, and strained his eyes left and right to see further down the alley. Not realizing it, he began to softly sing, *"...da spit tay cat wit da mot'eatn ear."*

A large gust of wind heaved against the window, hitting it with debris from the alley right where his face pressed against it. Startled, Jimmy jerked back and fell off the bench.

He almost cried out, but the thought that Del might be in trouble kept him quiet.

He lay there listening for any stirring roommates, when he heard a strange tapping noise. Three quiet taps at the window.

Deh? he wondered. *Dat you?*

He crept back onto the bench and slowly raised his head to look out the window.

A fluttering shadow scared him, but he didn't look away. Things were still scuttling down the alley as the wind continued to blow, but he thought he had seen a shape.

Bravely pressing his face to the window again, he saw another shadow flutter up to the garage roof across the alley. A brief flash of lightning, far in the distance, illuminated the object. A large shiny bird sat on the garage roof peering at Jimmy, its enhanced shadow darkening the orphanage window.

Jimmy saw the bird for a brief moment as he unknowingly called to it, "...*da spit tay cat wit da mot'eatn ear.*"

Another flash of lightning and the bird was gone.

After a few minutes, Jimmy quietly closed the shutters and latched them, hung up the old coats and tiptoed back to bed. He quickly dropped off to sleep thinking about the beautiful black bird he had just seen.

Around the corner of the big sleeping room, Josephine stood in the shadows of the dark hall until Jimmy had settled back into bed.

What's he doing now? she wondered. The last thing she needed was another all-night symphony from creep station.

CHAPTER 16

Sunday

"Ouch! What is this?"

Sharon woke early the next morning to a burning sensation running over her shoulder and up her neck. Her blanket rubbed against an itchy area, which sent ribbons of pain shooting to her head.

Looking into her bedroom mirror, she saw swollen curls of rash streaking up her neck and encroaching onto her right cheek.

"Oh my God! What is this?" she cried, gently touching the enflamed marks.

Just her luck! She tries to be a good person, and this is what she gets. Sure, she has to bend a rule every now and then, but she doesn't deserve to get some weird rash, especially the day she was going to work a stag party and make fifty bucks! Who can dance in a negligee with swamp crud growing up your face?

Walking to the kitchen to start a pot of coffee, she saw the old book laying on her séance table and remembered part of a strange dream she'd had last night.

Something about a bird flying around… dropping seeds into the swamp that grew into giant talking snakes, or something like that. Weird.

The image quickly faded, and she thought no more about the book on the table.

After a quick breakfast, she threw on loose clothes and headed out the door. She would drive into town and see if she could find some cream for her rash. Living this far out on Barataria road had the advantage of few prying eyes, and it wasn't terribly far from the city, but when it came to quick conveniences, there were none.

She drove north and passed the old swamp road. She'd heard there had just been a gator killing down there and wondered if it was anyone she knew. Usually these things didn't make much news, but there was something odd about this one, apparently.

As she drove past the abandoned Crown gas station which sat at the end of the swamp road, she suddenly thought of Chocolate sodas. She hadn't thought of them in years, but something about the quiet Sunday morning reminded her of driving home from church with her parents.

Her father was an honest, but uneducated trainyard worker. Her mother did her best with the money they made, but it didn't go far. Sunday afternoons typically included a stop at one of the few gas stations that was open to check the air and oil. Even though her father did this regularly, he used the stop as an excuse to spend a few cents on his only daughter; this usually meant a treat from the soda machine.

Her friends always said that Yoo-hoo was the best, but she preferred *Chocolate Soldier* – *'Cold or hot it hits the spot'*. She remembered wishing that the tiny red soldier on the side of the bottle would come to life, slay a wild beast and whisk her away to a magical land. There, she would live in a fairy tale and have five children, one more beautiful than the next. Her prince would be very handsome.

Her mother's voice brought her partially back from her daydream: *You have your health and good teeth. What else does a girl need?*

Despite her mother's utilitarian view on her late-arriving womanly assets, she *was* a caring woman and loved her family. *Maybe she deserved a call.*

Sharon knew they hadn't spoken in quite a while, but was having trouble remembering exactly how long it had been. *A year? Surely not over a year and a half.*

A year and a half really?

Despite the embarrassment she still felt from the affair, she thought her mom really did deserve a call. Maybe some of the fallout *had* been her fault.

She could still make amends.

She would call her mom when she got home.

The party is tonight.

She would call her mom tomorrow and save her the lie of what she was doing tonight. She would call tomorrow.

A movement in the shadows of the old gas station caught her attention and pulled her back to reality. She thought maybe her landlady's dog, Millie, had escaped the backyard fence again. If that were the case, she'd pick her up on the way back and deliver her home. Who knew, maybe the old lady would knock a few bucks off the rent.

Watching for the dog in her mirror, she saw another shadow and got the impression that it may be a person. Maybe her landlady was already out looking for Millie.

Her car's not there.

Well, maybe someone was finally trying to do something with that old building.

She knew that many people had tried to repurpose the old gas station before, but they never lasted long. If someone was trying to work it again, they shouldn't expect much traffic to come along. The gasoline pumps had long been removed. All that remained of the station was the graying cinderblock building, the rusting metal roof that stood above two vacant pump areas, and the road sign that kids had thrown rocks through for years.

She drove on, wondering what anyone would be trying to sell on this side of the river, but remembered that a fruit or vegetable stand would show up there occasionally and people would reuse the flimsy wooden stand that the original proprietor had left.

Approaching the Mississippi River Bridge, she swung her car to the side and slammed on the brakes.

"Shit! It's Sunday!" she said, letting her head fall against the tattered headrest.

"Damnit."

Besides the fact that most everyone would be heading to church, no store would be open today, not on a Sunday in the South.

Her burning rash protested at this and sent a searing pain up the side of her cheek and into her right ear.

"Owww!" she said as she looked sideways into the rearview mirror. Her heartrate jumped as she imagined the rash somehow crawling inside her ear and deep into her head.

Dismayed at her situation, she turned around and drove toward home, wondering how she would make it through the day. The burning was getting worse.

As she approached the old gas station again, she slowed to see if anyone was there, or if she could catch a glimpse of the dog. The old wooden cart was untouched, but she caught a sense of movement through the large front window of the building.

She pulled to the shoulder and sat with the car running. The rash felt as if it were pulsing now, irritating her, a beacon throbbing out to an unknown presence. She scratched at the rash, which sent a bolt of fire down her neck and back.

She squinted through the foggy car windows, messing with the defroster controls that never seemed to work when needed. She was positive she had seen movement. Why she cared, she wasn't sure, as her landlady never gave her a break on rent. But if some hobo had decided to take up residence just down the road from her, she wanted to know; plus, if someone was looking to muscle in on territory she regularly worked, she wanted to know that as well.

Feeling for the switchblade in her purse—and having walked an alley or two in the past—she felt comfortable enough with the open area around the old building. She got out of her car—where the cold mist felt good against her rash—and walked as far as the old fruit stand. She surveyed the area, and all looked normal—it was an abandoned building after all—but then noticed, sitting on an old rocker next to the front door, two of the rattiest Voodoo dolls she had ever seen. At least, she thought they were Voodoo dolls. She was certain those hadn't always been there.

New Orleans was flush with Voodoo dolls, skulls, orbs and other assorted gris—the Creole term for anything that may be used as a charm—but one typically did not lose a Voodoo doll, and you never threw one away. That was a sure way of offending whatever spirit was attached to the doll.

She also knew from dealing with the soothsaying community that the proper pronunciation of gris was with a long E sound like *free,* but preferred the more sinister sound which rhymed with *this.* Swamp people were known for taking liberal shortcuts with words, and she hated the extra work it took to form the long E sound in the back of her throat.

The blessing of gris—where inanimate objects were *blessed* or imbued with a magical power—was a decent money-maker for her. And although she knew she had little to no real power, she had seen some things in her past that made her a true believer; some people had truly awesome power. And gris could consist of anything from amulets and lockets, to small bones and trinkets; sometimes even a bundle of sticks tied with twine could be blessed or cursed and used to great effect; sometimes to terrible effect.

Just as she was about to return to her car, the front door of the gas station creaked open with a rusted jangle from an old bell.

She watched as a peculiar old man walked out of the interior shadows.

He stood in the doorway and looked at Sharon the best he could. At least, she thought he was looking at her.

She could see from the length of his arms and legs that he had been a tall man in his youth—probably over six feet tall—but because he was so hunched over, and because his knees seemed to be compressing before her very eyes, he barely stood five feet tall. And although he leaned heavily on an old walking stick, she perceived a constant struggle for him to keep his balance.

The strange man stood for a moment in the doorway and Sharon wondered if he could even speak, when he suddenly twisted his head sideways and breathed a ragged breath of air.

"Good morning, miss," the strange man said in a voice from another time.

She was so surprised by the sight and mannerisms of the strange man that she nearly didn't hear his greeting.

"Oh, good morning," she replied.

At first, Sharon couldn't understand what was so unsettling about the man, but slowly realized that his dress was completely inappropriate for someone who had just walked out of an abandoned gas station in this part of town.

His heavy rain slicker dragged against the ground due to his stoop, and all but covered his old wool pants and cowboy boots; a dark shadow masked his shirt, which appeared to be ornamented with a number of small leather bags strung about his neck; an old hat covered his head, which appeared to pull him forward. But the oddest thing he wore were a pair of tortoise-shell sunglasses with blue mirrored lenses.

"Pardon me," the strange man said in a gentlemanly proper voice, "is this your residence?" The hat and glasses obscured most of his face, and his mouth portrayed no emotion.

"Residence?" Sharon asked with concern. "No, this is a vacant building."

"Oh, of course," the man said. "I meant to say, is this your property? I was simply resting out of the weather."

"Oh, I see. Well, no, it's not my property, but… say, do you need help or something?"

"Help? No, why?"

"Well… you just kind of seemed… I don't know, a bit wobbly."

The strange man considered her for a long time, then said, "Just getting my sea legs about me."

Sharon wasn't sure what to make of the response, and mentally calculated the distance between them.

"Ok then," she said. "I thought maybe you were setting up shop or something."

The strange man considered her for a long time again, then said, "Oh, what type of shop?"

Sharon shrugged her shoulders. "I don't know. I thought you were selling something, is all." She turned to walk away.

"Sell?" the man said. "No, I rarely sell, but I often trade." A fierce wind blew at this and buffeted Sharon where she stood; oddly the wind seemed to miss the strange man completely. *Maybe the building blocked—* Sharon started, then said, "Trade? What do you trade?"

"Gris," the man said, raking the bags that hung about his neck.

"Hmm, I guess you just don't have it all out yet," she said, trying to look over him and through the station door.

"Oh, I only carry a few... specialized items," he said as the blue mirrored glasses followed her.

"That so?" Sharon asked. "What would that be?"

With a shaky hand the man raked the bags again.

"Gris, you say? Just what you have there?" she said, pointing to the bags around his neck.

The man touched the bags gently. "Special gris. For special... conditions."

"What about those?" Sharon pointed to the old Voodoo dolls laying in the chair.

The two ratty dolls looked a hundred years old to her. One appeared to be a miniature doll, only about four inches tall; it had stubby arms and legs, no attempt at hair or clothes that she could see, with bright red beads sewn in for the eyes. It sat on an overstuffed doll of a dog—or a cat, she couldn't really tell—that had one ear half torn off and a tail that was coming apart so that it looked like it was two pieces. They were stuck together with a long hat pin. Even though they looked like Voodoo dolls, Sharon couldn't see the telltale signs of stitching, and wondered what they were made of.

Stepping slowly through the door and resting his hand on the rocking chair, the man looked at the dolls and patted them gently, as if petting them, and said, "Oh these? They're not for sale."

"Why is that?" she asked.

Looking at her for a long moment he finally said, "They bite." And a distorted, toothy smile broke across his face.

Sharon waited for him to break into a laugh, signaling the punchline, but his face resumed the reserved look of a mortician.

She cleared her throat and turned to go back to her car when she heard the old man breathe another ragged breath.

"Pardon me, madam, for being so bold," he said, "but that is quite an ugly rash you have there."

Self-consciously touching her face, she said, "Oh, yes, I was just going to get something for this."

"Of course," the man, said nodding his head slowly. "But I doubt anyone will have what you need."

Casting a questioning glance his way she said, "Really? Why is—"

"I'm familiar with this rash," the man said, now standing only a few feet away from her.

The quick and silent movement startled her as she stared at herself in the mirrored glasses.

"Fascinating," the man said.

"What?"

"Oh, I'm sorry," the man said. "I was referring to your eyes. How lovely."

"Oh," Sharon said with relief. She was used to people commenting on her multi-colored eyes, but not within the context of an ugly rash. "Thank you. Odd mix of genes, I guess."

He nodded slowly. "Indeed."

"But, about the rash?" Sharon prompted.

"Yes, yes," he said, inspecting her closely from his hunched position. "That's quite aggressive. It's been a few years, quite a few actually... but... I know just what you need."

He shuffled through the many bags that hung about him, and upon finding one he held it out and said, "Put this under your pillow at night. In about two weeks, you should start to see it fade."

"Two weeks? I can't wait two weeks, I have... well..."

"Well what?" he said, listening intently.

"I just can't wait two weeks. Don't you have anything stronger?" she asked.

"Stronger? Hmmm... yes, I could make something stronger, but..."

"But what?"

"You must understand, the stronger the gris, the more... the consequences."

"Consequences?"

"Poor word choice. Affects, really."

"Oh... OK, yes, I get that. But how fast can you get rid of this?"

"Quite fast, but you must give freely."

"OK, but—"

He went to work quickly, opening the small leather bags, picking an assortment of items. He picked a fragment of parchment from one and a small piece of bone from another and crushed them between his fingers. This he let fall into an empty bag he produced from inside his trench coat. He produced a small bone knife from another pocket and cut a lock of hair before she could protest, then very carefully scraped a few flakes of dying skin from the rash. He crushed all of this again between his fingers and dropped it into the same bag as he mumbled to himself.

She thought it sounded like an incantation, but couldn't tell.

He closed the pouch tightly, tied it to a cord around his neck and dusted his hands.

"There, all finished," he said.

"That's it?"

"Yes. As I said, all finished. Your rash will begin to fade in an hour and will be completely gone by morning."

"Really? Are you sure?"

"Quite sure," he said.

"OK… don't I… need to take the gris with me or something?" she asked.

"Oh no!" he exclaimed, patting the bag with affection. "As I said before… special gris. This will pull the source of the rash to it, away from you, so it no longer manifests itself… outwardly."

Sharon self-consciously touched her face again.

"So what's the cost then?" she asked shrewdly.

"Cost? Oh, no cost really. As I said before, I prefer to trade."

"Trade what?" Sharon watched the strange man as her own image came into sharp focus, reflected in the blue mirrored glasses. It looked as if her image was shimmering a sensuous dance.

"Oh, I see," Sharon said. "You want to *trade*. Well… whatever." She couldn't imagine that the man had much stamina at all, and if the gris actually worked, she'd be glad to show her appreciation to him.

"When and where? Here?" She looked at the road for any traffic.

"Oh no," the man said. "May I call on you in an evening or two? To check on your… progress."

"OK, sure, but how—"

Turning around, she was surprised to see that he had already walked back to the door of the building. The Voodoo dolls were gone also, but she assumed he had snatched them up on his way.

He turned and looked in her direction once more.

"See you soon," he said as he broke into a wide, distorted grin.

CHAPTER 17

Sunday afternoon, Jimmy was pressed against the front window of the orphanage, face smashed flat, waiting for Del to arrive. They didn't always go to the movies, but Del had tried to visit Jimmy each Sunday since she had escaped the clutches of Sister Eulalie.

Del walked into the lobby and saw Josephine sitting behind the reception desk, reading a magazine.

"Hey, Del. The boy wonder has been waiting for a half-hour at least."

Del wrinkled the side of her mouth at the snide comment and walked into the waiting room. Josephine always had something to say about Jimmy, and it was hardly ever nice.

"Hi, Deh," Jimmy said as she walked through the door.

"'Hi, Del?' That's it?" she said with a curious look. "That's not very frien—"

She stopped short as Jimmy turned from the window. His eyes were red from tears.

"Oh, Jimmy, what happened?"

"I got in twouble," he said with his head down.

"Did you spill something again?" she asked as she led him to the reception desk.

Jimmy kept his head down as she signed him out.

Outside, she popped an umbrella and they headed down the sidewalk. After a block of walking in the cold air, she thought he looked calmer. "OK, so what gives, Jimmy Lareaux?"

"I'm yust causin' a watt ah twouble atey," he said matter-of-factly, nodding his head. "Twouble, twouble, twouble."

Del chuckled. "Oh, really? You don't seem like much trouble to me."

"Yep, da deva must have cwawed up my butt an eft a twouble turd."

"Jimmy!" she said, stopping suddenly.

"But I'm yust fawtin' twouble everywhere, Deh!" he exclaimed with his arms out. "Fawt twouble deh… fawt twouble over deh…"

"Who told you that?"

"Yosephine…"

"Yeah, that's what I thought. Well, don't listen to everything she says to you," she said, heading down the sidewalk again.

"Awn't you fwiends no mo?" he asked, catching up.

"Sometimes. I guess… Hey, I got an idea. Who wants to go watch the trains come in?"

"Dis guy!" He thumbed his chest.

After they'd had their fill of trains, Del and Jimmy walked slowly back toward the orphanage. The afternoon light, muted by heavy gray clouds, highlighted dark shadows under Jimmy's eyes.

"Are you feeling alright?" Del asked. "You look kinda tired."

"I tought you tuck in da winow ast night."

"Stuck in the window?" she said, then whispered, "Oh, our secret window?"

"Yeah, I heard a knock on da winow. I fought you got tuck."

"Someone knocked on the window? Are you sure it just wasn't the wind? It was pretty windy last night."

"No, it da biwd knock da winow. He fwew away."

"A bird?"

"Yeah, da win scaiwd him, but den I deamed of him an guess what?"

"What?"

"He could tawk!"

"He could? That's a pretty smart bird."

"Yeah, he petty smart, I guess. Den guess what?"

"What?"

"He teached me a song."

"The bird could sing, too?"

"Yep, he singed… uhmmm," Jimmy scrunched his face up like he had a lemon drop in his mouth.

"He singed… I forgot," he said throwing his hands up. With much concern he explained, "It just went in da ear, den in da utter ear and didn't come out!"

"Well that's—"

Lowering his voice, he said, "Den guess what?"

"What?"

"He got mad."

Del watched a change come over Jimmy's face.

"Got mad at what?"

"Cause I doan memba da song."

"Why do you think the bird got mad at that?"

"Cause, he give me bad deams."

"You had another bad dream? About what?"

Jimmy looked down at the grimy sidewalk and kicked at a gum splotch. "He made me deam of da issaad dat eat you head."

"What? Again with the wizard that eats my head? Who's been telling you these stories? Josephine?"

Jimmy barely shook his head.

"Then who?" she asked, giving him a quick one-arm hug. "There's no such thing as wizards, and certainly not wizards that eat people's heads."

Jimmy said nothing.

They walked for a while in silence. As they passed a display window of a Five and Dime, Jimmy stopped short and yelled, "Ook Deh, ook! Da issaad!" as he pointed at a large painted advertisement.

Del stared at the window for a moment before she realized what Jimmy was pointing at. The window reflected her confusion.

"This is what you've been dreaming of?"

Del watched the reflection of Jimmy nod his head slowly and lean into her.

"Jimmy, that's a lizard."

CHAPTER 18

E ddie wandered the streets of the French Quarter. The music venues were always open, but the Sunday evening crowds were tame compared to Friday and Saturday nights. He hoped the lull in traffic would allow him time to plead his case.

The repair shop wouldn't release his guitar on the promise of a check, and he needed a loaner. He hit every bar owner he knew about gigging, but no one would trust their guitar to him, fearing it would end up in a pawn shop. He even wiggled his right hand at them indicating that his extra finger always made for a killer set, but they simply shook their heads.

'Six-finger' Eddie—really five fingers and a thumb, but that didn't sound as cool—could pick out some crazy blues tunes with the extra digit. It truly sounded like two guitars being played at once. He was suddenly afraid that his days as a musical oddity may be over.

He walked south of the French Quarter following the Mississippi and found himself in the old wharf district. Dilapidated buildings rose up into the fog-rain like oversized crypts, reminding him of his encounter at the cemetery the night before. The old cobblestone streets were broken and warped and led him down a natural slope toward the river. The sweet smells of fried dough and rum gave way to the earthy smells of fish and men who lived in alleys. Somewhere down the dark water a foghorn blew.

The wharf lights cast a feeble glow through the dense fog that rolled in from the river, obscuring his view of the barges he knew to be anchored there. He met the occasional bum rummaging through a trash can and wondered how long it would be before that was him. Not long, he thought.

Turning into a dead-end alley he thought was open, he was surprised by a small group of teenage boys standing around a fire burning in a barrel drum. Before he could back out of the alley unnoticed, one of the boys jumped to their feet and circled around behind him.

"Well, well," the boy said, "look at dis peckerwood dat just strolled up in here."

The two other boys were on their feet and forming a circle around Eddie before he could respond.

"Hey boy, watchoo doin?"

Trying to steady his whiskey-legs, Eddie said, "Just headin' home, that's all," as he clutched his bottle tightly. He thought about making a dash, hoping the group wouldn't give chase, but knew he only had about a twenty-yard sprint in him.

"He's spyin' man, for da cops!" another boy said.

They closed in.

"Yeah, he look like a snitch to me, man," the third boy said.

"Da fuck you doin here, man?" the first boy asked as he shoved Eddie toward his pals.

The three shoved Eddie back and forth as they taunted him,

grabbing at his bottle then slapping up at his face.

"Take his money and let's split!"

Eddie laughed out loud at the thought of having any money to be stolen, but quickly regretted the outburst.

"Peckerwood, what da hell you laughin' at? You're about to get your a—"

Abruptly, one boy stopped and pointed over Eddie's shoulder toward the river. Eddie turned and watched as a peculiar man walked slowly up the cobblestones.

"Hey, man," the first boy said. "Look at dis dude. He definitely lost!"

The three boys turned, pushing Eddie behind them, and watched the strange man walk towards them.

He stood severely hunched at only five feet tall, supported by a cane, but looked as if he could be taller if his frail body could support it. His long overcoat billowed out behind him as if blown by an unfelt wind. An old hat shadowed most of his face from the feeble streetlamps, but dark mirrored glasses followed each boy with interest.

"Da fuck you doin, old man?" one boy said.

The strange man stopped several yards away, not answering.

"Old man, I said—"

Suddenly, another shape emerged from the fog. Eddie's arms prickled with goosebumps as the temperature fell around them.

"What da fuck is dat?" the first boy exclaimed.

Eddie watched as a huge, mottled gray animal walked forward. It was the size of a large wolf, with a broad chest—its head standing four feet tall. It had the eyes and paws of a cat. Its powerful face was scarred where tuffs of fur had been torn off—or fallen out due to mange. The left ear was nearly missing, as if it had been chewed off, and its tail had somehow been split in two, but each piece remained functional and swung about in different directions, like searching antennae.

Astride the cat-beast was a small figure; the tiniest man Eddie had ever seen, possibly only a foot tall if standing on the ground. The mutant was bald and appeared to be completely naked, with only a bumpy, brown rash covering its skin. Its stubby arms stuck out from its body as if no elbow joints had formed. It held onto nothing and appeared to be pinned to the cat-beast by a long thin metal spike that ran down through its shoulder and into the back of the beast. Its eyes looked like sewn red beads, never blinking.

"Good evening, boys," the strange man said as he stroked the beast's head.

The other boys looked to the first—the apparent leader—to speak. After a long silence the first boy said, "Who da fuck are you?"

"Me?" the man said quizzically. "Oh, that's not important at the moment."

Thick clouds of fog slid up the landing behind the man, seemingly pulled by an unseen force.

"Den what da fuck is dat?" the boy said, pointing to the beast.

The man nodded approvingly.

"I'd like you to meet Mr. Sandgrove," the strange man said, petting the beast again. "He's happy to make your acquaintance."

The beast breathed a ragged breath, gurgling through broken lungs, as long trails of slobber hung from its jowls. Subtle waves of steam rose from it, as if it had just finished a long run.

The boys exchanged glances.

"Da fuck kinda stupid name is dat?" the first boy said nervously.

The man stroked the beast a few more times, ignoring the question. "And this," he waved a hand toward the mutant, "is Toth."

The boys shifted their feet, testing the stability of the loose stones, and Eddie took a large drink from his bottle.

The first boy took a half step forward and said, "Better run off old man, before you get hurt."

The man cocked his head slightly as an odd shiver rippled through his body, vibrating the reflection of the boys in the dark glasses. Their images were reduced to fragments, fighting to stay in focus.

"Hurt? How so?" he asked.

"Man, I ain't playin' no game witchoo. Go on, or you get da same fate as da peckerwood," he said, pulling a knife from his back pocket.

The man watched them for several seconds. "Delightful!" he said, breaking into a wide, distorted grin.

The boy stood trying to stare the old man down. He shuffled his feet again and finally said, "Man you don't scare me. Just an ugly old dog wit a doll stuck on its back." He kicked gravel at the beast, hitting it and the mutant.

The beast hunched, ready to pounce, and bellowed a loud, wolfish howl. Its split tail twitched in anticipation as its claws protruded, piercing the old stones. The mutant on its back came to life with a surge of energy, standing up the best it could, eyes glowing red, and screamed out a high-pitched warble of gibberish, still pinned to the beast.

As the mutant stood, they all saw the long metal spike that started in its shoulder and protruded down through its rectum and into the beast's back. The mutant simply pushed with its legs and slid up the thin spike into a standing position. The mutant mouth never opened, but the eyes pulsed with demon fire; the crazy hellish thing spoke an ancient, foul language and one of the boys began screaming at the sound. The beast leapt straight into the air, landing on all four paws, which shook the hard cobblestones. The mutant slid down the needle and bounced off the back of the beast, only to come to life again with another surge of energy, cursing foul upon the wind.

The three boys broke and ran. The first one, down the river wharf, the other two back up the way Eddie had walked.

Without hesitation, the beast broke after the first boy with several loud barks. The mutant's arms and legs flung about wildly as the beast ran, its body bobbing from side to side on the long needle as the beast galloped after its prey.

A fragment of mutant gibberish trailed through the air and Eddie heard, "…aaeeeee, gob-blick-krickry! Ngyihng! Ngyihng! Ngyihng!"

They were quickly lost to the fog.

Eddie stood frozen as the terrifying scene unfolded in front of him. He looked at the nearly empty bottle in his hand, trying to decide if it was all a hallucination.

He really should get clean, he thought.

As if hearing this, the strange man looked straight at Eddie and smiled his toothy grin.

"Good evening," he said. "Pardon me for the… interruption."

"Interrupshon? Sheerosly?" Eddie said, looking around at where the group of boys just stood. "Who're you?"

"Oh, I'm what you may call a… traveling collector."

Eddie wobbled as a cold wind swirled fog and rain around him.

"Collector of what?"

After a long pause, the man cocked his head again and said, "Friends."

Eddie scratched absently at his rash as he pondered what the man meant.

The strange man breathed a deep ragged breath, savored the smell of the river, and said, "I say, that is a rather nasty rash you have there."

"Yeah," Eddie wobbled, "ish my bad luck rash. Man… what kinda dog—"

"Bad luck, you say? Why is that?"

"Man, you don't have the time…" Eddie trailed off, but not before wiggling his six fingers in the air.

The strange man stepped forward, inspecting Eddie closely. "Fascinating," he said, with a slight grin. "You know Eddie, I can help you with your rash. I'm also a bit of a… healer."

Something bothered Eddie about this comment, and he tried squinting the answer into his brain, but it didn't come.

"A healer, huh?" Eddie's eyes drooped as if being forced closed.

"Yes. Special gris, for… special issues."

"I got isshoo's a'right… got no money man… special gris… … fucked up…"

"You were a good musician, weren't you Eddie?" The man leaned in close. "God given talent, you could say."

Eddie nodded in agreement.

"Have a good ear I suspect. Can hear things, can *feel* things, that others… simply miss."

Eddie nodded again.

"I like music. A sin to throw that kind of talent away."

Eddie had heard this before, but couldn't remember where.

"I know what is causing your rash, Eddie. I can take this away and… some of your other issues, but you must give willingly. That is, you must agree to the… treatment."

Eddie nodded, almost asleep.

The man went straight to work, mixing the gris from the bags he carried; a snip of hair and a scrape of skin and he was done.

Eddie sat down hard in the alley.

"Good night, Eddie," the man said as he tied the new gris bag around his neck. "Your new life will begin very soon."

Right before Eddie passed out, a thought slipped through his mind. He didn't remember telling the man his name.

CHAPTER 19

Monday

F rank woke Monday morning to a distant ringing. He first thought his wife had slept through her alarm clock and started to nudge her, then remembered that she was gone. He rolled over and looked at her cold pillow still neatly fluffed. It seemed a physical incarnation of the cold day that was forming outside his window.

He closed his eyes, but heard the ringing again, only louder.

As his mind cleared, he realized he was hearing his own telephone ringing. *Dis prolly bad news*, he thought as he swung his heavy legs over the side of the bed. No one called him at 7:30 in the morning unless it was bad news.

Shuffling past the end of the bed, he grabbed his housecoat off the back of the door and made his way down the hall. Grabbing the phone off the wall he said, "Hello?"

"Frang, it's Henri GeeOHM."

"Yeah cap'n. What has you up this early?"

"Frang leesen, I got another body missin' da head."

"Another one?" he asked, rubbing his eyes awake. "Not a gator I guess?"

"No, dis no gator. We found da body down da wharf. Something chewed it apart pretty bad, but took a special interest in da head."

"Really, how so?"

"You go see, Frang. It's da lower wharf area, toward da bridge."

"Yeah, I know it. Not da first body dat showed up der. OK, let me get woke, den I'll head out—"

"And after dat, I need you to make a run on a missing person as well."

"Missing person? How long?"

"Got da call early dis morning. Jus' missin' since yesterday."

"Cap'n, it's still early," Frank said as he prepped the coffee pot. "Not even twenty-four hours old yet? We missin' da pope or somethin'? Why da rush?"

"I know, Frang, it's early to run it, but da landlady called it in. Da damn door was swingin' open dis mornin' an she's sittin' outside in da car watchin' o'er da place. Scared to go in."

"Ok, I get it, but why me? Don't you have—"

"It's close to da other bodies."

"Down Jean Lafitte area?"

"Yah, tis down toward da other missin' head, and da ol' man. You remember da ol' man, Frang?"

"Yeah, yeah, I remember. I was just out der. You think dey related?"

"I think dat we got a crazy man out der is what I think. Either dat or dis gator got up and it's walkin' around."

Frank chuckled briefly at the thought of a Saturday morning

cartoon gator strolling the park with a top hat and monocle, swinging a walking stick while whistling and tipping his hat to the ladies, then suddenly chomping someone as they walked past; but then his stomached turned.

"One more ting. You say you didn't find nothing at da ol' man's house, right?"

"Not besides what was left of da body with its guts thrown everywhere. But never did find da head. Poor old guy." He paused. "Dat just ain't how you expect to go."

"Yeah, yeah. OK, Frang, ok. You call later. Eh?"

"Sure, cap."

After Frank hung up the phone, he sat at the kitchen table and picked up two plastic bags—he still marveled at the invention even though the plastic bag was going on ten years old now, he thought. One still had the gator tooth from the site of the original body. The other bag had several large scales held together by a rotting membrane. Just two days ago this looked like gator skin that had been sloughed off, and now it looked like scales from a giant snake protruding from a hide-skin combination.

He thought back to when he and Del had arrived at Slim's place. As soon as they pulled up, Del had complained of a headache. One that she hadn't made any mention of until right at that moment. Frank assumed it was her squeamishness about seeing the body of someone she had just spoken to the day before, but hadn't asked.

He remembered that as he'd walked to the gangplank surrounding the house, the rising swamp was lapping around the support poles of the house, but he could still see where the ground had been torn and thrashed. Tracks, like those he had seen a day earlier, had been left in the mud, but were different somehow.

Upon closer inspection, it looked as if two sets of prints overlapped each other. The toe holes appeared to be a combination of human toes with claws extruding from them.

Besides the strange prints, an overwhelming smell of rotting meat had hung in the wet air, nearly causing him to gag. Looking around, he'd noticed a strange piece of flesh that he'd thought was the victim's, but after turning it over, realized it was a hybrid skin-hide that had been sloughed off in large sections.

At the kitchen table, his stomach turned over at the thought of the sweet, putrid smell. It was if the air had been coated with a thick oily substance that once inhaled, hung in the back of his mouth triggering a gag reflex as it threatened to slide down his throat.

He looked from one bag to the other, wondering what he was seeing. He felt a growing uneasiness that had settled about him since finding the first body. He was beginning to suspect that these weren't natural killings, but the alternative that kept pricking his mind was not one he wanted to entertain.

He finished his coffee and made an egg sandwich for the road.

At nine o'clock Frank pulled in front of his office and saw Del sitting on the top step. She had been waiting for him.

"Watchoo doing here so early Del-bell?" he asked as he huffed up the outside steps. Unlocking the office door, he said, "Chompin' at da bit on da new job?"

With a somber tone she said, "I was hoping you'd be here Frank. I wanted to ask you something."

Settling down into his protesting chair, he finally saw the unhappy look she'd been trying to hide.

"What's da matter?"

Looking at the floor, she said, "I was wondering… well… I was wondering if you might have some work that I could do around here?"

"But—"

"I'd work real cheap Frank," she said quickly. "You know, sort of like a, what do you call it? A starter rate?"

"But what about your new job?"

She shook her head quickly. "I don't… I don't think I'm going to have it long." She wiped at her eyes.

"But why not?"

She straightened in the chair as the cords in her neck stood out. "Because those two old reporters don't want to work with no n—," she clamped her lips in a tight, twisted line as her face flashed, "with someone like me."

Frank leaned back in his chair and looked out at the gray day. He knew the two guys downstairs and knew exactly what Del was facing.

"It won't always be like dis, honey. Gray, you know. Times are changin' pretty quick now, but it takes time for people to change. At least some people."

She nodded her head silently.

"In da mean time, I'm sure we can work somethin' out," he said, giving her a wink.

For the first time, Del felt like there was someone she could possibly trust.

CHAPTER 20

F rank drove to the old wharf where the third body was found. This one had drawn a small crowd of onlookers; during the day the wharf was busy with barge business and there were all sorts of people that passed this way.

"You stay back behind the line," Frank whispered to Del as they approached.

Frank spoke to a police officer, showed his badge, and the man nodded and let him through.

The body was covered, and Frank noticed that several other spots on the wharf were covered also, but they were smaller.

Frank peeked under the sheet. "Oh, lawd," escaped his mouth, along with his newly lit cigar. Dropping to the wet cobblestone, the cigar tried to escape the scene, but instead rolled into a pool of blood between the cobblestones. Frank looked longingly at the cigar, then cursed under his breath. Looking under the sheet didn't take long. He assumed the arms and legs were under the others.

He looked back at where the head had been, but his brain was struggling to process the image.

The back of the head was still intact, and seemed to be connected to the body with part of the spinal cord, but the face was gone, along with everything that should have been inside the skull.

The torso had not been eaten, but it looked like it had at the points where the arms and legs were torn off. Although the skull had remained attached, it appeared to have been licked clean of its contents, and laid there like a white, broken gourd. The brain was completely missing.

Frank shivered as he walked back to Del. "Come on honey, you doan wanna see dat."

"But what did you see Frank? I need to take notes or something. How am I ever gonna get—"

Frank walked ahead, not hearing her. He shivered again and realized that the hair was standing up on his neck. He knew it wasn't from the cold.

As they drove across the bridge, Frank answered yes-and-no questions for Del, but provided few details. His mind was running over the possible scenarios before him, and he felt he was running out of viable options.

Twenty minutes later they pulled up in front of a small two-bedroom house near the Jean Lafitte preserve. An agitated landlady was parked in front.

Frank turned to Del and said, "Let me go ta— Hey, what's da matter?" He saw Del rubbing her head.

"I don't know. Feels like another headache coming on," she said.

"How bout I leave da car run and you—"

"No, Frank. I want to help. I need to be able to do something!" she said with a cracking voice.

"OK, ok, let's go, den." Frank was concerned about her obsession with working and buying a house. He'd have to remember to talk to her about it later.

Exiting the car, Frank spoke with the landlady for a few minutes—who was quite animated about the time it took the police to get there—then entered the house after telling her he'd raise a complaint with the captain.

After a quick search for a body turned up nothing, Frank told the landlady she was free to leave and that he would lock up. She was only too happy to oblige as long as he promised to lock up, which he assured her again he would do.

Walking back into the house, he saw Del sitting on an old couch, rubbing her head.

"There's something wrong here, Frank. Something wrong with this house."

"How so?" he asked, eyeing her carefully.

"I don't know. I felt dizzy as soon as I walked in. I don't like it."

"Jus sit down for a minute. Dis won't take long."

He knew the main room had been used for séances. He recognized the tools of the trade of fortune tellers and mystics. He inspected the shelves and noted the standard cadre of mixed candles, incense and stones, tarot cards that were well worn, several small bottles filled with herbs and liquids, and a real-looking skull watching from the top shelf.

Turning to the table in the center of the room, he barely noticed a standard crystal ball when his eyes fell to a strange book that lay open and inviting.

The tattered book lay on the edge of the table. He immediately felt uneasy of the Frankenstein creation. He could tell from where he stood that the book had previously been in several pieces. The loose binding betrayed the act of manual gluing; the varying size and thickness of pages spoke to the dissection of different works; the worn edges showed the wear of ages, but the soul of the creation lay exposed for all to see:

~~ςεροε I~~ – Verset I

~~Ηελλιση σπιριτ ηεαρ με χλεαρλψ, γραντ ψου νοω φυλλ υσε ορ νεαρλψ,~~

Hellish spirit hear me clearly, grant you now full use or nearly,

Frank took a handkerchief from his pocket and carefully grabbed the corner of the book to close it.

"What's wrong with the book?" Del said, suddenly standing next to him.

Frank jumped slightly, causing the handkerchief to dance at the end of his fingers. "Doan know, but I don't like da look of it," he said, slowly closing it. "Gotta be careful with some of these things."

Frank looked around and seeing a newspaper lying on a chair, grabbed the front page and wrapped the book in it. "It's evidence for now."

"Where do you think the woman went?" she asked.

"Doan know dat, either. Kinda strange to leave da door open and your purse on da counter, don't ya think?"

"Yeah."

"No sign of struggle, but da people out here near da swamp live a different life. Our gal could be sleepin' off a hard night for all I know. One time I saw—"

Del sat down hard again in a kitchen chair and grabbed her head.

As beads of sweat broke across her forehead, she wobbled slightly as her stomach did a slow flip.

"You sure you're OK honey?" Frank said. "You look three shades pale."

After a long, slow breath Del said, "I just need to get out of the house. I need some air."

Frank helped her to the car and drove away slowly with the windows down, despite the incessant rain.

In the trees above the drive, a black gleaming eye watched them drive away, then flew off into the wind.

CHAPTER 21

Back in Frank's office, Del poured herself some tea as Frank jotted notes about the case in his notebook. The cold damp air had cleared her head, but a tiredness had fallen over her.

"So, do you think there's a real serial killer in the city?" she asked from the doorway of his office.

Frank pulled off his bifocals and rubbed the bridge of his nose. "Don't know. But whatever we lookin' at ain't good."

"Well if it's not a serial killer, then what?" she asked, watching him curiously. "Surely these aren't a coincidence?"

He leaned back in his chair and locked his large hands over his stomach. A fresh cigar, wedged in the corner of his mouth, sent curls of smoke around his head.

"Listen Del-Bell, dis city is old and it got lotsa secrets. What I'm thinkin' can't be explained real well, and certainly won't be goin' in my report."

Del squinted her eyes at him. "Not Voodoo again? Really, Frank?"

"Listen hon—"

The phone rang and broke their conversation.

"Yeah," Frank said.

"Frang, it's Henri GeeOHM."

"Yeah, cap. Was just writin' some notes. What I do you fer?"

"Frang, about da body on da pier."

"Yeah, yeah, I was just—"

"You're off da case. I'll take it from here."

Frank held the receiver away from his ear and looked at it, as if he would better understand what he'd just heard by staring into the black holes.

"Say again, cap?"

"Yeah Frang, I'll take da case from here. I'll need your notes by dis evenin.'"

"OK…" Frank said slowly. "Any reason—"

"And Frang, you sure you didn't find nothing with da other bodies, right?"

"Yeah, dat's right," Frank said as he replayed the kitchen table scene in his head. "I didn't find nothing but a pair of bodies."

"Yeah, OK Frang."

The line went dead.

Frank sat and looked at the dead receiver in his hand for several seconds.

"What's wrong?" Del said.

Frank hung up the phone and pulled a long draw from his cigar. He clasped his fingers over his stomach and swiveled toward the window. Another cold gray afternoon was setting in by the look of the clouds, he thought.

What is his game? Dis don't smell right.

"Frank, what is it?"

The luxury of being a private detective was that you could choose your own cases, Frank's wife had told him once.

What is his game?

"Is something wrong?"

"I need to go see someone," Frank said absently.

"Who, Frank? What's going on?"

"Del-bell, I want you to stay he—"

"Come on, Frank. I'll help however I can. I won't get in the way. I really need this job and—"

"Honey, something's afoot and I don't think you should be—"

"Please. This is all I got. I don't have anything else." She picked restlessly at her low-bitten nails.

Frank sighed deeply and watched a cigar ash fall to the floor where it disintegrated in a small puff. He knew a bit of Del's history. The fire that had killed her parents had happened in his precinct.

"Yeah, OK. You come along if you want," he said, looking out the window again. "But don't question where we goin' or who we gonna see. I'm gonna let dis case take me where it wants to take me."

"OK, Frank. Whatever you say."

*

Sharon wandered an old path she had never seen before. The forest was thick and the giant trees grew together in a twisted canopy far above her head; grotesque and stickly fingers stretching out from twisted branches. The dim light of day cast a monotonous gray pall over the sodden air, illuminating the ancient breath of the swamp, swirling and heaving in unison with an even older heartbeat. The swamp sighed in anticipation of Sharon's arrival.

Sharon was remotely aware of her surroundings. She felt as if she were sleepwalking through a vivid dream that was not generated by her own mind. She saw shapes come and go; her body maintained its balance as she transitioned from path to forest floor; her mind heard the branches and brambles snag her torn nightgown, her bare feet felt the cold mud, but she walked on.

She felt she was changing somehow, but had no fear of it. It was simply a process that would happen. Soon, the body and mind of Sharon Frobije would not exist. What would exist in its place she did not know, but it would happen.

She felt a strange hollowness permeate her core. It could be described as hunger, but not of the stomach, of her entire being; her soul felt thin.

She looked blankly at the Spanish moss that hung throughout the trees. Somehow her eyes saw the moss differently. Instead of the mysterious *Grandpa's Beard* as she had learned to call it as a child, she now thought of it as the tattered souls of all the people who'd lived unfulfilling lives. Those people that never endeavored beyond their immediate needs and left so many God-given gifts to lay in waste. She now understood that part of her soul was hanging in the trees somewhere, the part she'd so quickly thrown away by making the choices she had. A feeling of dismay came over her as she felt she was doomed to wander these woods forever, looking for the last few good shreds of herself.

The beast watched upside-down Sharon defy gravity as she wandered the swamp-forest. The beast knew nothing of tattered gowns or souls. The beast knew nothing of lost time or the yearnings to replace the grains of sand at the top of the hourglass. The beast knew evil and fear. The beast knew want and despair.

The beast watched Sharon want-and-despair as it hung upside-down beneath a low branch of an ancient tree; its long claws anchored deep. Its cat-eyes followed her closely, dilating quickly when she stopped or stumbled. Its split tail swayed lazily, then twitched with anticipation, causing a sensation of life to travel through the metal needle and tease the mutant towards life.

The mutant, having slid to the top of the needle, was stopped from sliding off by a round, flat nail head. Its arms and legs stuck out and hung down slightly toward its head, twitching back to life in unison with the tension of the beast. A faint "*ngyihng…*" escaped its unmoving mouth with each pulse.

The beast had Sharon's scent now, and would never lose it. It closed its eyes and waited.

CHAPTER 22

F rank pulled to the side of Prytania Street and looked out the driver's window at the old three-story mansion that sat across from the Lafayette Cemetery #1.

Built in the 1840s, the mansion was a marvel of architecture that showed the wealth and eccentricity of the original owner, reportedly a man of French descent who made a fortune in the slave trade. The mansion and supporting carriage houses encompassed an entire city block, and was surrounded by an ornate wrought-iron fence.

The steep-pitched gable roof was obscured in the thick fog-rain, but Frank knew it challenged the live-oaks for sun as it towered skyward.

Third-story dormers looked out over the soggy streets, and were high enough to give view over the wall of the cemetery and onto the crypts within.

A large covered front porch stood ominously silent, all at once inviting and dreadful.

The arthritic oaks stretched their massive branches in all directions, some reaching over the street and nearly touching the cemetery wall, as if straining to snare an errant soul, living or dead, to feed its ancient roots.

The house was dark except for a faint flicker of light that came from a second-story window.

Frank pulled slowly around the corner to where the side of the mansion loomed large to his left. Halfway down the block he came to a large gated drive where gas lamps cast a dying light upon an ornate but foreboding entry gate.

Pulling up to the gate, he pressed a small button and said, "Bonjour, l'entrée s'il vous plait?"

Several seconds passed before a response came. "C'est qui?" said an odd voice.

"Armand, it is Frank Morgan. How are you, old friend? May I speak with you?"

"Mon ami! Oui, oui, come in!" Armand said through the crackling speaker.

Just then, the gate gave a loud shudder and the two pieces creaked apart with strained groans. If anything would wake the dead, Frank thought, it was that gate.

Frank parked inside the gate, then he and Del walked through an overgrown garden that sat between the old carriage house and the main residence. The garden was a clever mix of stone walk areas and lush plantings that still slumbered under the cold March weather. A large circular fountain accented the center of the garden. An eight-foot tall maiden, rising out of the black tarn, cast her cold granite eyes upon them; her face shown sad for all those who passed.

Frank considered walking around the side of the house to the front, but was surprised as the backdoor opened before they could ascend the steps to the large back porch. The wild hair of Armand

Baptiste stood out in silhouette from the dim glow of the kitchen.

"Bonjour! Bonjour! Come in, mon ami!" said Armand's bushy white mustache.

"Armand, how are you?" Frank said, shaking his hand and pretending to tidy his lapel. "Dapper as always."

Armand's short, slight frame hid the physicality that Frank could feel in his gripping handshake.

"Still toting boxes?" Frank asked.

A twinkle lit Armand's eyes that added magic to an already wizened face. "On occasion," he said with a wry smile.

"This is my friend Del. I hope we're not disturbing you."

Armand's bushy eyebrows danced. "No, no! It is so very nice to have a visitor now and then!" He waved his pipe over his head as if spinning a saucer on it. "Gets me out of my study, you know!"

Armand led them into a large kitchen that was cluttered to no end with relics and artifacts of all types. The lingering smells of a late breakfast still hung in the air, mixing with a very recent bowl of pipe tobacco.

Del thought Armand seemed at a loss with what to do with his new guests, and watched the curious man as he meandered around the large room touching random items.

"Let's see now..." Armand said as he turned in a slow circle, patting objects, "table... my what a mess, table... chair... pantry... yes of course, stove!" He pointed a triumphant finger at Frank. "Would you care for some tea?"

Del arched an eyebrow, wondering about the odd little man Frank had insisted they see.

"I 'spect Del would love some," Frank said, "but as for me..." He shrugged his big shoulders.

"Ah, but of course. Brandy it is!" Armand said as he started another slow circle to piece together what was needed for brandy.

Del watched in amusement as the impeccably dressed man walked around the kitchen, smoothing his smoking jacket and patting objects, playing a loose game of word association. His strong hands shot here and there with amazing dexterity, touching, straightening and patting objects. "Vase," which sounded like *Voz*, "basin, let's see now, basin... pitcher, ceramic, yes of course, cupboard!" He walked out of the kitchen into the foyer. "I moved the brandy to the sideboard!"

Frank turned and saw the crossed arms and questioning look on Del's face. He smiled broadly and gave her a wink and a nod, then followed Armand to the brandy station.

As Frank and Armand chatted friendlies, Del gazed around the large parlor room to which they had moved. Late nineteenth century furniture was arranged in proper sitting areas. Large, dark paintings looked down from the ten-foot walls. Tiffany lamps and wall sconces cast warm, kaleidoscopic light toward the dark corners. The deep, rich feel of the room enveloped her as she caught a glimpse of herself in a mirror, gaping at the room like Alice down the rabbit hole.

She had never been in a room like this before, much less an entire house. She wanted to love the dark, rich wood and thick carpets, but tried to push them from her mind. Whatever house she could afford— more than likely a small apartment—would never look or feel like this one, so why think about it at all?

"Now Frank, mon ami," Armand said after a while, "what really brings you here? Is it that small package you have so carelessly wrapped and failed to acknowledge?" He tilted his head toward the book that sat next to Frank.

"Dis..." Frank said, touching it lightly. "Yeah, dis is part of da reason." He tapped his foot nervously on the floor, wondering how to start.

Armand puffed on his pipe, eyes twinkling, as he watched Frank.

"Well, it seems we got a… bone problem," Frank started.

Armand nodded thoughtfully. "Yes, I have read about the poor souls. Squeezed right out of their eternal sleep, it seems."

"Yeah, well, some of 'em ain't been asleep long. And…"

Armand stopped nodding.

"And, der missin' lotsa parts."

Frank went on to describe the three bodies he'd investigated, and the state that each was found in.

"The head you say, was missing? How so?" Armand asked as he strolled the room, touching objects as if recording the strange story with a secret word association being passed into the objects.

"Well, da arms and legs were torn off," Frank said, "but we found em. And da head was… well, part of da head was der. Da back skull. But…"

"Yes?" Armand asked, watching Frank intently.

"But uh, da face was gone and da brains were missin'."

"Really?" Armand said, touching a bust of Pallas Athena, storing the brain part of the story there. "The brains were missing," he told the bust quietly. "Cut out I suppose?"

Frank shifted his girth on the couch and sipped his brandy. As the liquid courage warmed his belly he said, "No, I believe they were et out."

A shrewd look crossed Armand's face as he turned from the bust. "And why do you think they were… et?"

No one noticed that Del's headache had seemed to return.

"That skull was clean as a whistle. Almost like it'd been licked clean.

And… looked like teeth marks on da part dat was left."

"What type of teeth marks?"

"Big damn dog maybe. Can't tell for sure. Whatever it was, it damn near bit through his arm before it ripped it off."

"And the other bodies," Armand asked. "Were they… equally violated?"

"Heads were gone, but da bodies were worse. And…"

"Yes?"

"And there were tracks. Hard to tell if they were animal or… or human in one case. They were kinda muddled together."

"Fascinating," Armand said as he walked absently out of the parlor.

Del looked quickly at Frank and gave a *What gives?* shrug. Frank was hoisting himself off the couch when he heard, "Follow me please! Up, up, up!" from somewhere outside the room.

Del and Frank walked out of the parlor just in time to see Armand disappear over the top of a long staircase that curved gracefully up to the second floor. The staircase originated from a large foyer that led to grand oak doors at the front of the house, and created a regal entryway that looked up to the room Armand was now in.

Del was the first to the top of the stairs and looked on in amazement at the room in front of her. At the top of the stairs was a large half-circle room that overlooked the grand foyer they had just stood in. The large alcove was lined floor to ceiling with ornately carved bookshelves, also constructed in a large, half circle that followed the contour of the room. A librarian's ladder hung from a metal track at the top of the shelves, which could be slid around from side to side to reach the uppermost ends. Part of the second-floor ceiling—floor to the third— had somehow been cut away and fashioned into an interior dome that rose to the third-floor ceiling, narrowing until it poked out of the roof.

There, a stained-glass dome finished the structure, which allowed ghostly colors to muddle together and creep down the interior curves. A large working table sat in front of the shelves and was covered with old books, loose manuscripts and several candelabras.

By the time Frank reached the top, Armand had already chosen several volumes from the shelves and was walking in a slow circle behind the table, stalking the final book. "Let's see, flood of 1785… yes flood, city plans, yes, dyke plans," he touched books seemingly at random, "no, not dyke plans… city, swamp… yes of course, Bayou Road!" he said triumphantly. "Have you ever heard the strange story of Dr. John?"

CHAPTER 23

Eddie wandered the streets in a sleep-like trance since waking late that morning in the cold alley on the wharf. He looked like any other junkie, dirty and stiff with cold. He walked like an old man, shuffling shoes of despair along the bumpy road of life; his youthful gait gone like a flash of pubescent dreaming.

He saw the world in grays, blacks and blues, the colors of a bruise, permanent and abusive. He saw the detritus scutter about the streets and cling to his pants; he skittered with the trash.

He felt a strange hollowness permeate his core. It could be described as hunger, but not of the stomach, of his entire being; his soul felt thin.

He wandered for hours until a cold wind caused him to pull his wet jacket around his neck. There he felt the remnants of his rash, nearly gone, but what good would it do him now? *Too little, too late, Eddie boy,* he thought. *What fucked up thing are you going to do next?*

With that thought, a raven flew out of the mist and landed on the branch of a tree that hung over a concrete wall. The rest of the branch draped into the St. Louis Cemetery #1. Eddie never saw the bird.

Eddie remembered that he had asked Marie Laveau for help a few nights back in this cemetery. A lot of good that did.

He shimmied through a side gate and looked left, then right. Something had drawn him in here, but he wasn't sure what. He could ask Marie for help again, but he didn't have anything to offer. He knew there were others he could ask for help, but once again, the unlucky ones like him didn't have it when they needed it.

The raven, sitting atop a high granite cross, pecked three times, sending an echo down one aisle. Eddie, hearing the echo, looked to where it came from.

He walked down the narrow aisle as the raven silently lit atop another vault toward the back of the cemetery. It pecked three times on that granite stone, sending an echo bouncing around a corner toward Eddie.

Eddie followed the new course and shuffled toward the back of the cemetery.

Finally, the raven lit atop a very old vault, pecked three times and waited.

Eddie slowly emerged from around the corner and gazed upon the vault. It sat in the last row of the cemetery, taking up more than twice the normal space and backed up to a large wall that separated the cemetery from a street. Wild vines grew out of the broken cobblestone and climbed the sides of the vault and over the wall. The raven flew to a tall baluster that protruded from the corner of the outer wall and watched Eddie closely.

Eddie didn't know why he was drawn to the vault, but he was. He walked up the three steps that led to the vault door and put his hands softly on the old granite. He thought he felt a slight vibration of life in the stone. Without hesitation, Eddie walked to the side of the vault, kicked off his shoes and climbed the old vines that led to the top. Once on top, he settled into a low crouch on the front corner of the vault roof. He began rocking slowly to an unheard tune; all the songs he would never sing. There, overlooking the cemetery, shrouded in a dense fog, Eddie waited.

The raven eyed him once more; satisfied, it flew off through the fog.

CHAPTER 24

Josephine grumbled at her next set of chores. She'd just finished a six-hour shift at the boring reception desk. No loving couple today looking for a seventeen-year-old throw-away. As if there ever would be.

She felt like her sad story only tainted her more. When people heard her story, they simply shook their heads politely, but then regarded her as something just less than a leper: druggy mother that always had the wrong guys around; parties with needles. *Poor thing,* she would hear some woman whisper, *but who knows what she may have.* Everyone would nod in agreement.

Her story was nothing like that of Del's. From the day Del had arrived, Josephine felt there was something about her; she held a mystique for Josephine and the nuns. The nuns pined over her in the beginning.

Poor thing, they would say, *such a tragic accident. Fire you know, loving parents, both killed trying to save their daughter, not knowing she had gone out the back. Yes, poor thing. Tragic. They must have really loved her. Terrible reminder, the scar and all. Yes, terrible. Poor thing.*

Josephine knew from the beginning that Del had a different aura about her. There was indeed something special in her. But from the moment Del had pushed her down to protect Jimmy, a spell was cast, and it was powerful. Josephine, being slightly younger than Del, didn't know what it was at the time, but she knew now that it would never release her.

Entering the girls' shower area, she retrieved the bucket and mop from the cleaning station—which was nothing more than the first shower stall on the right, stuffed full of mops and brooms—and began filling the bucket with hot water. Sitting on a small bench, watching the steam roll out, she thought of the last time she saw Del before she'd left the orphanage. Wanting to make a clean break the morning of her release, Del had taken a late shower the night before. Josephine had waited for her on this very same bench, intending to tell her things.

She had waited as the agonizing minutes ticked along, watching the steam roll up from Del's own stall. She stood up just as the water went off, but froze at the sight of her languid movements as she walked out of the steam. Del seemed not to notice the spell she held over her, and simply walked to the mirror with towel in hand. Josephine said nothing. That image, and the fact that she had not told Del what she'd wanted to, had tortured her sleep ever since.

Even Del's scar held a mystique for Jo. As embarrassing and terrible as it was to Del, Jo thought it gave her an added sense of beauty in a rough and damaged sort of way.

Kicking the bucket of soapy water, she felt her breathing increase as she silently cursed her inability to change her situation. She knew she would be out of the orphanage in another few months, but right now that was a lifetime. Del was finding her way in the world now, without her.

She slowly rolled the bucket and mop out into the hallway and pretended to tend to her chores, all the while playing the shower scene over and over in her mind. After a few minutes of lackluster sloshing, she heard a sound that instantly set her nerves on edge. Jimmy the boy-wonder was headed her way, singing.

"Owipop, owipop, oh, wow da owipop, owipop!" POP! He made a sound with his finger and cheek. *"Owipop, owipop, oh, wow da owipop, owipop!"* POP! He repeated immediately.

When she saw Jimmy come around the corner, walking backwards of all things, her mind went red. How Del could stand up for the boy-wonder night after night was beyond her comprehension. Without thinking, she placed the mop in the bucket and sent it rolling silently down the hall toward Jimmy.

Still walking backwards, counting ceiling tiles or something else equally as stupid, Jimmy sang, *"Owipop, owipop—,"* and stepped against the bucket, which sent him toppling over backward, spilling soapy water down the hall. "OWWW! I FEHW DOWN!" he yelled out, flailing around the slick floor.

Josephine stood silently by the shower entrance until she heard Sister Eulalie storming down the hall. She quickly went in and flushed a toilet, waiting for the nun's arrival. At the right moment she stepped out of the shower area into the hall and exclaimed her surprise at the mess Jimmy had made. Sister Eulalie already had Jimmy up by the collar and was hauling him off for his punishment.

Josephine couldn't guess at the degree of punishment, as it really depended on the Sister's mood. The *Dying Cockroach* was a favorite she would give to the boys for mild transgressions; made to lie on their backs in the hallway, with their arms and legs straight up in the air, quivering from exertion. She wouldn't make the girls do that because of their skirts, but the *Chair Pose* would work the legs just as hard. Of course, swats, hand slaps and pulled hair were dished out regularly, fast and efficient. But for the really bad ones, anything the Sister associated with an unclean soul, there was *Sin Washing*. Surely, she wouldn't make Jimmy do that, Josephine worried.

CHAPTER 25

Frank and Del settled into a cozy sitting area in front of the working table. The area bordered the banister overlooking the foyer below and Del could see where they stood earlier if she craned her neck to look over the back of the couch. Frank sat in a large wingback chair and Del on the coziest oversized loveseat she had ever seen. Armand had lit a fire in the old fireplace that stood to the right of the giant bookcases on the side wall. It sat at the top of the curving staircase they'd just ascended. After tinkering with the flue damper to adjust the draw of oxygen across the fire, he wandered slowly behind the table, touching different objects as if gathering bits of the story in his mind. He puffed on his pipe and began.

"Dr. John was a real character in the mid-to-late 1800s, in both the figurative and literal sense. He was a real person. A free black man, originating from a tribe in the Congo. The history of how he settled in the area is a bit muddled, but there are documents of him having ownership over a few businesses, some land, etc."

Armand refilled Frank's brandy and poured Del her first glass. She was eighteen after all, Frank had explained.

"Figuratively, he was quite the character. He had several wives, several run-ins with the law, and he reportedly was quite proficient in the black side of Voodoo."

At this Del made a *hhmmpppfff* sound with her nose and fidgeted in her chair.

"Del-bell," Frank said as he waved her to be quiet.

"It's alright, Frank. Not quite the believer I see," Armand said, nodding at Del.

"Well, I just—" Del began.

"No, no, quite alright. I wasn't a believer in the beginning either."

"It's just that… well, I thought there was a serial killer or something on the loose," she said. "Some *real* explanation for what's happening. I didn't think you were associating this with Voodoo, Frank."

Armand interrupted Frank's defense. "Miss Del, I'm not asking to embarrass you, but what do you know of the Voodoo religion?"

Del shuffled in her chair again. "Religion? Well… I know this city runs on the mythos of Voodoo because the tourists eat it up." Frank whistled and nodded again at the word choice. "But besides Voodoo dolls, love potions and… zombies, not much! And what's religion really got to do with it anyway?"

Armand's bushy face smiled. "Fair assessment of the commercial aspects," he said. "But religion just may have everything to do with it."

He waved his hand at the giant bookcases behind him.

"I'm an academic, you see. A professor in a previous life. And formerly quite the skeptic," he said pointedly at Del. "But all that changed one day when I could not explain what I had seen with my own eyes, so I went searching. First it was one book, then it was two. After a while," he waved at his surroundings again, "I was *toting boxes* as dear Frank would say. Boxes upon boxes of writings and manuscripts. Anything I could get my hands on to explain the phenomenon." He gazed out the window and watched the rain drizzle down the pane. "My financial state was such that it allowed me to indulge my curiosity to quite an unhealthy and obscene degree." He touched the books on the shelves lovingly. "And I'm afraid I must say that I have become quite obsessed with this field of study, and have collected quite a large volume of research on the topic."

"What did you see?" Del asked.

Ignoring the question, he paused to refill his own glass, savoring the tension in the room.

"Forgive me for delaying so, but I am quite enjoying the company. Rarely do I get visitors that… indulge me," he said with a tip of his glass. "Mais je digresse. Dr. John, as he was known by the locals, aka Jean Montanee, was a real person who practiced the real religion of Voodoo his whole life, as far as we can tell. His exploits were legendary and built him quite the following of believers. He used his considerable influence to his benefit whenever possible."

"Sounds like a snake-oil salesman to me," Del said.

"Yes, one could say on the surface that several of his dealings were quite suspect, but when you dig below the… mythos," he said, smiling at Del, "there are also credible sources to corroborate some very incredible claims."

"But what does this have to do with the dead bodies?" Del asked impatiently.

Armand nodded politely, happy that Del had arrived at the point he needed her to be.

"The Voodoo religion is not unlike that of Christianity," Armand said, "although it was born from the strife of several enslaved nations, not the strife of the Roman or Spanish Inquisitions.

"The views on life, death, the soul, basically the same. Loas, the same as spirits, are present. In fact," he said, leaning on the table to gaze at them both, "the two religions actually share saints! Did you realize that?"

Del wrinkled her forehead in disbelief.

"St. Peter of all things!" Armand said.

"St. Peter?"

"Yes! Fascinating, don't you think?" Armand said as he randomly organized loose manuscript pages. "Of course, the entities originally had different names, but the purpose of the higher Loas, aka Saints, were to perform similar functions, such as *'Keeper of the gate to the spirit world'*, etc."

At this, a thought shimmered in the far reaches of Armand's mind. It was the shadow of a thought he felt desperate to capture.

"...and who's to say if that is true or not?" Del said, snapping Armand's attention back to the conversation. Her face challenging the credibility of his last statement.

The thought was lost.

"I'm sorry, where was I?" Armand said. "But of course, religion. As I was saying, with any religion, where there's light, there is also dark. And as we know, there are very dark things to consider in the Voodoo religion, perhaps just as dark as in Christianity."

Incredulous, Del said, "Just as dark? OK, maybe I can see your point that Voodoo is more than just superstitious mumbo-jumbo, but to say that it's just as dark as Christianity, how can you make that statement knowing that Voodoo is known for zombies and Voodoo dolls?"

Armand admired Del quietly for a moment and saw that Frank was watching intently.

Finally, he said, "My dear Del, I stated that Voodoo is *perhaps* just as dark. How odd is it that one group is ridiculed for believing in zombies and Voodoo dolls, when another group is revered for their ritualistic eating of flesh and drinking of blood?"

Del shuffled in her chair. "OK, I get that the *idea* of communion is cannibalistic but—"

"Not to mention," Armand interrupted, "the revered groups belief in demons… possessions… and exorcisms."

For this, Del had no answer.

Frank let Del off the hook by clearing his throat and asking, "But what of Dr. John?"

Taking the hint, Armand said, "Of course, of course! How I have rambled! Anyway, the exploits of Dr. John paint him as an opportunist when it came to selling love potions and the like, but remember, he was from West Africa and grew up through a slave trade that mixed tribes from Africa with those of Haitians as they returned home. These tribes had deep beliefs in spiritualism built upon thousands of years of practicing natural healing and medicine. In fact, the earliest known surgeries, sometime around 3000 B.C. I believe, were attributed to the African tribes in Egypt—"

"The Egyptians?"

"Yes, that's right. Well-established trade routes throughout Western Africa, all the way over to Cairo, made the transference of knowledge fairly easy. The African tribes were performing brain surgeries long before the Europeans."

Armand paused to repack his pipe and let the significance settle over Del. Frank brushed cigar ashes from his stomach after helping himself to a bit more brandy.

Armand continued. "So, we now have a mix of people from a

continent twice the size of the U.S., that have thousands of more years of innate knowledge, and we call their religion mumbo-jumbo." He shook his head in disgust with his hands in the air.

Del nodded with understanding, but Armand saw the questions still hanging on her lips.

"But what of the dead bodies and Dr. John?" he prompted as Del nodded. "The darker reports of his... experiments, suggest that he studied, to somewhat of a successful end, the practice of necromancy and—"

"What?" Del jumped. "The raising of the dead?"

"Yes, my dear, but not only the raising of the dead, which is actually the spirit, but the binding of the spirit to a corpse. For reanimation, you see. Only... he reportedly didn't always use... human corpses. Quite often to monstrous effect."

A bellowing gust of wind shook the large house at that moment, causing all three to jump and fall quiet.

After several seconds of listening to the straining windowpanes, Armand continued. "There are accounts of his ability to summon a spirit, and in some cases, bind it to an object. Sometimes the object was as simple as a crudely made doll," a dread understanding washed across Del's face, "and sometimes it was a corpse. However, on occasion—"

"There's more?" Del asked.

"On occasion, the spirit was bound to a monstrosity."

Del looked at Frank for a hint that this was an elaborate spook story, but saw only grim agreement.

"What do you mean, 'monstrosity'?" she asked cautiously.

Armand considered his words carefully. "Imagine a spirit being pulled from its shadowy depths—its everlasting sleep—and *awakening* into an inanimate object such as a Voodoo doll. The spirit is aware it is on the other side again, but it's unfamiliar with its own form; not able to move; simply… stuck for eternity. Quite horrifying when you think about it. But now imagine the spirit is bound to a corpse, one that was formerly animate."

Armand's voice lowered as he imagined the horror. "The spirit recognizes the body shape, and in rare occasions can somehow re-animate the limbs, perhaps move what is left of the mouth or the eyes. But then… there are those that are bound to the most horrific fate. Bound not to a human corpse, but to that of an animal. An unholy union. Those, my dear, are the monstrosities; a human spirit bound to an animal's body; mad beyond comprehension; driven by animalistic need; tortured by the fleeting dream of one's former self. There are very few reports of these types of bindings, but those I have found coincide with reports of similarly mutilated bodies, and always with the brains eaten out.

"So you see, this is why the dead bodies, and particularly the teeth marks and transformed tracks reminded me of the strange story of Dr. John. I believe Frank may be looking for a monstrosity."

CHAPTER 26

A Monstrosity

Yes! Fearful monstrosity!

Oh, the horror of the thing! Cursed, cursed souls, you unerstan'... twisted and cursed, beyond imagination... yeah... beyond imagination.

I prayed these images would be burned from my mind, but they haunt me like a hellish specter.

I remember now! Oh! The horror I recall! And the poor wretched Toth. They speak of abominations as if they understood!

But what of the others? Alas, tell me the others have not been cast down this deep! How will they ever be found? How will they—

Wait.

Yes, of course, let's see... the others, the others... the story... the cemetery, no not the cemetery, ...the vault, Eddie?

Yes of course! The book!

The wind will carry the words.

CHAPTER 27

The wind leaned into the house, creaking the timbers down to the foundation. Frank cocked his head and listened to the house complain. Above them, several branches were somehow blown onto the roof and fell against the domed skylight, causing stickly finger-shadows to crawl down the interior curved walls.

Del thought she heard a voice on the wind, but said nothing.

Armand returned from the kitchen with a large tray of meats, cheeses and two bottles of wine. They were too far into their conversation to stop now, he had stated. Besides, he was in need of an excuse to open a good bottle.

After grazing over the first course—that was well explained by Armand, who also seemed to be an amateur sommelier—Del wandered behind the large worktable where Armand had given his lecture earlier that afternoon. She ran her fingers lightly over the books, wondering at the mysterious knowledge that must be hidden within the old leather hides. Armand watched her quietly as he and

Frank lit another round of pipe and cigar.

"Do you have a favorite?" Del asked, suddenly turning away from the giant shelves.

Armand puffed and considered. "They're all unique in their own way. Some very old, some very strange. I'm fascinated with them all really, but—" he walked around on her side of the table, "this one," he carefully pulled a raggedy looking book from the very center, "fascinates me the most," and carefully laid it on the table.

"Sweet Mary and Joseph," Frank whispered.

"What's that, mon ami—?" Armand started, but stopped dead as he looked at Frank's face. "What is it?"

"Where'd you get dat book?" Frank said, standing up slowly.

A strange look crossed Armand's face. "This is a grimoire I acquired from a bookseller late last year. Why?"

"What'd you say?" Del asked. "A grim…"

"Grim-WAH. It's a book of ma—" Armand stopped, watching Frank raise his hand.

"It's a book of magic," Frank said as he held out the package wrapped in newspaper that he had held all night.

"A book of ma—?"

"Yes, Del," Armand interrupted quietly. "A book of magic. Sometimes spells, sometimes stories, but… What do you have there, Frank?"

Frank walked slowly to the table, set the package down, and poured himself some more wine.

Armand took the package and laid it next to his own book. He slowly removed the paper and marveled at what lay before him.

"Frank…" he whispered.

"What? What is it?" Del asked.

"Frank, where did *you* get *this*?" Armand was looking at an eerily similar copy of the book he had just pulled off his shelf.

"From da house of a missin' person. She lives down Jean Lafitte area. Near da first missin' head."

Armand slowly opened both books and took a sharp intake of breath. He looked at the books from the bottom and could clearly see they had both been pasted together from sections of different books. They both had false covers on them.

Armand quickly flipped the pages simultaneously, letting his finger scan the pages for similarities.

"Oh, Frank. What have you found?" Armand said.

"You tell me. What'd I find?"

Armand continued scanning pages, but then quickly flipped his book open to a marked passage.

"Oh, hell," Frank muttered without even reading the words.

Armand looked at him for a brief second, then flipped the pages of Frank's book to nearly the same spot. He dropped his arms to his sides and stared in disbelief.

Del watched both men carefully consider the books in front of them.

"OK, guys, what's the—"

"A grimoire is a book of spells and incantations," Armand said. "Many people kept books such as these, but some grimoires are believed to actually hold magical abilities themselves. Infused somehow with old magical properties.

"I stated that this was my favorite book because it has a passage in it that appears to be part of an incantation. It was unclear to me if any other verses actually existed, until now."

His hands found the page in Frank's book, then found the passage that started with:

~~ςερσε I~~ – Verset I

~~Ηελλιση σπιριτ ηεαρ με χλεαρλψ, γραντ ψου νοω~~
~~φυλλ υσε ορ νεαρλψ,~~

Hellish spirit hear me clearly, grant you now full use or
nearly,

"It's true…" Armand said quietly. "I can't believe it, but it's right here in front of me."

"What's true?" Del asked. "And why is there the same writing in both books? Are they copies?"

Frank came around the table so he could read the passage from Armand's book straight on. At first, he thought it had the same passage; it was clearly the same shaky script that had been translated from a very old language. But upon closer inspection, he saw that the words were different.

"No, my dear Del, they're not copies," Armand said. "Although they were certainly written by the same hand. It appears that our mystery author, after achieving a painstaking translation, found it necessary to separate these two passages and preserve them in different copies of the same book."

"Why would someone do that?" Del asked.

Frank said, "Dis is dangerous writin' right here."

"Perhaps," Armand said. "But who's to say? You can see in the earlier pages of both books, they appear to be a collection of minor spells, and in some cases, a simple list of herbal healings." Armand turned to a page of Frank's book. "Recipes to cure a colicky baby; wart removal;

ah, here's a love potion." Flipping further. "Interesting. Something about our own Jean Montanee: *...a free Negro of the blackest color... country marks.* Interesting."

He flipped a few more pages.

"But most of this appears to be very *White*."

Del looked at him with questions.

"White, mild, innocent magic intended to help or heal. With the exception of course of your *hellish* verse," Armand said. "My book, on the other hand, is a bit stranger." He flipped to an early page. "*Incantation for the Red Raven*. Who ever heard of such a thing? A red raven?

"*The Bone Gourd Ceremony. The Bluebird Hex.* Here's one: *Scourge of the Death Rock*, how fascinating! And strangest of all, a reference to *The Unbinding Spell*—whatever that may be—on a later page, which appears to have been torn out of the book. Most frustrating."

Frank was sitting back in his chair, shaking his head slowly at the dangerous path he felt they were on.

"But, the piece de résistance of course is my verse three, which appears to be a continuation—with possible gap—of your verse one."

Del leaned close and read the scrawling script:

~~ςερσετ III~~ - Verset III

~~Ωιτη δεμον–ωιλλ I ωηολλψ βινδ, ψουρ ταττερεδ σουλ, βλαχκ ηεαρτ ανδ μινδ~~

With demon-will I wholly bind, your tattered soul, black heart and mind

~~Το με ψου σεε, φορ I αμ κινδ εξχεπτ το τηοσε I δοτη αβηορ.~~

To me you see, for I am kind except to those I doth abhor.

~~Εϖιλ τηινγσ ωερε δονε το με, βυτ νο ωορσε εϖιλ χαν τηερε βε,~~

Evil things were done to me, but no worse evil can there be,

~~Το τηατ ωηιχη I ωιλλ διε το σεε, υνλεασηεδ φρομ βεψονδ αβγΕΛ σ δοορ.~~

To that which I will die to see, unleashed from beyond abgEL's door.

~~Υνλοχκ ιτ σπιριτ, I βεσεεχη, φορ I δεσερϖε ρεϖενγε γαλορε…~~

Unlock it spirit, I beseech, for I deserve revenge galore…

~~Θυστ ονε νιγητ? Νοτ εϖερμορε?~~

Just one night? Not evermore?

Del felt her stomach do a slow flip and she grabbed her head as a bolt of pain shot through her temple.

Armand watched her cheeks turn white. Frank was on his feet.

She stumbled a bit and Armand grabbed her arm to steady her.

"Let me sit down, please," she said weakly.

"Del, what's da matter, honey?" Frank asked.

"I'm sorry, I don't know," she said. "I just got dizzy is all. I think I've had enough wine."

Armand helped her back to the old loveseat, where she curled up with a crocheted blanket that hung over the back.

Frank walked around the table and stared at the passage that Del had just read. He started to turn the page and look at the other incantations, but thought better of it. He'd rather not touch the book at all.

Armand brought a glass of water for Del, then motioned for Frank to join him in the large wingbacks that sat in front of the fire; a small table sat between them.

"So, what we lookin' at, ya think?" Frank asked as he settled into the chair.

"It's quite the mystery, eh, mon ami?" Armand said. After tweaking his bushy mustache into two upturned swoops, he lowered his voice, glancing at a peacefully resting Del and said, "I think there's a chance you've found yourself a modern case of a possession," finger pointing in the air, "at a minimum." He stroked his beard. "A theoretical worst-case scenario… which admittedly stretches credibility, is that you're looking at some type of reanimation." He clasped his hands thoughtfully and gazed into the fire.

"Reanimation?" Frank said quietly. "You think dat's true?"

"Theoretical possibility. Even I, surrounded by all this," he waved at the towering bookshelves, "have trouble believing, but I'll tell you Frank, there is volume after volume of stories and reports on these shelves, and none of these books were written as fiction in the sense that we know it. These authors, and sometimes they were family matriarchs, sometimes priests, sometimes researchers like me, these authors believed what they wrote down. *Something* happened to cause these stories to be recorded. *That* I believe."

Frank rubbed his thick chin and stared at the fire.

"There's something else that I haven't mentioned, Frank."

"Oh, great. And what'd dat be?"

"I looked on the inside of your book. At the bottom of the first page, there's a small inscription."

"I didn't see it. What'd it say?"

"Trois de trois."

Frank understood the French, but not the significance.

"Three of three," Armand said. "And my book has a similar inscription. Written on the inside of my book are the words *L'un des trois*, 'One of three.' Whoever made these books clearly wanted to keep them separate, but still be able to put them back together, logically, at a later time. What's odd is that your book, although labeled as part three, appears to be fairly benign in nature. A *white grimoire* if you will—with the exception of that hellish first verse. My book, labeled as part one, has verse three of the poem and appears to be a... *grimoire strange*, for lack of a better term. Someone went to great lengths to obscure the structure of this poem."

Realization dawned, flickering with red firelight over Frank's face.

"Der's anutter book," he said flatly.

"Yes, mon ami. There's another book. And I fear what it may contain."

CHAPTER 28

As the dying embers of the fire glowed with failing light, Frank and Armand dozed, one then the other. The brandy and wine had finally overtaken them, and they slipped into a deep sleep.

The old house moaned its nightly sighs and the rain drizzled cold and relentless. A dark shape flew to the top of the glass dome roof and cast a feeble shadow into the study and across the open books. It pecked three times on the glass. It spoke an unheard word. The hand-written passages in the books shimmered ever so slightly, as if an ancient life, somehow stored within the pages, suddenly awoke, pulsing to life on a frail alternating current to breathe the cool night air. Del dreamed a fitful dream.

She dreamed of the books on Armand's working table; they were catching fire and slight wisps of smoke were floating up from them. All the magic contained within the books, meant to be kept secret and separate, was now mixing into something beyond that which the original author had intended.

The wisps floated above the books and curled together, living, entwined into shapes that faded from mind as soon as she thought on them. The fleeting thoughts were maddening to her. She was supposed to know what they meant, but the meaning escaped her.

The smoke formed a large cloud in the room, and she floated through it. The cloud smelled of burnt garbage and plastic, like a house and all its belongings burning, acrid to her lungs. Flames leapt out of the dark at her and burned the side of her neck, under her ear. As she floated through the cloud, she became a fifolet—a spirit of the night—and was leading someone deep into the swamp. She floated around one tree, then another, teasing the person as she glowed with a gentle silver light. She saw that a woman followed her, walking through the swamp in bare feet and a torn, muddy dress. Other fifolets floated quietly out of sight, vibrating to each other, waiting for the Del-fifolet to lead the woman a bit further.

As Del stopped floating, hinting that the woman would catch her, a green fifolet slithered out of the ancient mud and caught the woman's foot in its mouth. The woman did not scream but seemed to regard it with a breathy anticipation. It slowly devoured the woman's leg, gentle pulsations sliding up translucently. The leg was visible, as if a ghost snake shimmered around it. The woman, with one leg anchored to the ground, appeared to lay back upon the air, surrendering, and slowly drift to the ground, finally laying in the mud as the snake spirit moved slowly up her body.

The cat-beast, hanging beneath a low tree branch, dissolved into a large blue fifolet, misshapen and grotesque, and dislodged itself from the tree and descended upon the woman. It covered her body in a deep blue cloud and quivered as its misshapen form undulated over and over, changing shapes rapidly, then settling into a slow rhythmic movement.

Her arms and legs writhed slowly in the mud of the swamp and grasped at the changing shapes. She shivered, as if an exquisite pain coursed through her body, and opened her mouth in a silent scream. The green spirit, now slithering out the top of her dress, tongue sensing the air, struck once at her face, covering her mouth, then dissolving, slowly wiggled into her throat, stifling her screams. The body of the snake was still emerging from the swamp and devouring her leg, but now appeared to grow heavier and opaquer, pulling her body beneath the surface of the mud.

In her dream, Del floated above the woman and gazed into her multi-colored eyes, right before she slipped beneath the mud and disappeared.

Several minutes later, small gas bubbles began forming in the mud where the woman had sunk. They expanded slowly, finally popping when a small head broke the surface tension of the bubble. Five bubbles in all had expanded and popped. The large blue fifolet descended on the spot again and formed enough of its shape that it appeared as a four-legged animal lowering itself over the patch of excreted bubbles. It lowered a bloated stomach-shape into the mud and quivered. When it stood up, five teats stretched out thin from the cloud body. First, the bald head of a tiny creature appeared from the mud; eyes blind, tiny translucent beak tearing the end of the teat; then, a tiny neck that pulled a hairless body up, long and slender like an eel, with six short stubby legs with three-toed claws, clicking at the air; finally, as the tiny abominations pulled free of the mud with a slurping suck, a tiny split tail twitched in the night air.

Five abominations were pulled from the ancient swamp, all clinging to the teats of a beast that should not exist in any dream. As the beast-spirit took physical form, it sauntered off into the swamp. A strange shape on its back bobbing back and forth as if on a long pin.

Del screamed in her sleep, but the screams fell silent against an oppressive weight that filled the night air. The lightly glowing grimoires dimmed to a dark void and the raven flew off into the night.

CHAPTER 29

J osephine walked quietly through the dark halls of the orphanage. The nuns had made their final rounds for the night. Josephine had mastered the art of slow, deep breathing long ago—which Sister Eulalie would always listen for—so knew she was clear to venture forth.

All day the vision of Del emerging from the steam had stayed with her. Laying in her bed trying to sleep, it had teased and haunted her; she had to walk it out of her system.

Heading to the coatroom, she passed the boy wonder, who was sleeping peacefully, no doubt dreaming of giant birthday cakes, magic *owipops* and flying on the back of the angel Saint Del. She briefly thought of placing a dead cockroach on his pillow as a joke, but didn't want to deal with the morning commotion. Besides, it wasn't like she really hated him—she had actually felt kind of bad for the trouble she'd caused him this afternoon—but Del's desire to protect him had always baffled her, and her frustrations with her own situation were getting the better of her.

She slipped into the coatroom, donned an old, dark raincoat, quietly opened the obscured shutter and window, and slipped down to the sidewalk. She pulled the window down as far as she dared and stuck a small piece of wood into the jamb to prevent it from sliding shut. She was free to roam the night.

*

The thoughts in Jimmy's head had never been logically structured. He knew he was slower than the other kids—when someone told him—and knew that even the younger kids could learn things faster than he could, but he'd accepted that this was how God made him, so God must have wanted him this way. He never understood why God needed to borrow his whistler however—he tried very hard to whistle, but could only ever manage to blow spittle from his lips—but Del told him that he must have had such a great whistler that God needed to borrow it, and that answer suited him fine; he was glad someone could use it.

He always tried his very best at whatever was asked of him—even when it took him ten tries to make a King in checkers—and he always tried to remember to *"leave it all on the table"* as Del would say, although he also knew he had to pick up his games when he was finished, so he thought maybe Del had gotten that one wrong.

Because he always did his best, despite his shortcomings, he slept the peaceful sleep of someone who had attained all they could, with the God-given abilities they had; he had risen to his potential—with one exception.

Del was the bravest person Jimmy had ever known. The way he understood it, she had survived the fires of H-E-double-L, and he didn't know anyone else who had done that, not even the nuns. She had come to the orphanage to be his guardian angel, and if there was one thing that Jimmy aspired to be, it was brave. Brave like Del.

In his peaceful sleep, Jimmy dreamt an unpeaceful dream. The *issad* was chasing Del to steal something from her. She was lost in the woods and was yelling for Jimmy to help her. In his dream he could run really fast and he never fell down. He yelled to her and thought he heard her voice far away. Lassie the wonder dog ran in front of Jimmy and led the way. When he found Del, she was surrounded by a strange cloud of mist, and Jimmy knew it was the *issad* but couldn't see him. Jimmy was scared of the cloud, but threw a rock at it anyway and it disappeared. Del was happy and they ate cake.

∗

Josephine walked the alleys toward the French Quarter. She had made this trip before, but now that she was almost eighteen, she took the liberty to wander closer to the action and could hear music wafting through the mist like a siren's song. Once she escaped the orphanage for good, she would come here and get a job at one of the many music houses, cleaning tables or whatever it took. She would never look back.

She turned on a cross street and started up the next alley when she caught sight of a group of men huddled around a low fire in a steel drum. She stopped instinctively, her fledging street-smarts warning her to detour. One of the men caught sight of her and whistled attention to the others. Watching them from under her hood, she slowly turned and started to walk back the way she had come. This signaled her as prey to the predators, and the men began walking in her direction. Looking back over her shoulder, she saw the men and broke into a sprint. They followed with a loud whoop.

She sprinted down the sidewalk of the cross street and cut up the next alley she came to, hoping to throw them off by heading in her original direction, just up a different path. She heard them far behind, but still in pursuit, and made several quick turns, not paying attention to the streets she turned on. Several minutes later she stopped to listen and was satisfied to not hear anything behind her. She looked around to see where she was and realized that she had zig-zagged her way to the St. Louis Cemetery #1. She knew where she was.

As she walked the sidewalk that followed the wall of the cemetery, she derided herself, partially for her stupidity of almost walking into a bad situation, but also for being scared. How was she to break free of the orphanage if she couldn't handle a few drunks in an alley. She thought briefly of retracing her steps and confronting the men, but decided instead to brave the cemetery. That would be enough for tonight.

Squeezing through a loosely chained side-gate, she entered the cemetery and was immediately struck by a cold pall that fell about her. The legends of the old cemeteries were well known to her, but she always thought they were told by people less brave than herself. When the hair stood up on her neck, she wondered how brave she really was.

Pallid lights along the outside walls cast ghostly images over the cold stone vaults, emphasizing the finality of the place. Josephine walked slowly down the dark alleys and past the crypts, feeling the cold, wet stones. She was drawn to the back of the cemetery for a reason she could not explain. The further she walked, the greater the weight she felt lay upon her soul.

She turned a corner and stopped suddenly, staring at the faint outline of a strange man that stood in front of her.

Later she would think she saw him speak briefly to the vault that sat at the back of the cemetery, but her mind was immediately overwhelmed with a sense of excitement and revulsion that she couldn't separate.

The man stood with a slight hunch, nearly six feet tall, she thought, if he could straighten up just a bit. He wore a strange hat and a long overcoat covered with small bags, and carried a walking stick that she wasn't sure he needed. Despite the blackness of the night and the heavy mist that swirled around him, he wore dark glasses that shimmered blue.

Greeting her as if she had been expected, he said, "Hello, my dear. Whose acquaintance do I have the pleasure of making?"

Josephine shuffled her feet and glanced over her shoulder, looking for the exit. The rows of crypts were shrouded in a thick fog that fell about her the moment she saw the strange man, and she wasn't sure where the side-gate was from here.

The man stared at her with a face as blank as the stone vault.

"I'm Josephine," she said, trying to hide a crack in her voice.

"Come my dear, don't be frightened," he said. "Josephine?"

"Yes," she said, already regretting giving him her first name.

"And your last name, my dear?" he asked. "I know many people here. Perhaps I've met your family."

Glancing at the vaults, a name popped into her head.

"Laveau," she lied. "Josephine Laveau."

The man's head cocked unnaturally to the side and a convulsive shiver ran the length of his body. The image in the blue mirrored glasses briefly went out of focus.

"Laveau, you say? How interesting." He rolled his head from side to side. "How utterly, utterly, interesting." She heard small bones cracking. "That is quite a famous name you have."

She shuffled her feet again. She wasn't sure why, but she felt giving him that name had been more of a mistake than the first.

"Well, Miss Laveau. I am *very* pleased to make your

acquaintance," he said with the slightest nod.

"Why is that? And who do I have the acquaintance of ma... who do I have... who are you?"

The man smiled a telling smile, an indifferent smirk to her uneasiness.

"Why, I've been called many things. Depending on my profession at the time, of course," he said, leaning towards her. His long hands stroked delicately at the air as he wove his tale. "I'm a bit of a collector, you see, so were we transacting a deal, *Monsieur* would do; but I have a fair hand at healing as well, so if it were a bit of gris that was needed, then *Doctor* would suffice."

"Gris? Are you a Voodoo man?"

His hands stopped, and the thick fog seemed to stop with them, as if this time and place were frozen.

"Yes Josephine, I am. What ails you, my dear?" His voice twinkled upon the air.

She looked at her feet and pulled her jacket tight. She remembered where the exit was now, and adjusted her feet slightly, just in case.

"Do you make... love potions?" she asked, casting a quick glance at him.

"Love potions? But of course!" he exclaimed. "One small draught and he'll be eating out of your—"

Her mouth twisted sideways in a subtle sign of dismay.

The strange man stopped and inhaled a deep breath, seemingly tasting the thick night air. The blue mirrored glasses reflected the swirling fog as a bolt of lightning lit the sky behind him. He was momentarily silhouetted in an unholy light as Josephine's fate hung in the balance.

"Oh, I see," he said. "Pardon me. *She'll* be eating out of your hand."

She looked up just as he broke into a distorted, toothy grin.

A rumble of thunder rattled the ground, nearly causing her to bolt, but the thought of Del being hers forever held her strong. She shuffled her feet again and looked over her shoulder to the front of the cemetery. She saw nothing but heavy, swirling fog, and thought she had stayed there long enough.

Chancing a final question, she asked, "What does something like that cost?"

"Hmmm… now that is an interesting question. I take it you have no money?"

She snorted lightly at this. "No, not living in the orphan—, uhh, the uh… not living in the… Orpheum."

The blue glasses watched her carefully.

"It's uh… just some old hotel they're gonna tear down. I'm moving out of there next week, but uh… no, I don't have any money." She moved sideways toward the exit.

"I see," the man said calmly. "Then perhaps you have something to trade." Her backwards retreat reflected in his glasses.

"Trade? Uh…" she looked over her shoulder again, "Trade? Like what?" she said, stopping.

"I trade my services for many things, my dear. I am most fascinated by the interesting people I meet in this business. Perhaps you could introduce me to some of your friends."

"My friends?"

"Yes, I'm sure some of your friends have similar wishes. Perhaps some illness I could cure for them. Who knows? They may end up owing you a big favor after I cure their problems. They owe you; you pay me. We could have quite a partnership, you and I."

"We could?"

"Yes, of course! You want to get away from the... Orpheum, as soon as possible don't you?"

"The Or... uh yes, like I said, I'll be moving soon. I think."

"Yes, of course you will. And I believe you'll do great things when you do. In fact, as I'm sure you've guessed, I do more than just create love potions."

"You do? Well, I kind of thought—"

"Of course, you did. I can feel it, you see. You are always thinking. And if you let me help you, you will do great things, Josephine." She was listening intently now. "And this girl you desire. She will be yours forever."

"Forever?" she said quietly.

"Yes. Forever. For a fair trade."

She nodded slightly, hypnotized. "Yes, for a fair trade."

"See the large vault behind me?" He gestured.

She looked over his shoulder and watched as the fog parted to reveal the oversized crypt.

"Yes."

"When you're ready to trade, all you have to do is come and knock three times on the vault. When you do, I'll know that you are ready. But make sure you bring something to trade. Don't call me back without something to trade."

He began to walk backwards into the fog.

She suddenly felt rushed, and wished she had asked more questions. "But, but what if you don't like what I have to trade?"

He turned his back to her and walked into the mist.

"Make it good, Josephine! Make it good," he said.

"But, what—"

"Sin, Josephine. I love to trade in sin!"

As he slipped into the shadow of mist, a large bird took flight from a nearby crypt. This drew her attention to the mist-shrouded vault roofs. There, an odd shape took form. She thought she saw the outline of someone crouching on the top of the crypt.

She broke and ran.

CHAPTER 30

Tuesday

Frank, Del and Armand woke at nearly the same time the next morning. The fire had died to a cold gray ash; the large room was cast with a cold gray light which seemed to drizzle and drip down the walls, implying that even the tepid sunlight filtering through the rain-heavy clouds was water-logged.

Armand quickly set to making breakfast, circling many times in the kitchen to stitch together the mental notes for a breakfast larger than a poached egg and toast.

"Don't worry, honey," Frank said as they sat down over coffee. "I'll smooth everything over fer you when we get you home. Hell, half da damn phone lines is down, anyway. We'll blame it on dat."

"Thanks, Frank," Del said quietly, slowly stirring her coffee.

In the background they heard Armand muttering. "Let's see, silverware... yes, silverware, hutch, drawer. There we are... yes, spoons. Of course! The marmalade is in the cellar!" He walked out of the room twirling his pipe in celebration.

Del continued to stare blankly at the table.

"What's da matter? I told you—"

"No, it's not that, Frank. I don't think I'd be in trouble anyway. Mama Dedé has given me quite a bit of freedom since I've been there. It's odd, really..."

"How so?"

"I don't know. It's like... it's like she watches me from afar, waiting to see what I'll do. She sets the rules of the house, but gives me leeway to come and go."

"Well, you an adult now."

"It's more than that. It's like she's waiting for something... expecting something out of me, but I don't know what it is." She watched the drops of coffee drip back into her cup.

"Den what—"

"I had a really strange dream last night," she said, "and can't get it out of my head. It was so vivid... and disturbing."

"I didn't sleep so well myself," Frank said. "Lotsa things on my mind. Too much talk of spooks and—"

"It was this crazy big ghost snake," she said. "I was in a swamp floating around and... crazy stuff. I don't know, it must have been the wine."

Armand had returned from the cellar and was stopped in the kitchen door, listening intently.

"What, honey? Tell me," Frank said, sensing Armand's curiosity.

"I was floating around like a spirit and the ghost snake... well, some other things were flying around with me, but I think the snake came out of the mud, first as some kind of green spirit, but then it started eating someone that was following me, and then—"

"Zombi!" Armand said suddenly, making Del jump.

"Oh! Gosh, you scared me. Sorry. I didn't know—"

"You dreamt of a large spirit snake? A green fifolet that became a giant snake?" he asked.

"I guess, something like that. Did you say 'zombie'?"

Resuming his professorial position on the other side of the table, he set his hands firmly in front of him. Fearing for breakfast, Frank took this as a cue to man the skillet.

Armand said, "Yes, but let's not dismiss this dream as wine-fueled meanderings of the mind, and let's approach the topic with the proper introduction."

A question rose on Del's face, but Armand continued.

"Le Grande Zom-BEE!" he pronounced, slapping his palms on the table.

Del sat frozen for a long minute, trying to determine what to make of this new bit of information and the theatrical delivery.

Armand slowly circled his side of the table again, forming the story in his mind.

A snide question slipped from Del's mouth: "OK, what's the Grand Zombie?"

Armand twisted his mustache furiously. "Please, my dear… too much contempt before breakfast."

"I'm sorry, I didn't mean—"

"No, it's alright," Armand said. "It's hard for *me* to believe this possibility." He breathed deeply and settled himself. "Le Grande Zombi is the spirit that is most closely related to Monsieur Jean Montanee—our dear Dr. John. As I stated last evening, he was involved in things much darker than simple curses." His voice lowered to a whisper. "Some texts claim that he was able to raise and control the dead—the spirit, of course. However, they often took forms other than that of a human body."

Del picked slowly at her breakfast as Frank ate from the skillet. Armand packed his pipe with his favorite breakfast tobacco.

"But what does this have to do with me?" Del finally asked. "Why did I dream of the snake?"

A matchhead flame, held to his pipe bowl, brightened Armand's eyes briefly. Del flashed back to the dream, the fire she came through, the swamp, the woman with multi-colored eyes, the abominations.

"What is it?" Armand asked, watching her face.

Rubbing her head slowly as if to massage the vision into focus, she said, "I just remembered… something about a fire… and something about a woman. A woman was following me, or… really, it seemed like I was leading her, somehow. Leading her to the snake and to the…"

"To the what?"

"Something happened in the dream. Some… things were born. The woman, and another spirit…" She trailed off.

Del felt that her dream was more than just the meanderings of a wine-muddled mind, that it had more meaning for her, but what, she couldn't imagine.

Armand stroked his beard knowingly and said, "We need to speak with someone who is more… attuned to this channel. My academic research will only take us so far."

"Who dat?" Frank asked, lighting his own breakfast cigar.

"She's quite knowledgeable. I've consulted her on occasion. A fair practitioner, I've heard. She goes by the name of Mama Dedé, perhaps—"

"WHAT?" Del yelled out. "Mama Dedé?" She looked questioningly at Frank.

"Oh hell," Frank muttered, as the tip of his cigar drooped from his mouth.

Armand looked from Del to Frank. "You know of her?"

"Yeah," Frank said slowly, "we know her."

"What's going on, Frank?" Del asked.

Frank puffed his cigar to life and studied her closely.

"Don't know, honey. But somethin' is happenin'. Dis ain't all coincidence. I'd say dat somethin' is about to get out of control, and if anyone will know what to do, it'd be Mama Dedé."

Armand was circling his thoughts again. "Let's see… Grand Zombi, incantations, spells, yes spells… grimoire, oh yes, grimoire white… verses, oh my, grimoire… strange, yes of course! Have you ever heard of the famous feud between Dr. John and Marie Laveau?"

CHAPTER 31

enri Guillaume sat in an unmarked car at the corner of Prytania and Valmont, a block away from Armand's house. His large body was stiff from spending the night in the car, but he dared not get out and stretch now that the feeble light of morning was seeping through the clouds. He'd followed Frank yesterday on a hunch that he hadn't reported everything he'd found at the body sites. Henri had an intuition, a sense about things that he had honed over the years, and he felt something was wrong. There should have been more evidence.

Perhaps Henri made a mistake by pulling Frank into this, considering the potential ramifications. He knew Frank was a good detective, and thought he was an honest one, that's why he had called him. All he was supposed to do was collect the evidence and bring it back. *Why hadn't he done that?*

Henri twisted a small black onyx ring on his right-hand pinky finger. The ring felt cold despite being attached to his large hand. The ring would never give warmth, he knew that. It would only take, but there was purpose in that.

Henri scratched at the side of his mouth were a fever blister had started. He looked in the mirror and saw a nasty red bump at the corner of his mouth. He couldn't remember ever having one before.

Movement now; lights on; increased smoke from a fireplace. They were waking up.

Finally, after nearly another hour, Henri saw the large iron gate open. Frank's telltale red car exited the inner grounds and turned toward Henri. Less than a minute later, Henri, laid out nearly flat in his seat, watched as Frank and the girl from yesterday drove right past him. From his awkward angle, he couldn't see the girl very well, but could tell she was young.

"What are you playin' at, Frang?" he said aloud.

He started his car and watched as Frank turned off Prytania. He quickly swung his car around and followed.

*

Sister Eulalie had made her morning rounds and sat at her office desk, irritable and impatient. She was preparing for her meeting with Dr. Morosé, head of the city asylum, about a special legal transfer. She and the doctor had a long working relationship; the orphanage, caring for those less fortunate souls, could only do so much, and for only so long; the city asylum had its purpose as well. She hadn't used it often, but with special situations it was a useful, and convenient, alternative.

The meeting wasn't what had her on edge; she was physically uncomfortable; she was starting to itch. Last night she had noticed a slight rash on her lower abdomen at the fold of her hips. She had thought it was a laundry issue, but this morning the rash had already spread down her inner thighs. If the vows of chastity weren't trying enough, the unfamiliar sensation was maddening. Her legs tingled at every movement of the heavy habit, brushing against the rash, distracting her thoughts.

She stood up and paced the room, randomly moving the two chairs in front of her desk. The kids seemed especially noisy this morning, and they grated her nerves. She could hear the vile boy singing his ridiculous songs all the way down the hall. She would be free of that sinful child soon enough, she hoped. She closed the door and turned, bumping into a chair, which sent itchy fire down her legs again. Her breath rose in a stilted gasp. Her mind was consumed with input; senses gathering; her body itched as her mind flashed over a crowd of young faces; smooth, beautiful young faces. She sat down hard in her chair. The heavy bounce helped for a moment, but her mind was made up; there would be a Sin Washing tonight. The faces of the young girls flew through her mind like a slide carousel; someone had sinned worse than the others; she didn't know who at this point and didn't care, but someone would attend her Sin Washing tonight.

CHAPTER 32

Del jumped out of Frank's car as soon as he pulled up in front of the orphanage.

"I'll only be a minute," she said as she held the door. "I want to tell Jimmy I didn't forget him yesterday."

"OK, Del-bell," Frank said, "but don't dally or you and I both be in trouble with Mama Dedé when we get you home."

Del wrinkled her mouth into a *whatever you say, Frank* look and winked at him as she shut the car door.

Ugh, dat girl, Frank thought as he pulled a fresh cigar from a box on the seat.

Josephine beamed a smile from behind the desk as Del walked in. "Hi Del! Hey, you look great. I was just—"

"Look great?" Del interrupted. "I slept in my clothes last night." She signed herself in.

"Oh, I… well, you still look great," Josephine said. "I'm glad you're here. I wanted to talk to you."

"Not now, Jo. I just stopped by to say hi to Jimmy. Maybe later?"

Josephine stood up and lightly touched Del's arm. "I like when you call me 'Jo,'" she said quietly. "I know you're busy, with your new life and all…" Del started toward the inner door. "But it's about Jimmy."

"What?" Del said, spinning around. "What about Jimmy?"

Josephine pulled Del out of view of the window in case Sister Eulalie was lurking in the hall.

"I saw the man from the asylum this morning. He met with the Crow," she said.

Del knew this was the older kids' code word for Sister Eulalie, but thought it was unwise to say it in the open.

Josephine leaned close to Del's ear and whispered. "They were talking about Jimmy. She's going to send him away."

"What?" Del said, grabbing her by the shoulders and pulling her straight out in front of her. Josephine felt a flush of blood rush up her neck as she saw the fire wash over Del's face and settle in her eyes. A combination of fear and fascination caught her breath.

"Are you sure?" Del said, holding her tightly.

"Yes, I… I heard the Crow say that since his birthday just passed, she could make the legal transfer. Del, I'm sorry."

"But that's not right. He's only sixteen!" Del paced the room. "What the hell is wrong with her? Doesn't she know—"

"I think it's because of his… well, you know. But there's more, Del. I need to talk to you. There's more I want to… there's more I need to say."

"I've got to get Jimmy out of here, somehow," Del growled under her breath.

"Del, please," Josephine said, following her around the room, "please listen to me. I'll help you! I'll help you with Jimmy!" Her voice cracked with desperation.

Del stopped and stared at the girl who constantly wanted to smooth her jacket sleeves; whose green eyes were always following her, searching for confirmation, pleading for a signal. Realization dawned over Del's mind.

"You'll help me with Jimmy?" she asked, breaking the spell.

A breath of disappointment slipped out of Josephine, deflating her momentarily. She felt tears of stress water her eyes, but could no longer hide them. She looked into Del's face. "Yes, anything. I'll help you with anything."

"I need to see Jimmy, then I have to leave. I need to think about what to do, but if you can help, I'd really appreciate it."

Josephine beamed again. "Yes, anything. We'll talk soon, then. When you think of what to do, we'll talk."

Del left Jo standing in the waiting room and walked back to where Jimmy was playing in the corner of the cafeteria. He sat by himself beneath a window facing the wall, a small bag of marbles spread before him.

Not being able to keep up with the other kids, he generally played alone when Del wasn't there. He tried very hard to work his thumb and finger to shoot the marbles properly, but resorted to simply rolling them back and forth. He had learned to roll them towards the wall after several had dropped down the air vent in the floor.

Del watched as he spoke quietly to the marbles. She wondered what magical thoughts he was conjuring, and hoped they were pleasant.

Not wanting to disturb his daydream with her sour mood, or with concepts of *institutions* that he wouldn't understand, she turned and walked out.

She rode silently in Frank's car, replaying the scene of Jimmy playing alone. She had told him what she had learned of the Crow's plan, but he had no answers. *Sometimes these things don't have good endings, Del-bell,* he had said. At that moment she hated Frank for his common sense. That wasn't the right answer at all.

Frank parked in front of the halfway house and gave Del a look of apprehension.

She felt a swell of emotion collect in the back of her throat; all the disappointment of the day culminating in small daggers of insult. And she threw them at Frank.

"What's wrong with you?" Del asked sharply. "You act like Mama Dedé's gonna put a curse on you or something."

Frank felt the sting of her words, but knew that she was struggling. "Come on honey, let's get you inside."

*

Henri watched Frank pull up in front of an old two-story house with a large backyard. The yard, like a lot of those in the old section of the city, was subdivided by odd smaller buildings; old stables converted into detached garages; old servants' quarters converted into lease rooms. Frank and the young girl got out of the car and walked straight into the house without even a knock. Henri drove slowly past the house and realized why. A small wooden sign above the door announced: *St. Augustine Transitional Home for Girls.*

The girl was an orphan. *What are you doing, Frang?*

Henri drove slowly past the house and through the city, letting his thoughts run. He wasn't sure what the girl's relationship was with Frank, but sensed that these two were playing at something they didn't understand. How was Frank—and possibly the girl—related to the bodies? Was Frank intentionally misleading her? This new turn of events was concerning. But what to do was the question.

Several minutes later, he arrived at the city morgue and without showing a badge, walked straight down to the autopsy room. He was well known there.

He was disappointed that there was only one body to inspect. The first body had been lost to the swamp according to Frank, and was exposed to the elements the longest, so there was really no surprise about the state of the remains; the old man however—Loo'siana Slim— was the second in order, which Henri presumed meant that he would be more intact, but maybe he misunderstood what was happening. But the third body, the teenage boy from the wharf, was mostly intact and held telltale signs.

Henri opened the door to the autopsy cooler and pulled out the sliding tray that held the remains of the third victim. Opening the cadaver bag, he stared down at an incredible sight. *A white alabaster bowl*, he thought immediately. How strange.

The inside of the skull had indeed been licked clean. The face was completely missing, although the lower jaw had somehow remained intact.

Henri scratched absently at the corner of his mouth where the fever blister was getting worse. It had started to form a few days ago. He paid it no attention.

He let the fingers of his other hand trace the inside of the skull, feeling the bumps and grooves; the brail of the dead. They slid across the whole of the alabaster bowl. They toyed with the sharp, jagged breaks where the skull had been cracked with incredible force. Nicking his finger across a sharp sliver of bone, he pulled his hand back and watched a drop of blood fall into the skull-bowl, staining it with a trace of life. He watched as a second drop joined the first, meandering to the bottom of the bowl, drawing his attention down.

He absently stuck the cut finger into his mouth as his eyes wandered to the subtle sign of teeth marks along the inside of the skull, near the jawbone; they were clearly animal teeth marks. He imagined whatever beast had done this gnawing against this side of the skull, slobbering into the base as a long tongue snaked out, lapping at the last morsels of brain tissue. As he looked closer, he saw clean striations against a back molar. The beast had left its teeth marks on one of the victim's teeth. Henri reached down, grabbing the scarred tooth, and pulled it from its socket. Not noticing the bits of nerve that clung to the tooth, he dropped it in his top pocket.

CHAPTER 33

Frank and Armand arrived at the St. Augustine Transitional Home for Girls at 7:30 in the evening in separate cars. They both felt terrible about falling asleep the night before, and bringing Del home so late that morning. Frank explained to Armand that Del had not gotten into trouble, but that Mama Dedé was none too happy with Frank, so they should probably not mention what a grand time they had last night.

As they ascended the steps of the halfway house, Frank turned to Armand and said, "Now remember, my time with Mama Dedé goes way back. As a young detective, I had to make use of her skills on more den one occasion."

"I never took you for a recipient of charms and spells," Armand said. "Are you a closet practitioner Frank?"

"No, nothing like dat, but she's good at knowin' things dat shouldn't be known, dat's all I'm sayin. And in da early days, she kinda had more den one job, if you get my meanin'. So we kinda ran into each other a lot on da street."

Armand nodded his understanding. A lot of Voodoo practitioners had multiple occupations.

Walking into the house, Armand was struck by the dichotomy of currents he felt flowing beneath the veneer of the transitional home for girls.

The front sitting room was furnished with old donated furniture; clean, but badly worn. The mismatched styles of lamps and chairs gave it a whimsical, clumsy look that the matching slipcovers could not hide from his antiquarian's eye.

The plaster walls had been patched and painted many times, and although not offensive, gave the air of a matriarch wearing her best regal face against the cruel process of aging youth.

The overall smells were homey; meager meals, enough to satisfy small bellies, had been cooked with love and stretched together with donations from the community. But at the same time, it smelled antiseptic and sterile, indicating a flow of too many bodies transitioning from one state of uncertainty to another.

These feelings and smells Armand had anticipated. What surprised him the most was the feeling that beneath all of this, there was a vast well of supernatural activity hovering just out of sight. It was as if this place pulsed with an energy that wanted to be consumed, flowing from a dark well of knowledge, bristling in anticipation of being released.

Del descended the stairs looking clean and fresh. Both men noticed how vibrant she looked. Her dark hair and freckles perfectly accenting eyes full of a mysterious knowledge.

As the men greeted Del in the foyer, they heard heavy footsteps trundle toward them down the hall. A moment later a stout, round woman filled the width of the hallway entrance to the foyer.

Del looked at Frank with a sly, knowing grin that indicated she sensed his nervousness. Frank shot her a look of consternation and brushed his shirt again.

"Well, well," Mama Dedé said. "Look who it is. Standin' here like you in a bread line waitin' for a coffee!"

Her short gray hair betrayed her age, but her smooth black face and sparkling eyes spoke of wisdom and caring. Frank waved cigar smoke away from his face, then brushed invisible ashes from the front of his shirt.

"Mama Dedé. How you been?" Frank said politely. "Been a long ti—, well… it had been a long time until—"

"Yeah, it *had* been a while, hadn't it, Frank?" Mama Dedé eyed him with hands on her wide hips. "Until you showed up here 'dis mornin' bringin' my girl in after all kinda hours!"

"Oh, now Mama Dedé," Frank said with a low head, "I explained all that dis morning, it got to be kinda late you see an—"

"Mmm-hmm. This I know."

Del watched Frank squirm with fascination.

"Who da fancy man?" Mama Dedé said, ignoring Frank's discomfort and nodding at Armand.

Stepping forward, Armand took her hand gently and said, "Armand Baptiste, at your service, mademoiselle." He nodded slightly. "I'm a fan of your… abilities. Your reputation precedes you."

With wide eyes and a rock of her hips she said, "Ooo wee. At my service!" She inspected Armand, then sent a dismissive glance at Frank.

"OK Frenchy, you wit me. Frank, da coffee's in da pot. Del honey, show Frank where da cups are. And don't break my good cups Frank."

She turned and led Armand down the hall. "How you like your coffee, Armand?"

With a twist of his mustache he said, "Hot and black, mon chéri."

"Ooo wee! Mon sherry!" she said, shaking her hips again. "You alright, Frenchy. You just fine wit me."

"Hot and black times two Frank!" she called out over her shoulder as they disappeared down the hall.

Frank looked at Del with chagrin. He understood what his punishment was to be for bringing Del home so late.

The side parlor off the kitchen was a shadow of its former glory. The ten-foot ceilings still held an air of aristocracy, but the smoke-stained wallpaper and peeling plaster spoke of faded glory. An old upright piano sat against one wall, and mismatched chairs lined the walls for extra seating. The stone fireplace opening was edged with short drapes that were tied back to reveal a type of altar surrounded by candles. A large round table sat in the middle of the room, and candelabras stood on every conceivable surface.

As Mama Dedé lit several candles, a soft glow drew stark shadows from the corners of the room, like dark moths to a flame.

Frank sat the serving tray of coffee on the big round table and took a seat next to Armand.

Del had never been in the parlor before, as it was always kept locked, but suddenly realized there was far more to Mama Dedé than she knew.

Once the idle chatter passed, Mama Dedé began: "OK boys, out wit it." She looked from Frank to Armand and settled there. "Why'd you call dis meetin'?"

"Well Mama Dedé," Frank said, "we think we got us a bad problem."

She looked at Frank, resting her chin on the back of her folded hands and said, "Can't Armand tell da story?" Turning to Armand she said, "That's a handsome mustache, Armand. I admire a man that can grow such a handsome mustache. Why can't you grow no mustache Frank? Yes, that's a handsome mustache alright."

Frank sat open-mouthed, with the tip of his cigar drooping down.

Mama Dedé turned back to Frank with a wink and said, "Oh Frank, lighten up. I'm just jerkin' ya! Get on with your story now before I need to pee."

Frank perked up and repeated the story of the dead body in the swamp, Loo'siana Slim and the boy found on the dock. Mama Dedé assumed a more serious posture and listened intently.

When he reached the part about the skull being licked clean, she leaned her girth back in the chair. It protested loudly. Her fingers locked over her round stomach.

"So why you comin' to me?" she finally asked. "You need protectin' from da man you chasin'?"

"Tell her about the grimoire," Armand said.

Mama Dedé eyed Armand carefully. "What grimoire?"

"Yeah, I was gettin' there," Frank said.

He then told her about the book he'd found in Sharon's house, which looked identical in some aspects to a second book.

"A second book," she said. "Where?"

At this point Armand lifted a thin leather satchel he'd been carrying, placed the bag in his lap and patted it lightly.

"What you got there, Frenchy?"

Armand nodded slowly and took the books from his bag and placed them on the table.

Mama Dedé leaned forward in her chair and inspected the books for a moment, then opened each one carefully.

She muttered under her breath and nodded as she read; many spells and incantations she recognized. When she finally turned to the poem verse in Sharon's book she drew back with a gasp.

"Oh lawd," she said quietly, reading it slowly.

She looked from Frank to Armand, and they both nodded to the second book. She flipped a few more pages, then found the other passage.

"Oh lawd, say it ain't so."

Armand pointed his finger at his grimoire and said, "'L'un des trois.' One of three," then pointed at Sharon's book and said, "'Trois de trois.' Three of three."

"Oh my Lawd! It cain't be!" she said, struggling to stand up. She walked quickly to a shelf and pulled down a small book. It was a bible. "The Lawd needs to help us all now. 'Specially you."

She turned and looked at Del.

Slow surprise crept into Del's face. "What do you mean, me?" she asked.

"It's about time we had a chat honey," Mama Dedé said, smoothing the edges of the old bible before gripping it tightly. "If this thing is happening, we got to see how far it's gone and see if it can be undone. You got to be ready."

"Ready? Ready for what?" Del said. "How does this have anything—"

Mama Dedé raised a heavily ringed hand and said, "Hush up, girl. Now all of you listen to what Mama Dedé has to say."

The candles flickered angrily in protest against the heavy gloom that fell about the room.

"I think you all are talkin' about da Gris-gris man, you know that?"

Del jumped at the word. "Oh my god, you know that name? My friend Jimmy was just singing a weird nursery rhyme about him."

"Jimmy? That boy you was tellin' me about?"

"Yes," Del said. "He got in trouble the other day for singing a strange nursery rhyme about… this man. It got stuck in his head and he couldn't stop singing it."

The group looked from face to face, judging the others' concern.

Mama Dedé said, "Da Gris-gris man is bad business. An old spirit dat got killed off a long time back. If it came back somehow, ain't nobody safe. 'Specially you." She looked at Del again.

Throwing her arms up, Del started to protest.

"Quiet. Just listen."

"But how—"

"Quiet!"

"Mama Dedé," Armand said, "if I may. You just said 'the Gris-gris *man*,' but then described it as a spirit that got killed off. Which is it?"

"It's both. Or at least, it's some combination of both. It started as a man. A long time ago a man named Dr. John got to be—"

"Dr. John?" Armand interrupted. "Jean Montanee, also known as Dr. John? Who had the famous feud with Marie Laveau?"

"That would be da one. They lived da same time you know; eighteen-hundreds there about. They both got to be mad powerful in da Voodoo ways. Marie, she used hers for good… and for makin' money, but mostly for good. John, he got to workin' it da other way. Oh, he made plenty of money with it, I hear, and helped lotsa people too, but sometimes he did bad business. Black business."

"And that's why they called him the Gris-gris man?" Armand asked.

"After he got to doin' da black business and shapin', he changed. People say that somethin' inside him just snapped. Some people say it wasn't even John no more, and that it wasn't really his fault, 'cause he got tricked. Either way, people got afraid to say his name for fear of callin' da spirit after 'em, so they took to talkin' about da Gris-gris man so people knew da difference."

Armand nodded thoughtfully. "Did you say 'shaping'?"

"Yeah, shape changin', shapin'. Stories say that he got so good wit da old Voodoo spells, he could call up spirits. It was one of them spirits that taught him how to shape."

"Wait," Del said, "we're talking about a legend of someone being able to change their shape? Really?"

"Yeah, that's what they say."

"No, I meant we're *really* going to explain the recent murders with this myth?" Del said.

"Del," Frank started.

"No, that's OK," Mama Dedé said. "I know da girl don't got da belief. She got to work her mind to it."

"But real shape changing?" Armand said. "What could he change into?"

"That's da problem. John did all kind of black business: tricked people out of money, cursed people for money, let dead folks speak through him for money, even tried to raise a few dead folks I heard, but don't know if he did that. And he could change into about whatever he wanted, but when he got to shapin', he usually picked a mean ol' animal like a wild hog sometimes, or a gator."

Frank choked on his sip of coffee and coughed loudly, interrupting the story. "Sorry, sorry," he said through a strangled voice, coughing again. "A gator?" Frank asked. "He change into a gator?"

"That's what they say. I hear that he got so used to it, and if someone done him wrong, he'd trick 'em and change them into somethin', then eat em up! Yeah, da Gris-gris man was bad tricky.

"He thought he was da trickiest, until he crossed Marie. Then he met his match."

"Marie Laveau, you mean?" Armand asked. "Yes, what about her? Was their feud real? And if so, what caused it?"

"Yeah, it was real, alright. Some say that he was Marie's mentor in da Voodoo, but some say she was his. Anyway, when John started cattin' around after she had the baby, she—"

"What? John and Marie had a child?"

"Two, actually. A boy and a girl. They both had some other kids already, and never were right for each other, but they couldn't keep away for a while. They were each other's own, dark drug, if you know what I mean.

"But when he went back to cattin' and she kicked him out, he got to doin' more black business. Finally, she cut ties with him completely and that's when da feud started.

"For kickin' him out, and causin' people to think he was more of a charlatan than an actual priest, he cursed all her chickens dead. They just up and died the same night. The next mornin', da maggots already had 'em and da meat couldn't be saved. So, in return, she cursed his mule to come up lame and it tripped and fell on his favorite dog and killed it."

"Fascinating," Armand said.

"Yeah, well it wasn't so fascinatin' when da children got killed."

"Oh my. I had no idea."

"Yeah, that's when it got really bad. John was so mad about his dog and mule, he up and cursed her oldest boy with consumption and he died right in Marie's arms; wasted away in under a month I heard, despite everything she tried to do. He thought he'd knocked her off her throne with that—he was none too happy with people sayin' she was da Queen of Voodoo anyway, you see. But all he did was call up da black streak in her."

"The black streak?"

"Yeah, she did good to hide it most times—control it really—but she just couldn't hold it back when he cursed her son dead.

"She waited, month after month, thinkin' about what to do. All da time, John crowin' like da *Cock a da Rock*, sayin' how he'd taught her a lesson. That was, until she sent the Pox down on his oldest daughter *and* him, but it wasn't—"

"Smallpox? But wasn't that very common at the time?"

"I didn't say it was da smallpox, Frenchy. John's oldest thought she was da *Daisy of da Field*. Mean damn girl the way I heard it. Always tellin' people her daddy was gonna curse 'em and such. Threatenin' all da boys—especially Marie's oldest. Anyway, Marie finally fixed 'em both. She cursed 'em with horse pox."

Frank whistled his chagrin as Armand searched for a reference.

"Horse herpes, Frenchy," she finally said. "Big ol' pus-filled blisters that just kept comin' back. On both of 'em. Town folks were sure there was only one way you could get horse herpes, and teased that poor girl to no end. It finally drove her mad, and she couldn't even look at herself in the mirror. Wandered off into da swamp and could be heard wailin' of a lonesome night. Some say that John would leave food out for her, but she never came back to da house, only wandered da swamp until she just disappeared one day. Left John to think about her every time he looked in his own mirror and saw the pox on himself.

"So, after that, they stayed out of each other's way. That is until he got bound to da spirit, then he couldn't control himself anymore. He was less man then, and more spirit, but it was da spirit controllin' him. Marie da one had to put him down."

Mama Dedé stopped and sipped her coffee. The others sat silently as they absorbed the fascinating story.

Armand said, "Pardon me for asking, but there are some things that are… confusing me. So, I had heard about the feud, and several other details, but most of this came from the historical research I've done on the topic. However, you refer to most of your story as something you have heard. John and Marie lived over a hundred years ago. Surely there is no one around claiming to have firsthand knowledge of these stories."

"No, I doubt there'd be anyone still alive what saw these things."

"Then how—"

"People don't have to be livin' to talk."

"You mean…" Armand started. His mind spun from the realization of what Mama Dedé was saying.

"Yeah, I hear from Marie from time to time, when I'm trancin', you know. Been a long time, though. She been quiet a long time now. But that how I know she da one put him down when he got bound."

"That's another thing," Armand said. "You said he got *bound*. Bound to what? Then, you said she had to put him down. What does that mean?"

A hard gust of wind rattled the house and the candle flames cowered. Agitated shadows emerged from deep corners, then retreated.

"Da way I hear, John thought he had da spirit under control— that da spirit that taught him how to shape—and John thinkin' he was so tricky, he was gonna make that spirit do his biddin', and fix Marie once and for all. But it was da spirit that was trickier than John. I guess it liked it when John shaped into a gator, and one day just bound him tight, only da shapin' hadn't gone all da way, you see. John was part man and part gator, and had already bound himself to the spirit, and da spirit just stuck him tight. In that form, havin' da mind of a man *and* animal, he just went mad. People say you could hear him howlin' crazy in the swamps at night; growlin' and gnashin' about. Lots of people got et up during that time. They said if you only got your head et up, then it was ol' John trying to get himself back right."

"Get himself back right?"

"Yeah, he was tryin' to become more man than animal, by eatin' up people's brains."

"Jesus, Mary and Joseph," Frank groaned as he stared at Armand.

Del sat in quiet disbelief as she rubbed her forehead where a dull pain had settled behind her eye.

"So how exactly did Marie *put him down*?" Armand asked.

"Well, after da killin' and eatin' of heads got so bad, people was comin' to Marie askin' for gris to keep da damn thing away. See, they used to call him da Gris-gris man, but he wasn't a man anymore, really. At least not in the sense that we think. When you're doin' that black business, da old magic seeps into your soul and changes you. After a while, you just become something different and can't go back to how you started.

"So, when it got bad like that, she called up some men to set about trappin' him. Kinda like they do wild hogs. They figured if they couldn't catch him when he was in spirit form, maybe they could catch him in his physical shape, assumin' he was still stuck tight. Sure enough, one day they all come a runnin', yellin' they'd trapped him. Marie had been—"

"Excuse me for interrupting again," Armand said, "but what did he look like?"

She deftly balanced her coffee cup onto its edge with a thick finger and looked at him. "Frenchy, you got an unhealthy fixation with this story, if you ask me."

A flash of alarm went through his eyes as he looked from her face to the cup and back.

"Purely academic, I assure you," he said.

She watched the look of concern slowly leave his face. The sparkling eyes of the enigmatic professor returned.

"By da point they trapped him, I hear he was part man, part gator, and part boar. He never gave up tryin' to get unstuck from da one form and damn near got out of it. Don't ask me how. Maybe by eatin' up brains that weren't human, but he had turned into an abomination.

"Anyway, Marie had been trancin' off and on for days and somehow, she figured out the unbinding spell. She went down to da swamp edge and unbound him right in da cage. When the spirit got unbound from the body, it flew off in the swamp in a flash of blue light. But he had been bound for so long, there wasn't much of da man left and he kinda… fell apart right in the cage. I hear they took the parts of him that was man and gave him a proper burial. The other parts that fell off, they threw 'em back in da swamp."

With a pale look Frank asked, "They threw 'em in da swamp? What were da gator parts dat fell off?"

"Skin and teeth mostly."

The group sat in silence once again as the wind moaned its opinion. The house seemed to remember the story, and its windowpanes rattled like nervous teeth.

"I don't know what to think," Del said, breaking the silence. "I… I just don't know."

"You feelin' OK?" Frank said. "You been rubbin' on your head a lot."

"Just a headache is all. This whole idea gives me a headache."

"So, are we now saying," Armand began, "that we believe he has come back? The Gris-gris man? Are we saying he's been reanimated?"

"Don't know about reanimated," Mama Dedé said, "'cause there was nothin' left of him. Maybe he got called back and rebound somehow—I mean the spirit. Maybe someone called that hellish spirit back and bound it again."

"Hellish spirit, indeed," Armand said, tapping a grimoire. "But which spirit are we speaking of? The original that John called up? Or the spirit of John himself?"

"Don't know. Maybe they got mixed up with all da bindin' John was doin'. But don't think we only talkin' 'bout one spirit. Before John got stuck, people say he had created some bad things, and those spirits— sort of like a fifolet I guess—would hang around and follow him of a night. Ghostly lights floatin' off around him. They say he could talk to 'em, even when he wasn't shapin'."

Del sat straight up in her chair. The candlelight cast harsh lines of fear upon her face.

"What is it, honey?" Frank asked.

"My dream," she said slowly, "from last night. After we read the grimoires, I had this really strange dream and—"

"Oh lawd! You read da books!" Mama Dedé exclaimed. "What's wrong with you two?" She glared at Frank and Armand. "Lettin' her read these books! Now listen, you got to know, da Gris-gris man is as bad as they come. I don't know if John started off like that, but after he raised that spirit, and got changed, he was all evil. You cain't be readin' things you don't understand! Now, what about this dream?"

Del quickly explained the dream of the fifolets, the woman, the snake and the abominations.

Mama Dedé made the sign of the cross, then put her hands flat on the table. "Oh lawd, we got to work fast now. And Del honey, you got to stay in this house 'til we figure out what we're gonna do."

"What do you mean?" she asked. "I still don't understand how this has anything to do with me!"

"He knows who you are," Mama Dedé said. "Or at least, he knows where you came from. Somehow, he's come back, and I'm afraid he knows you're here. He may not know where you're at exactly, but he can sense you. Them damn spirits of his can sense you."

"I'm sorry, but I don't believe any of this! And even if I did, why would he know about me?"

"Because of who you are honey! There's lots in your past you don't know, but I'm afraid he can sense you 'cause of who you are."

"And who would that be?" Del asked. "An orphan girl who—"

"You a Laveau, honey. Your momma and daddy tried to hide it, tried to keep other people from knowin' it so you could decide on your own what you want to do with it, but it's true. Marie Laveau was your way-back great-grandmomma."

CHAPTER 34

Sister Eulalie stalked the corridors of the orphanage barking sharp, quick orders. Her hope of ridding herself of the foul boy was to be delayed. Complications due to his condition required additional paperwork, but it would get done eventually. Besides that annoyance, the rash she'd noticed this morning had gotten worse. Her stomach and inner thighs itched with a maddening fire that consumed her mind. The Sin Washing couldn't start soon enough.

As she walked past the girls' shower room, she heard the distinctive sound of a mop bucket being put away. She entered the shower room and the choice was made. Josephine was just finishing her chores.

"Come with me, girl," the Sister said quietly.

Josephine turned and saw Eulalie standing before her; heavy breaths betrayed her intentions. Small tears sprang to Josephine's eyes as her stomach turned to acid. She quietly followed the nun.

Inside the Sister's room, Josephine set to making a bowl of warm soapy water as the nun adjusted the folds of clothing beneath her habit and settled herself in a chair, propping her feet on two short footstools. After the customary short sermon about washing our sins away, she simply said, "Begin."

Kneeling at the side of the chair, Josephine closed her eyes and slowly lifted the wet washcloth beneath the folds of her habit and between her legs.

Several minutes later the nun's arm came around her shoulders and pulled her close against her rough habit, burying Jo's face into the fold of her arm and torso. "Faster. Wash faster girl," the nun said.

Josephine, struggling to breathe against the heavy material, did as she was told and washed faster. She was now sweaty and itchy herself but knew not to stop. She heard the nun's breathing change and felt a sudden jerk as the nun reached across with her other hand, grabbed her hair and pulled her head against her clothed breast as her legs clamped around her hand. Several more minutes of direction and she was finished.

If the nun ever looked at Josephine during this time, she didn't know. Josephine kept her eyes shut tight.

"Get out," the nun said flatly, ending the session.

Josephine, forgetting to drop the washcloth into the bucket, left the room without thinking. She walked quickly through the dark hallway to the shower room, stripping her clothes as she went. She tossed the Crow's washcloth down with her pile of clothes. Crying, she threw herself into the shower before the water could heat up, gasping as the cold water shocked her. The sensation numbed her body to match her mind. She stood for several minutes staring blankly at the wall, then fumbled for the soap. She scrubbed herself furiously. She couldn't get the smell of Sister Eulalie off her fast enough.

*

The cat-beast sauntered out of the swamp toward its nest. Its stomach distended from its latest gorged meal and its teats swollen with nursing milk, it was ready to feed its young abominations again. They were ravenous.

The strange man held an abomination in his hands, caressed it and was pleased. He smiled at the sauntering beast as it reflected in his blue mirrored glasses. Patting its head, the man said, "Well done, Mr. Sandgrove, well done." And at that moment, both man and beast vibrated, causing wisps and streams of faint blue light to cascade around them. The streams mixed together in the air, exchanging energy, then flowed back into their bodies like a sharp intake of breath; man and beast were of the same essence.

The man inspected the abomination in his hands. The translucent beak was already tough and sharp, as his bloody fingers indicated. The three-toed claws flexed and clinched with a strong grip. The long weasel body felt smooth to his touch, but would toughen to a leathery hide over time. And the split-tail twitched in the air, always sensing.

The man dropped the weasel-thing back into the large mud nest where the others snapped at it in anticipation of eating. The thing mewled loudly for its size, snapped back blindly at the others, then settled into a unified sniffing of the air, smelling food nearby.

"And what of our guest?" the man asked lightly.

The beast turned toward a large mound between two cypress trees and snorted. There, buried beneath the rotting vegetation, Sharon lay motionless.

The man walked over and peered down into her face. To others she would appear dead, but she was not. Her breathing was non-existent, and her blood did not flow, but neither was it dead. One eye was stuck shut while the other stuck open, staring blindly out, like a broken doll.

He was unclear on her sense of being, at least the mental state of what was left, but could feel it reach out to him; it was a pleading thing. The man reached down into the mud and felt for a toe. He wondered if the weasels would like them. They would be but a morsel. His family was growing, and he would do anything for his family. Before he left, he lay his palm against the woman's forehead. He could feel her essence settling there, concentrating. It would only be a matter of time now. Sharon didn't know it, but she was getting smaller.

CHAPTER 35

Curled up tight, Del sat by herself in a large chair next to a window. After hearing everything Mama Dedé had to say, she felt very tired. *Related to Marie Laveau*. What did this mean for her? Her head laid listlessly on the thick chair back as she stared silently out the window. The window looked onto the inner courtyard at the back of the house and framed the dark night. Why had this ridiculous story of Voodoo landed on her? How was she to ever build a normal life for herself and Jimmy with this stigma hanging over her? She pulled an afghan around her shoulders and wiped her eyes. The wind outside, moaning, mocked her despair.

The others spoke in hushed tones. Del felt their fleeting glances. She hated the attention. A few days ago, all she could think about was starting her first job, starting a new life and maybe, just maybe, starting some type of family again by having Jimmy live with her. It was probably a pipe dream, she realized now. How would she ever accomplish this? There were too many things stacked against her. And now this.

She stood up and walked to a bookshelf against the wall. She looked blankly over the various volumes, not really reading the titles, but trying to think of what to do. The others watched her closely; she knew they were there but ignored them. They weren't allowed in her space of despair. She imagined a cold wall of solitude surround her, blocking them out.

She was deep in thought and barely noticed when Mama Dedé pulled a book from a shelf and placed it in her hands. Del didn't acknowledge her, only held the book until she went away. Turning back to the chair by the window, she curled up under the afghan, adjusted the small lamp on the table and opened the book.

It appeared to be a scrapbook of some kind, but also detailed the ancestors of Marie Laveau. A lot of people she had never heard of, nor cared to learn about.

She absently flipped the pages. After several minutes of scanning notes, she turned to an old newspaper clipping and began to read:

Daily Picayune, August 11th, 1866

The Strange Case of Mr. Sandgrove

> *On July 24th of this year, a missing person's report was filed for one Mr. Alphonse Sandgrove of 111 Bayou Rd., having last been seen on or about July the 18th in the vicinity of said road. According to witnesses, Mr. Sandgrove was last seen riding his horse towards the residence of Jean Montanee (aka Dr. John, aka Devil John), a reported Voodoo priest of the highest order, who holds a respectable estate bordering Bayou Road.*

> *The two men are reported to have an ongoing dispute regarding the untimely death of Mrs. Eleanor Sandgrove,*

who died in childbirth in March of this year, and who reportedly received a treatment of Voodoo blessings from the aforementioned doctor for the total sum of Seven Dollars.

The former dispute, filed at the local courthouse on April 3rd 1866, outlines the charges of Malpractice, Fraud and Trickery against the doctor, and requests the refund of Seven Dollars, for the cost of the blessing, and an additional payment of Fifty Dollars for the untimely loss of Mrs. Sandgrove.

Dispute notwithstanding, the two men have reportedly been seen arguing on or about Bayou Rd., creating a general disturbance of the peace.

In addition, after the disappearance of Mr. Sandgrove, who, according to relatives, had no plans to travel outside of the area, there have been reports of strange sightings and sounds in the vicinity of Bayou Rd. Witnesses say that late of night, a disturbing howl can be heard, sounding equal parts of man and wolf, and can raise the hackles of any who hear it. Additionally, some have even reported to have seen a strange animal in the vicinity that they believe is the aforementioned Mr. Sandgrove, who has been unnaturally transformed into the woeful beast as punishment for bringing accusations against the doctor.

This reporter believes that if Mr. Sandgrove is gone, he may have met a more natural, albeit untimely, demise, and does not put much stake in the belief of transformation through Voodoo rituals.

However, the question remains: Where is
Mr. Sandgrove?

Del felt her stomach do a slow flip as her head pounded for attention. There was something to this story, and to what she had heard tonight. The whole thing. She didn't know how, but somehow, she knew these things to be true. An air of helplessness washed over her, very much like the day she had learned she would be sent to the orphanage. A gray cloudy future lay before her; what lay beyond the clouds, she wasn't sure she wanted to know, but something was waiting for her.

*

Josephine lay awake with hot tears streaming her cheeks. She had taken the longest shower she could without drawing undo attention to herself, then went to bed. Confusion and anger spun her head.

She had to get out of this place. She had to. Her fingers clinched and spasmed as thoughts flew through her mind. She hated Sister Eulalie; she hated her for who she was; she hated her for what she had done to not only her, but to many kids; she even hated her for her desire to get rid of Jimmy. As weird as the kid was, he was actually pretty nice. She did like Jimmy, but he was the one thing that stood between her and Del. She could deal with Jimmy later. Right now, someone had to do something about the Sister.

She would have to kill her.

It surprised Josephine how easy the thought came to her. *Sure Josephine, just kill her. It will be easy. Just wish her dead and say the magic words. Abracadabra, you're dead, bitch.*

But how would you kill someone if you really wanted to? It needed to look like an accident. She didn't want to spend her life in jail. Did they keep poison around, she wondered? Could she get it into her food somehow? Was she really thinking about this, or…

Yes, she could kill her. Or at least, she could think about how to kill her. Maybe a fire? No, she didn't want to destroy the orphanage. Maybe she could choke her during a Sin Washing episode. *Choking leaves marks, stupid. Maybe you could smother her.*

Too bad she couldn't call up a demon and—

The wind howled a name that shook the old windows. The wind had been listening; listening to her thoughts, reading her mind. It knew what she needed.

It howled the name again. A dark name that chilled her blood and slowed it to a death crawl. It wasn't a voice she understood, but it was a feeling. She knew instantly what she would do. *The strange man in the cemetery*; the man who traded in sin. She would trade the Sister to the man in the cemetery. She would win Del, forever, and he could do whatever he wanted to the Sister. Forever.

CHAPTER 36

Henri Guillaume waved away the cobwebs that hung from the foyer ceiling and walked into the house at 113 Bayou Rd. Dropping his coat onto the chair that had sat there since before he was a boy, a small cloud of ancient dust swirled, announcing the latest four-legged inhabitants.

"Rats," he said as his nose flared, collecting dust mite samples. He scratched at his neck and the side of his face. The cobwebs and dust were irritating his skin.

He walked straight to the kitchen without turning on a light. Even though this wasn't his regular home, he knew it by heart. This wasn't the home that people would expect Henri to occupy, with his family's wealth and his upbringing. This was an old house, years past its condemnation date; a shack to some, an eyesore; a place of worship to others. Somehow Frank had found the two brothers in this house. *What a coincidence*—the entire police force looking for the Glapions and Frank finds them almost in plain sight.

He sat at the old wooden table and lit an oil lamp. He liked the feel of the dark, the void of possibility, the heavy weight of nothingness. Standing alone against the darkness, one small flame flickered its essence, a tiny, hypnotic wave of light and hope. Although just a small flame, within it lay the power to do terrible damage; great things could be undone by a single flame. There was always a flicker of hope, wasn't there? Something, someone, that stood out as a beacon. A poor lost soul that defies the odds; an orphan. Was she the tiny flame to be feared above all others? He would think on this.

Removing several files from a large satchel, he set them on the old kitchen table, vaguely aware of his visitors. He smelled them long before he heard them. Their musky essence—wet and moldering—lay a heavy scent on the dusty air.

Whiskers twitching, eyes aglow, the rats of Bayou Road and the surrounding wetlands skittered cautiously into the basement and eaves of the old house. Their long, dirty nails scratched a familiar sound into the walls, like the comforting creaks of well-worn boards.

He opened the files in front of him and turned each page with precision and care. He was always cautious of things he read for the first time. He knew to read them with one eye or the other, and to never read them out loud. Reading with one eye or the other, but not both, kept him from reading into a phrase unexpectedly. One eye comprehended while the other watched on in caution, a silent sentinel always looking ahead, skimming fragments, but never completing. Once the brain was trained for such a task, it was surprisingly easy to do, and he quite forgot it was something he had to learn as a small child.

Frang, what are you hiding? He had always been a good cop, a good detective. He had even mentored Henri in his early days, so why the deception now? He had had an unhealthy fixation with gators ever since the Glapion case that made him famous; the two brothers had used this house as a place of horror.

Henri pulled a gator tooth from his pocket and laid it on the table. One of his men had recovered it this morning from the first murder site. It took them days of hand-sifting through a layer of rotting sludge before they found it. It shone brilliantly in the candlelight, surprisingly white. In fact, Henri thought that it looked too white, as if it had never been used.

Everyone in Louisiana knew that gators could regrow their teeth, but they didn't typically just fall out with no sign of wear. These teeth looked brand new, only fully grown. *Did Frank plant them?* he wondered. If so, to what purpose?

He continued leafing through the files. Picture after picture drew closer scrutiny. Semi-mauled bodies, missing face, missing brain. He imagined himself there, an invisible spirit floating in the background, watching; maybe even as a fifolet.

What would he see? Would he see the man responsible for these attacks? The *beast* responsible? Lapping at the brains?

It was always the brain. How fascinating.

The wind pressed against the sides of the old house, squeezing through loose openings, stirring more rat dander into the air to settle over the cobwebs like a soft powder. A fresh sheet of rain drummed against the windows, pecking a hidden message to the inhabitants; *The time is near.* It was as if the wind were speaking.

His mind swam through a dark miasma; knowledge of the past; dreams of the future. How dark would it be?

The rain pecked again. Three times.

The future would be dark indeed.

*

Eddie sat silently in the cold drizzle, crouching over the large crypt he had ascended the day before. He was unsure where he was, but knew he was where he should be. He was unsure how long he'd been there, but knew it hadn't been long enough; not nearly long enough.

As if in a strange dream—maybe it was another delirium, but he didn't think so—he felt bits and pieces of people's lives as they walked past; heard bits and pieces of their stories, like a cacophony of instruments all being tuned at once. Their lives, at least parts of them, vibrated on a frequency that he could feel. He was a collection station, a radio receiver tuned to a specific channel. He was an archivist taking mental notes, storing clues for later use. He was a librarian of sin.

Crouching, feet and hands anchored to stone, shoulders hunched against the rain, he sat listening to the beautiful symphony of sin that flowed past him. If there was one thing he knew, it was sin.

When the young wife hurried down the sidewalk, in his mind he heard the notes of her latest affair. She did dirty things. She wasn't sure why she did them, but she did, nonetheless. Her name was Hope Menarvy.

When the old man walked by, he heard a fragment of the lie-song that was building in the man's head. A reason why he'd lost money, other than gambling it away, which was the actual truth. He had promised his wife he would stop and never lie about it again. His name was Harold Green.

As the beggar was mugged, just around the corner, Eddie felt an especially strong wave. Whether it was excitement or not, he couldn't say; more like a small shock his body now craved. When the teenage boy drove the ballpeen hammer into the beggar's skull, Eddie felt a bolt of heat run through the top of his head, down through his body, into his arms and legs, then out his hands and feet, straight into the stone. The heat-energy seemed to fuse his being together. He felt whole like he'd never felt before. The heat-energy forged his spine into a long curve; it was more comfortable now. It fused the inside of his arms to the outside of his thighs, permanently wrapping his arms tight around his legs. It stuck his eyelids to a perfect, half-open stare, watching forever; he didn't have to blink now. It accelerated the growth of his toenails, now curled over the edge, forming a connection to the stone as if he had been carved from a single slab. When the ballpeen hammer sunk beneath the beggar's skull, the boy's name who was still holding the handle sang in his mind, archived into the music library of sin with a special red stamp on the album cover: *Never to be checked out. Reserved for Him.* The boy's name was Leonard White. Eddie had met him once on the wharf of the Mississippi. Eddie had been a peckerwood then. But not now.

Eddie was now part of the tomb. No one noticed due to the heavy fog-rain, but he now blended into the crypts of the St. Louis Cemetery #1 like the other carved stone features.

Eddie was a living grotesque.

CHAPTER 37

F rank watched Del from across the room. She looked like she was dozing, but he imagined he felt her presence filling the room. It was a dark presence, different than the weighty gloom of the story, but no less dangerous. Frank began to understand why he had always been drawn to help Del. She was here for a reason. He could not have guessed it would have ever been a reason such as this, but he felt he needed to protect her now more than ever.

"So, she's really a Laveau?" Frank asked quietly.

Mama Dedé nodded and squeezed her bible again. "I've known since da day she came. I could feel somethin' in her, but wasn't sure what it was. It bothered me out of several nights sleepin', so I had to trance on it. Marie came to me that night and gave me a vision. It's foggy now, but it was Del's face dissolvin' backwards into her momma's face. It kept rollin' backwards, face after face. Somehow it still looked like Del's eyes, but the face kept changin'. I knew that I was seein' her momma, then her momma's momma, and finally it just ended with Marie. That's when I knew for sure."

"Fascinating," Armand said, shaking his head slowly. "Simply fascinating."

"A lot of people related to a Laveau somehow, Frenchy."

"Oh, I know, and that's not what I meant exactly." Armand stood and moved to the bookcase. Each hand rubbing fingers excitedly as if sprinkling a fine invisible powder. He began touching books at random, although none of them held the clues he had hidden in his own library.

"The power," he said finally, "where does it come from?"

"Da power?" Frank asked.

"Yes, where does the power come from?" Armand said, turning towards them. "I realize that many things are passed from parent to child. That's heredity. It's in the genes. But the power to trance?" He waved a hand at Mama Dedé. "The power to bind, or to unbind? Where does it come from? It can't simply be learned. Some people have it, some people don't. Why is that?"

They exchanged glances, but did not speak. The flames danced the answer onto the walls in an ancient language, then erased it without warning.

Mama Dedé watched Armand carefully. Appreciative of his careful questioning.

"It's just der I guess," Frank offered. "Always been out in da world floatin' around, waitin' for someone to pick it up." He leaned his girth back into the chair and considered his cigar with a scholarly look. "Hell, maybe it just floats around the universe until someone comes along dat can use it."

Armand slapped his hands together and pointed at Frank, causing him to ash his cigar onto his shirt. A low curse slipped from the side of Frank's mouth as he slapped the ashes away.

"Genius!" he said, still pointing at Frank.

Frank's mouth dropped open, letting his cigar droop forward. "Well I—"

Armand started a slow walk around the table, fingers sprinkling invisible powder at three times the speed of his walk. In his mind, he touched invisible books in his study; a candelabra here, an old wood carving there. He knew the clue was close; he just needed to visualize where it was in his library mind.

"Let's see, universe... yes universe. Stars... galaxies... no, not galaxies. Stars... constellations... yes of course! Have you ever heard the strange story of Otto the Younger?"

Del raised her head from the chair, watching as Armand did his strange word association ritual. She smiled slightly in the dark, thinking this crazy group of people, as mismatched as they were, would make a wonderful family. Jimmy would even fit in here in some odd way.

The pleasant thought quickly turned sour as an image of Sister Eulalie flashed into her mind; the wicked witch flying on her broomstick.

She buried her face in the afghan and quietly wiped the water from her eyes.

Armand continued without an answer. "*The Diary of Otto the Younger*—quite a tragic story—was an actual diary found, oh... in the 1920s I believe, in a previously unknown tomb in Egypt. The diary details the final days of a young boy trapped in the tomb—quite a tragic story—hiding from nomads who had just killed his entire party. He desperately details the findings in the tomb: strange carved constellations—*not of this sky*—hidden chambers, strange figures, and hieroglyphs that describe a universal energy, that some people evolve to. That is, of course, if the translations were correct. Actually, there was a wild idea there about *assisted evolution* I believe, but can't recall the details. Anyway, the hieroglyphs apparently described how individuals who came into contact with an ancient storm, or perhaps some debris from it, had undergone a transformation and were somehow *tapped* into this universal energy."

He paused, realizing he was now rapidly circling the table. Frank's cigar still drooped from his mouth.

"This transformation manifested itself in different… abilities. Some were good, and some were… evil. It was quite the sensation when the tomb was found, especially when researchers realized that the young boy, Otto, and his grandfather had made the discovery sometime in the… 1840s, if I recall. After the party was killed, the young boy hid until the nomads tired of searching for him."

"What'd they do?" Del asked from her chair.

Armand turned to her and paused, considering his words carefully. "Like I said Del, it's quite a tragic story."

"What'd they do?"

Armand cleared his throat and said, "They closed the tomb with him in it. The tomb was then buried with sand. It wasn't rediscovered until sixty years later."

The room fell silent as dread settled over them. Only the candles spoke in their silent, ancient language.

"How old was the boy?"

Armand cleared his throat again and twisted his mustache. "He was almost twelve."

Del laid her head back against the chair and said nothing. Jimmy was sixteen, but sometimes had the mentality of a twelve-year-old. She couldn't imagine how terrible it had been for young Otto.

"And how you know all dis, Frenchy?"

"It's an interesting area of research for me. I'm writing a book on ancient curses and their origins. Quite a fascinating topic. This is how I came to know of your expertise." He motioned to Mama Dedé. "And of course, the famous Marie Laveau and Dr. John." He looked at Del, and suddenly felt his own enthusiasm misplaced. Del turned her face to the floor.

"Sorry," he said. "I simply…" He let the sentence fade and took his seat.

Mama Dedé and Frank exchanged glances. Frank simply shook his head. He already thought they shouldn't be down this path.

Turning her attention back to Armand, she said, "So what you sayin'? You think we got us an Egyptian curse now too?"

Resuming his professorial tone, he said, "Oh, I don't know about that. The Voodoo mythos, at least, how it came to Louisiana, is well documented. It came here with the slave trade, primarily from Haiti and West Africa. And although we never pulled slaves from Egypt, it *is* the same continent. Who's to say that whatever transformation supposedly happened in Egypt—well, it was simply documented there, I guess the transformations could have happened anywhere—but who's to say that the people who were *transformed* didn't migrate throughout Africa and get swept up in the slave trades?"

Del listened intently and finally said, "What else do you know of the curse, or whatever it is?"

"Let me be clear: I'm not talking about a curse that can be turned on or off. The theory here—and it is still just a theory—is that some people in the far distant past came into contact with something that changed them somehow. Fundamentally. A… Darwin's *natural selection* of the cosmic order. The ability to perform these seemingly magical tasks is simply an outcome of their abnormal evolution."

Frank whistled his skepticism.

"I know," Armand said. "I know, it all sounds crazy, and I may be way off. It was simply that your mention of the universe was too much to ignore.

"There is more, however."

"Oh lord," Frank said.

"Tell it," Del said. "Tell us whatever you know."

Armand sat, shifting in his chair, and suddenly wished he hadn't remembered the story.

"Well, there was one more thing."

Everyone waited silently.

"The diary also mentioned something about the God Set, the Egyptian god of the underworld. He was also believed to be the God of Evil, Chaos and… Storms, of all things. He was described as… as a half man and half animal, with the head of a Jackal and two tails."

No one noticed the color drain from Frank's face.

"'And they become like Gods,'" Del said quietly.

Startled, Armand stared at Del. "Yes, how did you know that?"

"I don't even know why I said it. It just popped into my head," Del said. "Have you heard it before?"

"I read it once," Armand said. "It was one of the last things Otto ever wrote in his diary."

CHAPTER 38

Wednesday

M ama Dedé woke the next morning drained of energy. After Frank and Armand left, she had spent most of the night trancing, determined to figure out what all of this meant. Even though she had warned Del of the danger, she didn't think the girl fully understood or appreciated it. Hell, maybe she didn't fully understand. The Egyptian story that Armand had laid on them was a new variable.

The trancing sessions always left her drained and invigorated at the same time. Her spirit could float free of its earthly bond, expanding in all directions. This left her mind ringing clear as a bell. Her body, however, bore the brunt of the trance, her energy stores tapped beyond capacity. She slept heavily after a trance, the knowledge of the universe settling into her mind.

After waking, she lumbered to the kitchen in a large robe and slippers. Del was sitting at the kitchen table gazing into her coffee.

"Watcha thinkin', honey?" Mama Dedé asked, pouring herself a cup.

Del stirred her coffee and watched drops desperately cling to the edge of her spoon. They clung tightly, defying gravity for a surprising amount of time; tinsel strength far beyond her capacity. Regardless of their inherent strength, the drops fell and disappeared into the swirling black void anyway. She felt like she was each drop of coffee, getting smaller every time, weaker; a small black drop in a large cosmic ocean hurtling towards a giant, sucking void.

"Oh, just that I'm suddenly the target of a fairy-tale monster from a period of time I know nothing about. Just waiting for my prince charming to come along, give me a kiss and save me from the dragon."

Mama Dedé chuckled. "That's good, girl. You keep that sass. If this thing is true, you're gonna need every bit of strength you can muster."

"But how do we know?" Del asked. "How do we know if this is true, or just... just some weird coincidence and a couple of nutty old—although kind of interesting—men who like to tell spook stories?"

"Who, Frank and Armand? Heh, they nutty alright, but that don't mean da story ain't true." She joined Del at the table and grabbed her hands. A more serious look had never been on Mama Dedé's face.

"Listen to me now," she said in a low tone. "I heard from Marie last night. It wasn't very clear, kinda faded, like a T.V. channel that's goin' out, but it was her. She came to me early on in the trance. She knows that somethin' is happenin.'"

Del tried to hide the disbelief on her face by looking into the void of coffee.

"It has somethin' to do with that boy you know."

Del's spoon clanked into the bottom of her cup, sending angry drops cascading across the table. "What boy? Jimmy?" she said. "What's wrong with him?"

Mama Dedé grabbed her hands, demanding her attention. "I don't know for sure, but listen: there's somethin' you got to do. I don't fully understand why jus' yet, but you do what I tell you."

*

Del walked through the double-doors of the orphanage and didn't bother signing in. She had seen Jimmy staring out the window of the waiting room and knew something was wrong.

"He was crying all night," Josephine said, jumping up from behind the desk. "I tried to talk—Del…?"

Del walked straight through the next door and saw not the child-like excitement she normally saw in Jimmy, but instead a boy she hardly recognized.

Jimmy turned toward her from the window and sank into a small waiting-room chair next to the window. The dark circles under his eyes suggested sickness or malnutrition. He reached his hand up and spoke her name, but it came out as a mouse squeak. His hand fell to his lap and his head lolled against the back of the chair.

In two long strides Del was at his chair, sliding on her knees as she thought he would tumble forward onto the hard linoleum.

"Jimmy! Jimmy, what's wrong?" she asked, hugging him close. "Are you sick?" She felt his head for fever. He was cold and clammy, but still managed to feel wet with sweat.

"I tied, Deh," he said. "I fought you dead and I—"

"Dead? Jimmy, I'm not dead. I'm right here," she said, smoothing his hair back from his forehead. "Why would you think such a thing?"

"Bad deams." He started to say more, but now that Del was here sleep was quickly overtaking him.

"You had a bad dream again? Did it keep you awake? Josephine said you were up all night. Were you scared?"

"I fought you dead," he said weakly. "I deam da iissard tied to eat you head. Den I saw ghost people, and den… some bad fings."

"What bad—never mind. It was just a dream. I'm fine. I'm right here."

"But I doan wan' you to die, Deh. Da iissard wan' you to die, but I doan wan—"

"Wait, just wait!" she said, holding his hands tightly. "Why do you think the iissa— Why do you think the lizard wants me to die? Did the lizard talk to you in your dream?"

Jimmy thought about this as he rubbed his tired eyes. "No Deh, you talked to me in my deam, ony it wasn't you, but it was kinda you. You sang da song to kihw da iissard. You said sing da song Yimmy and I singed it but now I doan 'member it and now you gonna die 'cause my 'tupid head can't 'member da song."

"I'm not going to die, not for a long, long time. And neither are you. I'm going to get you out of here and you're going to come live with me." She looked over her shoulder in case the Crow was looking through the door window. "I don't know where we'll live yet, but I'm going to get you out of here. I need to do some things first. I don't know how long it will take, but I may not be able to come visit you for a while."

"But why?"

"Don't worry. I can't explain now, but I need to ask you to do something for me."

Jimmy perked up slightly at this. "What Deh, kihw da issarrd?"

"What? No. You stay away from the iissa— from the lizard. If you see him…" She suddenly wondered how far she should take this line of thought. "Jimmy, have you seen the lizard? Has… has the lizard seen you?"

Jimmy thought again on this. He felt happy that he could help Del. "No, I doan see da iissard. My deam see da iissard. Dat why he can't see me. He can't see my deam."

Del felt a slight wave of dizziness hit her as she considered the implications of what Jimmy was saying. She couldn't believe this was happening.

"Jimmy, you said I sung you a song in your dream. But you don't remember it?"

He shook his head weakly.

"Not even a little bit?"

Jimmy scrunched his face into concentration. Del knew that he would do this all day if she asked him

"Aarrgghhh… come out 'tupid tong!" Jimmy said.

"That's OK Ji—"

"It tuck, Deh. It fwew in but won't fwy out!"

Del chuckled at this and gave Jimmy a hug. "That's OK. Maybe it will come out later. If it does, try to remember it, OK?"

Jimmy nodded enthusiastically.

"And Jimmy, one more thing." She looked directly at him. "I need you to be really brave until I come and get you, OK?"

"Bwave da 'ion?"

"Yes, brave like a lion."

At this, Del walked Jimmy back to his bed, and despite the morning hour, tucked him tightly in. He was asleep almost immediately.

Looking around the unusually quiet orphanage, Del saw Josephine hovering in the shadow of the hall. She had been at the desk when Del ran in, but she wasn't sure where Jo had been during her talk with

Jimmy. She was concerned with how much Josephine may have heard.

Josephine walked quickly to Del, nearly skipping as she looked over her shoulder at the empty orphanage.

"Where is everyone?" Del asked.

Grabbing her jacket sleeve, Josephine tugged at Del's arm and pulled her towards the back hall that led to the showers and back offices.

"The Crow and most of the other penguins are out with the rug rats," Josephine said, "on some sort of field trip. Del, I need to talk to you."

Josephine stopped inside the entrance to the girls' shower room. She remembered sitting on the bench not long ago waiting for Del to finish her shower. She knew her time was short.

"Jo, I need a favor from you. I need to ask—"

"Anything," Jo said. "Ask me anything." She smoothed Del's jacket sleeves again from shoulder to wrist, willing herself not to grope her arms altogether. "But first I have to say something."

"Jo, I need—"

"Please wait. Please listen." Jo looked at the dark hallway, trying to detect any light footsteps, afraid her time has flying away. She felt a blush rush up the sides of her torso. She felt this every time she thought of Del, now. She saw herself slightly disconnected from the scene, gazing at Del, pawing at her arms, but couldn't stop herself. "Del, I wanted to say..." She didn't want to scare Del off, but she had to say this one thing. "I want you to know..." The blush flowed up her body, releasing waves of heat up her neck, turning her cheeks a warm, inviting pink. She felt dizzy. She swallowed hard. She thought she was fainting. She focused on the smallest thing she could see: a tiny freckle on the side of Del's mouth, right near the edge of her lips.

It was a hidden freckle, she'd never noticed it before, but she had never been this close before. It was intoxicating to be this close. No one else knew of this freckle, she was sure of it. It was her secret. One of the many secrets she would know about Del. Jo wasn't sure if she was still speaking or not. Del's lips moved ever so slightly, maybe a word, maybe a light sigh, she wasn't sure. She thought her lips quivered an invitation. Yes, her lips had invited her. She was sure of it now.

Without thinking, Jo grabbed the sleeves of Del's jacket pulling her forward, arched up on her tiptoes and kissed Del with a passion she had only dreamed about. All the dreams, all the words she had rehearsed were practice for this one, lone kiss. She couldn't say any more.

Del, surprised beyond action, stood still and let the kiss happen. Finally, grabbing Jo's shoulders, she held her out straight, breaking the spell. She saw Jo blink slowly, as if coming out of a dream. Pleading eyes looked up at her.

Del's mind swirled with confusion. *This is what Jo wanted to tell me? How... How did I not see this?*

Del wasn't sure how much time had passed; it was speeding up and slowing down to the point she felt like she was in a carnival room. The floor was tilting over her head and she was tipping backwards. Somewhere in the distance she heard a voice, small and desperate, a pleading voice, a warm voice.

"Del, please say something. You're scaring me. Just say something."

Del blinked several times and looked around. She was still standing in the girls' shower room, and the world had not turned upside down. Hordes of demons were not coming through the floor to take her to hell, and lighting had not destroyed the church as the Crow would sermonize. She felt her heart pounding in her chest and realized she wasn't having a heart attack after all. Her pulse settled.

She took a long slow breath and looked at Jo. Suddenly, something that Mama Dedé had told her flashed through her mind. She saw Jo looking up at her in anticipation. Del understood.

In one quick move, Del slid her hand from Jo's shoulder to the back of her neck and pulled her forward. She closed her eyes and let Jo kiss her again. She may have kissed Jo back, but wasn't sure which direction it was going. She ran her fingers up the back of Jo's neck and cradled her, kneading her fingers through Jo's long brown hair. She felt Jo sink towards her when she did this. After several seconds, Del broke the spell again and pulled her hand away. Jo's eyes shimmered with joy. Del tucked her hand into her jacket pocket, rolling her fingers together, saving her prize.

"Del, I… Thank you. I just wanted…" Jo stammered and swallowed hard. "I… I just… That's what I wanted to say… I'm here for you, Del. I'll help you. Whatever you need. With Jimmy, anything… I'll help however I can."

"I know you will, Jo," Del said. "Thank you. I know."

"Say my name again. Just once more."

"Thank you, Josephine."

CHAPTER 39

A Treacherous Name

Oh! Treacherous, treacherous name!

I beg of you never to speak it! I pray the wretched word shall never pass my ears again!

Haunted! Cursed! The bane of my torment and anguish for more years than I can recall!

Why I hate the name so has been lost to me, but it is poison! A curse rolled into a single word! A...

Wait... I do recall... something... something about the name... it is from a dream that pricks my mind.

But alas... What became of the name? Was it not lost? It is a curious thing.

All but lost to the ages I'd say... only wh—

Of course! It has come to me at last!

The wretched name was upon the wind.

And into the tempest it did fall.

CHAPTER 40

D el left the orphanage with confused thoughts running through her head. She tried to process the events of the morning, but felt more at a loss than ever before. Her life had become a whirlwind; a tornado, uncontrolled, wreaking havoc wherever it went. Her life had been unleashed on the few people around her she cared about, and had only brought destruction. She didn't know where her life was going, but had to get it under control somehow. She knew she had to find the strength, and just a few hours ago had taken the first step to that end: she had agreed to learn from Mama Dedé.

The short bike ride back to the halfway house helped to clear her head a bit, but her mind was still racing. She was nervous and excited at the same time. She could feel… life, speeding up around her. Things were now in motion that she didn't understand, but she knew she would be part of them. In fact, she somehow felt she was the center of the storm, maybe even the catalyst. She wondered if she really did have an unknown power. She had heard several stories of people with strange abilities; sometimes good, sometimes bad, but mostly good, she thought. Why couldn't she have something good? Even though she was an orphan, it wasn't her fault—at least she didn't think it was. If she had some type of natural power, she would use it to help people. She would help Jimmy. Maybe this was the thing she needed to help him. She would learn what she needed from Mama Dedé, just enough to get past this ghost thing, and then she would help Jimmy with the rest.

Part of this sounded ridiculous and immature to her, but the thought of having another way to help Jimmy superseded all other thoughts. She would learn this Voodoo stuff to help Jimmy.

As she entered the halfway house, Mama Dedé greeted her with a solemn nod, turned and walked down the hall to the parlor. Del followed without a word.

The other kids that stayed at the halfway house had been sent across the city to retirement homes to do chores. They would spend the night there. The house would remain nearly empty until the next morning. Mama Dedé hoped that would be enough time.

Inside the parlor, the information from last night flooded back into Del's mind. A heavy weight settled back around her shoulders, causing a dread to shadow her face.

The two women sat around the large, round table where just the night before, Del had been the child in the room; talked about in third-person as if she was not there; wondered over as if she were an oddity; feared slightly, although none would admit it.

The two women wondered about each other. Were they on nearly equal standing? Had the elder woman misinterpreted her own trances? Was Del the center of this whole thing?

The older, settling her girth into the same chair she always used for readings, seances and trancing, had reached the peak of her abilities long ago. Although she still picked up a new spell now and then, she knew there were certain things she would never be able to do. Mama Dedé was excellent at reading signs and concocting the standard love potions and good-luck charms. Her trancing abilities were nearly unmatched, which gave her a unique perspective on people's lives. She could trance almost back to the very start of a person's issue, which gave her an uncanny ability to create a remedy, even if the unfortunate person had suffered for years. However, she knew she would never match Marie Laveau or Dr. John. She would never have the ability to raise the dead or bind the soul. The power simply wasn't in her.

The younger, lithe and limber, sat cross-legged in a chair across the table and exuded an aura that none could see but everyone could feel. A powerful river of life flowed through the younger woman. It wasn't bravado or arrogance; it was purer, but just as dangerous. Del seemed to sit atop a deep well of life, a dark well that held many secrets. Secrets that wanted to rush forward, upward and outward, to be known and consumed. No one knew what power may lay within that well.

The heavy smell of candles and incense was cloying, but settled Del's nerves. When entering the parlor, she had noticed that dark curtains had been pulled over the windows. Not a ray of light seeped into the room from the gloomy day. The only light was generated by one of the dozens of candles that were burning, although even they seemed to cast a dark, half-luminous glow over the room.

"Now listen, honey," Mama Dedé said, "da only thing you got to do is follow what I say. When it's time for trancin', you'll know, den you just let your mind relax. I'll lead da way this time, but at some point, you'll be able to do dis on your own. It'll be like you're searching in a big dark closet for interesting things. You understan'?"

"Not really," Del said. "Well, maybe. But I got what you asked for."

"Already? We don't need it today, but you got it already, huh?"

"Yes," Del said, taking the tiny, nearly weightless bundle from her pocket.

"OK, put it in dis here jar. We cain't get it mixed up, but we'll figure out why we need it later."

Del reached her hand out and carefully placed a lock of Josephine's hair into the small jar.

"She didn't ask you why you need it?" Mama Dedé asked.

Del thought about the surprise kiss that had stunned her, then the second kiss that she had invited to happen, which gave her the opportunity to run her hands through Jo's hair. "No, not really," Del said, looking down at the table.

Mama Dedé saw something in Del's face, but simply said, "OK, now give me a lock of your hair."

"Why?"

"Cause dat's how I'm gonna keep track of you when we start. Da first lesson in spells is dat if you want to control someone, even just a little, you got to have something from 'em."

Del fingered her own curly hair, thinking about being controlled by someone. She didn't like the thought of it. She looked up and saw Mama Dedé watching her patiently. Del sighed and looked around the parlor room once more, then pulled a small lock of hair and handed it to the woman.

"Do you give dis freely?"

Del wrinkled her forehead as the side of her mouth curled. "Yeah… I just gave it to you." She didn't understand the question.

"Good," Mama Dedé said. "Cause people got to give freely, otherwise, da spell can go bad."

"You mean, you just can't control anyone you want with Voodoo?" Del asked.

"It depends. If you want to help someone, you always got to ask if they want help, and if they give freely. That makes da best magic. Some people, especially those that get a little tricky, try to cast without askin'. Sometimes it will work, but sometimes the person can... pull away from da spell. That's how spells go wrong."

"Then how do you cast a love spell on someone?" Del asked. "Do you ask the person's permission for that?"

"A love potion? Honey, that's a suggestion spell, not a controllin' one. Hell, it's part coffee, some Ginko, a little Ginseng root... and a lot of sweat."

"What? Coffee and sweat? Are you kidding?"

"No, da Ginko and Ginseng is good for da blood. Gotta get da blood moving for love. The sweat, that gets da person's scent in their nose. You know... hormones."

Del wrinkled her nose in disgust.

"Don't knock it till you try it, honey."

"Mama D, seriously?" Del tried to hide her embarrassment, but her cheeks betrayed her.

"Ha! You young girls. By the time I was your age... Well... let's not worry 'bout dat."

Del let a rare smile color her face as she cast a knowing look at the woman.

"Ok, then," Del said. "Why the coffee?"

"Easy. Stimulant. Got to make 'em horny quick, before they see someone else! Ha!"

"Oh my gosh!" Del said, covering her ears in mock surprise but real embarrassment. She suddenly realized that within the last twenty-four hours she had been elevated from a thing of amusement, to a person who could be trusted with an adult conversation.

Mama Dedé let out a belly laugh at Del's embarrassment. Del chuckled in response.

Del felt that the stress of the last few days had been bottling up inside her. In fact, ever since leaving the orphanage two months earlier, the heavy weight of stress had been bearing down on her. Watching the old woman belly laugh caused her to break into her own string of laughs, releasing the pent-up stress.

As tears streamed from Del's eyes, she knew it wasn't all from laughter, but welcomed the camouflage. After several more belly laughs, both women settled to an occasional giggle, then announced their readiness with a deep sigh.

Del's brown rosy cheeks gleamed with a youthful, inner radiance. *Yes,* Mama Dedé thought, *the well of life is deep with this one.*

Mama Dedé pulled a small gris bag from a hidden pocket in her dress. It was made of a deep green silk and had a small silver tie around it. She pulled a small piece of tape from a dispenser on the table and carefully stuck the hair to the piece of tape, then stuck the piece of tape to the inside of the gris bag. She pulled the drawstring tight and tucked it away.

She gave a knowing smile to Del, patted the bag under her dress, and nodded. She unlidded a tea pot that had been sitting in the middle of the table and a pungent, slightly familiar scent took Del back to her childhood. She had smelled this before.

Mama Dedé poured two small cups of the dark black liquid and said, "OK good, now drink dis tea."

Del hesitated for only a brief second, then felt a rush of trust overwhelm her and flow out toward the old woman. She picked up the small teacup and drank it.

"Now, repeat after me."

The trancing session had begun.

Del repeated the words she heard. At first, it was a strange sensation, as the words came slowly from Mama Dedé. Eventually—how long, she couldn't tell—it was no longer necessary for the next line of the incantation to be spoon-fed to her. Soon, Del repeated the words at the same time Mama Dedé spoke them. When it first happened, it almost took Del out of the trance, because she had never heard this chant before and wasn't sure where the words were coming from, but she stayed focused and quickly fell back into step. Soon, the two women were incanting in sync.

Del felt the room slowly peel away around her. The walls seemed to dissolve, along with the roof and floor; suddenly she sat at a table that floated in the middle of nowhere. She was not scared and felt no wind, so she thought she must still be in the parlor room. She thought briefly about the chair she sat in, which she assumed was still sitting on the wooden floor of the halfway house, but when she thought this, she felt herself slipping out of the trance again, so let the thoughts of physical things fade from her mind.

In her mind she now floated above the chair while Mama Dedé held her hand. They floated into a white, cloudy space void of color. A faint sound tickled her mind. It was a strange sound, but familiar somehow; the sound of a single drop of water, only in reverse. A drop of water that she somehow knew wasn't falling *into* a well, but was falling *out* of one. Her well of life was deep, but every few seconds, another drop was sucked out of it with a strange, backward sucking sound.

She listened to the drops of water as they were sucked out of existence. *How many drops have disappeared since I've been sitting here?* she wondered. *Eleven? Twelve?*

She tried to count the timing between the drops; why, she wasn't sure. She soon realized that the drops were *evaporating* once every two or three seconds. This thought gave her a bit of relief, as she had felt like her own life had sped up immensely since leaving the orphanage, and the constant ticking of the second hand always reminded her she had just lost another moment of her journey towards freedom.

She felt a tug on her mind. Mama Dedé was trying to show her something.

They slowly floated through the white clouds. Del started to see shimmers of color beneath the white. She heard the old woman's voice—from inside her head—tell her to focus on the yellow shimmer up ahead. As Del concentrated, she saw a scene form in her mind. Somehow, she was looking at the halfway house and two women that were sitting inside of it. The cold drizzle of the day was there, but could not be felt. Shadowy movement shimmered just outside of her view and somehow she felt it was a car passing by on the road. She liked the feeling of trancing; it was pure freedom.

Mama Dedé spoke in her head again. "Del, I want you to think of a place now, or a scene. We'll see if you can conjure an image."

Before Del could ask, an image of the orphanage flew into her mind. She was looking at the waiting room.

Del tried to back away from it. *Why this image?* she wondered. *Of all the things I could think about!*

Mama Dedé felt her struggle against it, but held her mind tight. "Just stay with it."

After several more seconds, Del concentrated on the image and it began to clear. It had the slightest yellow tint to it, but mostly looked just it had this morning. She saw the hallway that led to the large sleeping room. She was aware of some chatter and movement, but it was faint. Suddenly she saw Jimmy, still asleep in his bed.

Mama Dedé was seeing the same thing as Del. *What does the boy like?* she asked.

I don't know, Del thought. *He's always trying to catch butterflies.* And as soon as she thought the words, Del saw a butterfly form in the scene. She heard a faint exclamation from the old woman, but ignored it. She watched as the butterfly grew to the size of a bird. It changed colors several times until it became a wild palette of crimson red with blue and gold trim on its wings. Jimmy suddenly saw the butterfly in his dreams.

How is this—

Quiet honey, Mama Dedé thought, *just concentrate.*

Del watched Jimmy as he watched the butterfly. She didn't know how this was happening, or if he was dreaming other things, but she was certain he was seeing what she had just created.

The butterfly flapped lazily in the space of Jimmy's dream, floating on a warm breeze of love that radiated from Del's mind. She saw the wonder in Jimmy's eyes as he watched the magical thing. He cracked a toothy smile and waved at the butterfly, eyes shimmering with wonder. The butterfly, seemingly of its own accord, flew slowly around Jimmy's head, then tickled his nose with a velvet wing and disappeared. Jimmy went right back to sleep as if nothing had happened.

OK honey, enough for now, Mama Dedé thought. And as fast as it had happened, the trance was over.

Del opened her eyes slowly and let them focus on the familiar parlor room. The old woman was staring at her from across the table.

CHAPTER 41

J immy hopped through the grass after a blue frog. He was careful not to jump on it—and he didn't want to scare it—but he was trying to teach it to talk, and the best way to do that, he thought, was to pretend to be a frog himself.

He had been chasing a butterfly, but it flew up into a tree and turned into the frog. It sat there for a minute, then hopped out of the tree and looked at him. It had winked its left eye and tried to tell him something—at least he thought it was the frog's left eye, until he thought of himself as the frog, which meant he'd be looking the other way, and if he was looking the other way, he was pretty sure it would have been his right eye. Jimmy thought it was strange that the frog would get this confused, which is why he had to teach it to talk so he could ask.

The frog hopped three more times and turned around, looking at Jimmy, waiting. Jimmy hopped one big hop and landed to the right side of the frog. He giggled at what a good hopper he was.

The frog winked its right eye this time—although Jimmy thought the frog still had them confused—and hopped a big hop and landed on a lily pad in a small pond. There it sat.

Jimmy never wondered where the pond came from, only why the frog didn't want to talk to him, and sat still for a long time, letting the sun warm his back.

The frog croaked at him from the lily pad, the slight movement of which sent small ripples out across the pond, and Jimmy could see something reflected in the water.

Finally, Jimmy crawled the few remaining feet to the edge of the pond and gazed into the water.

On the right side of the lily pad, the sun reflected bright. As he looked at the sparkling water, he saw that he was playing a game of tag with Del. He waved at her reflection, but didn't think she could see him.

On the other side of the lily pad, the sunny reflection faded to dark. The ripples seemed higher there, as if someone had thrown a rock into the water. Jimmy could see little water bugs skittering across the ripples, leaving tiny indentations on the surface. They were the ugliest bugs he had ever seen and he wanted to look away, but one of the bugs was looking at him. As Jimmy watched the ugly bug, it suddenly stood up on its hind legs—it had several pairs—and started spinning around on the water. A little whirlpool grew beneath the spinning bug and suddenly sucked it down. The whirlpool slowly grew larger until it began sucking the other bugs down, along with bits and pieces of debris that floated on the surface. After several minutes, there was nothing else to consume, so it started floating toward the lily pad and the refection of Del.

Jimmy suddenly felt that Del was in trouble. The whirlpool was heading straight for her, but he didn't know what to do. The ripples in the pond grew higher, distorting Del's reflection. The blue frog clung to the tilting lily pad, watching Jimmy. It was waiting to see what he would do.

Jimmy watched the whirlpool as it moved closer and closer to Del. He suddenly thought he heard a tiny voice—it was Del's voice—cry out for help. He looked around, but only saw her distorted reflection in the ripples. It was as if the ripples were washing her away somehow; with every wave of water, a small piece of Del was washed away. She was dissolving.

The frog watched carefully.

Jimmy looked around again and started to yell out, but no one was there. He was in an endless field; the sun was almost gone behind a set of large black clouds, and the whirlpool was coming after Del.

Jimmy suddenly remembered something that Del told him once. She had to go away for a while, and he was supposed to be brave while she was gone. Maybe the pond was where she had to go—he wasn't sure—but she needed help now.

He started slapping the water, trying to make the whirlpool go away. He was now on his knees at the edge of the pond, leaning as far as he could over the water. The whirlpool was almost within reach, and if he stretched just a bit further, he might be able to slap it away.

The whirlpool was larger now, at least a foot across, and looked like it went straight to the bottom of the pond. There was nothing but a black hole in the center and it was sucking everything it could into it. The lily pad seemed to cling like magic to the side of the swirling water as the water slid beneath it. It tilted severely as part of it drooped into the black void. The frog sat watching. As Jimmy stretched his arm out in one final attempt to slap the whirlpool away, he felt his knees sink into the soft side of the pond, which caused him to tip forward. He was falling into the pond.

As if knowing, the frog looked once more at the spinning black void, then at Jimmy, and suddenly leaped into the whirlpool. In slow motion, the frog disappeared over the edge of the water and into the black void. Satisfied, the whirlpool abruptly stopped, and the ripples faded to a shimmer.

Jimmy was still falling. For a brief instant he knew that Del was safe, but he was still falling. He flailed his arms as he fell forward. Instead of the cold water of the pond, he fell into a void of clouds that was filled with strange colors and sounds. He thought he heard Del in there as well, but her voice was quickly drowned out by a loud bellowing laughter. The voice wasn't laughing at Jimmy, it was just an echo, but it was a scary voice. Jimmy fell forward, out of the cloud of blankets he was wrapped in, and hit the floor of the orphanage with a thud.

"Oww, I feh down!" he cried as he blinked his eyes open.

Josephine had been watching him from the corner of the room where she had been doing her chores. He had been thrashing through a fitful dream. Del had left just a few hours ago after tucking him in, but the only thing Jo cared about was that Del had given her the best gift she could have ever given. Hope. She loved Del, and now knew that Del was at least receptive to her. She was close to getting what she wanted. Very close.

Suddenly the back door of the orphanage came open behind Jo and a stream of kids washed down the hall and into the main sleeping room. The noise rose to a low thunder, but was split by the sharp lightning voice of the Crow. "What's that wretched boy doing on the floor again?"

Jo tried to ignore the Crow, but felt her dark presence behind her right before a sharp pain shot through her ear as a thumbnail dug into the soft tissue of her ear lobe.

"Watch that wretched boy," the Crow said, tugging her head around. "And keep him out of my way. Your time here is almost over. I'd hate for anything to delay your departure from our loving establishment."

With that, the Crow was gone, flying away to torment someone else.

Jo felt hot tears rush up the inside of her head and spill over her eyelids. There was nothing that was going to keep her from Del. Not the orphanage. Not Jimmy. And certainly not the Crow.

Jo's mind flooded with hate and longing, a dangerous mixture. The longing for Del was the hope that kept her sane in this awful place. The fear of losing Del was suffocating. She'd rather die. The hate towards anyone who tried to stand between her and Del... well, that simply wouldn't happen.

Jo knew that it was time to talk to the strange man in the cemetery.

CHAPTER 42

Frank and Armand walked into the halfway house at 2:00 pm. They had been talking all morning about the startling discovery made the night before, that Del was a descendant of the famous Marie Laveau. After their long talk in the morning, they had a long lunch at Frank's favorite pub, and were quite happy with themselves by the third Bloody Mary.

"And how are my two favorite gals dis morning?" Frank said proudly with a warm, sleepy-eyed look.

The two women looked puzzled, then, watching Armand fluff his mustache in the mirror, realized the men weren't just naturally happy to see them.

"Well, well..." Mama Dedé said. "Look at da peacocks that just strolled in here. You boys puff your chests anymore and you'll bust some buttons!"

"Mon chéri," Armand said grandly, "why does a peacock strut?"

The women exchanged looks again.

"Because, it is in its nature to do so!" he said, tipping forward slightly.

"Heh, Frenchy, I think I liked you more before Frank rubbed off on you," Mama Dedé said, pouring them both some coffee. "Now drink this and get your minds right. We got some things to talk about."

"Indeed, indeed," Armand said, sitting down at the kitchen table.

Mama Dedé said, "We got us da genuine article," as she looked at Del.

Del blushed a bit and fidgeted in her chair.

"Do tell," Frank said.

Mama Dedé described the first trancing session they'd had.

"Our girl got da knack. She got more than just a knack. She got the raw power."

"How do you know?" Armand asked.

After describing the scene with the butterfly, everyone beamed at Del.

"Fascinating," Armand said. "Simply fascinating. What did it feel like, Del?"

"Well, I don't know. Sort of like floating... and dreaming at the same time, although I was completely aware of what was happening."

"Fascinating," Armand echoed again.

"And in fact," Del said, "I was super aware of everything. Like I'd had too much coffee. My mind, it was... tingling, sort of. Excited. Especially when I first heard the water."

Mama Dedé clanked her spoon in surprise. "What do you mean, honey? What water?"

Del shrugged her shoulders and took a sip. "Couldn't you hear it? I don't know, it was just water dripping. It seems silly now that I think about it, but at the time I thought it was someone's life-force dripping. Weird, huh? I got the sense that it was little moments of life dripping along, but it could have been my imagination."

A look of concern fell over the old woman's face, and she was silent for several seconds, but not wanting to put too much emphasis on this knowledge, quickly changed the subject. "Don't be worrying about those drips. They ain't nothin'. You just worry about the colors and how to read 'em. We got a lot of work to do, still."

Del wrinkled the side of her mouth at this, but said no more.

"Colors?" Armand asked. "What do you mean?"

"It's just how you can tell if a trancin' scene is old or new. Da whole scene looks different, da area, da people. Just different."

Frank rolled his cigar in his mouth as he tracked the conversation.

Armand slowly twisted his bushy mustache on both ends, as if winding the springs of his mind to a careful calibration. The lights in his eyes dimmed, then brightened as his mind fixed around the concept Mama Dedé was explaining.

"You can actually see other people, well... the remnants of other... entities, when you are trancing?" Armand asked.

"That's da best way to think on it, I guess," she said. "There's a lot of colors in a trance. It takes a while to get used to seein' um. At first, they just all swirled together like a cloud. That's what Del was seein' today. With more practice, she'll start to see more color, but it'll all be mixed up, like da color of mud. But as you get stronger at the trancin', you can finally see 'em. They scenes, you see, scenes of things that gonna happen or might happen or already happened somewhere.

"You can always tell da old scenes, they kinda got a little hint of red to 'em—a haze. Da older they get, da red gets darker and faded as they move away from you. Da scenes that ain't happened yet—they still comin' at ya—look a little blueish. Just a little hint around the edges. But what makes trancin' really hard, is seein' da colors that other people have left; who's been watchin' da same scene."

The two men listened in disbelief.

"It's like this," she continued. "So when you seein' a scene, if someone *else* has been trancin' on da same thing, they leave a bit of imprint around da edge of da scene as well. Sort of a… a faint color trail. It's like a very faint fingerprint of your… essence, I guess. Each person looks a little different, and you can tell if someone has been trancin' around da same scene as you because you can see a bit of their color around da edge. One of da problems is that you don't know if that essence was just recently there, or they was there a long time ago.

"I've seen people leave purple smudge marks, sometimes a wispy line of orange or yellow. Pretty faint most times, and those are better trancers. Some people can trance, but never see anything, so they don't really leave a mark. You just feel 'em pass right by. They never see nothin'. Marie Laveau now, she leave a dark green shimmer around da edge of da whole scene. Don't matter if it has a red-haze or blue-haze, you can tell it was her, once you know what to look for. She tells me I leave long wisps of yellow, runnin' up and down. Just a real faint yellow."

"We can do it," Armand said suddenly, looking at Frank. "I was skeptical this morning, then over lunch, well, the liquid courage helped, but now hearing this, I think we can actually do it."

Frank nodded slowly in agreement.

"Do what?" Del asked.

"We have a plan to trap and kill the Gris-gris man."

*

An hour later, the four still sat around the kitchen table. Mama Dedé had been quiet while listening to their plan.

"But we ain't got da spell yet," she said sternly. "Marie unbound that unholy spirit years ago 'cause she knew the right spell!"

"But what if that's not the only way to kill him?" Armand asked. "If he took a physical form, if he's *bound* to a form, it's a form that can burn, correct?" He looked around the table for agreement. "It's not like he's bound to a rock, or something that can't physically be destroyed."

The old woman sighed deeply. "We don't know how he came back, so we don't know what he's bound to, but I would agree that it's most likely a person, or a body at least."

"Someone read from the books, though," Armand said, "didn't they? Isn't this what started everything? Isn't this how he came back?"

"That's da only way I know," Mama Dedé said.

"But where is the third—"

"Or people," Frank said, interrupting, sending a spark of ash onto his stomach and slapping it away frantically.

Armand's thought process was visibly broken as he watched the shower of sparks with annoyance. He thought the clumsy detective routine didn't always fit Frank, and wondered if he hadn't learned how to work it advantageously into his mannerisms over the years.

He remembered playing poker with Frank and some guys from the local newspaper one time, years before. Frank, thinner then, had the same bumbling routine, and always with the cigar. Just when someone was on a winning streak Frank would spill his drink or drop his cigar in his lap; never obvious, always discrete; Armand had lost his shirt to Frank that night. "What was I saying? We were just talking about—"

"Der's been three deaths dat we know of, and a missing person. So we're sayin' he could look like any one of dem? Jesus, Mary and Joseph."

Drawn back to this other interesting theory like a moth to a flame, Armand said quietly, "Yes, or any combination, I suppose."

Frank watched Armand. "What combination?"

"The monstrosity, mon ami. Remember when we spoke, just a few days ago—"

"Hell, it seems like we just thought it," Frank said.

"Yes, I agree. Time is moving quickly; against us, I'm afraid," Armand said. "But when we first spoke of this… legend, for at the time that's all it seemed to be, we knew of references to *unholy bindings and monstrosities*. Alas, we must remember that whatever we are looking for, it may not look like what we'd expect."

"But you think we can trap it, and kill it?" Del said.

"Yes, I do," Armand said. "With all the knowledge sitting at this table, I believe we can lure it—especially now that we've learned what a wonderful trancer we have—lure it, trap it how we described, just long enough to set the fire, and kill it. For good."

The looks across the table were of cautious optimism.

"When do we do this?" Del asked.

Armand looked at Frank. "When do you think we can have things ready?"

"Maybe… tomorrow night?" Frank said cautiously as his eyes twinkled.

Armand felt the slightest unease at the odd look of anticipation on Frank's face. What did he just see?

Mama Dédé rubbed her hands nervously. "I don't know, I don't know. I just wish we had da unbinding spell. I've tried to get it from Marie before, but she always fades away when I start thinkin' on it."

"It'll work," Frank said, bolstering everyone's confidence. "I think this is our best shot. It'll work."

He looked around the table and nodded enthusiasm toward each person. Each person nodded back.

The plan was set.

CHAPTER 43

F rank and Armand left the halfway house right after they met with Mama Dedé and Del. They both had prep work to do.

Frank watched as the St. Augustine Transitional Home for Girls—now the impromptu Voodoo Training Center for Fighting Legendary Monstrosities—grew smaller in his rearview mirror. Despite the cold mist that still hung about the city, he cranked his window down and let his arm hang out the side as he drove. The cold air was refreshing. The heavy fog-mist quickly formed large beads on his fat cheeks, but he relished in the wild, fresh air. He felt more alive today than any time he could remember since his wife's death. He would let his instincts guide him.

He breathed a deep breath and felt a sense of calm overcome him. He knew he was putting Del at risk by including her in the plan— Armand had originally disagreed with him—but it was the only way, Frank was sure of it. In fact, he wanted it this way.

He backed into his driveway and stopped right before the garage door. He killed the lights, then walked around and opened the large trunk. He raised the old garage door, flipped on a light and began collecting his items.

Twenty minutes later his trunk was full with four hand-forged steal wolf traps his grandfather had used, spikes, a sledge hammer, two cans of gasoline, an Old Judge coffee can full of red brick dust that he had taped a plastic lid over, a bag of dried High John root, several old gunny sacks, and his twelve-gauge shotgun.

Looking around the garage, he scanned across his old work bench. *Is dat really necessary?* he thought. *You want to walk dat path again?*

Maybe.

He walked to the work bench and opened a large drawer. He withdrew a small, expertly crafted wooden box. Within the box was a black leather diary and black cloth bag. He took both.

Frank had one more stop—or at least a drive-by—to make before he went back to the halfway house. Ever since the first body appeared, something had tugged at the back of his mind. It was a splinter under his nail that he couldn't quite reach.

As he drove the half-flooded roads out of the city, he thought back to an old case. The Glapion murders. The case that made him a semi-celebrity around town had been a gruesome one: husband and wife murdered in the most brutal manner, a long trail of suspects and clues, brutality, rituals.

He had found them in a shack at the edge of the swamp. They had been kept alive for nearly two solid weeks, the coroner had said. This was based on the condition of the severely emaciated bodies, and the fact that the wife was still alive when he found her. She was gibbering in a state of madness as she frantically tried to reattach her husband's arm; she never realized that she was in fact holding his thigh bone the entire time.

She died within hours of being found, and never spoke a coherent word besides the single sentence she repeated over and over:

Ouvre baye pou mwen, Papa!
Ouvre baye pou mwen!

The translation was:

Open the gate for me, Papa!
Open the gate for me!

The grisly scene was a Voodoo ritual that had gone bad. Two brothers claimed to have heard voices telling them how to call up an ancient spirit, but a vessel was needed for it to attach to. They kidnapped the couple and kept them alive—how was never determined—in order to keep the bones, meat and organs as fresh as possible while they constructed their masterpiece.

Both of the man's legs had been taken off—at different places— along with both of the woman's. This, according to the coroner, was a nearly impossible feat, considering they lived through the entire operation. Both of his arms were eventually removed. Three of the legs had been woven onto the pelvis of a wild boar skeleton with barbed wire. The man's arms had been connected to the boar's shoulders, but the original front limbs of the animal were left intact. The skeleton had a total of seven limbs. The muscles of the man's legs had been sown haphazardly around the bones, in the belief that when the spirit was bound to the skeleton, it would know how to make the limbs move. The spine was from the boar, giving the skeleton an abnormally long gait, but the head had been replaced by the skull of an alligator, which had been attached via barbed wire as well. Once the skeleton was assembled, the two brothers commenced to placing the organs.

It hadn't occurred to Frank before, but a deep dread settled over him as he realized how closely the facts of the old case aligned with the clues—and theories of legends—of the case that he was dealing with now.

The case was solved to a satisfactory degree, but justice was never officially served, considering the two brothers never made it to trial. The gruesome facts were told the first day of their capture—they were all too happy to recite their plan, and talked like cocaine freaks on a two-day binge—and considering they were brothers, no one thought it abnormal to jail them in the same cell. However, no one thought they would be found dead after having chewed each other's tongues out, either.

The two brothers were listed as *agitated* in the rounds log by the night guard. They were both awake at 11:00 pm. By 6:00 am the next morning, they had managed to chew the others tongue off and write

Ouvre baye pou mwen, Papa!

all over the cell walls in blood before they died.

Frank came out of his daydream as he turned onto Bayou Rd. He hadn't been on this road in years, but just seeing the name on the old road sign snapped him out of his dream and back into reality.

He drove slowly down the two-lane blacktop road as he approached the old farmhouse, and stopped before turning into the drive. At this point, the house was much closer to a shack, but somehow remained standing as if by sheer will alone. The old drive had once been covered with a thin layer of shale, sand and creek gravel, but only a few stubborn patches of the hard gravel pack remained; the rest had become part of an ever-extending overgrown field.

Frank was surprised to see what looked like tire tracks through the high weeds. Someone had recently been there, and whoever it was knew where the original drive was.

He pulled his car into the drive and followed it around to the back of the old house.

He looked carefully around the weedy area, and thought he saw tracks that led to the side porch, which would take him to the front of the house; he preferred to enter through the back.

The back door was protected by a large covered back porch with a rusty screen door that creaked in the wind on ancient hinges. He looked at the crud-covered padlock that secured the door; it hadn't seen a key in decades, he was sure. Some quick work with a small prybar and the old door gave way. Like most doors this age, the internal locking mechanism no longer worked, and the padlock hinge was connected by decaying screws; the heads popped right off with a bit of leverage.

Entering through the back led him straight into an old kitchen. The first thing to hit him was the dead smell of the ancient house. It smelled of sweltering attic rafters, old moldy basement beams and a hundred layers of dust and cobwebs. It was a heavy smell, of age, rot, and death.

The gloom of the day hid the marks on the floor, but his eyes were instantly drawn to a disturbance on the table. He lit a withering candle that sat there, and marveled at what he saw: fresh marks in the dust.

Someone had recently been sitting in 113 Bayou Rd., very recently. They sat a folder or pile of papers on the dusty table and leafed through them. Frank could still see some straight lines in the dust as the paper-folder was pushed around, moving the dust.

He suddenly felt his time was very short.

CHAPTER 44

Sister Eulalie paced her office in agitation. She had returned several hours ago from the field outing with the younger kids to see that wretched boy, Jimmy, lying on the floor again. His transference to the state mental hospital couldn't happen soon enough as far as she was concerned. Some people just took up space, and the world was too crowded already. Besides, God had a way of thinning the herd; she was sure He had something in mind for that one.

Her mind could barely focus on the task at hand—preparing for an evening funeral service. A member of the local parish had specifically asked for her to speak, so there was no way she could avoid it, but her rash was almost unbearable now. She thought she may need to see a doctor, but the thought repulsed her. Some degenerate, leering man looking at her private parts, putting his large dirty fingers all over her. She'd have to have several Sin Washings to get clean after that.

Why did the men in her life—granted, there had only been her brothers and uncles, long before she entered the church—have to have large, dirty fingers? And her doctor as well? She couldn't bear the thought of one more large, dirty finger touching her down there. That's why the Sin Washings had to be handled with small, delicate hands; clean hands that weren't contaminated, that could wash the sin away when the need arose.

If God only had a way of thinning the herd of all the sinners, she thought. Not only would the world be a better place, she wouldn't have such a need for all of the Sin Washing sessions. She felt as though something was about to happen; she felt as if all the sin in the world was being concentrated through her body and manifesting itself as this terrible rash. *Maybe she had been chosen for this. Maybe this was a test, after all.*

She would bear the burden.

She had a way of dispelling the sin that collected through her— not of her own doing, for it wasn't her sin manifesting itself down there—and now realized what she must do. She must increase the Sin Washings, for she was helping God rid the world of this terrible plague.

*

Several hours later, Sister Eulalie entered the St. Louis Cemetery #1 with a small congregation of mourners. The cemetery had to be lit with torches, as the electric had been out in this part of the city for several days. The dark clouds hung like a shroud over the entire city, but felt especially heavy over the cemetery, as if a burial shroud had been placed over every person there.

Eddie suddenly shivered in ecstasy.

He had vibrated slowly all day, as a constant stream of sin pulsed through him. This place was electric, he felt. He wasn't *aware* that he felt this, as he no longer had the capacity for individual thought, but somehow it was right; he was a weathervane turning in the wind of humanity.

He no longer knew *where* he was, or where he had ever been, although he had a faint memory—a feeling really—of an old barrel of apples, where the weight of everything pressed down on the apples below; all the detritus from the top, all the sweat that leached out of the skins, slipped and dripped and fell through the openings between the other apples, to settle at the bottom where the softer apples—already bruised or damaged—were subject to a greater weight from above. This caused them to falter even faster—from the inside out—and rot. The juice collected there was sweet for an instant, but quickly turned sour and putrid. It stank at the bottom of the barrel, and Eddie loved it.

His sin-radio-antennae suddenly vibrated with a strong signal. It was difficult to determine who it was, due to all the weeping and moaning. Every mourner felt that they had done something wrong to the recently interred.

Eddie's mind quivered; a tuning fork vibrating at the perfect pitch. There was no outwardly obvious sign of his exaltation—to those in the cemetery, he was a grotesque and pompous addition to an oversized crypt—but there was excitement nonetheless, and to his master, he was a lightning rod. The electricity he collected was of the oldest kind; it collected in his calcifying head, ran down his spine, pulsed through his arms and legs and flowed into the unholy crypt he perched upon. From there, the electric sin flowed into granite stones and disappeared into an unholy channel. Somewhere on the other end of the channel, an abomination listened.

Eulalie Agnus Washington. The name suddenly came to him through the din of sin.

Sister Eulalie, you are a sinner, and you have an itch, Eddie vibrated. Suddenly years of events passed through his mind: thoughts, scenes, actions. The Sister who thought herself a saint.

Sin Washing? Oh, how he vibrated. His master would be pleased. The apple had certainly rotted with this one. Suddenly another name flashed from Sister Eulalie and popped into his head:

Del...

Del... La...

What is this name?

Del.. Larue...

Del Lavau...

More images flashed through her head:

Del, Jo, Del...

Jo... Del, Del, Del...

The wretched boy?

The terrible, terrible, wretched boy?

Eddie wanted to find *his* channel. He wanted to hear the song of the wretched boy. He sounded wonderful.

As Eddie focused on collecting more information on the names, his thought-link with his master weakened. He was too excited to notice. He had to figure out who these other names belonged to. If they were prominent in the Sister's mind, Eddie felt they were important. He concentrated.

Jo. For some reason her song was slightly familiar to him, but he didn't know why. He felt he had sensed her before.

Del. He tingled again, but for a different reason. It wasn't a sin signal he was picking up—at least not much compared to most—but he vibrated just the same. She had a beautiful song. Somehow, she was important.

The wretched boy.

Nothing.

Eulalie Agnus Washington—Sister Eulalie—felt strongly about the wretched boy. *He must be very bad,* Eddie thought. *Why doesn't the name come to me?*

The wretched boy.

Nothing.

The pure boy?

That couldn't be possible.

The cast of mourners were leaving and the signals were fading, but Eddie had already recorded the names. One of them went straight to the top.

His master would be pleased.

*

The strange man sat cross-legged on a mat of leaves. His old body swayed slightly, as if blown by an unfelt wind; a *dark* wind that only dark entities could feel. He had been like this for hours, conserving what energy he had; trancing when he could. He had to feed again soon; his energy was low. The regeneration process had sapped his energy stores. The sustenance from the two men in the swamp had been enough for him to come into existence—including Mr. Sandgrove—but the boy on the wharf had been all for the beast; for the breeding; for their family. And the family was always hungry.

The beast, Mr. Sandgrove, swayed unconsciously, in sync with the strange man, for they were of the same essence.

The beast stood up, done with its nursing session, and felt its teats stretched and pulled. The weasels were growing fast, and had become too heavy to lift out of the mud while they held on by their beaks. The weasels, true abominations, gnashed and mewled at the escaping dinner. The beast snapped back at its own offspring, clutching one in its powerful jaws and yanking it away from a teat with a slight ripping sound. The beast shook it several times in reprimand, then dropped it back into the nest. The motherly instinct had nearly left it.

It walked over to a rapidly shrinking mound, sniffed around in the mud, then bit several toes off a small foot. The foot was much smaller than it had been the day before, and would hardly satisfy the growing brood, but the beast tossed the toes into the middle of the nest as a distraction, and the gnashing began anew. It then climbed a tree, locked its long claws around a branch and swung around, upside down to sleep. Toth the mutant slowly slid down the long needle, only stopping on the flattened end that resembled a nail head. A low sound escaped its mouth as its stiff arms and legs stretched out from its sides, a sound that indicated a meager wave of life had been created by the static friction generated by sliding against the metal rod. "Ngyihng…"

CHAPTER 45

Josephine sat on the bench in the girls' bathroom rubbing her earlobe. The Crow had cut a small gash in it when she'd grabbed her earlier in the day. Jo wanted to kill her then, but fortunately the Crow had left for someone's funeral, and she'd had a few blessed hours of peace. Now that the Crow had returned, it only reminded Jo of how much she really hated her.

Her face streamed with hot tears as she tried to remember all the bad things the Crow had done over the years. She wanted to remember so she wouldn't lose her nerve; she wanted to remember because tonight was her night. She would trade the Crow to the strange man in the cemetery, completing her side of the bargain, and have Del forever.

She had a partial plan worked out in her mind, but it felt rushed. However, the Crow's time had come. No one else in the orphanage could do anything about her. Del had been the only one who the Crow didn't have total dominance over. Why, she wasn't sure, but Jo knew there was no love lost between those two.

What had the strange man said to her?

"But make sure you bring something to trade, Josephine. Don't call me back without something to trade."

How could she bring the sister to the cemetery?

Suddenly, she heard Jimmy hopping down the hallway towards the girls' bathroom. She knew he was hopping because of the accompanying *wibbit... wibbit...* she heard with each large jump.

She watched quietly as Jimmy hopped right past the door and down the hall. A thought tweaked her mind like the light of a distant lighthouse. It passed quickly and almost faded away, then swung back around and shined in her mind again, brighter the second time around.

She would trick the Crow.

She suddenly knew how to get the Crow to the cemetery; at least, she thought it might work. Her mind raced. Her time was short. Now that the idea struck her, she knew it had to be tonight. She couldn't wait any longer.

Josephine quickly walked down the hall after Jimmy. Turning a corner, she saw the Crow's office light on behind a closed door. *Perfect*, she thought.

"Jimmy, quiet down," she said in fake reprimand. "Come here, I have something to ask you."

Jimmy turned around and hopped back to her.

"Can you keep a secret?" she said, just loud enough to permeate the old frosted glass window in the Crow's door. She watched it for any sign of movement.

"Ah, secwet," Jimmy said loudly. "Yeah, I can keep—"

"Shhh," Jo said as she caught a sign of movement. The Crow had moved close to the window behind her closed door, listening.

"This is a big secret, Jimmy. So, don't tell no one, OK?"

"OK."

"I'm supposed to go see Del tonight."

"Deh? Can I see De—"

"Shhh, I'm supposed to go meet her tonight, but it's after hours and I don't know how to get out."

Jo knew where Del's last secret exit was, as she had just used it. But the Crow didn't know, and it was eating her alive that Del still had a secret over her.

"Do you know where Del's secret door is?"

Jimmy thought about the promise he had made to Del never to tell anyone about the window, and was trying to determine if *the secret door* was the same thing. He wasn't sure if this would be breaking the promise or not, but before he could form his answer Jo responded, "You do? That's great. And you'll show me tonight?"

Jimmy stood wondering how he had just given the secret away when he hadn't said anything.

"OK, that's great. Thanks, Jimmy," Jo said, watching the shadow behind the door. "I'll wait until after bedtime, when everyone else is asleep, and you can tell me where it is, OK?"

Jimmy was happy that Jo wasn't mad at him any longer. She always seemed to be mad at him, but thought it was because he had knocked over her mop bucket more than a few times. Still, he wasn't sure what he had said, if anything that—

"OK, great. Thanks Jimmy. Come on, let's get ready for bed," Jo said as she quickly pulled him back up the hall.

Jimmy's face scrunched as a thought quickly passed him. He still couldn't guess how he had let the secret slip, but was now looking forward to his pajamas, and let Jo lead him down the hall.

Jo gave a silent prayer that this would work.

An hour after the lights were turned out, the last nun finished her walkthrough of the open sleeping area where the smaller kids slept. Jo knew the timing by heart. She lay there thinking of Del and what their life would be like when they were finally together. Forever.

Quietly, she slipped out of bed, pulled her sneakers on and threw on her jacket. She walked out of the smaller, more private sleeping area she shared with the older girls. There was only one other girl her age in the room, and she was snoring loudly.

Jo moved like a mouse between shadows, and looked absently over her shoulder for effect. She couldn't see the Crow, but felt that she was lurking somewhere. She slipped into the back coatroom, not risking a fake conversation with Jimmy—she hoped the Crow wouldn't realize that—and quickly removed the old raincoats, slid open the window and slipped out into the night. She would wait outside for a sign that the Crow was following.

In less than a minute, she heard the telltale squeak of a rusty hinge; someone had opened the front door of the orphanage.

Jo quick-stepped up the alley, planning to leave fleeting sounds in the dark—just out of sight—for the Crow to follow. She turned left at the street, away from the orphanage, and didn't risk a look back. She walked slowly, half in, half out of the shadows to make herself easier to follow. Her plan was working.

Inside the orphanage, Jimmy peeked his head out of his covers and looked around. His long nap that day had left him full of energy, and the thought of seeing Del was exciting. He put on his Bugs Bunny house shoes and walked quietly to the coat closet. The coats had been moved to the side and the window was slightly open. He remembered to put on his yellow raincoat, then looked once more behind him. There was no one in the closet, so it was safe to go. With great effort, he raised the window, climbed onto the wooden bench, and stuck his legs out the window, just like Del had showed him. He dropped the few feet to the ground and was proud that he didn't trip. He looked up and down the alley—which was scarier without Del—and thought how happy she would be to see him. Suddenly, he saw someone walk quickly across the front of the alley on the main street that ran in front of the orphanage.

That must be Jo, he thought. He would follow her and surprise Del.

Quiet da mouse, quiet da mouse, he thought as he followed the fleeting shadow. He giggled to himself at what a great mouse he made.

*

Jo wound through the streets in a manner that she hoped would confuse and frustrate the Crow. She didn't want to lose her, but wanted her to be good and mad by the time the strange man came. Hopefully he would think she was a decent trade.

She turned the final corner and saw St. Louis Cemetery #1 looming before her. The mist seemed especially heavy there, even though she was already dripping with water. The front gate creaked with delight as she pushed past it, as if wanting to announce her arrival. She stole a look over her shoulder before she entered, but couldn't tell if the Crow was behind her or not.

The crypts of the cemetery seemed to lean precariously in all directions, mocking her tenuous sense of safety. She thought back to the last time she had been there—just a few days past really—but couldn't recognize any particular crypt as a marker. She turned left, then right, then left again, and suddenly had a sense that she was moving in the right direction. It felt colder suddenly; the mist felt heavier; she moved towards the back of the cemetery.

As if understanding her needs and desires, the thick fog parted slightly, and she saw the outline of a double crypt looming against the back wall. She wasn't sure, but she thought she had seen a man crouching on that crypt the last time she was there. It must have been her imagination. Now all she saw was an oversized gargoyle. The ugliest thing she had ever seen.

Eddie vibrated in ecstasy.

Jo walked to the old crypt, ascended the three wide stairs, and without hesitation knocked three times on the chamber door. Echoing… echoing... forevermore.

She watched the mist swirl about the cemetery in increasingly thick clouds. First it moved slowly, sluggish in its power; winding the forces of the universe out of an ancient stasis. She heard the faint creak of a gate. Her time was near.

Suddenly, a shadow appeared out of the fog; a hooded shadow, slightly hunched. The Crow had followed her.

Jo stood still, not knowing what to do next. The Sister walked forward cautiously, looking from side to side. Her eyes seemed to glow in the deep gloom.

"What are you doing out after hours?" The Sister scowled through the mist. "I knew you were just as bad as the other one. There will be punishment for this!"

Jo inched back toward the shadow of the crypt. She hadn't accounted for what to do if the strange man didn't show up.

Eddie was vibrating on high now. His mind was red hot with the pulse that radiated off the nun. This was the signal he had picked up earlier in the day. It was glorious.

"Well? Speak up! What are you doing out here? Tell me where your little girlfriend is, you wretched girl!"

Just as Jo started to break and run, she heard it: another slight squeak from the old gate at the front of the cemetery.

Her heart leapt into her throat as she retreated to the back wall and waited.

An instant after the gate squeaked, the strange man formed straight out of the fog; one minute nothing, the next minute, blue mirrored glasses glinted from the gloom; oversized eyes that saw everything.

The nun heard a noise over her shoulder and spun around quickly—still quite agile for her age—and saw the man at the front of a long row.

The cemetery was formed from long rows of crypts, with a few wide aisles that split the cemetery longways into sections. Several narrower aisles formed horizontal paths and crossed the cemetery in a confusing array of passages.

The nun and the strange man eyed one another. Jo couldn't be sure, but thought she saw the man twist his head far to one side, as if cracking an old joint, then saw a shiver run through him as he appeared to fade in and out of her vision.

A trick of the fog, surely, she thought.

"Who are you?" the Sister said, trying to control her voice.

The man walked slowly toward her, but trailed outside an unseen circle; an imaginary force that seemed to emit from the nun. He turned right, down a small aisle, and walked out of sight, behind a crypt. They were thirty feet apart, but had several crypts in between them.

"Good evening, Josephine," the man said. His voice floated across the mist and down the aisles in a staggered, disorienting manner, arriving in her ears at slightly different times. It had the effect of a strange echo, and she heard, "Josephine… …osephine… …osephine…" ripple across her mind.

"Thank you for calling me... ...alling me... ...thank you... ... alling me."

Jo's stomach twisted and pushed into the back of her throat. A pungent smell of stress-sweat rose up out of her jacket and assaulted her nose. She felt dizzy. All she could do was lean against the cold wall and watch.

"So, you've come to trade, is that it Josephine? ...osephine ... osephine...

"I hope you've brought something good to trade... ...something good to... ...brought something... ...good to trade..."

The man walked from around a crypt and into a slight open area in the middle of the cemetery that joined the aisle where the nun stood. Jo could now see the man and the nun—good versus evil—at the same time. Although, the thought crossed her mind, she wasn't sure which was which.

He sniffed the air several times, took several more steps toward the nun, and sniffed again. The two circled each other like gunmen at the beginning of a duel.

Raising the cross from around her neck and holding it straight toward the man, she cawed again, "I said, who—"

The man raised his hand and silenced her. They were fifteen feet apart. He leaned forward precariously, and sniffed the air once more, then did a peculiar thing; he licked his lips.

A look of revulsion crossed over the nun's face as her lips quivered in disgust, "I warn you," the Crow said, "stay away from me or—"

The man took three graceful steps sideways: slow, deliberate, elegant steps to an unheard melody; a deadly dance hypnotic. He was cutting the angle between Jo and the Crow; Jo was nearly behind him now against the back wall of the cemetery, the Crow straight in front of him.

"Delightful!" he said as he stared at the cross, then broke into a distorted, toothy grin.

The nun swayed slightly, as if nearly fainting, then steadied herself, she had been holding her breath the last several seconds.

"What is this?" she croaked. Looking past the strange man, she glared at Jo. "What have you been doing out here with this... this man?" She took a few steps back.

"I say, that is a rather nasty rash you have there," the man said, holding a crooked finger in the air. He stuck the finger into his mouth, tasting the air again. "Yes... quite a nasty rash indeed!" His head tilted wildly to the side.

The sister stole a glance at the front of her habit. "How did—" She glared at Jo, anger twisting her dark face. "You vile girl!" she blurted. "You lying, vile little girl! I don't... I... Oh, you need a session! Yes, that's what you need, a long session with a certain doctor I know! You and that wretched boy! I'll send you both off to the asylum for the rest of your long, miserable lives!"

Eddie vibrated beyond capacity. He was a dense magnet pulling in a glorious song of sin and expelling long sighs of ecstasy to his master. He was a dark star with the gravity of a thousand suns. He was a black hole of sin, collecting everything that ever occurred, and once over the event horizon of his mind, he spewed out the tattered remnants of a dark humanity to all who would listen. Those remnants were fragment thoughts from his channel of sin that got mixed with other thoughts that radiated from the minds in the cemetery. These were all important, he felt. He had to collect them all as quickly as possible. He wouldn't miss a note.

Sin Washing, vile, Sin Washing, Jo, Del, session, the wretched boy, washing, rash, faster girl, faster, Jo, Del, Del, the blank boy, Jo, washing, Del, Del, Del!

The strange man shook his head and waved an old hand in front of his face, as if swatting away a swarm of gnats. The flood of thoughts coming from Eddie had suddenly overwhelmed him, and he was only catching a portion of what Eddie was sending him. *Sin Washing, Jo, … wretched rash, girl, …faster, Jo, Del, boy, wash… Del, Del…*

Annoyed at the confusing swarm of thoughts, the strange man shut Eddie from his mind until he could finish his trade.

"Josephine, come forward," the man said.

The Crow countered, "Josephine, you get back to your room this instant!"

The man held his hand out to his side and calmly said, "Josephine, if this is what you have brought to trade, step forward."

The sister, still not realizing what was happening, watched as Jo walked to the side of the strange man.

"There is a price when making this type of trade, Josephine. Trading in sin is a tricky business, and requires a delicate balance. It is a scale that none can cheat. You will carry a small balance for making this trade, but alas, what is a small price to pay for getting your ultimate wish, eh?"

Jo looked at the man, swallowed hard with a dry throat, and nodded her head quietly.

"Do you give this sin freely in exchange for the undying love of Del?"

"Yes," Jo said as she dropped an old washcloth into the man's hand.

A puzzled look came over the Sister's face as she saw the item; it looked vaguely familiar. Suddenly, a look of horror and understanding spread over her face; the washcloth. It was the washcloth that Jo had used during their last session. The nun felt a deep cold settle over her.

Suddenly, Jo caught a glimpse of movement to her left. The eyes of the beast glowed through the heavy mist; a ragged breath steamed the night air.

How long it had been there she didn't know, but it was clearly on the hunt.

The beast stalked forward slowly, head low and forward, sniffing the air, eyes unwavering. A slow methodical movement expanded powerful lungs, the hair on the back of its thick neck stood in ragged spikes, a long trail of slobber hung from its jowls, long claws clicked against the cobblestone from behind thick pads.

The mutant Toth, still pinned to its back, appeared to smile from its red-bead mouth as its bead eyes stared out forever.

As the beast raised its head to look at the strange man, Jo noticed something hanging beneath its neck. Connected by a thick strip of leather—from what type of animal Jo couldn't tell—a small doll hung. Smaller than a child's doll, but larger than a Voodoo doll, the half-chewed doll of a red-headed woman hung sideways beneath the slobbering mouth; a plaything for a monstrosity. Its matted red hair was caked with mud, one multi-colored eye stuck open like a broken doll. Several toes appeared to have been chewed off.

Jo imagined for a brief second that the doll looked at her, pleading.

A scream formed in the nun's chest, but before it could break forth, two loud barks and a wolfish howl from the beast froze the sounds in her throat.

With one powerful leap the beast covered half the distance between it and the nun and landed in a full sprint. She only had time to shuffle one foot backward, which snagged on an old brick, and in slow-motion she began a slow fall backwards.

As her other leg kicked into the air for balance, the skirt of her habit separated rudely in the air just as the beast landed between her feet and clamped onto her pelvis with the jaws of a demon. Her eyes flew open in embarrassed surprise before the pain of the bite registered in her brain. She was lifted off her feet by the powerful jaws as the first scream gurgled out of her throat. Anchored with powerful claws gripping the bricks, the beast held its prey high. The nun screamed a high-pitched sound of hell and grabbed the back of the beast's head, trying to relieve the lightning of pain that shot up from her groin. Her eyes rolled back in her head as she gasped in another deep breath and let out a manic wail of sounds that caused her tongue to flop crazily out of her mouth, as if the beast had bitten it loose from within her stomach.

Toth came to life and nearly flew off the needle that pinned it to the beast. The blast of hellish life that traveled out of the beast and up through the needle in its rectum excited the mutant body into motion. Its red-bead eyes stared wantonly under the nun's skirt as its dead mouth mocked her screams.

The strange man burst into a long, bellowing laugh. With each breath he jammed his walking stick into the ground with delight, cracking the bricks and trembling the dead stone.

The beast shook its prey twice, causing a strange gaggle to emanate from her throat, then with another powerful leap, bounded off into the mist.

Toth swung wildly on the long needle, dead arms and legs flailing about in an uncoordinated mockery of the nuns own flailing limbs. As the unholy trinity bounded into the night, the last thing Jo heard before she fainted was a strange stream of gibberish floating back from the mutant, "...uunngghh, ttagaa bligh nagaa, Ngyihng! Ngyihng! Ngyihng!"

CHAPTER 46

Thursday

H enri Guillaume pulled up in front of the St. Augustine Transitional Home for Girls at 7:00 am. It had been a very long week already, and Thursday was starting off to be its worst day.

He ascended the steps, but before he could knock, Mama Dedé met him at the door.

"You were expecting me?" Henri said through the screen door.

The big woman eyed him as she sipped at her coffee. "No, but I can smell bacon a *long* ways away. And you," pointing her cup at him, "smell like bacon."

Flashing his badge through the screen, he smiled politely and asked, "May I come in for a minute? I have a few questions I need to ask one of your girls."

"Who?" she asked, still blocking the door.

"Please, it'll only take a minute. Del will want to hear dis, I think."

"What?" Del said from the hall. "Who are you?"

"My name is Henri GeeOHM. I used to work with Frang," he said, twisting the onyx ring on his little finger. "Something has happened at the orphanage. I wonder if you can—"

"What's happened?" Del said. "Come in and tell me!"

Henri walked into the front room and looked around dismissively. Mama Dedé eyed him suspiciously over the rim of her cup.

Henri told the women that three people had somehow gone missing from the orphanage last night: Sister Eulalie, Josephine and Jimmy. No bodies had been found, and no sign of foul-play had been detected. The police where at quite a loss. Henri knew—from the orphanage records—that Del had recently been discharged from the orphanage, and had visited there several times in the last week, visiting Jimmy, which is why he was at the halfway house.

"Jimmy's missing?" Del said. "How can that be? He wouldn't go out by himself. He doesn't even know how to—"

Her mind flashed back to all the times she had helped him squirm out the back window of the coat closet, all the while Jimmy praising her for how smart she was. Her stomach turned sour with the realization that she may be partially to blame.

"Yes? How to what?" Henri asked.

"Nothing," Del said. "The doors are locked at night. He couldn't get out without someone's help. The Crow must have done this."

Henri waited.

"Sister Eulalie," she said finally. "Some of the kids call her... the Crow. It's just a nickname... but what's being done to find Jimmy? Is there a search party? When will—"

"I see," Henri said. "A nickname." He looked around the room again, and after a long pause asked, "Have you seen Frang lately?"

Annoyed, Del said, "Well, just—"

"Who?" Mama Dedé interrupted. "Frang?"

With irritation Henri exaggerated the words: "Frangk Morgan. Have you seen him lately?"

Taking over the conversation, the large woman sipped her coffee slowly. "Oh, da ol' Glapion detective?" she said. "I ain't seen Frank in quite a while. A long while. Why?"

"It's an internal matter," Henri said. "Some evidence has been misplaced from a case he—"

Henri stopped, suddenly wondering why he was explaining himself to this woman. "Well, you call me if you hear from one of them, yes?" He handed a business card to Del.

"Yes, of course," she said, grabbing the end of the card.

Still holding onto the other end, Henri tugged Del's hand to bring her eyes to his. "Larouche? Your last name, it's Larouche?"

"Uh… yes, that's right. Why?"

Henri released the card and shrugged. "Sounds familiar, dat's all. Have a nice day."

After Henri left, Mama Dedé closed and locked the door and led Del by the hand to the kitchen.

Sitting at the table, she said, "Now listen, honey. I don't know what happened to those people at da orphanage, but you stay clear of dat man. I—"

"But I have to go find Jimmy! He's lost! He can't stay out by himself. He—"

"Now just wait a minute. We got things to do. You gotta get your mind right for—"

"And why did he ask about Frank?"

"Well he—"

"And why did you lie to him about the last time we saw Frank?"

"Well I just—"

"Where is Frank, anyway?" Del asked. "He left yesterday afternoon, but hasn't come back yet. And what do you think he meant about missing evidence?" Del thought back to the alligator teeth.

"I don't know, but listen: I got to go out and get some things, you know, for—"

Del had already tuned out the current conversation, thinking about how to find Jimmy. "What? Oh, yes, for the… trap, right?"

"That's right. Now don't go out of da house. And don't let no one in 'til I get back, unless it's Frank or Armand. You understand?"

Why is the captain looking for Frank? Del wondered.

"You understand?"

"What? Oh, yes. Lock the doors, blah, blah."

"'Blah, blah'?" Mama Dedé said. "Now listen here—"

"Oh, did I say that out loud?" Del said with a sheepish grin. "I'm sorry, I just—"

Mama Dedé was already up from the table.

"I'm runnin' my errands. You stay put, Miss Blah Blah."

Surprised amusement crossed Del's face as she watched the woman leave.

As Mama Dedé shuffled down the hall, Del heard, "'Blah, blah' my black ass…" trail back at her.

*

As soon as Mama Dedé left the house, Del prepared the tea and went to the parlor room. If she couldn't leave the house, she would find Jimmy another way. She would look for him by trancing.

Mama Dedé had told her that they needed to trance together several more times before Del could do it on her own, but this was an emergency. Besides, Del had done pretty well her first time—exceptionally well, in fact—so this time would be no different.

The quicker she could find Jimmy, the quicker they could be finished with this Voodoo guy and she could go on with her life.

Even though it was early morning, she had to light several candles. The power was intermittingly going out, and currently it was off again.

She settled her mind and drank the strong tea. She recited the incantation from memory and felt her mind start to expand.

Just like before, she felt the room peel away from her. The walls and floor dissolved. She was suddenly floating in the middle of a bank of white clouds.

This time she noticed the faint colors more quickly; *they are different scenes,* Mama Dedé had told her. She had to look for different scenes. She wondered how she could find Jimmy in this endless dream-world, but if he was lost or in trouble, she would do whatever she needed to help him. *Maybe I need to think of a scene that Jimmy would be in.*

She thought of the orphanage.

The orphanage came to her mind in a broken vision; muted tones of gray gave her the sense of where she was, but there were strange flecks of red and blue around the images as well. She remembered Mama Dedé saying something about the red and blue colors, but didn't recall what it meant. As she looked from one scene to the next, she felt her weightless body tilt and roll slightly according to where she was looking.

As she looked around—not with her eyes, but with the disorienting feeling of movement—she felt on the verge of doing a somersault, as if underwater. When she *leaned back* in her mind to follow a scene that was unfolding above her head, she felt her entire body tip backwards—as if she were a gimbal spinning on several axes—and she could see a different part of the cloud-image behind her. She noticed subtle color differences here as well, and somehow knew these were scenes she could go and inspect; scenes of what, she didn't know.

She then *thought* herself to look at an image to her left and slightly down. Her weightless body pitched forward, and her crossed legs floated under and behind her, tipping her head forward. She was nearly upside down in her mind, but felt right-side up somehow. It was disorienting, but she thought she could control it.

Del felt a strange power surge into her being.

Her skin tingled with it.

She was electric.

She focused on the swirling gray scene in front of her. Streams of color morphed and moved in and out of the image: fat, vague streams of color were pierced with spikes of a different hue; slowly turning clouds of color twisted and contorted; all indicating an image or thought or moment that was changing before her very eyes.

In her mind, she never saw Jimmy, but floated out of the secret window somehow. As far as she knew, only she and Jimmy knew about the secret exit, so she assumed he'd slipped out of the window the night before. This image had a slight red tinge around the outside, and looked as if it was aging quickly.

She floated into the alley—one that she knew very well—and saw a shadow pass down the street by the alley opening. She floated to follow the shadow.

Somewhere in the trance-dream she heard a spoken fragment, *quiet da mouse*, and her heart leapt.

Jimmy had gone this way! Why did he sneak out?

Her pulse climbed.

Her body tilted from side to side as she struggled to follow the invisible trail in her head. She felt like she was being sucked along by a magnetic wind; a dark gravity pulling her to a lifeless void. Suddenly a new image rose up before her; a cemetery loomed large and foreboding. She was overwhelmed with the smell of the dead—some for a hundred years or more—and felt phantom hands—long motionless—reach at her mind for attention.

She wanted to get away from this place of horror, but was certain Jimmy had gone this way, so she dove further into the dream-trance. Fleeting images shot past her like a movie reel out of control. She saw crypt after crypt, then a faint image of Jo flew by her.

She looked down and to her right and her mind-body rotated forward effortlessly. A new color caught her attention, and she looked further down, which was now up. She meant to stop and inspect that color-scene closer, but spun right past it, failing to stop as her legs floated over her head. As she spun forward, she looked back over her shoulder and to the left, and her gimbal-body spun faster in a twisting somersault way. Her crossed legs came around her side, then spun over her head. A wolf-dog came and went; she saw stars and people floating through them; Jo was hiding; the Crow was near! She looked left, then right, and caught a glimpse of something else, but it disappeared only to come flying past her feet again, then around the side of her head. Her head fell forward as her legs sped-up behind her, causing her head to fall forward even faster. A strange man and Jo; blurred lights; giant worms with mandibles; tiny blue lightning like a thousand filaments. She was spinning rapidly now. Her head was gaining weight, which caused her gimbal-body to spin and twist. The wolf-dog again; a man in space with sparkling eyes; a demon named Ali; the Crow. The colors of the scenes were a rainbow blur. Her stomach floated up into her throat, then sank into her right leg.

This caused her to tilt sideways and spin in a new direction. She was spinning out of control and floating in all directions at once.

Suddenly, a loud voice bellowed laughter in her head and the deepest wave of dread settled over her. She'd never heard the sound before, but it was familiar nonetheless. The sound was of evil, and evil made the voice. Something had found her.

She tried to orient on the voice. She knew it was stationary because she could hear it come and go like cars passing on a freeway. A distant scream. A gibberish, mutant voice.

The bellow seemed to fuel her spin, causing her to accelerate; an unseen breath that blew her, tumbling into insanity. She felt her mind start to slip away.

She spun forever in all directions, helpless. She was bound and unbound at the same time. She struggled to stop, to call out, to wake up, as the bellowing voice held her suspended. She thought briefly of Jimmy and her inability to save him—she couldn't even save herself. Her first time trancing and she slipped into a trap somehow—let herself get caught. She had no special power. She had nothing.

As she spun, she suddenly felt a new sensation, as if layers of her mind were being peeled back. Something, or someone, was stripping her mind naked, searching for something; a vulnerability.

She was helpless to the bellowing voice. It laughed and cajoled. Her mind was left exposed, naked for scrutiny and leering. *That* was the feeling she hated the most; the leering. Sister Eulalie leered at kids from time to time, including Del, but this was different. She suddenly felt exposed. The bellowing voice had violated her private thoughts, and was somehow leering at her, probing her essence, and it found her wanting.

Tears sprang from her eyes as she spun helplessly. She called out weakly for help, with both mind and voice, but no one heard. Her energy had been spent. The words flew away too quickly to be coherent. They sounded like partial words from a skipping record player, feeble syllables of madness.

As consciousness faded, the last thought to escape her mind was— *Jimmy...* And as her mind went blank, the last voice she heard was a loud bellowing laughter, then she was left helpless in the dark.

CHAPTER 47

Frank and Armand walked into the halfway house Thursday afternoon and instantly knew something was wrong. They had left the house the day before to gather their items for trapping the Gris-gris man, and had just arrived back. A palpable sense of gloom clouded the air.

Frank grabbed Armand's arm and motioned for him to wait. He reached instinctively for his shoulder pistol, although he didn't carry it regularly now, and briefly thought about retrieving it from his car. He scanned the room, then walked lightly down the hallway towards the back parlor.

Armand was surprised at the stealth the heavy man suddenly showed. The image of the bumbling, lovable man with cigar ashes on his shirt was gone; a deadly serious man now walked in his place.

As they approached the parlor, they heard a distressing sound. "Oh lawd, come back honey. You hear me? You got to come back!"

The men stepped through the door of the parlor and saw Mama Dedé hovering over a couch. Del was lying there, motionless.

"What happened?" Frank asked.

"She got stuck, Frank! Lawd help us, but she got stuck!" she said, dabbing Del's forehead with a cloth. "Oh, what have I done? Too soon. It was just too soon."

"Stuck? Stuck how?"

"She stuck in a trance," she said. "When I left this mornin' for errands, she must of went to trancin' herself. I think she was looking for that Jimmy boy. Oh, lawd, what are we gonna do?"

"Looking for Jimmy?" Frank asked. "Why? What's happened since yesterday?"

Mama Dedé quickly told the men about the visit from Henri that morning, the missing people from the orphanage, and how she found Del when she had returned.

"How do we get her out of the trance?" Armand asked. "Can't we simply wake her up?"

"No, no. We cain't force her awake. She won't come back right. She got to get her mind free first."

"Free? Free from what?" Armand asked.

"When you're trancin', your mind is tied up in seeing da visions, making your way through da scenes. It's easy to get confused or lost. But it's not bein' lost that I'm worried about."

"What else is there to worry about?" Armand asked.

"Trancin' is like lookin' at da outside of every house you can imagine. Each house has a whole lot of scenes and images of things that have already happened, happening now, or may gonna happen. Most times, seein' the scenes is like lookin' through a window. But sometimes... sometimes it's like lookin' through a door. If da door is open and you pass straight through, you may not be able to get back."

"A door? To what?"

Mama Dedé dabbed at Del's forehead, then fixed Armand with a cold stare. "The other sides."

Frank and Armand exchanged concerned looks.

"Sides?" Armand asked.

The woman nodded in silent agreement.

Armand stood up and began a slow pace about the room, letting his mind run free. He absently touched objects, but not as haphazardly as before. He was in deep controlled thought.

"Frank, you have your items, I suppose?" he asked into the room.

"Yep."

"And I, mine," he said, winding his mustache again. Still staring into space, he said, "Mama D, if we give you some time, you know, watch the house, watch over Del, do you think you can locate her? Do you think you can find where she's gone?"

"I might be able to," the woman said, wringing her hands. "I just got to!"

"How would you even start?"

"Remember, you can see scenes as well as da remnants of people who have been trancin' around those scenes. I 'spect if I land on a scene that Del was lookin' at, I could tell that she'd been there."

"Fascinating. And where do you think you'd look first?"

Without hesitation the woman said, "Da orphanage. She's looking for Jimmy, so I think she'd start with da orphanage."

"Very well, then," Armand said. "We'll secure the house and start setting the trap." Looking at Frank, he continued, "Are we still in agreement that the courtyard outside will suffice?"

Frank nodded slowly. "Yeah, it'll do fine. Stone garden surrounded by servant houses. High fence surrounding da rest. Privacy. Once da fire gets set it should go fast, so once anyone see's da flames, da deed should be done. Besides, da damn clouds is so thick, I doubt anyone will even notice."

"Ok then," Armand said, "we'll arrange what we need. In the meantime," looking at Mama D, "you find Del."

*

An hour and a half later, the two men sat at an old wrought-iron table in the cobblestone courtyard behind the halfway house. As Frank had mentioned earlier, the halfway house—previously known as the Prudhomme House—had been grand in its day. Mimicking Armand's own home, only on a smaller scale, the Prudhomme House had been built with modest-sized out-buildings; some had been used as servants' quarters in the early days, and some had been converted to work sheds or garages.

The courtyard spanned the rectangular distance between the house and the outbuildings. Dead gardens spilled over the sides of stone planters that ringed the outside of the courtyard. A small grassy circle, ringed with smaller stone planters, pinpointed the center of the yard, which used to hold a large round table for outside family dinners. Now the grassy circle was a brown scar inside a larger moss-covered area of limestone paths.

Around the inside of the courtyard, between the stone planters and partially hidden by overgrowth, the men had carefully placed everything they thought they'd need to trap the Gris-gris man—at least for a few minutes—until the fire could be started. The plan was to lure the man into the courtyard, where any one of several traps would catch and hold him. They didn't have access to a steal hog cage as Marie did when she dispatched him so many years ago, but several of Frank's wolf traps had been set around the courtyard, staked down between the paver stones and covered with old gunny sacks.

In the center of the dead-grass area they had constructed a small wooden shrine to Dr. John—based on Armand's research—that included a bundle of High John Root, a bottle of Absinthe and several chicken feet tied in a bundle. Neither man was sure if they were truly dealing with Dr. John, or the transformed spirit that had become the Gris-gris man, but felt the correlation was close enough that it may actually work.

Carefully hidden around the edge of the grass circle was a thin layer of red brick dust, designed to keep him held inside the ring. The circle was open towards the gate facing the road—through which they hoped he would enter—and would be the only way he could escape, assuming one of the wolf traps didn't snare him, or he wasn't interested in the offerings.

However, Frank and Armand didn't plan on giving him much time to inspect the goods, and had several small coffee cans of gasoline placed all over the courtyard which they would light first, to block his exit, then to ultimately dispatch him entirely. The largest can of gas sat right beneath the offering table, and was tied to the others with a network of twine rope. Once alight, the rope would burn quickly, but not before one good pull would overturn several of the other cans spilling gas across the entire stone courtyard.

"You think you can really call him?" Frank said, mopping a mixture of sweat and mist from his brow.

"Yes, I believe I can," Armand said. "I studied every volume I had on Dr. John last night. I feel like I have a very good understanding of what he is drawn to."

Frank watched Armand absently twist his mustache.

"Or at least, what he was drawn to when he was... well, before, when he was still a man."

"Whatchoo think he'll look like?" Frank asked, admiring a new cigar. "Da Devil himself?"

Armand thought for a long moment. "I'm not sure, mon ami. Whatever it is, whatever... shape he has assumed, we should be careful to remember that it is pure evil beneath its surface."

Frank nodded slowly as he lit his cigar.

"And you'll be ready, yes?" Armand asked. "With your... you know, just in case?"

"Oh, what, dis?" Frank pulled his pistol from its shoulder holster. "Yeah, if it comes down to it, dis will stop him. But you think you really got to do da other thing? You gonna read from it?"

"Yes, mon ami," Armand said. "As you say, if it comes down to it, and he isn't attracted to the offerings or the other chants I've found, I'll read from it. I'll read the verses from the grimoires."

*

Del spun helplessly in her mind—a crazy-mad gimbal spinning out of control—for what seemed like an eternity. Somehow her mind had slipped—or was slipping—away from her, and she was unraveling. She felt the rough edges of her mind splinter off and fly away. She felt the spongy hemispheres being ground down, polished out of existence by the insanely spinning orb she had become. She was becoming invisible.

She couldn't remember how long she'd been in this state, but knew that it hadn't always been like this. She thought she remembered a past life, some of it good, some of it bad. She had parents once, she thought. Somehow, she felt their presence in the dark, or at least a remnant of them, but she didn't know where she was, and she felt a lot of things. Not all of them were good.

She couldn't remember how she got there. A faint dream of a vision showed her an old parlor room that somehow smelled familiar, but it was mixed with the black and white ghost of an orphanage and the smell of death. Although, what was smell in this nameless void anyway?

All she could think about was stopping. Somehow, she knew she had to stop spinning, but something was propelling her. The loud bellowing voice; the black death-wind was making her spin. She had to stop spinning before she flew apart completely.

*

"Fools!" Mama Dedé suddenly said from the back porch. "Lawd if we're not lost and you fools are talkin' nonsense!" She turned and solemnly walked back into the house.

Frank and Armand quickly joined her at the kitchen table where she had nearly fallen into a chair. Her face was ashen and sweaty, and she wrung her hands in dismay.

"What is it?" Frank said. "Did you find Del? What have you seen?"

Mama Dedé steadied herself and looked at each man separately. She suddenly buried her face in her hands as a large sob wracked her heavy bosom.

"Oh lawd, lawd… What have I done?"

"Please," Armand said quickly, "the news. The suspense is unbearable."

"I cain't find her. She's lost."

"Lost? Surely you mean—"

Slapping her hands on the table, she said, "I said what I mean!"

Realizing her own anger would not help Del in any way, she shook her head and grabbed Armand's hand, then reaching to Frank's hand, she shook them both hard, squeezing them tightly. "I went looking for her right after we talked. I started with da orphanage and was able to find her right away."

"Well, if you found her right away, then—"

Mama Dedé shook her head and silenced Armand. "She started there. I know because I could see her essence. She has an essence like no one I've seen before. But I still couldn't find her."

She released their hands and went to the counter by the coffee pot.

"Here, let me make some fresh," Frank said.

Without responding, she opened the far cabinet door and pulled down an old bottle of Cognac and three small glasses. She poured herself a short dose and swallowed it quickly. She set the collection on the table, knowing that Frank would do the rest, then continued.

"I saw were she was," she said. "I even saw where she went. At least for a little while. Then I heard it, but it was too late. I heard him laugh. A big, horrible laugh, far off. I tried to find Del in that scene, but she was gone."

"Who are you talking about?" Armand said. "Who was laughing?"

"Da Gris-gris man," she said. "I don't know how I know, but I do. It was da Gris-gris man that caught Del in her trance."

The two men looked at each other as fear spread across their faces. This was far beyond their ability to help.

"What can we do?" Armand asked. "There must be something we can do to help. You just need to guide us."

She explained that after she'd found Del's trail, she went looking for her, and that's when she heard the laugh. Del should have been there somewhere, in one of the scenes, but Mama Dedé only found a trail of her.

"Wait, watchoo mean, only a trail?" Frank asked.

"Yes, fascinating," Armand said. "What does her essence look like?"

Mama Dedé looked at Armand and thought for a moment. Her eyes told two stories.

"Silver droplets," she said. "Da prettiest little silver droplets you ever saw. I never seen anyone leave hard shapes like that before. No, usually da color is so faint, you think it's a trick of light, but not Del."

The woman cast her eyes toward the table.

"What's wrong?" Frank said.

"There's something else," Armand said. "There's something else about the silver droplets, isn't there?"

She breathed a long, slow breath.

"They streaked," she said. "Most looked pure. The ones I could see anyway. But some are streaked."

"Streaked with what?"

"Black."

The group sat a long time. No one wanted to be the first to imply anything against Del.

The minutes ticked along.

Finally, Armand broke the silence. "Silver droplets. Beautiful silver droplets. That should make it easy to find her again, shouldn't it? If we stay here, Frank and I, we'll stay here and… continue with our plan. You get some rest, we'll watch the house, then when you're ready, you go back to trancin' and find her. You can follow the droplets, right?"

Mama Dedé looked at Armand and Frank with something very near shame in her eyes.

"It's not that easy, Frenchy."

"Why? Why isn't it that easy?"

"I can see 'em, I just cain't follow 'em."

"Why not?"

"Da droplets, they scattered in all directions."

CHAPTER 48

E arly that evening, the two men finished their dinner of crawfish etouffee and checked the courtyard for any last-minute preparations. Mama Dedé had just awoken from a late nap, and was preparing to start trancing again. She was going to look for Del, but also to try to contact Marie; she felt that having the unbinding spell was the only way they could truly get rid of the Gris-gris man, despite what damage Frank and Armand could inflict.

She checked on Del, then walked outside. "So, you boys ready, I see. You sure you want to try this?"

"Yes," Armand said. "We feel we're as prepared as we can be."

"OK, then, there's nothin' else I can say. But first sign of anything, and I mean *anything*, you come ring this back bell, three times. If I'm still trancin', I'll hear it and come right back out. You hear?"

"We hear ya," Frank said. "But we ain't waitin' around to kill him. As soon as we slow him down, we gonna kill him."

"Just be careful. And don't forget this bell."

Frank nodded and turned back to the traps, cans and ropes.

Armand inspected his offerings, then looked inside a leather satchel he had slung around his neck. He hadn't transcribed the verses, but knew where the first two were marked in the books. He'd read from them if necessary.

Frank had gone around and lit several torches to illuminate the courtyard—careful of their spacing near the gas cans. The electric had been out all day, and deep layers of clouds now blocked all moonlight. Somewhere a nearly full moon was shining, but not there.

Frank settled himself on one side of the covered back porch, nearest to the gate. If the Gris-gris man was to make an appearance, he'd be able to quickly block his exit by tipping over the torch near him, which would ignite the gas he had poured along the cobblestones near the entrance.

Armand sat behind the makeshift offering-table they had constructed, facing the open gate. He could see Frank to his right, sitting on the porch, and the old stables-turned-garage to his left. He hoped he was obscured behind the glare of the torch that lit the eerie courtyard.

Both men waited.

At the beginning of the evening, Armand had called Dr. John's name and requested an audience. Although most of the text he had read required him to simply leave the offerings and let the enigmatic figure appear in his own good time, Armand thought they couldn't leave anything to chance, and specifically invoked him by name.

As the hours ticked by, the two men watched each other through the deepening gloom; two fireflies signaling each other with glowing embers; cigar, cigar, pipe; smoke signal, pipe, cigar.

Armand checked his pocket watch and noted that it was now ten minutes past the bewitching hour; midnight had come and gone without so much as a stray cat visit. There was nothing left to do,

Armand decided. He lit another small torch next to him, now casting enough light to read by—which was also the signal to Frank—opened his leather satchel, and removed the Grimoire White.

Armand read aloud the first part:

> "Hellish spirit hear me clearly, grant you now full use or nearly,
>> Of my soul for use and toiling, at the work of evil lore.
>> This damned soul is ripe for taking; in its core with trembled shaking,
>> Hunger-lust pang never slaking, begging at your ghostly door.
>> Use me spirit, just tonight, that I may unlock Abgel's door;
>> Just tonight, no less, no more."

The words were upon the wind.

In the St. Louis Cemetery #1, Eddie heard the hellish words and vibrated on high. Someone was invoking the spell. "Sing," came a raven-voice in his head, and Eddie's stone mouth sang the second part of the spell.

> "I call to you, by way of chanting—lest a demon voice be ranting,
>> Ranting in my wretched mind to call you up from days of yore.
>> I summon you to evil deed, your voice as one my mind will heed,

*Seeking someone sure to bleed, to right a wrong done
to my core.*

*Use me spirit, just tonight, that I may open abGel's
door,*

Just tonight, no less, no more."

Armand had just opened the Grimoire Strange as the soundless chant of the stone grotesque fell still. Not realizing the spell was falling in order, he started the third passage.

"With demon-will I wholly bind, your tattered soul, black heart and mind

To me you see, for I am kind, except to those I doth abhor."

The words were upon the wind, and dark clouds, swelling with evil intent, hung low in the sky, waiting to give birth to a fury that would rain hell upon the land; just a few more words needed to be spoken.

Suddenly, a dark figure strolled slowly out of the mist beyond the gate of the courtyard. Armand saw movement at the edge of his vision and quickly closed the grimoire. The spell was broken.

The clouds—quivering in anticipation—cried an angry protest of thunder at the interruption and roiled with dark fever.

The figure outside the gate moved slowly, a limp or walking cane stuttering their gate. Armand watched between flickering flames, catching glimpses here and there of the dark figure. A second figure appeared next to the first. There was no mistaking its powerful stride. The beast breathed a ragged breath as it stepped forward and the mist flew away in fear.

Standing just outside the gate, the two figures seemed to inspect the courtyard carefully. The hunched figure turned its head slightly from side to side as the beast breathed deeply, flexing its nostrils, detecting something.

The blonde doll that hung below the neck of the beast stared with one pleading eye stuck open; watching the remnants of a life it used to know. The mutant Toth sat inanimate on a long needle, waiting for a static spark of life.

Without moving his head, Armand sent his eyes searching for a sign that Frank was ready to spring their trap. There was no ember glow.

The two figures stood just outside the open gate, sniffing, shuffling.

The beast, split tail twitching in anticipation, shook its head savagely, howled a wolfish bark, and bit the limping figure in the side of the leg. The bite thrust the figure forward into the courtyard, where it began a feeble run toward the center.

Everything happened at once.

CHAPTER 49

The silver droplets of Del had been scattered to the wind. Thrown in all directions, they floated aimlessly in the space that used to be Del, like stars of the universe.

Mama Dedé floated in her trance, looking upon the sparkling remnants of Del's essence, despair turning her own yellow essence dark and muddy.

The woman could see the faintest sheen of red around the silver droplets. She knew this meant that a scene was old and moving away from her, but she had never seen the red sheen applied to someone's essence before—or what was left of it. Looking around at the sparkling remnants, she was surprised to see a few droplets with the slightest blue sheen to them. But how could that be? How could there be a new part of Del?

Maybe the whole of Del was still intact, she thought. Maybe the blue-sheen silver droplets were simply pieces of Del moving in a different direction. If so, they must be flowing towards her.

As the woman looked around in her mind, she floated away

from the scene she was in. The further she floated away, the more droplets she could see. And now that she was able to detect the slightest red-sheen and blue-sheen, she saw a breathtaking sight. Like gazing at the Milky Way galaxy on a clear cold night, she realized she was looking at the universe of Del. Beautiful silver droplets, like stars in the sky, had been flung away from each other with a great force. Up close, they looked to be flying away at such speed that they would never come back together, but she now observed that they were flying away at a *decreasing* speed. The droplets were slowing down ever so slightly and drifting toward each other. Her essence, somehow—like gravity to a dust particle—was trying to pull back together.

The woman, now clearly understanding how to follow the path of Del, floated in a new direction and moved back into the stream of Del's essence. She would follow it to her core.

After what seemed to be hours of following her trail, Mama Dedé saw something she had never seen before; a huge spinning orb made of the same, beautiful Del-silver, but with melting streaks of the purest black flying around the surface. Deadly fingers of electricity coursed off the orb and raced around the surface. Here, the droplets were no longer flying away, but were held in stasis; frozen in time. Slowly, one by one, they fell back into the Del-orb with a violent explosion. If the droplets were the outer essence of Del, the violently spinning orb was her core. It was a terrible and beautiful sight all at once.

If Del somehow returned from this, the woman thought, she would never be the same.

But could she return in time?

*

Del was exhausted. She had struggled against the bellowing voice-wind for hours, for days, for her entire life. Her essence had almost blurred out of existence.

The dark voice spoke in her head. "I know what your heart desires most Delphine, for we are the same, you and I!"

Del was liquid. She felt the core of her being sink to her center and start to solidify; some base element of her essence was reforming.

"We are special Del," the voice said. "Special beyond comprehension. Formed from knowledge long forgotten. Superior in all ways. Singular in purpose."

Del could still hear the voice, but felt it no longer propel her out of control. She was somehow regaining some control over herself. Instead of fighting the spin, wasting energy trying to stop it, she would control it.

"Our abilities," the voice continued, "to trance, to tread the past, to read the future, is fundamental to our nature. We are elemental."

She used its energy to spin even faster; a white-hot orb of universal essence; collecting mass; increasing her gravitational pull; she was reforming.

As the Del-orb spun beyond comprehension, a new thing started to form. No one knew it yet, but the new thing would be awesome and terrible.

"We draw people to us that we can use," the voice continued, "misfits, degenerates, the sinful; people that crawl on their bellies and grovel. We help them and they do what we command. The world is made of the powerful and the meek. You and I are powerful, for we are of the same flesh and we have become like Gods.

"I'm coming to see you soon, Delphine. You and your family of misfits; especially the blank one. Yes, I know of the blank one. It's unclear why I can't see him, but I know he is near. With you and the blank one, we will all be whole again. We will be a family soon, and each one will be whole."

*

Armand watched as the hunched figure stumbled forward into the courtyard, where its overcoat opened and two weasel-like creatures dropped to the ground. New to their first hunt, the weasels mewled and gnashed their beaks at air and shadow. They could smell food, but were mindless creatures and snapped at each other for several seconds. Finally realizing they were free to kill and eat at will, their six legs found their footing and they scampered toward the deep shadows, with their claws sending a menacing *tica-tica-tica-tica* sound echoing into the dark.

Armand, now trying to track the scampering abominations in the dark, stepped sideways causing the chair to scrape against the courtyard stone. The weasels heard him instantly.

A flash of light illuminated the unfolding scene. On the other side of the courtyard, a torch had been tipped over, igniting a small can of gas. The quick explosion blew the can apart and sent flames shooting in all directions. The stumbling figure spun around in confusion, trying to escape the flames, and tangled themselves in the carefully hidden ropes that tied the cans of gas together. Several cans spilled their contents onto the stony courtyard and caught fire. The beast howled its shock and anger at the trap, sending a jolt of life to the mutant Toth, who gibbered a mad protest. With spider speed, one of the weasels, catching Armand's scent, scampered toward him in the dark—six dagger-legs tapping a death march along the way— and stepped onto a hidden wolf trap. The steel spring snapped shut in an instant, cutting its head clean from its unnatural body, where it rolled to Armand's feet in the dark. The beast howled a mortal wound as it felt the essence of its offspring snap out of existence.

The stumbling figure reached the center of the courtyard as if to claim its prize, only to throw the hood from its head and scream, "He has returned, Del! He has come for you!" At that moment, the flames reached the limping nun and she caught fire.

Frank, suddenly seeing the nun inside the circle of flames, shifted in his chair, betraying his position to the beast, who caught his movement from the corner of its watchful eye.

The beast reared its head and howled an unholy wail as it stood on its hind legs like a stamping horse, slamming its heavy paws into the ground. The energy from the beast sent an overload of life into the dead mutant, causing it to shoot up from the beast's back and spin around the needle like a child's toy. The ridiculously spinning mutant screamed its unholy gibberish, "..Aaaiiieeeeee!! …glb …glb … chkryyyy!" and landed facing backwards on the back of the beast. The unnatural energy that passed between the two would sustain its life for several minutes, and it stood up, sliding up the heavy needle, and gibbered at the night.

Armand started toward the burning nun, but the entire courtyard was now in flames. The trap had worked too well; there was no way to get to her.

The nun screamed her apocalyptic warning once more before realizing she was on fire. Suddenly, as if directed by a silent voice, she turned and ran towards the house.

Armand saw her intention and had time to yell but one word of warning:

"Del!"

*

Frank saw the nun stumble forward as his attention was drawn back to the gate. A giant wolf—or something very near one—had just howled its angry warning and turned its powerful head in his direction. As he pulled his pistol, a ludicrous thought passed through his mind: *somehow a child's toy got stuck on the back of that wolf*, then he raised his hand and fired.

In one strong leap the beast covered half the distance from the gate to Frank. Its second leap took it into the path of the bullet and a small piece of its left shoulder was sheared away, along with the right foot of the mutant. The force knocked the beast sideways out of the air and onto a burning patch of courtyard.

The nun hit the back porch as Frank's chair caught on a warped board, tipping him backwards out of his chair. She crashed through the backdoor and stumbled into the kitchen; flaming pieces of clothing fell from her as she careened down the hall yelling for Del.

Armand, five steps behind the nun, ran to Frank as the beast—now alight—ran wildly about the courtyard, gnashing at its burning fur.

Grabbing Frank's gun, Armand managed one wild shot as the beast leapt out of the courtyard and into the night. The mutant, still riding backwards, glared and gibbered at Armand as it swung wildly from side to side; it would remember his face.

The next thing the men saw was the nun—having crashed through a top window and bounced off the back-porch roof—land with a sickening thud onto the stone courtyard.

They both realized the horror of the situation at the same time. The house was in flames.

CHAPTER 50

Jimmy wandered the dark streets looking for Jo and Del. He couldn't remember how long he'd been out there. He had fallen asleep underneath some bushes, then heard a strange noise that woke him up, so he'd left. Someone had been nice enough to leave part of their apple on the sidewalk for him, so he ate that, but he was still hungry. He thought he heard voices ahead of him in the fog, but could never catch up to them. He would go back to the orphanage if he could remember the way, but he couldn't even tell if it was day or night now, so he kept walking.

Ever since he'd left the orphanage to follow Jo, his head had been singing a new song for him. He wasn't sure how his head knew the song without him knowing it, but some things worked in mysterious ways, Del had told him once, and Del was always right.

Suddenly he wondered if Del was singing to him. Maybe she was trying to tell him where she was! If he could just remember the song, he'd be able to find her. He decided to sit down and think really hard about the song, and soon he'd find Del.

*

Jo came upon a surreal sight as she turned the corner to the halfway house. The entire house was in flames!

After waking up in the cemetery that morning, she'd wandered the streets for a long time, wondering what to do. She knew the horrible memories from the night before had really happened; it hadn't just been a crazy nightmare. But where would she go? Now that she had traded the Crow to the man in the cemetery, she wondered when he would fulfill his part of the bargain. When would she get Del? Deciding this was her chance to be free of the orphanage for good, she wandered the streets until the idea to find the halfway house came to her.

Her heart dropped when she saw the flames. She wondered if this had something to do with the strange man, but let the thought pass out of her head as she sprinted towards the house. If Del was in there, she would need help.

Frank and Armand had just entered the smoke-filled kitchen when the front door of the house was flung open. A water-logged girl had just run into the house, but the sudden gust of wind caused the small fire in the hall to leap to the ceiling and crawl towards the back of the house. The two men were knocked back by a hot blast of air that slithered like a night-demon over the ceiling.

"Mama D!" Frank yelled. "Wake up! We got to get out!"

Armand was frantically throwing water from the sink at the door of the parlor, which had been shut tight during the trancing session. A piece of the nun's habit had fallen off there, and the fire had quickly climbed up the old wooden door. The water had no effect.

Frank, seeing no possibility of stopping the fire at this point—for he assumed the top floor was burning also—pushed Armand aside and with one large heave of his shoulder broke through the burning door of the parlor, landing hard on the parlor floor.

Jo and Armand quickly followed, and all were stunned to see Mama Dedé still sitting calmly at the table while Del laid on the couch, both oblivious to the fire.

Frank went to shake Mama D, but remembering her words from earlier in the night, Armand grabbed Frank's arm and said, "The bell!" then ran out of the room.

An instant later, three loud frantic rings could be heard from the back doorbell. Mama Dedé instantly opened her eyes and started coughing.

"Oh lawd! What happened?" she said wearily.

"Never mind," Frank said, pulling her to her feet. She was weak from the long trancing session, and had to lean her great girth onto him.

Jo was trying to wake Del up as Armand ran through the door. "Don't!" he yelled. "Just grab her feet. I'll get her shoulders."

Frank led Mama D out the front of the house. Armand and Jo followed closely, carrying Del.

Flames had crawled across the entire ceiling and were inching down the walls. A wild gust of wind sent them blowing into the middle of the hall in a last ditch effort to stop the group's escape. A long hot flame licked at Jo and caught her on the left side of her neck. She screamed in pain, but never let go of Del's legs.

The group stumbled down the front steps and tumbled into the small yard just as the upstairs windows blew out. The house was completely engulfed in flames. They got into Frank and Armand's cars, still parked in front. As the group drove away into the night, they watched as the roof began to cave in. The St. Augustine Transitional Home for Girls was no more.

Jo watched out the back window in shock as they drove away. Amidst the hellish scene, she caught a fleeting glimpse of a shadow that darted away from the house. About the size of a large cat, she thought, but the gooseflesh on her arms told her it was something different.

CHAPTER 51

Armand settled the weary group into the spare rooms of his house. The open second floor—primarily used for his research—was surrounded by more rooms than he could ever use.

He lit a fire in the upstairs fireplace and poured brandy for himself, Frank and Mama Dedé. Jo was attending to Del, who had been laid in her own room.

The group sat in silence for several long minutes, replaying the events of the evening.

"What we gonna do now?" Frank said, breaking the silence. "How da hell we gonna kill dis thing?"

Armand twisted his mustache delicately, puffed his pipe, then said, "Somehow he knew it was a trap. How did he know?"

"He's tricky," Mama Dedé finally said. "Da Gris-gris man is bad tricky."

Jo joined them at the fireplace, took a cup of tea and quietly said, "She's still sleeping. She'll wake up soon."

Each person cast a look around the group; none were confident this statement was true.

"Did he really know it was a trap, or did he just suspect?" Frank asked.

"Does it matter now, mon ami?" Armand said. "Maybe he knew, maybe he got lucky, regardless, he knows we're after him now."

"Where did the nun come from?" Frank asked.

"What nun?" Jo said with wide eyes.

"I'm pretty sure dat was Sister Eulalie from da orphanage," Frank said. "I hate to think how she got involved with these unholy doin's."

Jo sat in silence, wishing the conversation to go away, or at least that no one would send a question her way. Her mind was spinning with the implications of what she had done.

Mama Dedé turned her girth towards Jo and said, "Honey, what was your name again? And how did you get tied up in this mess? What were you doin' out so late?"

Jo shuffled her feet and swallowed hard, hoping no one detected the nerves that she felt shimmering across her face. "Me? Uh, my name is Jo. Josephine, really. I was… I… I'm a friend of Del's from the orphanage. I snuck out and was coming to see her."

Mama Dedé eyed the girl and thought back to her visit from Captain Guillaume. Wasn't Josephine the name of one of the people who had gone missing? The woman knew that someone wasn't telling the truth, but at this point couldn't be sure who.

Frank leaned back in the large chair, causing it to groan. "Seems like a lot of people been sneakin' out of dat orphanage," he said, watching her closely.

Realizing that she was still under interrogation, Jo said, "Oh, uh, yeah, I guess."

"Or go missin," Mama Dedé added.

"You know anything about Sister Eulalie?" Frank asked Jo. "Der seems to be more to her... well, der *was* more to her than people seemed to know."

Jo shuffled her feet again and sipped at her tea. "Yeah, I guess there was."

"And that poor little Jimmy boy, he gone missin' too," the older woman continued, watching Jo closely.

"What? Jimmy is missing?" Jo asked with dismay. Her stomach turned at the thought of her own implication. "When?"

Mama D continued, looking straight at Jo: "Yeah, been missin' about..." she thought back to the morning visit from Henri, "a day and a half now. I hope nothin' has happened to dat boy. Del would be fit to be—"

A strong wind suddenly burst through the room, causing the candles to snuff out all at once. Smoke flowed backwards down the chimney and blew into the room; sparks flittered like angry fireflies onto the hardwood floor—dying an uneventful death.

Armand jumped up to address the errant window, but the look on Mama Dedé's face stopped him. She stared in fear down the dark hall.

The old woman stood slowly, but motioned for everyone to stay seated. "Quiet," she whispered.

Each person turned and followed her gaze. They all saw a faint, shimmering apparition, but each would remember it differently: Armand would claim to have seen a very faint orb, glowing in the dark; Frank would claim to have seen an eye, oblong and pulsating, forever searching; Jo saw a fiery, white void, dangerous and beautiful; but Mama Dedé was the only one to see the truth: a radiant, terrible face, morphing from one state to another, struggling for existence.

She spoke quietly. "Del, is that you?"

The quivering apparition slowed in response to the old woman. It pulsed an unnatural light that flowed along the walls like a quicksilver tide.

"Can you hear me?"

"You speak," the thing said.

Mama Dedé prayed silently then said, "Yes, I do. Who are you?"

The thing considered this for a moment. "I am Del."

Jo began to whimper. Mama Dedé stared to the two men to keep the girl silent.

"Del, honey? Where are you?"

The thing hovered silent for several seconds, then sputtered, "I was Del, I was Del, I was Del, Del, Del."

Mama Dedé crossed herself and breathed a slow, shuddering breath as the apparition shifted in front of her.

"Where is Del now?"

A murmur emanated from the cloud: "I am Del."

Armand quietly relit the candles and stood watching as another vision of Del appeared in the dark hall, a more physical form that appeared behind the doppelganger cloud.

The flickering candles, drawn by the powerful gravity of the physical Del, excitedly cast their warm glow her way, illuminating her shimmering form in the cold night air.

The group saw a beautiful and disturbing site; the teenage Del was no more; emerging from the dark was a woman—still the same biological age, but infinitely older in spirit—that appeared to stand out from the night by an unnatural force. Her physical form cut against the dark shadows, as if the forces of the world had no effect on her. She appeared to float down the hall, drifting on a wind of great knowledge.

Del stared into the open space where the others sat, looking past their existence to something far beyond them. Each member of the group was but a fleeting image in a giant tapestry that Del now saw.

Upon laying her in bed, Mama Dedé had rummaged through the old closets and chest of drawers and found an old white nightgown that she had changed Del into, removing her smoke-tainted clothes. It was the shimmering night gown and soft tread of her bare feet that now gave Del an otherworldly appearance.

Her hair was pulled back by on old silk scarf—a makeshift tignon that fell gracefully to one side—which helped highlight her high cheekbones and glowing brown skin. An unseen wind ruffled at her nightgown, accentuating her lithe body, and giving her a look of constant movement.

"Del," Mama Dedé whispered.

Jo clamped both hands to her face and stifled a gasp. Tears of happiness and fear sprang to her eyes.

"Del, honey," the woman said, "are you back?"

Del saw the faces looking at her and heard the voices, but they were part of a fabric that didn't seem whole. She was unsure if she was still trancing, or if this was another trick she had to avoid.

She stared past the group and into the deep shadows of the room. She wanted to fall back into those shadows, where it was dark and safe.

Armand poured a cup of tea and walked to Del, who stood at the edge of the room. He saw in her eyes that she was still lost. He wondered at that moment if she would ever fully return.

"Here," Armand said, handing her the cup. "Drink this and come sit with us. We're glad you're feeling better."

Armand looked at Del and, in that moment, knew she was different.

How, he could not say, but he felt that if he looked at her for too long, her eyes would pull him into a deep void, and he would be lost. He imagined that he saw the beautiful silver droplets with black stains floating deep within her eyes; a dark and terrible power coalescing behind a beautiful face—a deadly combination.

Del sat quietly holding her cup of tea, not drinking. She stared into the fire and watched the flames. The tapestry of voices continued to speak around her, but the words came in tatters.

Mama Dedé finally took the cup from her and set it on the table.

The group asked her questions and she nodded and replied "yes" and "no" when they asked if she was well or needed anything. Finally, when Armand mentioned the house burning, Del's mind engaged.

"The house burned?" she asked calmly.

Mama Dedé nodded. "Da whole thing. But you don't worry about—"

Del turned to Jo. "And Jimmy?"

Jo looked around at the others, then said, "We'll find him Del, we'll—"

"'And they become like Gods,'" Del said to no one.

A long silence dragged out as each person looked to the other for an indication of how to respond to the odd statement. Finally, Armand broke the silence and said, "Yes, that's right Del. Otto the Younger wrote that in his diary before… well, that was one of the last things he wrote. Why do you say?"

"Someone mentioned it recently."

"Who?" Armand asked gently. "The… man?"

"He's not a man. But yes."

Armand looked around the room again for support on what to say next.

"He's creating a family," Del said. "I don't know why, but it's a family that he wants. I know now that I have to kill him."

Frank's cigar drooped down again for the third time tonight. "Watchoo mean honey? We done—"

But the look of calm detachment from Del's face stopped Frank's words from forming any further.

"Why do you think he wants a family?" Armand asked gently.

"Because he told me. We are the same, he and I. He wants each of us in his family... in some form or other. Somehow we are the same, and I have to kill him."

She looked from one person to the next, and no one spoke. She saw a different level of horror on each face as they considered the possibility of becoming a member of that unholy family.

Each person saw something different when they looked back at Del: victim, savior, monster, but they all felt the same thing: Del was different, and would never be the same.

"I have to sleep now. In the morning I'll trance, then I'll know what to do. I'll need your help. I'll know more tomorrow."

Frank looked at the clock. It was nearly 3:00 am. He started to protest, but let it die as Del stood up and walked back to her room.

She was preparing to meet the Gris-gris man.

CHAPTER 52

A Late Hour

Alas, the hour grows late and here we are.

We are so very close now.

Yes, I feel that we are very close to the end of our journey, yet... for one of us...

That is to say, I fear we will not end at the same place, you and I, for my essence is...

Oh, fearful mind! Cowered, I am. Hanging on the words of a stranger.

A kind soul you are, yes, for guiding me so. A sinful soul? Well, who can cast the first stone, really? But a stranger that has helped ca—

Alas, I dare not speak further of it, for it is a tenuous thing. I fear the slightest breath may cast it away.

But soldier on you must. Yes, if I, by some unfortunate fate, cannot continue our journey, you now are the only one who can soldier on.

I believe it to be fate, and...

You must do it for Del.

CHAPTER 53

The beast limped into the swamp camp and lay down heavily on its right side, nursing its torn left shoulder. The mutant Toth, pressed into the mud by the pressure of the long needle, lay silent. It did not miss its right foot, as it was not aware of its parts.

"Poor Mr. Sandgrove," the strange man purred as he stroked the beast. "What have they done to you?" He laid a hand on the heaving side of the beast and felt the ragged wound that had torn flesh not an hour earlier.

The strange man shivered as he drank in the pain. The reflection in the mirrored blue glasses momentarily went out of focus as he vibrated with intensity.

"And Toth," he continued, "your foot is missing. Alas, you haven't been using it much lately, but you simply don't look whole without it. Let's see what we can do about that."

Rooting around in the abandoned nest, he found the remnants of a big toe. "This will work just fine," he said. Pulling a small needle from a gris bag around his neck, he pierced the rotting toe, sprinkled it with powder from a separate bag, whispered a quiet prayer, then shoved it onto the meaty stump of Toth's leg.

Smoke rose from the end of the leg, then the toe bubbled and hissed around the edges as it merged with the body of the mutant. Soon it was not only permanently attached, but completely covered with the same brown leathery bumps of mutant skin.

Turning his attention to the laboring beast, the strange man grabbed a handful of mud from the swamp floor and put it in his mouth. He inspected the taste—appreciating the age of the swamp— then took powder from a gris bag and a long, stringy piece of sinew and swallowed them all. He chewed the mixture thoughtfully. Finally, he leaned in close to the ragged wound and with a sudden convulsion, vomited brown, sticky acid over it. The wound sizzled and popped, singeing the hair wherever the acid landed. Slowly, the wound closed over from the meat-patch saliva.

As the beast lay panting a labored recovery, the strange man struggled to his feet. The trees quivered with worried anticipation; the abominations—only four now, he knew—felt the pain flow out from their paternal source and gnashed at the night air with a mewling whine. He sensed the weasels were close; he could feel them, but they hid in the dark shadows, feeling the loss of one of their own. His family was suffering.

"We need nourishment," the man said to the creatures of the swamp. "Just a few more family members and we'll be whole again. I feel that we shall find our precious Del soon, and the blank one. The others, well, we'll find places for them all. Yes, they will all have a place in our family; some will nourish us completely, and the others... the others will join us forever."

*

Jimmy sat behind an abandoned building and sang his song. This was the same song that had played over and over in his head ever since he'd left the orphanage. It was a strange song with no music. He didn't understand the words, but felt it was important, so he tried very hard to remember it.

He shivered against the cold night and wondered if he would ever get back home. He wished he could stay with Del, and didn't understand why she had gone away. Somehow her *time was up* at the orphanage. He was sad when he'd heard that, and hoped his time was never up.

His heavy eyelids drooped as he started to doze. He'd had scary dreams ever since leaving the orphanage, and didn't want to dream anymore, so he tried his best to stay awake. The more he sang, the longer he could stay awake, he thought.

Quietly, a heavy mist began to swirl about him. He watched the clouds twist and morph as if a micro-storm was forming just beyond him. The longer he watched, the more the clouds looked like familiar things. He first saw the orphanage, and was very excited that he was almost home, but then remembered that he was lost, so he thought it must be someone playing a trick on him. He then saw several shadows move away from the orphanage and float down dark streets. They went the same direction for a while, then disappeared. He saw several faces start to form in the dark clouds and huddled closer to the cold wall. He remembered Del's warning about strangers, and took that to heart. He remembered the game that he and Del would play by trying to see shapes in the clouds, but there were no elephants or giraffes here. Eyes seemed to form in the clouds, and the faces surrounding them were ghost faces. They twisted into shapes that didn't look like normal faces. The mouths were either missing or were giant holes, large enough to eat you with, my dear. He sat very still and thought, *quiet da mouse, quiet da mouse,* as the eyes looked in all directions. The song with no music flew into his head again, only louder this time. Again and again it sang. The eyes hovered in the clouds, turning, rolling in all directions. They looked forward and backward at the same time. They were the eyes of a monster.

He clinched his own eyes shut and pretended to be a tiny mouse, not moving, and let the song flow through him. A strange little noise caught his attention; a tiny scratching sound somewhere in the dark— maybe another scared mouse, he thought. If it was scared, he should try to protect it, but he didn't know how. The mouse probably couldn't see the eyes, and he wanted to warn it to run away, but like the frog, he wasn't sure if he could teach it to talk. He chanced a look at the swirling clouds again and the eyes were now those of a giant; large and watery, they hung in the air right above his head. They had floated closer to him, but still couldn't see him. The eyes were angry.

Far off in the distance, two faint shimmering lights suddenly appeared. They hovered close to each other for a long time, then finally moved toward him in a slow, wavery dance. He imagined they could be small fairies or ghosts floating in the air. He had never seen a fairy or a ghost, but was sure he didn't want to see one tonight. Somewhere in the dark he heard the mouse scurry about again. It made a strange sound for a mouse that was sure to draw the eyes to him.

Tica-tica-tica-tica floated in the cold night air as the far-off lights drifted closer.

CHAPTER 54

Friday

J o walked into Armand's kitchen after a few hours of restless sleep. The sweet smell of pipe tobacco hung in the air and mingled with the aroma of strong coffee. Mama Dedé sat at the kitchen table and eyed her as she entered.

"Couldn't sleep?" the woman said to Jo.

"Not very well. I was worried about Del."

"Mmm-hmm."

Jo shuffled her feet as she debated on sitting down or going back to bed. The older woman had been watching her ever since she showed up last night.

"Take a seat," she said, and nodded at the cups Armand had set on the table.

Jo sat quietly and poured her coffee. She looked at the sugar bowl sitting in front of the woman but didn't ask. She sipped at the strong black coffee and tried to hide the bitter taste as it wrinkled her face.

"Heh," the woman sniffed and pushed the bowl towards Jo.

Nodding her thanks and spooning more sugar than she intended, Jo sipped and failed again at hiding the cloying sweetness she had just choked down and that now swirled in her cup.

"Pssh, girl, you about da worst liar I ever seen," Mama Dedé said as she settled back into her chair, holding her cup on bosoms that spilled onto the table.

"What? Why do you say—"

"Don't waste your time, honey. I done heard everything you can come up with, and plenty you cain't imagine."

Jo looked at the sugar bowl and felt a sick feeling rise in her throat.

"You and I are gonna get straight, right here and right now. I can find out what I need to know. I have da sight, you know." At this, Jo's eyes widened to small saucers. "But I ain't got much time, so don't go wastin' it. And more important, Del ain't got da time to waste, neither. So, you straighten up and tell me how you involved."

Relief rushed over Jo as she inhaled a deep breath and started her story. She told her of how she first met the strange man in the cemetery, the promise he had made to her, and how she had tricked the nun to follow her that night. With a final gush of air, she told the woman about the beast and seeing the nun as she was carried away. She was honest when she said she didn't remember anything after that, and had wandered the streets trying to think of what to do.

When the story was done, Jo sat slumped in the kitchen chair; tears brimmed in her eyes. The truth had drained her, and she felt tired again. She felt like she could sleep for days.

Mama Dedé sat looking at the young girl and did not speak. She could sense the heavy burden that lay upon her. She knew part of it was regret, and felt it was appropriate, but part of what the woman felt was something the girl could not yet fathom. Like Jacob Marley, Jo had forged the first link of an invisible chain that would hang about her forever. She knew people called it different names: a stain, bad karma, sin. Regardless of the word used to describe it, in the end—and if heavy enough—it would drag her down to the same dark depths.

*

Armand quietly ran his hands over his books in the second-floor library. He knew that his guests were beginning to stir, but he was intent on finding something that could help them. He was hoping there was a lost tome or hidden scrap of parchment that would expose a clue as to what to do next. He puffed at his pipe and twisted his mustache as if these acts would materialize the hidden clue. He drummed his fingers on the large worktop table and rearranged papers to no effect. He walked around the table and looked at his books from a different angle. Gazing over the shelves, he spied an overstuffed folder laying in one corner. It was his research folder for his book on the origins of spells and curses. An inner excitement sparkled in his mind as he walked to it. He puffed his pipe to a chimney stack as his fingertips danced together; a safecracker preparing for his job. He sat the folder on the worktable and began carefully thumbing the pages.

After several minutes, he came to some clipped pages from an old newspaper. It was the article about Frank when he solved the Glapion murders. *Yes, this is it.* He scanned the pages carefully.

Armand had forgotten he even had the clippings, but had stowed them away as part of his research. The Glapion murders were sensational when they'd happened, but wouldn't have made it into his research if not for the strange passages that were written on the walls.

In both the house at 113 Bayou Rd. and the jail cell, the strange words of:

Ouvre baye pou mwen, Papa!
Ouvre baye pou mwen!

had been written. The translation of course being:

Open the gate for me Papa!
Open the gate for me!

A cascade of legends flooded Armand's mind, and he turned from the work table with a sick flush; a sinister word association dizzying him. He spoke freely to the room. "Missing heads, abominations, yes…, tricky spells… oh yes, ouvre baye Papa, Gris-gris man, ouvre baye Papa Legba, Dr. John, Gris-gris man, Legba."

"Legba?" Frank said, rubbing sleep from his eyes as he walked toward the stairs. "What are you on to?"

Armand sprinkled invisible dust in the air with both hands. *Legba? The trickster god of the underworld? What had they stumbled into?*

"Yes, mon ami," Armand said quickly, scooping up books and folders, "that is what I said. Legba." And headed down the stairs after him.

Jo climbed past them both, carrying a tray with coffee and toast for Del. She smiled weakly at each one.

Armand set the books on the table with a heavy thud, where Mama Dedé had just spoken with Jo. He waited for Frank to be seated. He looked at them both with a twinkle in his eye.

"What you got, Frenchy?"

Armand grinned slyly. "Nothing more than a theory, but an interesting one indeed."

"It don't have flying 'gators, do it?" Frank asked.

"Mon ami, this is serious," Armand said with a tinge of hurt. "Please, indulge me."

Frank traded the cigar in his mouth for a sausage and mumbled some words of agreeance.

Armand had already begun. "Our theory so far has been that the Gris-gris man is an altered version of Dr. John, who, through his Voodoo practices, raised a spirit—which one, we don't know—but raised a spirit that gave him extra powers. Only the powers were a trick, and caused John to be trapped in a terrible state, and we know the rest."

Frank nodded his sausage in agreeance again. "Stho?" he said, holding the sausage with his teeth.

"But what if it goes further than that? We explored on this briefly a few nights ago, when I mentioned the tragic story of young Otto, although I took the theory too far into Egypt. But then when Del mentioned that the Gris-gris man wanted a family, I was struck by what an odd goal that would be."

"How so?"

"If I was just raised from the dead, I'm not sure a family would be the first thing on my wish list. I'd probably want my body back, then—"

Armand saw the expression on Mama Dedé's face and stopped.

"He does have his body back," she said.

"What? How do you know?"

"That girl up there," she said quietly, "da one tendin' to Del right now? She's seen him."

"What? How?"

"She made some kinda deal with him. It involved da flamin' nun that burned down my house."

"Fascinating."

"Frenchy, you better stop being so damn fascinated about my house burnin' down or I'm gonna—"

"Oh, forgive me, mon chéri, that's not what I meant. How in the world did the girl get involved?"

"That's a long story that we ain't got time for, now get on with your theory and let's hear it."

"Of course, of course. Oh my, where to go now... So, if he has his body back—"

"And don't forget about dat blasted wolf-dog, cat, whatever it was," Frank added. "Dat was da ugliest sumbitch I ever saw. I hit it, but der's no guarantee it's dead."

"The dog, of course! Or, the beast really. No, mon ami, I doubt it's dead. I fear it is fed by a source other than mere mortal life."

"Why you say dat?"

"The thing on its back, did you get a good look at it?"

"Da doll? Just a glimpse right before I shot its horse."

"That doll, I believe it was alive."

"Bully you say! Why you think—"

"Because after you fell off the chair, I—"

"Da damn leg caught on a board!"

"My pardons," Armand said with a slight bow. "After you were disabled, I caught a glimpse of the wolf-beast galloping away. Somehow—I think it was your shot—but somehow the *doll* got spun around. Right before it galloped out of sight, I swear I saw the doll's face come to life and then... then I heard it gibber at me."

Frank whistled his belief and leaned back in his chair, reflexively brushing some foreign debris from his shirt.

"But I digress, we were speaking of..." and Armand had to sprinkle invisible powder with his fingers to pull his mind back to its task, "Del… let's see, not Del, family… family, yes, something about… yes of course! Papa Legba!"

"We were?"

"Yes, yes, now please, no more interruptions. The diary of Otto the Younger mentions—however briefly—several Egyptian gods in conjunction with some very strange hieroglyphs and constellations. These gods are too numerous to discuss now, and will only confuse the theory, but it caused me to wonder what they may have in common. Any ideas?"

"You da professor, Frenchy."

Armand calibrated his mustache slightly.

"They all have messengers. In fact, depending on one's interpretation, they all have *the same* messenger. Of course, this messenger god has different names: Eschu, Anansi, Elegua. But with the African people, he's best known as Legba. The trickster god. He is supposedly one of the worst to deal with. He is the only one that can pass between worlds, and controls the gates to them. He presents himself as an old man… and travels with a dog."

Armand waited anxiously for his audience to process the story.

Frank and Mama Dédé exchanged glances, then turned back to Armand.

Armand's hands adjusted invisible books in the air. "Don't you see the similarities? A god that can pass between worlds, a trickster; strange evolving powers; two ancient cultures—the Egyptians and Africans—that share the same continent; migrating slaves; merging religions AND a grisly murder where both the perpetrators and victims called to the same deity: *ouvre baye Papa.*"

"Da Glapions," Frank said.

"That's right, Frank, the Glapion murders, your own case, may be the key here."

"Dat was bad business."

Armand nodded. "Black business, I'd say."

Concerned reality clouded the faces of his audience.

"Once again, it's just a theory, but I believe there is a chance that our problem is far older than we originally thought."

After a long silence, Frank said, "So how does dat help us now?"

"Well, if the spirit that Dr. John raised all those years ago really is Legba, we'd have to find a very ancient spell to deal with him. I have most of the Egyptian Book of the Dead transcribed here in these tomes." He patted the large pile. "If I can find the right spell, we may be able to—"

"Stop!" Mama Dedé said, slapping her hands on the table. "Don't be talkin' about readin' one more thing from a book you don't know nothin' about! Now I've done told both of you, these books aren't to be fooled with. You done read from two grimoires already, we don't know where da third is hidin', and now you talkin' about reading some Egyptian books? Do you know what is supposed to happen if you read from da third–

"Damn!" she said, clamping her mouth tight and sitting on her hands.

Frank and Armand exchanged knowing glances; Mama Dedé clearly had not meant to go down this line of conversation.

"The third... what?" Armand asked cautiously. "You mean the missing grimoire?"

She gave them both a scolding look. "That's exactly what I mean."

"But I thought you weren't aware of the existence of the three books? That first night when Frank and I came over, I pointed out that there was One of Three and—"

"I know what you pointed out. I just made believe that I didn't know much so you two knuckleheads wouldn't go on asking me about da damn third book!"

Armand looked slightly hurt as he closed the top book of his stack and took his seat. He tweaked his mustache slightly and began cleaning his pipe.

"Oh, pecker up, Frenchy. If I'd bit you, you'd a felt it. Now here's da only thing I'm ever gonna say about da third grimoire."

Both men adjusted in their seats like school children.

"Those books—primarily just da one hellish spell—was separated into three parts a long time ago. I hear that no one knows exactly what da third book says, but it's da last piece of a spell that should have never been thought of, and it'll trick you."

Armand raised his hand slightly and cautioned a question.

"What do you mean, *IT* will trick you? Don't you mean *him*?"

"Damn Frenchy, you're all over da theory, and just for the record, I think you may be right. I think old John maybe did call up Legba by mistake. But just as I said before, da legend is that you won't know you reading da bad part of da spell until it's too late. Once you do, and if da other parts have been read in da right order, da spell is cast—da binding spell—and you have to deal with whatever you just conjured, or whatever you just bound yourself to."

"But how would someone ever be tricked into reading a spell book that they didn't want to read?"

"Cause it don't look like a spell book! And some folks say that it don't even have spells in it, except for da last piece, but somehow it tricks you into reading them all in order. Then..." She hesitated, thinking she had already said too much.

"Yes? What then?" Armand coaxed.

"Then, da last thing you see is a sign from da demon who created da unholy thing."

"A sign? What kind of sign?"

She sighed heavily, not wanting to speak the words. "Something—I don't know what—but something appears in da third book once da spell is set. Some type of... death-chant response."

"What? A death chant?"

"Yeah, a death chant. A message from da demon. It just up and speaks to you somehow. And God help da poor soul that sees it. That's all I know and that's all I'm sayin', so don't go on askin'. And that's why you two cain't be readin' from just any ol' book!"

With that, she heaved herself from the table and marched toward the stairs that led up to Del's room.

CHAPTER 55

Later that morning, Del emerged from her trancing session and walked into the second-floor library. She hadn't left her room all morning. Frank was napping in a large chair by the cold fireplace, and Armand was hovering over some old papers.

"Good morning, my dear," Armand said, looking up. "Are you… better?"

Del nodded. "Yes, thank you. I…"

Armand watched her search for words.

"Thank you for helping me last night. You know, when you offered the tea. I wasn't quite sure if I was still trancing or not, or if I was… out yet. I had seen so many visions, I wasn't sure what was real."

"Yes, I understand. Well… sort of. To be honest, we weren't sure…"

"If I was real?"

Armand chuckled. "Yes, exactly. How did you know?"

Del looked at the large bookshelf and wondered if there was anything in Armand's books that could explain what she had experienced. She doubted there was.

"It's hard to describe. I was lost for so long—actually, I don't know if *lost* is even the right word. I was *not here* for so long, I wasn't sure what was real. Eventually, I saw a scene form—you all talking in front of the fireplace—and I was drawn to it. I watched it for a while, but was... well, I was afraid that I was dead and that I was watching it as a ghost. Crazy, huh? Anyway, I tried to reach out. I tried to get your attention, but it was like no one could hear me. I wasn't even sure if I was speaking. I tried to project an image out and get someone's attention, then I saw a door open and—"

"Excuse me for interrupting, but what type of... door?"

Del watched as Armand tweaked his mustache.

"Not like a normal door, but somehow I saw a way... through. It was a new path I could take, and I suddenly wanted to move from where I was, *out*, to the scene I was watching. I've never felt that before, but I'll have to ask Mama D about it. Then, I was walking down the hall and could see you all sitting, but it was very far away. The hall was stretched somehow, and you all looked very hazy, like I was seeing you through a cloud. Someone was speaking to me, I think. Did I say anything?"

Armand thought back to the strange conversation Mama Dedé had had with the apparition. "No, not that I recall."

"Hmm, strange," Del said. "That part must have been a dream. But suddenly I got to the end of the hall and you all were sitting there. I don't remember going to bed, however."

Feeling that they had already ventured too far into dangerous territory, Armand shifted the conversation. "I must say, you look quite lovely in the kanga. It's much better than the old blue jeans and sneakers." He gave her a quick wink.

"Is that what you call this?" Del said. "I just thought it was an

African dress, and it fit. But, why do you even have something like this in your house?"

"Oh, it's quite fascinating, really. It appears that the former owner of this establishment was very eccentric, and amassed quite the collection. She collected themes of items and stuffed them into every conceivable corner of the house. When she passed, I purchased the home as you see it. Alas, you ended up in the African room last night. How did you sleep after...? Well, are you recovered?"

"What do you know of my... trancing issue? At the house, before last night. Did she say anything?"

"Mama Dedé? Oh no, ever the discrete one. She just said that you... got tripped up."

Del looked at the sleeping Frank and smiled slightly. She thought back to the time when she was trapped and everything she saw. She didn't understand most of it, but thought that Armand might.

"When I was... trapped, and spinning, I saw a lot of strange things. I remember Mama D describing how scenes move toward or away from a person, and it wasn't that. It was like... I was seeing things that I only imagined, or... that don't exist, somehow. Does that make any sense?"

Armand twisted his mustache to a different calibration and studied her closely. "Give me an example."

"Well, for instance, I saw a man floating in space with glass eyes."

"Fascinating," Armand said quietly. "What did he look like?"

"I'm not sure. I didn't even see his face, but somehow I knew it was a man. At first, I was scared of him, then I was scared *for* him. I don't know, it may have just been a hallucination."

"And his eyes where glass, you say?"

"Yes, well... maybe not glass, but they sparkled, like the stars."

"Really? What else?"

"I don't know, just a bunch of weird images. What do you think they were?"

Armand puffed at his pipe thoughtfully and considered Del carefully again.

"She's got da sight," Frank said from his sleeping-chair. "Simple as dat."

Armand thought he was correct, and nodded his agreement.

Del accepted this conclusion as fact. She now knew that it was true, although she didn't know how to interpret most of what she'd seen.

"Can I speak with you both downstairs?" she asked.

The two men followed her without question, which was soon to become the norm.

*

The small group sat around the kitchen table and waited for Del to start. The two men had cooked up a late brunch while Mama Dedé and Jo had rummaged through the upstairs closets, forming interim wardrobes for themselves.

Finally, Del spoke.

"I need to say something, then I need to ask for something."

The group waited in reverence.

"I have to apologize to each of you, but for different reasons."

She looked at Frank first. "I'm sorry for all the times I dismissed your concerns, when I didn't believe you. I do now."

She turned and looked at Mama Dedé. "I'm sorry for not listening to your instructions earlier. I... I thought I would just play along with this *Voodoo stuff* and get past this and go on with my life. I know now that this *is* my life."

She looked at Armand. "I'm sorry for dismissing you in the

beginning, as well. I thought your stories were crazier than Frank's."
Armand nodded some agreement to this.

"And for you," she said, turning to Jo, "I want to apologize for taking something without asking." Jo wrinkled her face in question. "The last day I saw you… at the orphanage," Jo's face lit up with the warm thought of Del's touch, "I took a strand of hair without you knowing it." Del watched the wheels turn on Jo's face until realization dawned across it in painful waves.

Jo swallowed hard at the feeling of being pulled toward Del that day, but now felt an equally strong revulsion.

Quietly Jo said, "You… you needed it to control me, didn't you?"

Del nodded.

"And… when the house burned…"

Del nodded again.

"You lost it in the fire."

"Yes."

Waves of confusion crashed over Jo as she suddenly realized the smell of the sausage grease and cigar smoke was turning her stomach sour. It surely wasn't what Del had just said to her, because she didn't care what Del said. It had been a stupid schoolyard crush in a terrible place, where no one cared about anyone anyway, so nothing about Del mattered. It never did. Her breakfast started to come up, but she held it back.

"Jo, please, I want you to understand—"

Jo waved her off and stood up. Her legs almost betrayed her, but if she could survive the Crow, she could survive Del. She willed steel to flow into her veins, which hardened her against the betrayal. She squeezed the muscles in her legs as tightly as possible to steady herself against the hurricane force of Del's words. "Excuse me," she said, nodding to an impossible understanding, and smiled weakly at the dishes on the table. She left the kitchen and went upstairs to her temporary room. She had to leave this place as soon as possible.

After a long uncomfortable pause, Del looked up from the table and let each person inspect the shame in her eyes. She exposed it for all to see and did not hide it. She cleared her throat and said, "Now I need to ask something of each of you."

The group looked from one to the other and waited for the request. "What would dat be, Del-bell?" Frank said.

"I need a hair from each one of you."

The room fell silent.

"You do?" Frank mumbled past his cigar, with wide eyes.

"Yes. The Gris-gris man is coming for me and Jimmy; for all of us actually. I need to meet him before he is at full strength. And I'll need you all to come with me. I think you each have a part to play."

"We do?" Frank said.

"Yes. Marie showed me each of your faces this morning."

"You heard from Marie?" It was Mama Dedé's turn to be surprised. "Thank da Lord! Did she give you da unbinding spell?"

Del shook her head slowly.

"No? Then how we suppo—"

"She won't give it," Del said.

Mama Dedé tried to shake the confusion from her head. "What do you mean 'she won't give it'? She unbound him once before. It's da only thing we have to—"

"She says the words are too dangerous to be upon the wind. We are to go and meet the Gris-gris man and she'll deliver the—"

"More dangerous than da binding spell?" Mama Dedé stood up and stalked the kitchen. "We got half da damn binding spell suddenly been found. Who knows where da last part is, what can be worse than that?"

Del twisted in her chair, then finally said, "I don't think she'll give it to *me* for some reason."

Mama Dedé looked at her from across the room. "Why you think that? You a Laveau honey, you—"

"I don't think she trusts me with it," Del said quietly.

"What? Why, that's a bunch of nonsense. You kin and—"

"I don't think she trusts me with it because there's something wrong with me. There's something else that I don't know about myself."

"Well… now I just… I just don't know why that would be." The woman sank back down in her chair.

"I think I'll find out tonight," Del said.

"Tonight?" Frank said. "Why to—"

"We have to call the Gris-gris man tonight. We can't wait any longer, which brings me back to my request. I need a hair from each of you."

"And why is dat again?"

"So I can control you when the Gris-gris man comes."

CHAPTER 56

L ater that day, Frank and Armand sat in the second-floor
library quietly smoking. Earlier in the day, Frank had driven
home and grabbed his second pistol. He cleaned each one
thoroughly as he sat next to the roaring fire.

Despite the afternoon hour, the house was dark from the
oppressive clouds. The rain was threatening another downpour. The
Number One power station had flooded the night before and plunged
a large section of the city into darkness, sending a feeling of complete
isolation over the drowning city.

Armand settled his mind by rummaging through old manuscripts.
He had resigned himself to the fact that a magic bullet was not in his pile
of worn and smelly books. He looked at the mountainous shelves and
suddenly felt silly and small. How could he imagine fighting an ancient
spirit with these books? He shook his head and joined Frank by the fire.

Frank puffed a large cloud of smoke into a perfect ring and sent it
Armand's way. When Armand looked up, Frank quietly pushed the
second revolver to him.

"Der's da safety," he said. "Keep it in your pocket just in case. I doan know what we're fixin' to see out der tonight."

"Thank you, mon ami. I wish I had something to give you. A good luck charm or... something. Alas, all these things," he pointed around the room, "and not an amulet in sight."

Mama Dedé puffed to the top of the stairs. "Ooo, wee! Frenchy... we gonna... have to put my... room on da bottom! These stairs... like to kill me!"

She sat down heavily in front of the fire.

"What were you sayin' about an amulet?" she said.

"Well, I was just thinking—"

But then a small cloth bag landed on his lap. "Here's your good luck charm, Frenchy. Put it around your neck."

Armand's eyes sparkled at the gift as he gently inspected the bag.

"I'd hate for somethin' to happen to that handsome mustache tonight."

Another bag landed on Frank's stomach, causing him to ash cigar sparks in all directions.

"Now Frank, don't go and burn up all da good luck I just made for ya."

"No, no, not at all," he said, smiling. "Much appreciated."

"Well, these will help, but they ain't magic bullets," she said. "I don't know what we're fixin' to see tonight, but you two managed to not get your brains et out da other night, so there's still some hope for you."

"Indeed," Armand said proudly as he inspected himself in the mirror over the mantle. The gris bag hung prominently around his neck.

"Jo's gone," Del said suddenly from the hall.

Frank looked up in awe as he watched yet another version of Del emerge from the dark. The orphan girl with the tattered jean jacket and sneakers was gone, she was transforming. She now stood before them nearly complete. *Del the Spirit Hunter,* Frank thought.

Having rummaged through the closets, Del had replaced her worn sneakers and tee-shirt with used but sturdy knee-high brown leather boots; jeans and white shirt; a well-used leather motorcycle jacket and a loose tignon to tie her hair back. Several protective amulets and a small silver cross hung around her neck. Mama Dedé had already drawn a protective symbol—a veve, the woman had called it—onto the back of the jacket with a pen knife and bleach so it would never come off.

Frank whistled his awe. He thought the young girl had become a beautiful young woman overnight.

Mama Dedé looked upon a woman who had been cast into hardness by an unnatural process. An *unraveling* that most could not survive; tempered by unnatural forces. The problem with tempering, she thought, was if it was done too quickly or at too high a temperature, it made the item dangerously unstable; the slightest imperfection would eventually cause a fatal break. She thought briefly of the black essence that had once swirled around the Del-orb, and wondered where those imperfections had settled.

Del looked over the group, then opened her jacket and took a gris bag from around her neck. She walked to Mama Dedé first, who—without asking—pulled an old gray hair from her head and said, "I freely give this." She then turned to Armand who did the same and said, "I freely give this. Use it wisely."

Del then turned to Frank, who had watched the others with surprise. So willingly they gave themselves over to Del. Why was that, he wondered?

Frank stammered a weak question: "So… what you gonna… why you need dis again?"

"When we see him tonight," Del began, "and we will see him. He won't be alone. I can sense others that surround him. And you've already seen a few of his creations. I'll be trancing, and while I am, with these hairs, I can best protect you all if I can control you to some degree. However, it will be difficult to protect myself, which is why I need you all there."

Frank ignored the questioning glance that Armand sent his way. From time to time, throughout their long friendship, Armand had done that, Frank remembered. He turned his attention back to Del.

"Do you know da spell yet?"

Del shook her head no.

"Mon ami?" Armand prompted.

Frank ignored him.

"Please, Frank," Del said. "It's important that you trust me."

After an uncomfortably long pause, Frank plucked a gray and black hair and muttered, "I give it," then placed it in the bag.

"Thank you," Del said.

"What about Jo?" Frank asked.

"She left sometime after breakfast," Del said quietly. "I went up to her room to apologize again, but she was gone. I was hoping to... well, it doesn't matter now."

"She didn't leave a note?" Mama Dedé asked.

"No, just this." Del held up a hairbrush.

The same question passed between the group in an instant, but remained unspoken, for speaking of such a delicate thing could change its very nature.

As the silence settled and the flames waited in anticipation, Del finally spoke.

"It's time to find the Gris-gris man."

CHAPTER 57

The group arrived at the St. Louis Cemetery #1 shortly after 7:00 pm. With them they carried the few items they thought would be of use: pistols, gris bags, torches, and a life-altering belief in Del.

They stood at the main gate and quickly reviewed the plan again; Del would trance and communicate with Marie. The unbinding spell would be delivered, at least they were all trusting that it would be; Mama Dedé would trance and watch over Del; Frank and Armand would watch over them.

The cemetery had been pitch-black for days due to the loss of the Number One power station. The men set up the torches and lit them as the two women drank the bitter tea from a thermos and prepared. As the torches shone against the sharp stone corners of the dead, Del nodded to cach person, then walked to the large double crypt at the rear of the cemetery. Marie had given her a picture of it in her last trance. It was the crypt of Jean Montanee, aka Dr. John, and now served the Gris-gris man. An unholy creation looked down from the top of the crypt, watching her with stone eyes.

Mama Dedé quickly laid down a large circle of brick dust around the group using the torch circumference as a rough outline. She didn't have much, and cursed herself for not thinking to bring more.

Silent against the dreadnight, Eddie vibrated in anticipation.

Del knocked three times on the chamber door—per Marie's ghostly instructions—and stepped back inside the dust circle in the center of the cemetery. There she waited.

The fat black clouds were the first to respond. With a purpose that could only be described as *unnatural,* they sank close to the cemetery walls and formed a soft but ominous ceiling just over their heads. They rolled in agitation; a stomach lining black with cancer turned inside out. They dripped heavy raindrops that sizzled just outside the circle of torchlight like acid drops.

A crack of thunder—far off but echoing near—announced the coming of the strange man and his family of abominations. Things had been set in motion now that could not be undone.

Del suddenly felt rushed. Things weren't supposed to happen this fast, she thought. She still needed time to get fully into her trance. She looked around and saw that Mama Dedé was already standing quietly in the center of the dead, swaying slightly in the wind, chanting to herself. She had to hurry.

She closed her eyes and concentrated. An instant later she was hovering above her own body, and could see the ghostly horrors of the cemetery. The dead were coming out to watch.

The dead of the cemetery showed themselves in fits and starts— long dead fireflies from another time, blinking in and out of existence. Barely visible to Del's powerful inner sight, they looked like bleached, tattered leaves—ancient and fearful of something worse than death—

skittering around on the last day before winter. Brittlely dry, their life-well long run out, they chittered at the night and clung with fragile hope to the life-breath that Del and the others expelled, hoping desperately for one last taste of the living.

A dark raven manipulated the rising winds and lit on the bust of the grotesque that would watch forever in silence. The raven would hear its song once more before the night was through.

Del watched as the tattered spirits jockeyed for position just outside the magic circle of dust. Her trancing vision was different this time. She saw the strong aura of her friends pulse from their bodies in real time. It was as if she was looking at them with her eyes and mind at the same time. The heartbeat of their essence pulsed white, but with the faintest red-blue shift depending on if they were swaying by millimeters towards her or away. She was hyper tuned to every movement around her.

A low rusty creak announced the opening of the cemetery gate. The Gris-gris man had arrived.

The low, fat clouds twisted in anticipation of unleashing the storm that was building. A rumble, or growl, began low in the ground and rippled upward through the old cobblestones and escaped into the waiting clouds. The shock wave sent dust flying and vibrated the grains of red brick dust, distorting the shape of the protective circle. For now, it held.

Del began to spin in her mind, slowly at first, cautiously checking her newfound power. This allowed her to watch in all directions at once; the Del-orb, like a three-dimensional radar, sampling the life forces around her many times a second.

"Good evening, Delphine... ...elphine... ...evening... ...elphine." The voice echoed and bounced off the hard edges of the crypts and disoriented the group.

"Thank you for calling me... ...alling me... ...thank you... ... alling me."

Frank and Armand turned in a slow circle around the trancing women, looking for the source of the sound. They held torches in one hand and pistols in the other. All they saw was the black swirling mist.

"Thank you for bringing your friends to me... ...to me... ... bringing your friends... thank you for bringing..."

"Don't listen to him," Del broadcast into the minds of her friends. "He's lying and trying to trick you."

"On the contrary my dear... ...the contrary... ...my dear... I was clear with my deal... ...honest... ...clear with my deal... Three souls for the price of one... ...price of one... ...three souls... ...and you get Jo back... ...Jo back... ...you get..."

"That's not true! He's lying! Don't listen to him!"

"My dear... ...my dear... You're wearing gris bags... ...gris bags... ...the same as I... ...same as I... ...gris bags...

"But alas... ...alas... Mine don't have... ...don't have... ...the hairs of my friends... ...hairs of my friends... ...don't have... ...lying within... ...within..."

The Del-orb spun, watching the scene unfold below her. She saw the Gris-gris man at the main gate of the cemetery, but he looked different from the auras of her friends. In her trancing mind he looked not like a person, but a cloud of competing light; images struggling with each other for domination. He was a menagerie of souls, the essence of many, trying to take a dominant position within the vessel they were bound to. His essence was chaos.

Del saw the blue shift of his essence a fraction of a second before it split into pieces. One second, he was a cloud of competing color, the next, he had split into two: a man-sized shape and something slightly smaller, but in many ways more deadly. The strange man and beast formed out of the split and began to walk the cemetery.

Frank saw the beast first and raised his pistol, but the unholy thing faded back into the cloud that protected it. They now had a special relationship, Frank and the beast. One killing the other tonight was the only option.

Armand saw the mist swirl on the opposite side of the cemetery. They were being surrounded. A man-shaped figure hung just beyond the unnatural clouds. He could make out a silhouette; a hunched man leaning to one side; a walking stick in support; an old hat; blue reflections where the eyes should be. *How strange*, Armand thought. *Man... hunched man... dog? No not dog... beast? Yes, beast... Voodoo... spirits... Egypt? Maybe... Africa? Yes... Oh, what fools we have been.*

He feared they had made a terrible mistake.

CHAPTER 58

Mama Dedé searched and searched but couldn't find Marie. She was trancing alongside Del. She knew what was beginning to happen, but she had to find Marie and the unbinding spell. She couldn't understand why it had not been given to Del, unless... No, Del would never betray them. She knew the Gris-gris man was tricky; she had been warning them all along. Del wouldn't betray them.

Del was trancing differently than she had been taught. Mama Dedé only knew of one way, but Del's mind was in two places at once. She could see the silver droplets of Del around the cemetery scene that she herself was trancing on, but also knew that Del was simultaneously in another place. Where that place was, she didn't know.

The massive Del-orb she had seen reforming the day before was truly beautiful and terrible all at once. She just hoped that whatever powers Del had suddenly found didn't completely overwhelm the person she had been.

Mama Dedé turned her attention back to the cemetery scene just as a blue-shift formed around the Gris-gris man—something was about to happen. Even though she knew Armand was looking in the right direction, she caused a small light to flash in Armand's mind at the feet of the man, pulling his attention down. Just as she did, Armand saw four nearly invisible shadows fall from the man and scurry into the darkness. Armand heard a faint *tica-tica-tica-tica* in his mind as the abominations skittered into position. He gave a mental *Thank you.* He assumed that Mama D could somehow sense his appreciation.

A crack of lightning split the dark clouds somewhere over the Jean Lafitte swamp, briefly illuminating the dark cemetery. Armand looked to his right and the image of the ugliest gargoyle he had ever seen was silhouetted and burned into his mind as if from a camera flash. The gargoyle, perched on top of the oversized crypt Del had knocked on, seemed to be watching the unholy scene unfold, and for the briefest second Armand imagined that the eyes glowed slightly with an unnatural lust.

Somewhere in the dark the beast breathed its ragged breath. Frank thought he could make out steam trails floating up from its back, despite the cold, heavy mist that weighed against it. A large head hung low and huffed at the ground. Long trails of slobber hung glistening from its jowls as it anticipated its next meal.

"Delphine, my love... ...my love... ...elphine...

"It doesn't have to be this way... ...doesn't... ...this way...

"Join back with us... ...join back... ...your family is waiting... your family... ...for you to come back... ...come back..."

"Don't listen, honey," Mama Dedé said to everyone. "He's a tricky ol' bastard! You ain't part of his family."

Del spun faster, watching the spirits come and go. She had no idea why they had all gathered there, but the cemetery was full of them. It was becoming difficult to tell which spirits had been buried there and which were from the Gris-gris man.

"Oh, but she is, you see… …you see… …she is…

"Marie and I had become one you see… …become one you see… …offspring… …yes, offspring… …yes… was spread across this land… …offspring spread…

"Over the years the sibling lines crossed… …over the years… … yes, the lines crossed… and Del became the one… …yes, became the one… Del is the one…

"Who can harness the power… …the power… …she can harness… from both of us… …she can harness… …is the one…

"For we are elemental… …elemental… …for we… and become like Gods… …we become like Gods… …are elemental… …like Gods…"

Mama Dedé felt a heaviness grow over her as she watched the scene. Every time the words echoed on the wind, Del's essence quivered and changed by the slightest degree. The silver droplets of Del were as liquid, highly sensitive to the man's words, and responded in an unconscious way. The black streaks were a permanent part of Del now. Whether they were trying to surface or not, the woman couldn't tell.

A frantic skittering sound drew Armand's attention to the left, then to the right. He saw fleeting glimpses of the weasels as they ran from one shadow to the next. Their slender, six-legged bodies squeezing around corners and between stones as if they had no structure. They gnashed their sharp beaks at each other when they collided, then gnashed at the cobblestone. They were claws and beaks with a rudimentary brain stem.

Frank tracked the beast the best he could, but was distracted by the

Gris-gris man's words. *Del was the descendent of both him and Marie?* What sort of cosmic alignment was needed to bring the lines of brother and sister—or more likely, half-brother and sister—back together after several generations to create the perfect Voodoo priestess? And what sort of inherent evils came with the bloodline? The wind howled an answer and stung Frank's face with sharp bits of debris and sand in reprimand of his blasphemous thoughts. *And they become like Gods*, Del had said once without knowing why. The Gris-gris man had just said that. Maybe they were more aligned than Frank realized. He wanted to shoot and kill every supernatural thing in this cemetery, but didn't have the ammunition or time. He felt his opportunity slipping away. Another crack of lightning lit the cemetery. The ground shuddered and Frank watched as the protective circle of brick dust vibrated again, scattering the grains slightly further apart. A few more vibrations like that and the circle would be unrecognizable. He wasn't sure how much power the brick dust had, but decided he didn't want to wait until it was completely gone to find out. Mama Dédé saw his blue-shift movement right before he made it. She yelled a warning, but he was still fast for his age. The pistol shot rang out, and an instant later Del fell to the ground. The lifeblood of Del the Spirit Hunter dripped into the dry lifeless bricks of the St. Louis Cemetery #1.

The Del-orb wobbled from the wound, but continued to spin, caught by surprise by the unexpected shot. The spirits of the cemetery and the weasels of hell smelled the blood—for it was upon the wind— and went into a frenzy. They gnashed at each other, at shadows, at the wind, and skittered toward the fresh blood. The red brick dust held its own. The insane weasels ran straight for Del, but were repelled with the faintest shock of static electricity by whatever force the old woman had coaxed into the circle of dust. They gnashed their beaks at the surprise, ran back to the cover of shadow, then ran at the circle again, only to be repelled with a faint flash of light. Each flash of light produced a mild electric shock that singed the unholy flesh of the abominations, and the smell of burnt flesh drifted on the air. Frank couldn't see the other spirits, but felt their plan was quickly unraveling. The ground trembled again as the bellowing laughter of the Gris-gris man shook the night air. Hell was opening upon the cemetery.

CHAPTER 59

T he beast howled an angry warning and stood on its hind legs. Slamming its heavy paws onto the cobblestones, Frank had the ludicrous thought of a child's toy gone mad; a possessed rocking-horse with a deformed doll strapped to its back. Only the doll appeared to come to life each time the beast slammed its paws down. A strangled, glottal sound squeezed out of the mutant thing; first a *glla-glgu-glla* followed by a *ngyihng, ngyihng* as the thing sparked to life each time the beast lurched forward.

Frank fired again, this time hitting the stony ground in front of the beast. The bullet ricocheted and nicked the leg of the beast, sending it into a wild frenzy. The beast leaped straight into the air, landing on all fours, and screamed a blood-curdling howl. The energy from the beast surged up through the long needle, sparking the mutant to life, and sent it spinning crazily on its metal axis. The mutant screamed its mad gibberish into the night air, spewing ancient and foul curses. At the same time, Frank noticed another small doll—even tinier than the mutant—that swung wildly under the beast's neck. The tiny, broken doll with one open eye seemed to come to life with the violent energy that pulsed off the beast as well. The red-headed Sharon-doll screamed at the night and everything that had been done to it.

All the dead things were screaming.

Mama Dedé saw that Del had fallen, and came out of her trance. She moved to her side and inspected the wound.

"Frank, what'd you do?" she yelled.

"Where da hell is dat spell?" Frank yelled back. "Da brick line is failin!"

Mama Dedé had known the brick line was failing before Frank had announced it, but didn't have the spell. She lied to him and said, "It's comin' Frank, but what—"

"Watch the weasels!" Armand yelled and fired a ricocheting shot at a moving shadow. The hellish thing scampered sideways with the speed of a spider, legs lightning fast, then skittered a sideways path around the dust circle. The abominations chittered to each other, looking for a break in the dust circle.

The wounded body of Del lay in the center of the chaos as the Del-orb spun faster and faster, trying to get ahead of the melee. She felt the spell was coming, but couldn't understand why it hadn't been given to her directly.

"You're bleeding my love… …my love… …you're bleeding…

"Your friend shot you… …your friend… …tried to kill you… …kill you… …friend shot you…

"I'll punish him for you Del… …punish him… …Del I'll punish… …if you send him to me… …send him to me… …punish him… …you have the power… …the power… …you have the power… …don't forget the hair… …his hair… …send him… …send him… …send him…"

Frank heard the ominous commands and spun around, looking wildly into the night. The wind howled the haunted voice and carried it like a plague. The foul breath of the hellish spirit was upon the wind, and it stank like death. The living in the cemetery shrank from the stench; the dead reveled in it.

The beast watched the confusion pass through the small group and stalked closer.

The Gris-gris man circled the group slowly, fading in and out of the fog. Blue mirrored glasses wavering with tremors of excitement.

The weasels skittered in and out of the dark shadows, waiting for a chance to pass the circle. Waiting for a chance to feed.

Eddie vibrated silent signals to his master. The fear in the group was sweet and pungent.

Then someone spoke the words:

"Hellish spirit hear me clearly, grant you now full use or nearly,

Of my soul for use and toiling, at the work of evil lore.

This damned soul is ripe for taking; in its core with trembled shaking,

Hunger-lust pang never slaking, begging at your ghostly door.

Use me spirit, just tonight, that I may unlock Abgel's door;

Just tonight, no less, no more."

"Who said that?" Mama Dedé yelled. She was no longer trancing and couldn't tell. "Armand?"

"I hear it, but I don't know where it came from," he yelled. "It's a different voice."

Eddie vibrated on high. "Sing," came a raven-voice in his head, and Eddie's stone mouth sang in unison with the wind-voice.

"I call to you, by way of chanting—lest a demon voice be ranting,

Ranting in my wretched mind, to call you up from days of yore.

I summon you to evil deed, your voice as one my mind will heed,

Seeking someone sure to bleed, to right a wrong done to my core.

Use me spirit, just tonight, that I may open abGel's door,

Just tonight, no less, no more."

The Del-orb spun through a thousand scenarios. Scenes of red and blue flew past her mind. She searched for the right combination, but there were too many choices. Too many things were happening at once, and she didn't know which to choose or who to control. She was losing the battle.

The wind picked up the words and now several voices sang in unison. The third stanza of the unholy spell was spoken.

"With demon-will I wholly bind, your tattered soul, black heart and mind,

To me you see, for I am kind except to those I doth abhor.

Evil things were done to me, but no worse evil can there be,

To that which I will die to see, unleashed from beyond abgEL's door.

Unlock it spirit, I beseech, for I deserve revenge galore…

Just one night? Not evermore?"

As the third stanza was set upon the wind, a deep groan let out from the oversized crypt. The ancient granite shuddered and rumbled; the dust of the dead was caught up in the hell-wind and thrown away; tension twisted in the old stones until the seal gave way. With an explosion of rotting death air, the chamber door opened.

Peering into the crypt, Armand only saw a dark void. Its sheer blackness felt heavy and empty, as if a great gravity lay just beyond; a gravity that you could never escape from.

"There he is!" Mama Dedé yelled, pointing to a different part of the cemetery. As the others followed her finger, they saw the source of the new voice. On top of the cemetery wall stood Henri Guillaume. He was reading from an old grimoire as he held Jimmy by the collar.

The Gris-gris man bellowed a wild laugh that bordered on hysteria at the sight of the police captain and his captive. He knew the blank one was somehow the key.

Jimmy stood barely balancing on the tall cemetery wall. Henri had climbed him up on top of his car, parked outside the wall, and hoisted him up the rest of the way to have an advantaged view. He was a cold and miserable sight. His pajamas were nearly one color of dirt brown, and he shivered with a deep, bone-shaking cold. One house shoe was missing and the other—a badly stained Bugs Bunny—looked like it had been dragged out of the swamp. Tears of pain and confusion streamed down his face as he looked upon the chaos. His first sight was of Del lying on the cold ground.

"You found him... ...found him... ...you found... ...the blank one... ...blank one..."

"Dat sumbitch!" Frank yelled, seeing Henri standing upon the wall. "I knew it!"

"Bring him to me... ...to me... ...bring him..."

The weasels grew bold at the distraction and ran, snapping at the circle. In some places the dust had almost blown away completely and they tested its fading power.

Frank swung his pistol around and centered it on Henri. The tearing winds blew dust at his eyes. He couldn't get a clear bead.

"No," Del's voice rocked in his head. "Wait."

Del? Del, is dat you?

Suddenly Frank felt himself walking when he'd never planned to. Like synchronized dancers, he and Armand exchanged places without a word. Mama Dedé grabbed a torch, and with Armand began swinging at the weasels.

Armand raised his pistol just off his hip and put his finger to the trigger. His mind was occupied by swinging the torch with his left hand, so he never noticed his right arm moving. Suddenly a shot rang out as he pulled the trigger involuntarily. The head of a weasel exploded as it jumped into the shot path just as Armand squeezed the trigger.

The Gris-gris man, the beast and the two dead dolls all screamed when the weasel exploded. Each one of them felt the pain differently, but they were all grievously wounded.

A second weasel went mad and spun in a circle just long enough for Mama Dedé to smash it over the head with a heavy torch. Its neck snapped, but the unholy beak continued to open and close, searching for prey. She pressed down hard with the flaming torch. A thick scent of burning flesh rose in the air as she seared its head from its body. The Gris-gris man shuddered again and trembled.

"READ!" he screamed at Henri. With a silent command, he called his hellish family to retreat to his side. The beast howled its anger, but retreated into the shadows and ran around the outside of the circle. The weasels skittered back as well; *tica-tica-tica-tica* floating on the wind.

"Sing!" Del said inside Jimmy's head.

Jimmy looked around stunned, hearing Del's voice but not knowing where it came from. He began to cry harder. He thought Del was dead.

Henri oddly held the grimoire, not tight against the blasting wind, but lightly like a waiter carrying a delicate soufflé. Strangely, the book did not tip from his outstretched hand, nor did the pages flutter wildly. He didn't know how the book worked, but knew he had to be patient.

It was as if an unseen presence was turning the pages and reading the book to him. He felt the final words of the spell would soon be exposed; the voice on the wind had been reliable to this point.

Del cast a vision into Jimmy's mind: bees; Jimmy hated bees. He swung his arms wildly, trying to make them fly away. He had no idea why bees would be out on a night like this. He didn't like them because he was afraid of being stung, but then he heard Del tell him to be brave.

"Bwave da 'ion?"

"Yes, brave like a lion," Del said.

Without thinking, Jimmy swatted at the imaginary bees that had just flown in front of Henry and smacked him hard in the groin. Henri let out a groan and doubled over. Grabbing at Jimmy for balance, the large man toppled forward as Jimmy fell backwards.

"Jimmy!" Del yelled, as the sound of banging metal echoed over the wall.

Henri fell and rolled, jamming his shoulder into the hard cemetery floor, but kept hold of the grimoire. He stood up and walked out of the crypt shadows, looking for enough light to see the spell once it was exposed to him.

"Jimmy," Del said, more quietly this time. From her trance, she had watched him hit the top of Henri's car and roll to the ground. She knew he was badly bruised, but this was the last chance they had. She had seen every option possible, she had tranced on every scenario, and this was it. She had to get Jimmy to sing.

Del watched the unfolding scene, manipulated the group and spoke to Jimmy simultaneously. She directed Frank and Armand to fan out slightly, instead of standing directly between her prone body and the Gris-gris man. She knew where the beast would run next, but too many variations were nearly the same shade of blue in her mind, so she couldn't see exactly which would happen next, thereby negating a scene just a second behind it.

"Sing, Jimmy," Del coaxed. "I know you know it. Sing the secret song. But you have to be really quiet."

Jimmy leaned against the back of the car, listening to Del. He didn't know any secret songs, unless the song kept itself a secret from him, but he was pretty sure that was a different thing. "I doan know a—"

"Shhh…" she whispered to him. "Just speak to me in your head, Jimmy. Just think the words to me."

Jimmy thought of the made-up song he had been singing ever since he'd left the orphanage. Like a lot of songs, this one had popped into his head and never left, but he didn't understand the words.

Da ph'gn mglwa song?

"Yes! That's—" she almost shouted. *Yes, that's the one. Hurry!*

The Gris-gris man heard Del speak to Jimmy, and with a silent command sent the last two weasels up over the wall.

Armand, not knowing why he did it, picked up a handful of rocks and threw them over the crypt, away from Jimmy, sending the raven squawking into the wind. Little echoes of sound reverberated down the alleyway on the other side of the wall. The weasels, just topping the wall, skittered down the other side and blindly followed the false sounds, looking for running prey.

OK, Jimmy, now quiet as a mouse. Sing the secret song for me, Del spoke in his head.

Quiet da' mouse, Jimmy thought, and began to sing.

The words of the song were ancient words. To human ears they sounded glottal and phlegmy.

Ph'ng bwahla gwyhb'll uhl, Pk'yn vhmoha dwb'll duhl…

But to the creatures of the night, it was the sound of their undoing, for this was the *Unbinding Spell*, spoken in its most ancient form.

"Alas, what is that?" the old man screamed. "What is that sound?!"

No one in the cemetery heard the ancient song except Del and the Gris-gris man. Everyone else was focused on their mortal enemy, and who would make the next move.

Henri emerged from the dark shadows, waiting for the last verse of the hidden spell to be exposed. This was the *Binding Spell*, which was never meant to be found again, and had been kept secret until the unfortunate day when someone read from a book they didn't understand.

As the first syllable of the first word of the last part of the spell was uttered upon the wind, the dark void within the crypt began to turn. No one noticed.

Jimmy, quietly singing his song, had a sudden vision of the dream where he saw Del's reflection in the pond. He saw the small water bug create the whirlpool that grew larger and larger until it threatened to swallow her up. He didn't know why, but he felt the whirlpool had just come back.

CHAPTER 60

*Just one night not surely just, for break and maim and
kill I must;*

  *With this new power all will see, that hell hath come
upon their door.*

Henri heard the first two lines of the last verse spoken into
his head as the words appeared to him in the book. The
voices in his head were many. The voices that had exposed
the spell to him, who had driven his actions the entire time, who hated
him now but couldn't look away, those voices were many, and they
were upon the wind. Those voices would finish the spell, he knew. If
they could only do it in time.

The Gris-gris man, hearing both spells being spoken, panicked at
the slightest hint of the Unbinding Spell being cast, and tore at his
overcoat to get to his gris bags.

"Don't read that book!" Mama Dedé yelled, and ran at Henri. As
he walked into the dim light of the torches, she saw that he was a

man, not only possessed, but cursed at the same time. The same rash that affected Eddie and Sharon had started on Henri as a small fever blister. Forming near the point of sin-origin, the rash had spread out like a plague—a scarlet signal drawing attention to the source—and infected his mouth, throat and tongue. It had eaten through his right cheek and spread up to his eye, which hung nearly out of its socket. His tongue—working desperately to form the words he had killed to find, words that would bind him permanently to unnatural power—fought to stay inside his mouth, and in his frenzy, slipped out of the hole in his cheek, lolling crazily down the side of his face like a carnival mask.

> *I freely spill this blood of mine, and with a drop, do fully bind,*
> *My tattered soul, black heart and mind, to abgeL's beyond the door.*

As the words appeared, he pulled a small knife from his belt. This was the moment he'd been waiting for. He repeated the words as they came into his head while running a knife down the left side of his face, slicing a large cut on his cheek bone. His blood had been spilt.

Mama Dedé was upon him, and swung the heavy torch at him as he pulled his head back, causing her to catch the right side of his face instead of his head. The flaming torch easily broke through the remaining shreds of cheek skin connecting his upper and lower lips and opened a wide mouth-hole in the side of his face. His tongue flew back into place, then lolled around like a flopping fish tail. He screamed in agony and swung a wild knife hand at her.

The void in the crypt spun faster. Small flecks of dust and debris began to shimmy on the three steps that led up to the unholy resting place. One by one, the flecks hovered at the balancing point of gravity, then like a magic trick, were sucked into the void and blinked out of existence with a tiny *snap.*

Jimmy silently sang his song from his hiding spot. He knew the void was getting bigger and he knew that it was coming after Del, but she had told him to sing, so sing he did.

Frank and Armand stared in disbelief as the Gris-gris man dropped his long overcoat and searched his gris bags. Having thought the man clothed with an old brown shirt, the men were shocked to see that he was clothed with nothing more than old leather gris bags that hung over bumpy brown skin—infected and leaking. The same brown skin covered the mutant, but seemed to be in a constant state of sloughing off the old man. It was as if he was regenerating and melting at the same time.

"Oh hell," Frank muttered as he raised his gun and fired. Several shots hit the man, but seemed to have no real affect. Pieces of flesh were blown into the wind and carried away, but they melted back together just as quickly.

With a flinch of his hand, the beast leapt to the man's side just as he yanked a gris bag from around his neck. He grabbed the mutant Toth on its long needle and tossed the gris bag into the air. As the men watched the gris bag defy gravity in the neutral balance between the void and ground, the man yanked the needle from the spine of the beast and hurled it—with an inanimate Toth—toward the men. They didn't see it until it was too late.

Del's body lay helpless in the cemetery as her mind saw the ploy a second too late. She sent the warning to the men just as the gris bag was sucked into the void and exploded out of existence with an ear-popping sound.

Free of the mutant, the beast leapt a crazy leap and covered ten feet in the space of a second, just as Del's warning hit Frank's mind. He looked up in time to push Armand to the side as he thrust his pistol in the air and fired.

The airborne Toth—like a well-placed missile—sailed through the air and stuck inches deep into Armand's shoulder as he fell away from Frank and the beast. Armand screamed in pain and horror, sending a new jolt of life-energy into the mutant thing. Toth sprang to life and screamed in unison. With this new source of energy, a new magic happened. The face of Toth changed; the sewn red-bead eyes came to life and stared into Armand's face; like a newborn seeing the face of its mother for the first time, Armand's face was burned upon the mind of Toth, and the mutant would never forget it. The mouth came to life and tried to suckle more life, but only knew how to gnash and bite. Armand felt the hot sting of its bite as Toth bit off the outer part of his right ear with the frantic sound of "Ngyihng! Ngyihng! Ngyihng!" The arms and legs came to life, moving where there had never been joints before. They flailed at him, groping, kicking, trying to cling to this new precious source of life; to crawl inside and live forever. The makeshift right foot, a rotting big toe having been pinned on by a rusty needle, flailed and kicked on mutant legs, catching Armand in the mouth. The big-toe foot tried a feeble grasp at his mustache and lip, but only managed to lose small bits of skin in the process.

Mama Dedé staggered back from the knife blow as they both fell to the ground. The book fell from Henri's hand with a heavy thud, but never lost its place, hellishly intent on being finished.

As the two foes crawled toward each other, Mama Dedé intent on burning the book with her torch, Henri resolved to see the final words appear and repeat them, they watched in awe and terror as the book moved.

From the frantic light of her torch, as if driven by unseen hands, they watched as the book turned its own page.

CHAPTER 61

My chanting, spirit, hear it right. Bind us now on equal shore.

This I pray, forever more.

The Binding Spell had been cast.

Henri had read the words.

The Gris-gris man laughed in ecstasy as a toothy, distorted grin stretched his face. He waited for the newly bound soul to join with him, making him whole again.

The words were now upon the wind, and would forever haunt those who uttered them. This thing could not be undone.

The black void in the crypt, spinning madly as the magic words fueled its existence, suddenly sparked to life with a violent flash of lightning. A great heat burst forth from the void and momentarily lit the hellish scene in the cemetery with a bright, hot light. Smoke and debris spun around the opening of the void, hanging in suspension, before being sucked out of existence. The violent winds of doom sucked at the air, pulling everything to it.

Del, watching the mad scene from her trance, became suddenly aware of a strange sensation. Her floating gimbal-mind was free, but was still aware of her physical body lying on the ground. Her body felt lighter as the void-winds sucked at her, threatening to pull her straight off the ground and into the black void of nothing. She was almost out of time.

"Sing, Jimmy!" she screamed into the air. "Sing loud!"

Jimmy had been faithfully singing in his head as he tried to block out the scary sounds of the cemetery. He had sung the song so many times, it was now on autopilot, and he couldn't stop it if he wanted to.

In his mind he saw the void open wider. To him it looked like the giant mouth of a monster, and it was trying to eat Del. It was trying to eat everything in the cemetery. The image of the monster mouth and the image of the whirlpool from his dream melted together into one scene. Suddenly, Jimmy saw the blue frog floating on the lily pad. He remembered watching the frog cling to the pad in his dream as the deep whirlpool inched closer and closer to the image of Del. Just as he had thought it would suck Del's image down, the frog jumped into the whirlpool and scared it away. Jimmy also remembered Del telling him that he needed to be brave like a lion. He knew what he needed to do.

Very carefully, Jimmy climbed onto the car and pulled himself to the top of the wall. Looking onto the chaotic scene, he saw Del lying on the ground and the whirlpool-void getting larger. It was about to suck her down.

As no one noticed, he slipped over the wall and landed hard on the ground, inside the cemetery. As the strange song ran through his head on autopilot, he coaxed himself along with Del's simple instructions.

"Bwave da 'ion, bwave da 'ion," he said as he crept forward.

*

Frank felt his left foot slide backward just as he pulled the trigger. The unexpected movement caused him to fall back slightly, altering his aim. Del had seen the arc the beast was yet to leap and knew that Frank's aim would be slightly off. She didn't know how much she could correct it, though.

It was an overcorrection.

The giant mouth of the beast closed over Frank's hand as the bullet exited the gun. The range was too close. A wide hole blew out the side of the beast's mouth and separated the left side of its jaw from the skull, but did not kill it. The powerful jaw hung loosely to its head by the remaining skin and tendons. The beast somersaulted over Frank's falling body, flipped in the air and landed unconscious on the ground.

The beast did not move.

The Gris-gris man froze in disbelief. One moment wild with elation, the next, paralyzed by fear and confusion. His family was slipping away from him.

Blinking his eyes clear, Frank looked up as the Gris-gris man convulsed violently, tossing the old hat from his head; blue mirrored glasses reflecting a chaotic scene.

Standing before them, shirtless and bald, a hunched figure stood on the precipice of non-existence. The old man's skin, brown and putrid, fought to regenerate itself. His head, now exposed to the feeble light of the night, was forever rotting away by a violent red rash. The rash had eaten away most of the skin and some of the skull, exposing a fetid blob of gray material that was itself an abomination; part man, part animal. Being fed by the completed binding spell, parts of him were regenerating from Henri's own essence, but Frank had the sense that he was one body occupied by competing forces. A thing in a constant state of change.

Armand screamed somewhere to Frank's left.

The more he screamed, the more Toth came to life. The more Toth came to life, the more it fought to claw its way inside. Its mother was here finally. Its mother with the beautiful, handsome mustache. It would love its mother forever, if it could just get inside.

Frank rolled to his side and saw the mutant Toth chewing at Armand's ear. The needle had sunk deep in Armand's shoulder, preventing him from raising his right arm. His left hand fought to pull the thing out, but each slight movement of the needle sent bolts of pain shooting into his body, rendering the attempt useless.

Frank grabbed the unholy thing and thought he heard a mad gibberish word of "nooo…" eek out of it just as he yanked it from Armand's shoulder. He threw the thing into the night and thought of it no more.

He turned back and looked at the Gris-gris man, who was rapidly changing. The strange man appeared to have a faint aura of blue surrounding him. It was if part of his essence was being blown away. He spun in a slow circle, both laughing and screaming at the words on the wind. Two spells had been unleashed onto the night. The Binding Spell and the ancient words of the Unbinding Song swirled simultaneously on the wind. They were never meant to be spoken at the same time.

Del watched from her trance and saw the horror of Henri's undoing before he realized he was doomed. The blue-shift scene in her mind showed the terrible events set into motion. Henri, thinking he had bound his essence to the spirit that controlled the gates of hell, was now loose upon the wind, as his host began to come undone as well.

Her body suddenly moved, pulling her mind away from the

trancing scene. She saw her arms lift slowly, pulled by the violent winds being sucked into oblivion, and now saw her own demise. She had lingered too long to save herself. The last trancing scene to cross her mind was her body lifting off the ground and disappearing into the black void with a spectacular explosion. Her mind went blank as she tried to regain control over her own body.

*

Jimmy crept forward. He was almost to the crazy, spinning man. "Bwave da 'ion," he kept repeating, although he now wondered if this wasn't just a dream. He had been lost from the orphanage for so long, and had had so many things pop into his head that it must be a crazy dream. Del had told him that there were no such things as wizards that eat your head, so he decided he must still be dreaming. And in his dream with the blue frog, the void went away after it hopped in, and that's when Jimmy woke up. He decided he would just hop into the void like the frog had done and end this crazy dream.

He broke his quiet cover and ran with a clumsy gait toward the void.

The Gris-gris man, disoriented and failing, heard the words of the Unbinding Spell come close to him, then pass him by. He spun in the direction of the words and reached into the shadows, grabbing at the wind. When he did, the blue mirrored glasses were thrown from his face and his true nature was exposed for all to see. The rash had not only eaten away the skin of his head and part of his skull, it had eaten his eyes first, for the Gris-gris man always looked upon the great sin of his own making and could see nothing else. He was blind without the beast, raven, or the other abominations he had created, and could not even look upon Jimmy with his mind. Jimmy was beyond his ability to see, for he had lived up to every bit of his potential.

Frank and Armand pulled Mama Dedé to her feet as Henri unraveled. He was still on his hands and knees when they had kicked the book away from him, hoping to stop the spell. They pulled her away as his skin flaked off in long, papery strips. He shuddered violently in his crawling pose; a strange mannequin searching for a lost item—a recently departed soul.

Frank saw the boy far too late to save him. He was running towards the void as Del's body began to lift off the ground. It was a slight motion, be he could see first her legs, then arms, float free trying to escape gravity.

CHAPTER 62

"Jimmy, no!" Frank heard from overhead. He looked up to see a girl running along the top of the cemetery wall. She was agile and quick and seemed to anticipate the odd motion of the boy, as if she had run after him before.

The girl hurdled the gap between the wall and the nearest crypt and launched herself in the air from its roof. She overtook Jimmy with her fall and knocked him flat.

"Ow, I feh down!" he yelled as he rolled to a stop.

Jo fell and rolled as she saw Del's body lifting from the ground. The beast, only a few feet away from Del, had just been sucked into the void, sending brilliant blue tendrils of essence flashing into the night. Somewhere behind her she heard the strange man scream as it snapped out of existence. Rocks and debris blew past her and into the void, each producing its own *un-existing* snap.

Del's body was pulled from the ground again, balancing on the tipping point of gravity, just as she fully came out of her trance and opened her eyes. The mouth of a cosmic void stared her in the face, and she saw into the other side. Her mind was overwhelmed, and went blank. The time and space of the void beyond expanded her mind; strange visions burned ancient knowledge into her mind, altering it forever; unimaginable monstrosities looked across the void and saw her existence—and they would never forget her.

As Del's body tipped forward, Jo hit her with a hard tackle, which flung the two girls back to the ground. They landed lightly as the void pulled at their bodies. Jo didn't notice the angry vortex pull at her frame. She only saw Del.

Del, knocked back into reality by the hard blow, saw the horrors of the universe slip away and become the glistening eyes of someone who had once trusted her, and now smiled at her again.

Jo hugged Del and pawed at her leather jacket, smoothing it as her feet floated off the ground, dangerously close to the event horizon of the void.

"Del, Del, are you hurt? Tell me you're OK."

"Jo, how… where did you come from?"

Jo unconsciously squirmed up Del's body as her legs kept floating off the ground.

"I came back. I came back to you, Del, and you were gone. You were all gone," she said breathlessly. She felt as if she were on a high mountain with very little oxygen.

The gris bags had already been pulled loose of the old man as he stumbled against the force of the cosmic wind. With Henri's essence spent, he was unbinding rapidly.

"Jo, I was looking for you, but we had to leave, we had to—"

"No, no, don't explain. I understand. I was looking for you, too." Jo clawed at the ground without realizing why. "At first, I didn't know where to go, but then I knew. I knew where to go, somehow. It was if—"

"Jo, what's wrong?" Del said.

Jo grabbed at Del's jacket.

"Del, I wanted to tell you—" She felt her legs lift completely off the ground, and realization crossed her face.

She clung to Del, but saw that she was pulling her off the ground as well. She didn't want to lose her again, and clung tightly.

With all the strength she had left, Jo pulled herself forward and clutched at Del's jacket. She pulled her face close, and while looking into the wild powerful eyes of the girl who had pushed her down once to protect a little boy, she kissed her, with open eyes. She wanted Del to be the last thing she saw.

Del reached out to Jo's face just as the deflating body of the Gris-gris man lost its balance and went skidding toward the void. The cosmic wind pulled him into the same path as the girls, and a flailing arm caught hold of Jo's ankle. The strange man had almost completely unraveled, but the sudden jolt was enough to break Jo's tenuous hold. Her hands released, breaking the kiss, just as Del reached for her face. The cosmic wind sucked her back and Del was left with a strand of hair fluttering between her fingers where Jo's face had just been.

The Gris-gris man and Jo fell into the void at the same time and snapped out of existence with a blinding flash of light. As the void snapped shut, blue tendrils of essence sparked off a dying existence and flew away into the night.

The cemetery fell silent as the dead things slunk away.

Thrown back to the ground as the void snapped shut, Del's mind closed around the last images she had seen: the cosmic horrors of the universe, and the eyes of her friend slipping into them. Those images splintered deep into her mind, and the shards would be left to fester forever.

Frank and Armand scanned the cemetery, then ran to Del and lifted her motionless body from the ground. The only sign of life they saw was a small trickle of blood from her nose.

Mama Dedé inspected Del and cast a quick healing spell over her. She didn't know what injuries Del had, but hoped the spell would hold until they got her home.

The group looked around the cemetery in disbelief. *Was the Gris-gris man really gone? Were all the weasels dead? What about–*

"Jimmy!" Mama Dedé said. "Where's da boy?"

"Here!" Armand yelled. "I have him."

Armand pulled Jimmy from the ground, still dazed from his hard tackle.

"Let's go!" Frank yelled as the group hobbled together.

"Are we forgetting any—"

"Let's go, now!" Frank yelled again.

Eddied vibrated with shock and anger at the betrayal of his master. These vile people sent away one of the few things he loved, and the only thing he felt ever loved him back. He would remember the names of these people, for they all had a sin-song, and his God-given talent was to hear the music.

He sent silent messages into the night, searching for a receiver, pleading for a sign, but couldn't tell if his signal was being heard. He imagined that he felt the faintest pull on his sin-transmission, but was quickly fading without the unholy power of the Gris-gris man. He felt the undead life leak from his body like the fleeting warmth of an ember in the rain. The last thing to cross his dying mind was the name of the blank one. It came to him in a whisper as one of the fleeing cowards placed it on the wind.

Jimmy!

Then he faded to stone.

The battered group carried Del and Jimmy through the creaking gate and crammed into Frank's car. Without a look behind them, they left the hellish cemetery to the dead and drove off into the night.

CHAPTER 63

April 1963

A month later, on a warm Saturday morning, Del woke to the smell of bacon and coffee and heard the warm banter between Frank and Armand coming from downstairs.

The unholy storm that had plagued them for weeks during that cold March had stopped almost immediately after *that night,* as she had come to think of it. The clouds persisted for a few more weeks, as if desperate to cling to an old memory, before they finally faded away. They had all been clinging to old memories the last few weeks and would continue do so for the rest of their lives.

The high waters had finally subsided and, she was sad to learn, had left many dead. It seemed that during the hellish weeks leading up to *that night,* many other people, crazed either from the extended, dark isolation of the flood, or suffering from the fear of an uncontrollable rash—or both—had committed some of the most heinous acts in recent memory.

The police stations had been overwhelmed with the calls for help, and hampered by the intermittent electricity. Because of this, people were left to their own means. And some of those means were beyond explanation for a civilized society.

The people committing the heinous acts—and who were later apprehended—all had the same story: They thought the end was near, and were trying to atone for their sins, or trade them away by whatever means possible.

After *that night,* Del had spent a week straight in bed recovering from the mental and physical exhaustion of the ordeal. The thought of Jo and all she had seen haunted her relentlessly the first several weeks. Her dreams were tormented visions—like a trance state turned inside out—that sent her thrashing wildly in the dark. Sometimes she would wake, sometimes not, but in the morning, there was always a sign that Mama Dedé had been at her side the night before: a warm glass of milk; a cold pot of tea; the lingering smell of burned incense; always a gris bag; and several dangling mirrors hanging outside her windows.

Del hated the dangling mirrors because they reminded her of Loo'siana Slim—the first person she had met when this whole thing started—but she had also learned that there was a lot about the world she didn't know, so she pushed the bad memories of Slim and Jo to the back of her mind and tried to get out of bed each day.

It was just in the last few days that she'd taken to venturing out of her room to roam Armand's interesting old house—her house now, apparently—but she still tiptoed through it like a ghost that didn't quite belong. Mama Dedé had told her that it would take some time. Yes, Del thought, it will take quite a lot of time.

As she stretched out of bed, her eyes glanced over her nightstand and fell upon a small crystal jar that sparkled with early morning light. It was appropriate that the light shining through the window should hit the crystal just so, she thought. That jar held something very special.

She shimmied to the edge of the bed and carefully lifted the lid. A long strand of hair was neatly wound around a small thimble and rested inside. Mama Dedé said it was the strand of Jo's hair that Del had clung to after they'd brought her home that night.

In her mind, she ventured to recall a little about that night, but mentally kept her distance. The horrible memories were too quick to come screaming back.

She remembered coming out of her trance to the feeling of being thrown to the ground. She had almost been stuck again, she thought. Somehow, from the time she exited her trance to the time she saw Jo fall into the void, something had happened. Something, or someone, had *looked* into her mind. It was different than when the Gris-gris man had done it during her first solo trance. It felt more like great and terrible things had been imprinted on her mind.

Thinking back to the strand of hair, she also struggled with a vague memory of a scene that kept floating to the top of her mind. *Did Jo kiss me?* Maybe she was thinking of that day at the orphanage. Or maybe she had just dreamt it. But why? Had she kissed her back? She couldn't be sure but would—

"…of course! Have you ever heard the strange story of…" floated up the stairs and broke her chain of thought.

She giggled at the image of Armand twisting his mustache in preparation for a great debate, and Frank knocking ashes onto his big belly. Plus, her appetite was coming back, and between Frank and Armand, they made pretty good short-order cooks. She hopped out of bed, threw on her robe and went downstairs.

*

Frank and Armand were busy with breakfast when Del walked into the kitchen.

"Well, if it ain't Sleepin' Beauty!" Frank said, looking up from his large skillet of sausage gravy. "Come to grace us dis mornin' for breakfast."

"Good morning, Frank," Del said, pouring her coffee. "Mornin' Mama D. Thanks for the tea last night. Sorry I didn't drink any—"

"What? Nothing for me?" Armand asked, feigning insult.

"Good morning Armand. Your mustache looks very handsome this morning."

Armand's eyes brightened. "Why thank you!"

"Hhmmpff," Frank mumbled under his breath, "always da mustache…"

Ignoring Frank, Mama Dedé said, "Oh, honey, don't worry 'bout that. I was just up a-wandering around this big ol' house last night and needed to sit down and drink me a little cup."

"In my room?" Del asked with a twist of her mouth.

"Well, this house is so damn big I got to carry my drinks with me for when I need to sit a spell!" She waved her hand around the kitchen. "Armand, why you need such a big house anyway?"

Brightly he said, "Well actually, it's quite a fascinating story. You see—"

"Save it, Frenchy." She dismissed him with her hand. "After breakfast."

"Oh, OK, I—"

"So Frank, are you living here now, too?" Del asked as she dipped a spoon in his gravy.

"Del-bell?"

She saved a special hug for Frank. "Just kidding."

"Well, you know, I got to make sure Armand is takin' care of my two favorite gals."

"Mon ami?" Armand shrugged. "I haven't burned the roux once, not like—"

"Da damn roux wasn't burnt! It was supposed to be dat color."

The two women exchanged a knowing glance and let the morning banter fade into the background of homey noises that were quickly becoming familiar.

Del hadn't remembered the first several nights at Armand's, but as she lay in bed day after day, the creaks and groans of the house became familiar, then soothed her like the sound of an old rocking chair. It was as if the old comfortable house was inviting her to stay.

Her fitful dreams didn't allow her to think too long on the subject, until the night Mama Dedé came to her and said that Armand had asked them both to stay. It was a big lonely house, he had said, and seemed much brighter with them in it. She wanted to know if Del was OK with the arrangement.

The few other girls from the halfway house had already been assigned to new homes, and now it was just Del and Mama D. Del remembered that being the first time she had smiled, albeit weakly, in a long time, and slept deeper that very night.

She turned and looked out the back window of the kitchen onto the sunny, brick garden. It needed serious tending, but appeared to be great for attracting butterflies. Jimmy would love it here, even though his stay was temporary for now—due to the strange events at the orphanage.

Mama Dedé knew the foster system well and assured her that his paperwork was nearly complete. Mama Dedé would officially have custody of Jimmy until he and Del were older. They would decide what to do when the day came, but Armand had assured them that this was their home for as long as they wanted.

Walking onto the back porch, she breathed in the fresh morning air. She couldn't remember if she had ever felt this happy. She rubbed her shoulder where her wound was healing, and thought it would be a good day to get some sun on it. It was sure to scar, but that was how she was made—a series of small scars—and she was OK with that.

Jimmy rounded an overgrown planter, walking backwards, watching a pair of butterflies overhead. He tripped over a loose cobblestone and stumbled backward. Del held her breath, but Jimmy righted himself—with flailing arms—and stood, amazed in the sunshine.

"Hey, I dint feh down!" he told the butterflies.

"No, you didn't!" Del said from the back porch.

Jimmy spun around at the sound of her voice and peered through the sunlight. "Deh!" he said with a squinty smile. "You a seepy head!"

"Me?"

"Yeah. An you 'ate."

"Late? Late for what? It's Saturday. You can't be late for anything on a Saturday."

Jimmy considered this intensely for a minute, then said, "Fo da movies."

A smile broke Del's face that she couldn't hide if she had tried. "Well, Jimmy Lareaux, you are right again. We wouldn't want to be late for the movies on a Saturday, would we?"

"No, an you 'ate."

"For breakfast? How late am I?"

"No Deh, not beakast. Fo pwayin." At this he looked at his watch and decided, "You sic 'minunds 'ate Deh. Sic minunds."

"Oh well, then we better get some playin' in before breakfast. What are you doing?"

He turned to point where the butterflies had been, but they were gone.

"Hey, dey gone!"

"Yeah, they flew off."

"Weh'dey go?"

"I think they flew off to play the birds and the bees."

"No Deh, not da biwds da bees. Deh pwayin' buttafwy!" he said, and walked up the back steps shaking his head.

"My mistake, Jimmy Wawoo. My mistake."

CHAPTER 64

After breakfast, Mama Dedé drove Del and Jimmy to the movies. Frank and Armand sat on the back porch with their *after*-breakfast cigar and bowl. Their lives had changed drastically over the last few weeks, and each was adjusting at his own pace, but they thought they were progressing, all things considered.

Frank still stayed at his own place, but took to arriving at Armand's early in the morning to check on Del and eventually to take over making the sausage gravy, which Armand had no business making.

The night they'd encountered the Gris-gris man, upon returning home, they had carried Del to her—at the time—temporary room, and both men knew somehow that it was where she should stay. Frank would have certainly made arrangements, but his small Craftsman house was still filled with memories of his wife, and there was no room, mentally or physically, for another woman.

The new arrangement took on a life of its own almost immediately, and each person knew that it was good.

"So Del's lookin' good," Frank said between puffs. "Nice to see her up and movin' around."

"Indeed, she is," Armand said. "Fascinating. Simply fascinating how the psyche can experience something so traumatic, yet seem to bounce back after some good rest."

"Yeah, fascinatin'." Frank rocked his chair a few more times. "So was his eyes really gone, you think?"

"Mon ami! Please..." Armand said with exasperation, pointing to his pipe as if to say, *Before my second bowl is finished?*

"Well hell, we gotta talk about it someday. Don't we?"

Clutching his pipe in his teeth, Armand shrugged his hands to say, *I suppose.*

"Besides, I can't get da damn images outta my head."

"Yes, I agree," Armand said. "I worry about poor Del. How much of it do you think she remembers?"

"Hell, who knows? I just hope she forgets about me grazin' her before I die."

"Grazing her?" Armand rocked forward and leaned on his knees, peering at Frank. "Mon ami, you shot her in the arm!"

"I told you already. I didn't shoot her!" Frank turned away from Armand. "At least not on purpose. Da damn thing ricocheted was all." He puffed furiously at his cigar as Armand rocked back. "Damn near died myself when I saw her lyin' der. Holy Christ."

"Anyway," Armand said, "she seems to be well on the mend physically. Regarding what she remembers now, or may remember in the future... who's to say? Even if she does remember, will she believe?"

"How da hell could you not? Damn door to hell openin' right in front of us; crazy voices on da wind; and den you got da damn hell-dolls screamin' like banshees—"

"Mon ami, please," Armand said, touching his ear gently.

"Oh, sorry," Frank said, rocking some more, then said, "At least you didn't get yer *handsome mustache* et off!" and burst into laughter.

"That, my friend," Armand said, pointing at Frank with the mouth-end of his pipe, "is an excellent point," and laughed in response.

Armand went back to cleaning his bowl, and let the spring breeze blow some of his scarier thoughts away. Although some would not leave with a hurricane, he thought.

Frank watched him as a shadow crossed his face.

"Frank, what did you hear that night?"

"Hell, everything was jumbled. You askin' 'bout somethin' specific?"

Armand tapped his bowl out and looked at the deep shadows forming in the garden. *What unnatural things lie deep within those shadows, waiting for their turn to emerge?* he wondered.

"Well for one thing, do you think they're all accounted for? You know, the things he created. The weasels."

"Well," Frank said, resting his hands on his belly, "I kinda thought when he snapped out, all da other things went wit him. You don't?"

"I saw the beast get sucked in first. Well, I don't know which was first, Henri flaking apart or the beast—"

"I knew dat sumbitch was tainted," Frank said, pointing a finger at Armand. "Dat's why I kept da gator teeth to myself! It's probably how he got to Captain so quick after I left; cursin' people and what not. He sure was interested in dat Glapion case, I can tell you. Sorry, go ahead."

Armand continued. "After Henri and the beast, then of course all the chaos with Jimmy and Josephine happened, and… well, that poor girl… but when the Gris-gris man hit her, and the two of them… fell in, to whatever the void was, that was all I saw. I didn't see anything else fall in."

"Mmm, hmm," Frank mumbled. "Did ya see any… lights? Blue maybe? Real faint?"

Armand looked at the boards beneath his feet and thought maybe he would paint them this year. They were currently the color of a dull void, and he had seen enough of that color for an entire lifetime.

"Perhaps. Do you suppose some of them are still out there?"

"Don't know. Don't care to ever know, really. You?"

"I suppose not. As long as the little cannibal made it in."

A long silence passed between the men as they tried to piece together the missing scenes.

"It did make it in, didn't it?" Armand finally asked.

"Da little crazy doll? Hell—"

"It wasn't a doll, mon ami. With every bit of what sound mind is left in me, I believe that thing was alive. Not just bewitched, but somehow… alive. I felt its presence."

Frank whistled his disbelief, which deep down inside, was true belief. He was very afraid it was true somehow.

"When I yanked da damn thing outta yer shoulder, I threw it as far away as I could, but I cain't honestly tell you where it fell. Maybe we take a trip back—in da daylight—and look around for it."

"I've looked already," Armand said. "I've been there twice and it's not there—"

"Well den dat—"

"—but I did find part of the book."

Frank's cigar drooped down as his face went slack.

"Oh hell… what do you mean, *part* a da book?"

Armand rocked in silence, feeling the implication weigh heavily on himself. It was as if the entire house had hunched its great walls a bit closer to him. The porch shadows hung cold, feeling the dismay.

"The pages that Henri was reading from appear to be the missing pages from my very own grimoire. My *Grimoire Strange*."

"What da hell?"

"Yes, I always knew that part of my own book was missing, but as mismatched as the pages were, it was difficult to guess just what may have been there. Alas, now I know."

Frank puffed hard on his cigar, looking for an answer in the thick smoke. "So, dis means," he calculated carefully, "da third book, da missin' grimoire, is still missin'. Dat right?"

"Yes, I'm afraid so. That is to say, the book that we have referred to as the third book, which presumably is *deux de trois*—part two of three—is still missing."

"Then how da hell did da spell get spoke?

Armand nodded to the house. "You know she said the pages turned themselves, right?"

Frank stared at Armand through a thinning cloud of smoke. "It was awful windy."

"Yes, it was. Quite windy… Howling wind, I'd say. Kind of like voices."

Frank dropped his hands heavily on the chair arms and leaned forward. "I knew you weren't gonna let dat go."

"No, mon ami. This one I cannot let go. I asked you earlier what you heard that night, but I'll save you the trouble of stating it. Instead, I'll tell you what I heard."

Frank leaned back heavily in his chair, watching Armand, waiting for him to state the thing that Frank had wanted to forget the most, but that which would never go away. Ever.

Armand cleared his throat, relit his pipe and began.

"I remember Mama D. telling us about the book. I remember

her warning well because I knew the warning before she stated it. I'm a researcher, Frank. I live inside books and legends. I live inside the stories of old. I live for the turning of the next page where the thing is unknown. She warned us that once the spell was cast, that a secret part of the spell would show itself in the pages. As far as I know, no one has ever seen the hidden part of the spell, or, if they have, it has surely announced their doom, for any that look upon it are then known to the creator of the spell. That's how these things work, you see.

"What I wouldn't give to know if the hidden part of the spell actually appeared in the book that night. That hellish book... that... *Grimoire Dark*.

"But alas, the thing I do know, is that the words were upon the wind, because there were voices driving them, Frank. Not Henri's voice, not ours, or... his, but other voices. Thousands of them Frank, all saying the same words. And they were upon the wind."

The men sat in long silence, as they both knew this to be true. As they sat, a cloud passed overhead, blocking the warm spring sun, and a cold wind chilled them. For a moment, each man feared that their words had called something back, for they each believed with their hearts that once a thing was spoken, it could never be unheard.

"What do you think is out there, mon ami? Beyond the pages of our lives?" Armand finally asked.

Frank considered his cigar thoughtfully, and rocked his chair to the slow rhythm of the world. He considered all that he had ever seen or done. He considered the unholy things they had seen *that night*. He rocked this way for a long time until Armand thought he had forgotten the question. Finally, Frank spoke.

"Der's a few angels out there. Like Del.

"Der's a lotta good people tryin' to get better. Like Del.

"Der's some people fightin' der own black streaks." He paused. "Like Del.

"And der's monsters…"

CHAPTER 65

A Bid Farewell

The binding spell, long forgotten, with your chant has been begotten,

By you now, to bind us morrow, and you ask, 'On even shore?'

Fool you are for spirit speaking! Soon this demon will be wreaking,

hell, upon your spirit shrieking, burning to your very core!

Fool you were to go on chanting, dared to open Legba's door.

Just tonight? Ha! — evermore.

— Deux de Trois —

Alas! Alas! Your death-chant has come, pray to wonder where I am from?

The depths you see, ancient and dark, spawned before this time began.

You called me forth by page of book, this Grimoire Dark hiding the rook,

Your hands now hold the missing book; the words were always the plan.

Your words I hear upon the wind, we'll meet as soon as I can;

For I, Dear Reader, *am the Gris-gris man.*

A NOTE FROM
THE AUTHOR

I hope you enjoyed reading *A Grimoire Dark* as much as I enjoyed writing it. It seems to be true that we really should be careful what we read, for the path rarely leads where expected.

I also hope you caught the references to other authors and books I sprinkled within this story—some obvious, others not—but the one reference I hope was obvious was the call out to The Raven, by Edgar Allen Poe.

I knew I needed a spooky incantation for the binding spell—but of course, it had to be tricky—and when I came across The Raven again, I knew I had found the right structure. It was interesting to decipher the rhyme and meter of this iconic poem, then write something specific to the book, but in the same style. Granted, I understand it is NOT Poe, but just creating something in the same style was one of the high points of writing this book.

Anyway, for those interested—and possibly thinking back to *Once upon a midnight dreary*—here is the poem in its entirety.

The Song of Abgel

Hellish spirit hear me clearly, grant you now full use or nearly,

 Of my soul for use and toiling, at the work of evil lore.

 This damned soul is ripe for taking, in its core with trembled shaking,

 Hunger-lust pang never slaking, begging at your ghostly door.

 Use me spirit, just tonight, that I may unlock Abgel's door.

 Just tonight, no less, no more.

I call to you, by way of chanting—lest a demon voice be ranting,

 Ranting in my wretched mind to call you up from days of yore.

 I summon you to evil deed, your voice as one my mind will heed,

 Seeking someone sure to bleed, to right a wrong done to my core.

 Use me spirit, just tonight, that I may open abGel's door.

 Just tonight, no less, no more.

With demon-will I wholly bind, your tattered soul, black heart and mind

To me you see, for I am kind except to those I doth abhor.

Evil things were done to me, but no worse evil can there be,

To that which I will die to see, unleashed from beyond abgEL's door.

Unlock it spirit, I beseech, for I deserve revenge galore.

Just one night? Not evermore?

Just one night not surely just, for break and maim and kill I must;

With this new power all will see, that hell hath come upon their door.

I freely spill this blood of mine, and with a drop, do fully bind,

My tattered soul, black heart and mind, to abgEL's beyond the door.

My chanting, spirit, hear it right. Bind us now on equal shore.

This I pray, forever more.

The binding spell, long forgotten, with your chant has been begotten,

By you now, to bind us morrow, and you ask, 'On even shore?'

Fool you are for spirit speaking! Soon this demon will be wreaking,

Wreaking hell upon your spirit, burning to your very core!

Fool you were to go on chanting, dared to open Legba's door.

Just tonight? Ha! — evermore.

ACKNOWLEDGEMENTS

Thanks again to my wonderful wife Mary for the long hours reading and discussing this story, especially considering the content. You are right more often than I realize, and this book is better for it.

Also, many thanks to: Christina, Ryan, Lauren, Steve and Joe, the close family and friends who read this story in its imperfect state. I hope you recognize where your suggestions have been applied and realize that your words are now upon the wind.

MORE BOOKS BY D.S. QUINTON

Thank you for reading *A Grimoire Dark!*

It was a fun book to write and woke up a dark corner of my mind, so I wouldn't be surprised if we hear more from Del, Jimmy and the others at some point. I'm assuming Eddie will still being hanging around, waiting… and listening.

If you're looking for another read, maybe explore where the supernatural power came from. Remember, Armand had a theory about this, based on the diary of a very unfortunate boy.

That theory is FREE to download and read!

The Phoenix Stone – A Dark Beginning
Would you die to expose the secret of mankind's origin? Otto just might...

Desperate to journal his grandfather's discovery before his capture, young Otto hides in a secret Egyptian chamber avoiding nomads and flesh-eating beetles to chronicle an amazing story—How we began. Will the story be lost? Will the nomads find him? Or...does the unthinkable happen?

This short story is the dark beginning of all things.

Get *The Phoenix Stone* at www.dsquinton.com/my-books/

*

And as the dark beginning splinters into infinite shards of kaleidoscope dreams, one story tumbles headlong into the future of human evolution, A.I. and government conspiracies with the genre-blending novel...

Devel Django - A Dark Wave Journey

A near-future thriller that whispers at the fundamental question of humankind—Where did we come from?—and gropes at the undefined space between science and religion.

It is a unique tapestry woven with coarse threads of horror, hybrid metal synapses, and detailed with a fine, ancient brush from a long-lost palate of knowledge.

Get *Devel Django* at www.mybook.to/DevelDjango

A TASTE OF THE FUTURE

I very much hope you enjoyed *A Grimoire Dark*.

If you did and would like more in the same vein, here's a sneak peak at the second book in the *Spirit Hunter* series: *Scars of Redemption**…

*Also available on Amazon

PROLOGUE

I n 1963, a most unfortunate thing happened. A book was found.
The book had been wrapped in cloth, bound by twine, covered
in burlap, tied with rope and hidden in an alcove behind a false
wall in a den.

The city was New Orleans.

The book was a grimoire.

The day the Grimoire Dark was found, everything changed. Old
superstitions, arcane and forgotten, suddenly returned. Archaic
fears, once dismissed as childhood nightmares, resurfaced with
cold certainty. Ancient horrors, long buried, awoke. And the spirits
moaned that the dead would be many.

The greatest of the horrors, the Gris-gris man, terrorized the
Crescent City that year. Binding the souls of those who crossed his
path, he searched for a soul more coveted than any other, that held the
key to great power. He found the soul and nearly restored himself but
for the actions of a few brave people.

The night Del and an unlikely band of heroes fought the Gris-

gris man, her illusion of living a normal life shattered. Her unnatural abilities—considered a gift by some—felt like a curse to her and the people that died, *That Night* would haunt her forever.

Her wounds were grave, and recovering from the ordeal took time. Eventually, after many months, her dreams of a normal life returned, and she wondered on her future.

But dreams are never what they seem, and monsters are never where you look.

She thought her journey of nightmares had come to an end. Little did she know, it had just begun.

CHAPTER 1

D elphine Larouche often dreamt of the dead, but it was not often she went looking for them. Tonight would be different.

She knew that some individuals looked for dead *people (corpses)*: policemen, firemen, or grave robbers, for instance. Even newspaper reporters looked for dead people—when they were trying to scoop a big story. But rarely did they look for the dead *in their other state*. They simply didn't *know* the dead existed in another state.

How nice for them.

The remnants of last night's dream vanished as she grabbed the morning paper from the front porch. A fading smell of magnolia blossoms hung on the air. By the end of June, the scent would be gone.

She closed the large front door behind her and tiptoed down the hall. The floorboards were kind to her this morning; they barely squeaked. She hoped for twenty minutes alone with the paper before one of the others came down and asked for their favorite section.

She entered the kitchen, poured her coffee, and scanned the headlines.

"Equal pay *and* civil rights?" Del said to no one. She snapped the newspaper open and laid it on the kitchen table.

The morning sun cast a warm, airy glow into the room, but the effect was as if magic floated right out of the paper. In a way it did. The *Times-Picayune* was a treasure trove to her, bringing news of the larger world and making it all seem a little less scary.

She carefully flattened the crease where the paper had been folded. She did this from left to right, in order to push any wrinkles off the page. She leaned forward and sniffed (but not before verifying she was still alone). There was something about the smell of a newspaper that she loved. The woody, dusty smell of the paper, combined with the chemical ink aroma, triggered a special feeling, a promise of mystery, knowledge and freedom.

In the orphanage the newspaper had been her only link to the outside world, making it seem smaller and less scary. To Jimmy—the mentally handicapped boy she'd protected there—the paper was a constant source of fun. Besides the funny papers, it was good material for hats and other craft items—but never boats. He was afraid of those.

She read the headline again.

The Times-Picayune

June 10th, 1963

President John F. Kennedy Signs Equal Pay Act into Law.

To anyone reading the same story, the idea of equal pay for equal work should be obvious. Who would think otherwise? Although… the fact that it had to be made into a law in the first place…

As optimistic as Del was, she wasn't completely naïve of the world she lived in. How could she be? She was reminded of her place in it every time she tried to do her job as a newspaper reporter.

But you're not really a reporter if they don't even let you in the door.

Yes, there was that.

She couldn't claim anything about unequal pay when she didn't even get a chance to do the job. Over the last few months, as her wounds healed and the weather warmed, she'd diligently attended the satellite office of *The Times-Picayune* newspaper, waiting for an assignment. She remembered how excited she was when she'd learned she had the position. That was the day she nearly ran Frank over on the sidewalk. That day felt like it was far in her past now.

Granted, the editor had called the job an *internship*, which Del thought would include training, but was more like a trial. A test run, really. The only problem was that the guys in that particular office had no need of an intern, didn't want an intern, and especially didn't want one that looked like her. As the days became weeks, then stretched into months, the three men in the satellite office made a game of how they could get rid of Del. Often, it included running bogus errands all over town.

"Run across town to the print supply and see how many packages of Super White paper they have left. This batch is gettin' dingy," one of them would say. They'd all lean back in their chairs and laugh.

They'd ask for typewriter ribbons, several bottles of the new product called Liquid Paper—which they quickly nick-named White-Out, *"to fix all these dark splotches"*—and a hundred other useless items.

Finally, tiring of the game, they resorted to simply locking the outside door and pretending they couldn't hear her knocking, even though she could see them through the window.

Because she wasn't being given assignments, she had nothing to turn in. And because she was considered an *intern reporter*, with no assignments, that meant she didn't have a paycheck. When she spoke to the editor about her dilemma, he simply said to *make herself more useful*, and that was how she'd start climbing the corporate ladder.

Del had never heard the term 'corporate ladder' before, but began to wonder if it even had a rung for her to start with.

She pondered this, then turned her attention back to the paper and another article. She sipped her coffee and read. This one stated that the Civil Rights movement—which Del felt officially began with Rosa Parks on the bus—was gaining steam and would soon see significant gains under the current president. He, President Kennedy—almost too handsome for the office, she thought—had already had several meetings on the subject.

"Good morning, Del," Armand Baptiste said as he entered the kitchen. "What does the world have in store for us today?"

Armand, her kind benefactor, had reached the status of *eccentric surrogate uncle* in her mind. The kind who usually knows best, but may let you get away with more than he should.

"Equal pay! Right here in black and white. Can you believe it? And a lot more after that." She smiled and thought of the possibilities.

"Good for him," Armand said as he scanned the headline. "Mark my words, he'll do wonderful things for the country. All he needs is a little time."

Little did anyone know JFK's time was almost up. It would end less than six months later in Dallas, in the cold sunshine of a November day. But no one was looking for monsters then.

"I have to talk to my editor at the *Picayune* again," Del exclaimed.

"I need a real assignment. I'm missing out on the most important events of our time!"

Having poured his coffee, Armand turned towards her. The mouth-end of his unlit pipe became a conductor's baton. "Yes, how is the newspaper business? Are you getting—"

"No! I'm not getting anything." Del folded the paper and slapped it onto the table. She crossed her arms tightly over her chest. A rapid drumming emanated from beneath the table where her foot tapped out her annoyance.

"I see." Armand clutched his pipe between his teeth. "Well, perhaps a different office would—"

"I already asked. I have to report to the one I'm at."

"The one with the men that…"

"Yeah." Del nodded. "With the men that can't stand the sight of me." Her foot drumming became slow and deliberate. "I just need to land my first story. It doesn't have to be a major scoop, just a chance to show I can do it."

Armand stroked his beard. How hard it must be for her, he thought. Life wasn't fair, and she'd been dealt a hard hand to play. He saw greatness in her, but how it would manifest was yet to be determined. He hoped he could play some small part in that discovery.

"And my old typewriter," he said. "It's working out?"

"Oh yeah, it's great. I've been practicing. I'm up to thirty words a minute now."

"Thirty words per minute you say? Very respectable."

"I guess. I'd probably be faster by now, but Jimmy always wants to practice, right when I start. Says he's going to get a job at the newspaper with me."

"The young man idolizes you."

"I told him he has to learn his letters first. I'm teaching him." Then Del's face darkened. "It's not like they taught him anything in that orphanage anyway. All Sister Eulalie wanted to do was send him away because of his *condition*." Her foot tapping sped up.

"Please, the morning is much too pleasant to bring up those old horrors," Armand said.

Del sighed. "I know. But I'll teach him to write, just wait and see. And I'll teach him to type, too." Then she added, "You don't mind, do you?"

Snapping out of a deep thought, Armand was surprised at the question. "What? Why, of course not. It's your typewriter now. Do with it as you wish."

"Thanks. I'm sure it will help, if I can just get a story to work on."

"Well," Armand began, "you could always," and here he chose his words carefully, "*look* for your big story." He held up his hand and waggled his fingers just like Frank did when he would talk about her *trancing*. The wrinkle of Del's mouth told Armand that wasn't the best suggestion.

She knew that she could use her *gift* to go looking for something bad that was about to happen; she did have the sight after all. But the thought didn't sit well with her. It was like she'd be wishing for someone to get hurt or robbed, just so she could write a story. And she certainly didn't want to do that.

"I know, but… it just seems like snooping. You know what I mean?"

"I believe I do," Armand said. He began organizing the things needed to make breakfast. "And good for you for having the courage to stick to your convictions."

Del sighed again. "Yeah, if only everyone else did the same."

Armand smiled. Del was wise beyond her years, he thought. She just didn't know it yet.

"I guess it's a good thing Mama Dedé set me up with another one of her clients, huh?" Del traced a lazy shape across the newspaper. "Otherwise, I wouldn't have any money at all."

"That's right," said Armand. "Another client. Tonight. Yes?"

"Yeah."

"What do you think it will be? A haunting? A voice from the past?"

"Psshh… as protective as Mama Dedé is? It's probably someone who lost their keys."

CHAPTER 2

A grizzled hand lashed out of the swirling mist and caught Del on the back of the neck. Three jagged cuts opened her skin and ran across her left shoulder. In an instant, they burned with unnatural fire. She cried out in pain.

Del stood amidst a whirlwind of madness and faced her attacker. Dust and debris swirled around her, choking her breath and clouding her sight. This wasn't what she'd expected at all.

Her leather boots anchored her youthful legs to the rocking floor—she would not fall. The ends of her headband fluttered wildly—a rattler warning the attacker to be ware. Her light-brown face and sculpted jaw were locked in granite determination—she would not falter. Her eyes—sparkling and fierce—penetrated the dark gloom and saw beyond the veil. They were piercing flames of life in a storm of death.

The outline of the Spirit Hunter stood beautiful and deadly.

The shape of the spirit shifted, grotesque and wanting.

Debris hit Del's temple and rocked her head. A cut opened there. Her eyes closed on instinct and the phantom vanished.

She was alone in the room, so she couldn't fully trance out, leaving her body defenseless, but she couldn't fight the thing like this. In fact, she hadn't expected a fight at all. Mama D said this would be an easy one.

She spun around and leapt backwards, moving toward the center of the room. She knew the floor would warp when she did this—the entity was tricky—but also knew it was an illusion of movement. The floor was solid. But in her mind, and in the minds of people who'd recently stayed here, the feeling of falling forever was too much to bear. This malevolent thing before her was claiming the room for itself.

As she fought to maintain her balance, she remembered something Mama D had told her about *projecting*. It may be a way she could trick the specter, but she'd never tried it like this.

Her trancing had become stronger over the last few months. Projecting was similar, her mentor had said, you just had to imagine what you wanted to look like, otherwise you were just mirroring yourself in another place.

Just as the apparition reappeared—this time attached to the wall above the door—Del slipped out of the current moment and into her trance, projecting. She was instantly hovering above the scene and could see her own body still standing in the middle of the nightmare.

While trancing, Del could see everything. She was still surprised by this ability—only realizing she had it a few months ago. It was a feeling like nothing she'd ever experienced; it gave her the feeling of simultaneously floating and mindreading, but it was more than that. When trancing, she felt connected to something beyond her everyday life. There was energy, so much energy, beyond what people could see or feel, and she was tapped into it. She could observe people in a scene and even see a split second *in front of them*. She could sense the hands on the clocks waiting to move. She could feel the wood in the room age by tiny degrees. Now, on top of that, she was projecting an image of herself and feeling these things all at once.

From her trance she saw the specter hovering against the wall and became overwhelmed with pity. It wasn't a monstrous demon or hellish abomination at all—those she *had* seen—but was an old woman, barely visible, her essence nearly washed out. The spirit wore the rags of someone from a different time. She was very old, Del thought. New Orleans had been around a long time. The entity emanated profound sadness. She could feel it. Its outer shape—the one that Del's physical body and eyes were dealing with—was that of a monstrous swirl of dark smoke. It had enough power to fling objects around, which were possibly what Del felt cut her neck. It also had the ability to cast visions into the minds of the living; her mind thought the floor was falling even now. But Del didn't sense horror from the thing. She sensed fear. The old spirit was scared.

Del called out from her trancing mind. *Woman. I am here. Don't fear me.*

The phantasm twisted its head around and stared up at the image Del had projected above it—a shimmering silver orb that pulsed with energy.

The face of the old woman stretched into a grotesque mask of shock. The eyes bulged and popped. The mouth distorted with a long grimace, then disappeared into smoke, only to instantly reform as a face. The wretched thing twisted in fear as it clung above the door.

Then Del felt her body tilt.

The few seconds it took to trance out and observe the spirit were precious moments *not* spent maintaining her body's balance. She couldn't be in both places at once. She only hoped she could move between the two fast enough to *appear* that she did.

The spirit felt the shift in the air that announced Del's balance was leaving. Its attention turned to the body, preparing to seize upon it as it fell.

Del saw the spirit's intention to send an old vase crashing to the floor just where her head would hit. She slipped out of her trance and righted her body—her eyes sparking with fearsome light—and caught the vase before it broke. Righting her balance and locking her legs against a final descent of the floor, she slipped back into her trance and sent a fiery burst of silver light throughout the room. The spirit of the old woman looked from Del's body to her projected, silver-orb entity and back again. Del appeared to be in two places at once. And one version of Del was a monstrous cloud of energy.

The phantasm shrieked and flew from the room. Across the city, several sleeping people dreamed of a tattered spirit that night. It flew south into the swamp.

Del slipped out of her trance and collapsed onto the floor, exhausted. The session was finished.

ABOUT THE AUTHOR

D.S. Quinton was born in the Midwest USA and attended the schools of daydreaming, foosball, and mixology. His is an avid student of the unknown and grew up on Greek mythology, the Twilight Zone and Night Gallery.

He is the author of the Spirit Hunter supernatural thriller series and the Circus Sideshow supernatural oddity series, along with a few other interesting tales.

Although his guitar slide is rusty, the piano keys are warm, and despite the lure of many untraveled paths, his feet are generally moving forward.

You can find him at *dsquinton.com*, some social media platforms, or on his deck solving the world's problems with his wife and a good bottle of wine.

Made in United States
Troutdale, OR
07/22/2024

21463740R10257